A POINTED DEATH
FIRST IN THE POINTER MYSTERY SERIES

Kath Russell

Copyright © 2010 Kath Russell
All rights reserved.

Cover illustration of Nola Billingsley and her pointer dog, Skootch, by Ron Ruelle, www.ronruelle.com

A Pointed Death is a work of fiction. Names, characters, places and incidents are the products of the author's imagination or are used fictitiously. Any resemblance to real events, places or people, living or dead, is completely coincidental.

Printed by CreateSpace, an Amazon.com Company

ISBN: 1450563090
ISBN-13: 9781450563093
Library of Congress Control Number: 2010905541

THIS BOOK IS DEDICATED
TO THE ENTREPRENEURIAL WOMEN
OF THE BIOTECHNOLOGY INDUSTRY.
WHILE PRODUCING GREAT VALUE,
YOU HAVE KEPT YOUR DIGNITY
AND YOUR SENSE OF HUMOR.

PROLOGUE

The beefy hand of the liquidator, lifeline clogged with grease, sliced the air like a rattlesnake's head. I covered the hovering palm with twenties. Don London had auctioned the assets of my failed dot-com and was delivering the remaining equipment I could not sell, because it was leased, and I would have to pay it off, into the garage of my San Francisco home. New businesses are supposed to start in California garages, not end in them.

Don's crew rolled the last piece of equipment into the garage. The copy machine looked expensive and out of place sandwiched between my treadmill and the recycling bins.

"Better luck next time, Nola." Don hefted his corpulent frame into the driver's seat of his truck.

"Don't wish me luck, wish me venture capital."

"You entrepreneurs are a persistent breed." He slammed the driver's side door.

"Persistent or plain stupid!" My shout startled an umbrella-toting woman walking her poodle down the sidewalk of our peaceful, manicured block. Hell, there you go disrupting things, Nola Billingsley. You can never leave well enough alone. A rambunctious, independent woman who has to have the last word.

VI • A Pointed Death

As Don's truck pulled away, I turned and surveyed the stacked equipment. Over the copy machine, suspended from a redwood rafter, an artificial Christmas wreath drooped. All it needed was a rest-in-peace sash to become a memorial tribute for my defunct start-up. I owed $13,500 more on this collating colossus. Our dot-com's accountant had negotiated the lease in one of his last official acts before absconding with a sizable chunk of my capital. What a depressing end for an entrepreneur. I made my way along the narrow aisle that remained of my garage toward the kitchen and the scotch bottle.

The next morning, as I sat down to yogurt and coffee, I realized I had no place to go. My former offices, the scene of much pain and frustration as the business lurched toward collapse, were at least a destination. I looked across the table at my mother. Crap, you're a forty-eight-year-old woman with no visible means of support living with your mother. How low can you go?

Turning from the blaring television, Janie Belle read my thoughts. "You should reopen your consulting business. Why don't you call up some of your old biology contacts?"

"That's biotechnology, Mother. I plan to, but I have to tie up loose ends on the cyber-business."

My mother is a vibrant eighty years young. She has survived depressions, wars, hurricanes, miscarriages and cancer. She is a displaced Southern girl who wields her accent like a passport. Everywhere she goes, she brings a moving van chock full of eighteenth-century furniture, china, crystal, and family portraits. The gilt-framed, manor-born ancestors were all here on the Left Coast, hanging on the living room walls, mildewing genteelly in the California damp.

She lifted her coffee cup, pinkie curled. "Is there anything I can do to help?"

"Not unless you change your mind and learn the computer."

"Absolutely not! I am not going to start that at my age."

Janie Belle has mastered many things: needlework, stenciling, gourmet cooking, Girl Scout leading, duplicate bridge, gardening, even chicken farming. She also has conquered things technological. She handles the digital gadgets in the car with skill, channel-surfs with the cable remote, gabs on the cell phone, and nukes with the microwave, but she will NOT go near a computer.

I got Janie Belle an e-mail address once. I would come home to a cheery drawl, "Have I got maaail?" I printed messages off for her, and she answered them with handwritten letters on monogrammed stationery. She is complete, resolute, and content in a way modern women, especially we boomer women, can never be.

At this moment, the love of my life thundered into the room. Skootch E. Hurry is a pointer dog. I wish I could be more specific as to the exact breed of pointer he is, but we met at the SPCA and his lineage is a mystery. The "E." does not stand for anything; it is just that the dog has such presence, he deserves a middle initial.

At the pound, Skootch attracted my attention by wagging his tail against the cage so hard it bled. I took pity and brought him home. He is a spoiled, undisciplined, overweight slob, and the dearest creature on the planet. Janie Belle insists he dipped the tip in catsup. She says he is a con artist in dog's clothing. They are tight as shrink-wrap.

Skootch sauntered up to the kitchen table with a self-deprecating sway. This is a prelude to the Lunge. Eighty-pound Skootch, who fancies himself a lap dog, drapes his upper torso across your lap to get a better view of your breakfast plate. He spied my yogurt and harrumphed in distaste.

"Nola, why don't you take that mangy dog for a walk. He's so fat you can't see any of his ribs, and his privates are disappearing in his tummy roll."

Skootch left my lap for the greener pastures of Janie Belle's side of the table. Janie Belle continued, "It's your fault the canine is corpulent, you spoil him nonstop." The Lunge was repeated. Skootch's head lowered into position over her half-eaten breakfast. His tongue made fast work of the left side of the plate.

Janie Belle executed an ineffectual shove. "He must be twenty pounds overweight. How you can look the vet in the face?" The tongue swirled around the right side of the plate, a movement as elegant as Renoir's brushwork. Skootch aimed a wistful gaze at the butter dish. His neck extended outward in its direction.

The spunky eighty-year-old smacked him on the nose and pushed him off her lap. "That's enough! Y'all should be ashamed of yourself."

I took Janie Belle's advice and treated Skootch to a walk in order to procrastinate before calling former colleagues in the biotechnology industry. I drove Skootch to Fort Funston, a national preserve perched on the edge of the Pacific Ocean.

Fort Funston is an unspoiled expanse on the cliffs that rise from Ocean Beach. Hundreds of acres of native plants, winding trails, desolate beachfront, and Technicolor views spoiled by only one thing—bureaucracy. The Park Service had decided to make war on dogs. A band of control freaks fueled by an eco-religious fervor, these policy-wielding potentates wish to restrict the use of Fort Funston to, well, themselves and the birds.

The horseback riding clubs and the hang glider association, San Francisco's own indigenous air force, had the foresight to create legal barriers protecting their use of the park when the

City ceded the recreational area to the Feds. The naïve pet owners relied on the common sense and decency of freedom-loving people everywhere, and got screwed. Now dogs, which previously ran free, are leashed and led in the park.

As I pulled my station wagon into the parking lot, the weather was getting worse. The fog gathered substance and rolled over the cliff, a bully looking for a scrap. I saw a solitary dog owner wrapped in a slicker, hunkered against the cold. I did not see any park rangers. Weighing my chances as the first drops of rain hit my windshield, I decided it was worth the risk of a citation. Opening the door, I freed the caged canine and picked up a plastic bag, but not Skootch's leash. The rain pattered in approval.

I have a problem with authority, especially authority embodied in small-time functionaries who often magnify the scope of their power to annoying extremes. I know I am being petty, but I love getting around such people.

Skootch flew over the parking lot and on to the sandy dunes, picking up speed like a fighter jet on a flight deck. Then he threw himself into an elegant spin and ended in a seamless squat. He pooped robustly and flew off again. Without any elegance whatsoever, I trudged over and retrieved the doggy detritus.

I caught up with Skootch as he was about to enter the coppice. Most of Fort Funston is wide open, covered with low grasses, succulents and wild strawberry, but there are a few small stands of trees. The first one that guards the approach to Battery Betty, a pre-WWII artillery installation, always makes me apprehensive. There is something about the abrupt silence. You walk across an open stretch, deafened by wind and wave, and step into a dense tunnel of trees. The trees are remarkably effective at shutting out the sound, yet the breeze makes it through, causing the branches to move in the sanctuary. The effect is uncanny.

Skootch becomes fully alert in this place, collecting himself as consciously as a diver on a springboard. He walks in the middle of the path. A powerful scent can lure him to the edge, but he is cautious as he sniffs and always returns to the center. I was content to let him walk ahead of me. Rough-riding on the breeze, the fog penetrated to the heart of the coppice, obscuring my vision. Skootch picked up speed as he neared the end of the tree canopy. There is an elbow of land between the thicket and the concrete passage of the old military structure. It contains a riotous mix of plants, a peek-a-boo view of the ocean, another trash receptacle, and a convenient park bench.

The concrete battery is not Skootch's favorite place, because it produces first-rate echoes. He waits for me in the elbow, circling through the grasses, sampling aromas here and there. Once I enter the tunnel, he powers past me out the other end and congratulates himself on his bravery.

The fog was thick as mucous now. We'll have to cut our walk short, I thought, as I zipped up my jacket. Intent on the zipper, I nearly fell over Skootch. The dog was stopped in mid-trail at a full point, stiff and immutable as a statue. I had to overcome my shock because despite his heritage, Skootch never points anything but the refrigerator. Yet he pointed now, pointed the park bench.

I eased around him. "Is someone there?"

"Burf."

As there was no other reply, I advanced again. Skootch crept behind me, torso low to the ground, neck extended, growling from deep in the throat.

The bench reclaimed some definition from the fog. A person sat on it. As I grew closer, a gust cleared the immediate area, and I gasped in shock. A body slumped on the bench, propped with its legs wide apart and arms over the back rungs.

I jammed my hands in my pockets for my cell phone. Nuts, I'd left it at home. The elbow area became claustrophobic. There was not enough room for Skootch, a dead man, and me. Especially, since the slouching corpse was as headless as Irving's horseman.

I sprinted into the tunnel of the old battery. My choice was a mistake, but I could not make myself go back. The fog had accumulated here in a dense and dripping shroud. Not wishing to follow me into the awful scary place, but not able to leave me, Skootch began to howl. The reverb terrified both of us. My jog accelerated into a stampede, but the surface was too slippery for my leather-soled shoes. Losing my balance, I tried to recover but pitched forward instead. I narrowly missed knocking my teeth out. Scrambling to my feet, I started again but stumbled over something.

Winded now, I gasped for air and planted both palms to push myself up as Skootch reached my side. His body language telegraphed he was protecting me from something. He growled with certain menace at an object about two feet in front of my nose. It must have been the thing I tripped on.

This time it was the reverb from my scream that sent Skootch and me racing from that place. The scream I let out when I found myself face-to-face on the sodden floor of Battery Betty with the head of my former employee, the embezzler, Roger Chen.

* * *

CHAPTER 1

The police cars and other official vehicles filled the Fort Funston parking lot with merry flashes of red, blue, and yellow that bounced off the fog tent containing this particular three-ring circus. Skootch was locked in the back of the station wagon in high dudgeon. Having given my evidence, such as it was, I slumped in the passenger seat of a police car, feeling and looking like one of the sad clowns.

Exhaustion was setting in. I experienced the after effects of the adrenalin surge resulting from my grizzly discoveries, the sprint to my car, the drive to the ranger enclave, the hurried explanations to the rangers, the phone calls, the dash back to the parking lot to await the first response vehicles, the return trip to the coppice and the giving of my statement.

I sighed as I watched a knot of burly men emerge from the fog with a bagged burden on a stretcher. How many times had I wished such a fate on my ex-employee? Roger, headless, on a stretcher. My revenge fantasies had been creative, but never this unbridled.

Roger's body was borne along by four of San Francisco's finest. A fifth professional, a woman from the forensic team, carried his head with a certain detached reverence. Roger would have liked that. He was a lady's man. He would not have liked the plastic bag, though.

I glanced down at the knees of my jeans. The blood was dry now. I had knelt in Roger's blood in Battery Betty, although I did not notice it until I reached the ranger station. Covered in gore, I caused a stir when I burst through the door. I watched as the source of all that blood disappeared into the back of the coroner's van.

My tired mind sank back into memory. Roger started working for our company during a difficult time. We had hired a Web development company to build and test the applications and databases supporting our Internet business. The company failed us in terms of deliverables and deadline. We missed our launch date, losing the benefit of hundreds of thousands of advertising dollars. When the site launched, it was full of bugs and crashed repeatedly. The calls from angry customers rang 24/7.

Our controller decided to leave because he could not take the insanity of a start-up anymore. We placed an ad and interviewed seven prospective replacements. At the next staff meeting, we vetted the candidates and chose Roger. He was a Cal grad with great references.

Sally Harford, our marketing VP and an unrepentant transplant from the East, voiced doubts, saying that in his all-black outfit, designer glasses, and flashy rings, Roger did not seem accountant-like. This drew laughs from the Californians who were blasé about seeing eclectic attire in the workplace. Our content manager said we were lucky he was free of piercing.

One Wednesday, two months later, I answered the phone, anticipating a call from the head of my new development team with a report on the testing of our repaired shopping cart. I was anxious to hear her assessment. Our cart was full of glitches, and the previous week, subscribers were charged four times for one subscription, creating a customer services cataclysm. I grabbed the receiver.

"Hello, is this Nola Billingsley?" said the strange but pleasant voice.

"Yes." This was not my developer. I would make this conversation brief to free the line.

"I am Patricia Marx calling from American Express. We have observed unusual activity on your account, and it is our policy to contact the principal cardholder to alert them to unusually high numbers or sizes of transactions compared to the account's history."

My emotional antennae began to gyrate. "Which is it?"

"Both. We are seeing a significant increase in the number of transactions and in the amounts charged."

"What is our balance now?"

"Charges for the month are at $53,435. Of course, that represents transactions reported to us by merchants to date, not the actual amount charged, which can be higher."

My mouth turned dry as sandpaper.

"What are the purchases for?" I fought to remain calm.

"Furniture from Ikea, a lot of jewelry, a mink jacket, steel-belted tires. Oh, and a stay at Morocco Bay Resort in Carmel."

"Are they associated with any card in particular?"

"Well, yes, with Mr. Chen's card."

"I'll call you back."

Bursting from my chair, I slammed the receiver back on its cradle. I started down the hall but pivoted and retraced my steps to the office of my colleague, David Comisky. David, known to everyone as Dakota because he was born during a blizzard in North Dakota, was designing new pages for our site. I startled him when I rushed in. "Dakota, follow me."

"What's wrong?"

"Roger has stolen from the firm. I'm going to fire him and escort him out. I want you to back me up if the creep decides to make trouble."

Although he had acquiesced in his selection, Dakota had never trusted Roger. In his view, something was a little off. Dakota set his jaw and push himself up from his ergonomic chair. A quiet and respectful man, as far removed from violence as they come, Dakota was, nonetheless, a big believer in honesty and justice. Roger was about to get some, and Dakota would help make sure he took his medicine.

I strode down the hall and rounded the corner into Roger's office, moving across the room until I was standing over him. "Roger, significant irregularities in our accounts have come to my attention, and I am going to ask you leave the premises now."

Roger's unreadable eyes looked up over tinted lenses.

"You were late coming in this morning, but I believe you have collected your paycheck, so we are square on salary. Under the circumstances, there will not be any severance. If you have any issues about this, call me, but right now we want you to go." My voice was steadier than my mental state.

Roger looked uncomfortable, but the reason for that was dancing on the edge of my peripheral vision. Our accountant was enjoying pornography on company time. The image of a young girl with an inviting pout, her legs splayed wide, stared out from the monitor on his desk. At least it did until he clicked his mouse and my accounting program reappeared on his desktop.

Roger adopted a deadpan. At the end of my speech regarding the balances on his credit card, he made one of his own.

"I never take the card with me. I keep it right here in this file, so the charges can't be mine. Apparently, somebody has stolen my information and is using it to buy stuff. This happens a lot these days. I've seen it at other companies. Our insurance company will cover it."

"Be that as it may, please collect your belongings. If I find that I'm wrong, you'll be the first to know. My apologies will be profuse and heartfelt, but for now, get out!"

Roger mechanically tossed objects into his briefcase. "I suppose I could consult my lawyer." He snapped the case shut and rose.

"Whatever." I sounded as clipped as the click of the attaché.

Sidling past me, he returned to the subject of insurance. A vivid recollection of a day, weeks in the past, when he had bugged me until I found and loaned him the file with our business and liability policies, occupied my brain as we closed the gap between his office and the lobby.

"Companies build credit card fraud into their cost of doing business. The insurance guys expect a certain amount of it to go on. It's structured into your fees." Roger adjusted his gold neck chain.

By this time, Dakota had opened the front door, and Roger stepped out on the stoop at the front of our building. Start-up companies with no financing choose down-market lease space, and we were no exception. Our entry was devoid of elegant plantings, cool marble floors, and burbling water features. Roger stood on a cracking concrete apron abutting the parking pad.

"Your coverage is more than adequate." Roger warmed to his subject, but I cut him short.

"Save your breath, Rog." I tried to slam the door in his face, but it had a pressure attachment, one of the few things that worked in our suite. I had to put my back to it to accelerate its closing. The effect was more than anticlimactic; it was comic and demoralizing.

I set the lock, turned, and leaned my head against the door. Alice Ng, our receptionist, stared at Dakota and me, clutching a stack of files to her chest, her lips pulled into a tight line.

"Alice, tell Serge, Sally, Mac, and Ellen to be in my office in fifteen minutes. And crank up the coffeemaker. We're going to need caffeine."

I glanced out the window. Roger was on his haunches opening his briefcase on the stoop. He extracted his cell phone and punched a number. A smile ignited his face as the desired party answered, and he launched into an animated conversation I was sure had nothing to do with what had just happened to him. A female friend, no doubt. Roger had several of those. I wondered if this woman knew about his predilection for hot honeys on the Web.

The firing was no big deal to him, I realized. He had expected it. I remembered how few belongings he needed to collect. In fact, most of his things were already in the briefcase. I'd been had. I had been naïve, too trusting, and too preoccupied with business problems to check up on this guy, and it was going to cost me.

My managers and Alice assembled in my office. Alice and Dakota had passed on the basics, and the room buzzed with I-told-you-so's. I got the group's attention and explained what had happened, cautioning everyone to refrain from discussing the matter outside our immediate management circle.

"OK, guys, you need to understand that you cannot say what you might be feeling about this even though the facts are pretty much in." I stood before a row of angry faces.

"She means we can't call Rog a crook even if he is one." Dakota almost spat Roger's name.

I squeezed my right fist so hard, my knuckle cracked. "I owe all of you an apology. This mess is my fault. My reference checking stopped after I interviewed one of his supervisors. Can't remember how it came up, but she went to my alma mater. I guess I turned off my radar after that."

"Don't beat yourself up." Sally said.

"When I checked with Cal admissions and learned he graduated *cum laude*, I figured we'd found a winner. Call me a diploma snob."

Dakota rested his elbows on his knees and rubbed his temples. "Elite schools get their share of rotten apples."

"No kidding, and not all of them become lawyers." Sally's quip was met with forced laughter.

I dismissed all but Dakota, Alice, and my IT manager, Serge. The four of us would divide the tasks involved in collecting and reviewing Roger's files and going over our accounting records to determine how much damage he had done.

It was three o'clock in the morning when I found the forged bank drafts. Roger had written himself a few extra payroll checks. He had forged my name. It was not even a good approximation of my signature.

With the expert assistance of the personnel at American Express, we documented over fifty thousand dollars in charges of a personal nature attributable to Roger. The customer service people were efficient and polite; they also were clear that if Mr. Chen was an employee with an authorized corporate card, his charges were our responsibility.

Serge Washington, my IT manager, found multiple e-mails detailing Roger's purchases as he filled his girlfriend's apartment with trendy furniture and the latest appliances and swathed her body in silks. Roger also had been generous to himself and his male friends with tickets to concerts, charges at casinos and clubs, sporty tires, and enough gasoline to drive from here to Mars.

Serge left at eleven-thirty to hit the bars. The process of clearing Roger's hard drive of an extensive and disgusting collection of pornography had put him in a bad mood, and he needed a drink.

It took another hour to figure out how Roger had kept his charges a secret. Roger made entries for payments to American Express and other payees for amounts that represented the *actual* business purchases for that month, the office supplies, the software licenses, the shipping charges and the travel expenses. Thus, when I looked at our account balances over our intranet, they looked reasonable because they tracked to our usual pattern. As the expert at American Express had emphasized, it is all about patterns. Patterns that connote normalcy. Patterns of deception.

At six a.m., Dakota entered my office and slid into the chair next to my desk.

"You know what else we have to do."

I swallowed. Hard. "What?"

"We'll have to call every one of our online customers and advise them that an unscrupulous person might have their credit card information."

My heart nearly stopped. Roger was the person in our organization who reconciled the transactions that occurred on our Web site and dealt with refunds. With this responsibility came access to the secure side of our shopping cart and the credit card information of customers. He had the cyber keys to our city.

Dakota's eyes were moist. I could see he was feeling a tsunami of emotions. He was a founder of our company. We had fought hard to build and launch our Web business. At times, it seemed as if the entire galaxy was conspiring to keep us from achieving our goal.

Our first Internet customers were cause for celebration. Now our reputation was ruined. Roger had not only stolen money from us, he had also taken our good name and our pride. When word-of-mouth reached full cry on this, the reaction could destroy our fragile new business.

"Well." I managed a feeble shrug. "I guess it's a good thing we haven't had many customers. We only have a few hundred calls to make."

A rap on the car window inches from my ear brought me back to foggy Fort Funston. A man in plain clothes stood next to the police cruiser I occupied. I pushed open the rear door and rose to meet him.

"Ms. Billingsley, I'm Detective Filipe Barbagalatto." We shook hands perfunctorily. "You indicated to the first officers on the scene that you knew the victim. Is that right?"

"Yes, that's correct." I surveyed the scene around me. The initial arrivals who were in uniform had been joined by a horde of forensic specialists. Now, investigative experts had converged, evidenced by this homicide detective. "I recognized the victim because he used to work for me."

"Used to?"

"Yes, he was an accountant in a dot-com I used to run."

"Used to?" Barbagalatto's pen hovered over his notebook.

The guy needs a vocabulary infusion, I thought. "The business subsequently failed, but Roger was gone by then." I sagged back against the car door as the realization sunk in that my next remark wouldn't sound good. "I fired Roger for embezzling funds from my company."

The pen halted again. "So the victim ripped you off? He tanked your business?"

"No. Well, yes, he did rip us off and his theft certainly didn't do our company any good, but he's not responsible for our going belly up. We were compensated by the insurance company for some of what was taken."

"When did all this happen, and when was the last time you saw him before you found him here?"

"I haven't seen him since the day I threw him out of our offices." I shoved off the car and stood to my full height. "Listen, I've been working with the police for some time over Roger's crimes. I've delivered all the paperwork pertaining to this to people at the Hall of Justice."

"You don't happen to have that case number handy?"

"You've got to be kidding," I blurted before I could catch myself.

A calculating stare was my answer. I rubbed my forearms for warmth against the growing chill in the air and in the demeanor of my interrogator. He can't figure me for a bloodthirsty beheader! Yet, I had to admit that my stumbling on Roger's body was suspiciously serendipitous. Police do not believe in coincidence.

"I think you need to contact the officer heading the fraud investigation. His name is Bob, ah, Robert Harrison, and he will put you in the picture." I used my most helpful tone. A pair of caramel eyes under sun-bleached brows formed in my memory. I felt calmer, which was good because Barbagalatto was being as tenacious as Skootch with a ham bone.

"I'll do that, but you and I still need to get together first thing tomorrow."

On the morning after we discovered Roger's infamy, we divided the customer list and began phoning the unsuspecting buyers. I took a small portion of calls, because I had to make room in my schedule to contact the police, our legal counsel, the insurance companies, and the fraud unit of American Express.

American Express was knowledgeable and helpful. The insurance companies were blasé and efficient. Streams of forms spewed from our fax machine instructing me about information I would have to collect, copy, and submit with my claim for reimbursement under the employee theft provisions of our policy. Roger's skullduggery was a full-time job for me over the next few weeks.

After over an hour on the phone trying to penetrate the voice menus of the San Francisco Police Department, I slammed down the receiver and scooped up my car keys.

I eased my Saab onto Mission Street and turned right at the Ocean Avenue light after navigating around an articulated bus and several jaywalkers making for a popular produce stand at the corner. Young Latinos in baggy pants sauntered past wizened Asian women with net shopping bags. A Filipino couple pushed a high-tech baby stroller, and two ancient brown loiterers of indeterminate race leaned against a power pole festooned with multilingual posters.

A young girl, with ebony tresses longer than her skirt, rushed past my hood before the light changed. Her breasts bounced as she clip-clopped in and out of the crosswalk on her platform shoes. Appreciative, the Latino lads hiked their precipitous trousers. One fellow grasped a grand plantain from the fruit stand and gestured lasciviously.

I turned on Alemany Boulevard to make my way to the Balboa Police Station. I passed the Calmest Palmist's, the Happy Buddha Herb Store, the Brazilian Churrascaria, the Holistic Pet Clinic, and the An Loc Immigration Law Office, and turned left at the Tito Chavez VCR Repair, right across from the Slavic Cultural Center.

Ah, San Francisco. We blast incomprehensible languages at each other with boom boxes, give the finger to a dozen ethnic groups in a single block, and legislate multilingual ballots so long and hefty they give voters a headache and a hernia at the same time. San Francisco is the quintessence of diversity. We are proud of our rich texture but stressed by its consequences. We cannot communicate, compromise, or peacefully coexist; we muddle forward in a hair shirt of political correctness.

Some bureaucrat thought the Balboa Police Station was going to be such a nice place to visit, he had better hide it from the citizenry. The station is sequestered in a transit armpit created by the 280 Interstate, several ill-conceived on-ramps, and the Muni train terminus. There are signs to the station, which you can read if you happen to have a machete. I made three passes before I found the way in.

The desk sergeant was a sleek, compact thirty-ish Hispanic with enough electronics on his belt to control a small factory. I stated my mission. His attention wandered the minute I described the alleged transgression as a white collar, nonviolent crime against property. Listening to various yerps and squeaks from his belt, he assigned me to a svelte but less technologically bedecked officer.

This official took my name, phone number, and address and assigned me a case number. "Your case will be forwarded downtown to our special fraud unit. They're located in the Hall of Justice on the fourth floor. You can expect a call from the case officer in a week or so. Keep your case number handy. You'll need that when you call in or go for interviews." He nodded and turned away, sweeping a stack of file folders off the counter with a practiced hand.

That was it. SFPD's interest in my welfare was entirely bureaucratic. They wanted me to have a case number. I felt let down. Betrayed by every cop program I had ever watched. They never gave you a case number on CHPS. A case number never crossed Columbo's lips.

A week later, I dressed for my interview with Inspector Robert Harrison. The inspector had called just as the officer at Balboa Station had promised. As the president of a struggling start-up, I had slipped into the habit of wearing jeans. I rummaged through my closet and pulled out a wrinkled pantsuit. I took the suit with me to the bathroom hoping steam from my shower would soften the wrinkles and eliminate the musty smell.

Twenty minutes later, I arrived at the breakfast table. Janie Belle regarded the suit with skepticism. As a Southern Lady, she had never reached détente with pantsuits. When she spied the pearl necklace I had added, her left eyebrow, which had edged up into the danger zone, returned to its neutral position. "Pearls always add femininity to an ensemble."

"I'm not trying to be a femme fatale, Mom."

"Well, try not to forget you're a girl." Janie Belle eyed my unmanicured nails as I passed her.

Skootch headed for me with a tongue-lolling grin and a Good-Morning Lunge in mind.

"Hold it there, buster, I don't want any doggy hair on my suit."

Offended, he sat, alternating a look at me with one at the butter dish. I poured cereal in my bowl and tossed him a few kernels of my latest fad diet garbage before dousing it with fat-free milk.

"I'm headed downtown to meet the detective handling our case against Roger, and I have no idea how long I'll be. I'm taking him all the documents he requested. The stuff fills two storage boxes. I hope I can park close, because schlepping them is going to be a pain."

"Why don't you take one of the luggage cart thingies?" Janie Belle was ever practical.

"Because I'd have to go up in the attic and find the damned thing!" Our attic was a black hole where you could lose hours, days, even weeks searching for things.

My breakfast was over, because during this exchange, Skootch succeeded in executing a complete Lunge and polished off my designer cereal. A drop of milk formed at the end of one elegant whisker.

As I backed the Saab out of the garage, I noticed the sky. It promised to be a decent day. I headed for upper Market Street. The drive over the crest at Twin Peaks and down Market into the Castro District is a spectacular journey. Noe Valley, downtown San Francisco, Berkeley, Oakland, Alameda, Sausalito, Yerba Buena, and Treasure Island sunbathe before you. The Bay Bridge curves sensuously, a discarded piece of grosgrain ribbon, and aircraft carriers look like Tootsie Rolls.

The whole spectacle puts you in a mood that even the pierced denizens of lower Market, with their exposed and tattooed flesh, jangling metallica, and Jell-O-ed hair, cannot deflate. I have a definite love-hate relationship with my city, but at the moment, I was all hearts and flower power.

The traffic light turned yellow, and I slowed to a stop. A container ship made its way along the channel toward the Oakland depot. My eye strayed along the shore to Alameda Island. Our perusal of copious e-mails had revealed that Roger's main squeeze lived on Alameda. I wondered which of the buildings, winking in the morning sun, housed a considerable portion of my assets. Somehow, this woman had taken on the face of the cyber-whore. I pictured her visage bobbing up and down over Roger's shoulder as he rode her on a futon delivered from Ikea. Despite the panorama, my mood darkened.

The light changed. Traffic was testy this morning. Drivers switched lanes like metronomes as they tacked toward the Ferry Building. Suicidal bicyclists pumped their way forward between the surging engines.

Now in the flat part of the city, I exited and parked in a lot that promised not to bankrupt me by lunchtime. I hefted one box of documents under an arm and slung my shoulder bag over the other. Without the luggage thingie, I would have to come back for the second box.

The Hall of Justice swarmed with activity. I found the fraud unit and asked for Inspector Harrison. I was told to wait. Behind the receptionist was a taupe sea of battered cubicles stretching to a row of grimy windows on the perimeter of the room. People bobbed up and down in the cubicles as if they were jack-in-the-boxes in the quality control section of a toy manufacturer.

One man stood. And kept on going. When he stopped rising, he towered over all the other "jacks" at about six-foot-five. He exited his cube in a single stride and made short work of the corridor to the reception area. By the time he rounded the counter, he had his caramel brown eyes fixed on me. His right arm came up in an athletic swing, and a big, open hand came my way.

"Ms. Billingsley? I'm Bob Harrison."

His voice was warm, deep, and Eastern, possibly Southeastern. I shook his hand and found it warm as well. He gestured at a conference room to our right. I moved to retrieve my box of documents from the floor, but he intervened and lifted the box as if it were a bottled water.

The room was a modest affair boasting six chairs with frayed black tweed seats and a laminated table that looked as if it should be cultured for virulent organisms. A fake ficus skulked in the corner supported by the wall. Harrison placed the box on the table and attempted to slide it toward the middle. The slurry on the surface made that impossible. He picked the box up, repositioned it, and waited for me to take a seat before pulling out his chair.

"I looked over the case file and my notes from our phone conversation. Have you been able to obtain the original forged checks from your bank?"

"Yes, they're here with everything else you requested. At least they will be when I bring the second box up from my car. His e-mails should be helpful."

"Your company policy states that you have the right to access and read e-mails? I'll need a copy of that."

"Yes, it's here. We were careful about the wording of those passages in the employee manual."

He flipped off the top of the box and leafed through the materials. "Has Mr. Chen attempted to contact you since you fired him?"

"No. Not even to arrange pickup of his Janet Jackson concert tickets that arrived two days after I canned him."

"Purchased with his corporate card, I'll bet." Harrison did not take his eyes off the box contents. A tiny upward curve appeared at one corner of his mouth though.

"How'd you guess? I'm sure he was planning to entertain clients!" My ploy worked. Harrison looked up and smiled. He had a warm smile to go along with his hands and voice.

"Let's go get that other box, and I'll tell you how this is all going to work on the way." Harrison seated the stack of paper back into the box.

He ushered me out of the conference room and toward the main elevators. Pressing the button, he spoke to the receptionist. "Elsie, I've still got dibs on that room. We're getting some more docs from this lady's car."

A mousy man in shirtsleeves and crepe-soled shoes shared the descending elevator car with us, and we rode down in silence.

After erupting from the revolving exit door, Harrison squinted up at the sky and began to talk. "Here's how this goes. We review all the evidence. Then, we'll invite Roger in to tell his side of it. We'll see whether he comes in or not. If he's smart, he won't come or he'll come with an attorney. Once we have his response, we'll take the works to the D.A. The D.A. decides if there is enough here to move the case forward."

"How long does all this take?"

"Give it a couple months, give or take a few weeks for the D.A.'s office to kick it around."

"A couple months? You've got to be kidding! Roger could leave the country. Or, hey, he could bilk another unsuspecting company like mine."

"Yeah, he could, but the process is the process. Speaking of other companies, you did give me his resume and the notes on the interviews with prior employers when you were recruiting him?"

"Yes, it's all in these boxes. I can't believe his references were so good. You don't suppose those companies were hot to get rid of him and lied to make him attractive to the next unsuspecting employer?" My jaw clenched in anger.

"Could be. Employment law being what it is, companies are careful not to badmouth anybody."

Harrison lifted the second box from my trunk and tucked it under his arm.

"I can't believe we were so stupid. We didn't do a credit check on him. His references were excellent. People gave us much more than employment dates and job titles. We thought we were home free, and he turned out to be a damned crook. Stealing from us and the next minute commiserating about our development problems like a real member of the team. He even made suggestions in staff meetings!" My face reddened with my rising blood pressure.

We were back at the steps of the Hall of Justice. Harrison turned toward me. "Look. You've had a bad experience with a lifestyle criminal. This guy has no moral center. His goal is to achieve and maintain a certain manner of living. He wears the right clothes, goes to the right clubs, listens to the right music, and takes the right drugs. He has the right kind of babe hanging off his arm. Go south of Market Street, and you'll see dozens like him. They look like they've been cloned, or they've escaped from a rip-off version of the *Men in Black* movie." Harrison balanced the box like a basketball and rubbed his chin. "They only take jobs to get money to support their habits. If the jobs don't pay enough, they help themselves. The fact that it doesn't belong to them is irrelevant. They are part of the elite. You are outside that inner circle; you don't count."

"But what can small businesses do to protect ourselves? We have to trust some employees. I can't be everywhere." My shoulders slumping, I walked a few paces and half sat, half leaned on the broad masonry balustrade abutting the sidewalk.

Harrison followed me to the pavement's edge and rested the box on the second step. His lips pursed as he turned something over in his mind.

"Well, you could have put more checks in place to flag his kind of pilfering, but the thing is that with computers on every desk and the Internet and everything, the tables are tilted in their favor. If they're inside your firewall, stealing is as easy as the click of a mouse."

Harrison's eyes flashed, coming back into focus from his reverie, and his back straightened. Had he reached a decision, about the case or about me? He turned, facing me squarely. "Look, Ms. Billingsley, your case is not the only Chen case we're investigating."

"What!"

"I shouldn't be telling you this, but there is another company that has filed a similar complaint against your former employee. From my brief review of their documents, they have a firmer case than you do."

"And with all this, you still need months to bring him to justice?"

"Hey, I said there was a process we have to follow, and justice is the D.A.'s job. I'm in the apprehension game." Harrison reclaimed the box and ascended the stairs.

His stride was a match for the broad, imposing steps that evoked the grandeur of a nation devoted to law, and the majesty of its mistress, Justice. I, who was beginning to view her as a fickle courtesan, took two rapid steps on each level to keep up with the inspector.

We reached the landing, and Harrison paused before entering his private quarter of the revolving door. "Why don't you let us do our job and see what happens? We're lowly government types, not entrepreneurs, but sometimes we accomplish things with dumb brute force. You could be pleasantly surprised."

Grinning, he whisked into the rotating door, cutting off any rejoinder. I followed, winded from the sprint up the stairs. When I emerged, he was cutting a swath Moses-like through a sea of supplicants. Justice, I fumed, must have been a jogger, and picked up the pace.

As the elevator doors closed, I resolved to gain the upper hand. "Where are you from? You're no Californian."

"Nope, but who is?" Harrison rocked back and forth on his heels, his free hand in his trouser pocket. "I'm from Baltimore. I was with the homicide division there. Just been here four months."

"Where'd you go to school?"

"Hopkins."

"Really?" My estimation of Harrison rose. Several members of my family were Hopkins graduates.

"What possessed you to come here?

"Needed a change."

We returned to the conference room, and Harrison positioned the second box next to the first. He peeled off the top and began to extract folders. His eyes grew distant as they had before when he was deciding whether to tell me about the other company Roger cheated. He got up and closed the door, shutting out the sounds from the busy hall.

"I lost a partner while working on a case. She was a great partner and a greater person. She died in the line of duty at the hands of a real bastard. He's still at large. I needed to try something different after that. And find a new place."

"Oh." I had to look away. I don't know what I had expected, but it wasn't death. I had been thinking about my problems, and now the life experiences and feelings of another person made my problems seem mundane. "I'm sorry."

We looked at each other. The silence allowed the noise of the outer hall to reassert itself.

Finally, he sighed and turned to the paperwork.

We worked for several hours, and the parking fees due when I retrieved my car did almost bankrupt me.

Skootch's insistent barking brought me back to the chill of Fort Funston. Detective Barbagalatto and I had agreed to continue our discussions the following morning, and the crime scene team was wrapping up. Roger's body and the spectators were long gone. Unless you wanted to count the fog people, the ephemeral bodies of mist that moved across the open space, silent and deferential as Tiger Woods groupies on a bad golf day, the place was almost depopulated.

A uniformed officer headed my way, pulled off his cap, and wiped his forehead. I recognized him as the owner of the police car inside which I had been sitting before Barbagalatto had accosted me.

"I guess it's been quite a day for you. Thank you for your cooperation and patience." The officer leaned back and looked over his shoulder at my station wagon. "That's one agitated dog. He doesn't appreciate being kept away from the action."

"No. He's an action kinda guy."

"Better take him home and feed him or something."

I pictured the Lunge that would follow half a day of being cooped up in the back of a station wagon while no one listened to your entreaties. "Yeah, easy for you to say."

As I tried to settle behind the steering wheel with an ecstatic dog licking my cheek, I realized how cold and exhausted I was. Not as cold as Roger, though. Roger was cold as in the cold, cold ground. His heart, if he had one, stilled forever. Roger had pissed me off, but what dreadful thing had he done and to whom to end up murdered so horribly?

"Get off, Skootch!" I pushed the dog away from the gearshift to get the wagon out of neutral. Feeling my fatigue full force now, I drove to the park exit before realizing I needed to turn on my lights. I flipped the wand on the steering column and lowered the passenger window for my canine companion, hoping he would leave me alone.

As we headed home, I begged my conscience to manufacture a modicum of sympathy for my former employee. She refused. OK, it would be unprincipled to weep for a dead man when you hated his guts while his guts were still warm. Was that it? Feel pity for his family, came her reply. Hey, that's a great suggestion! I can do that.

Still, as I accelerated onto Sloat Boulevard, I could not escape the guilt for my lack of feeling. I thought I was an ambivalent turd, an insensitive dolt.

"I think not," whispered the familiar voice in that arch way she had picked up from her honors seminar professor. I froze at the stop sign, unable to go forward, my fingers whitening on the wheel.

The voice that was not my conscience continued. "You wept for me."

The hairs on my arms rose even though I knew Joyce was just in my mind. Joyce Strand, my roommate and confidant. My best friend.

"I still weep for you Joyce. I miss you. I miss you something awful."

"I know." The voice faded away.

Skootch left his window, impatient because the vehicle was not moving. He intended to nuzzle his chauffeur back into action, but he found something else more important to do. He needed to lick away the tears flowing down her face.

* * *

CHAPTER 2

The next morning began with Janie Belle's version of the Rebel Yell. "Nolaaaaaaaaaaa!" She comes to the head of the stairs and hollers. This strategy is effective most of the time. If it fails, she has a backup plan. She sends Skootch barreling up three flights of stairs to hurl his considerable bulk on top of me and launder me into consciousness.

Fearing Plan B, I rolled over. "I'm awaaaaaake, OK."

"If you had been awaaaaaaaake, you would have heard the phonnnnnnne. Pick up. Something. Something. Police."

I rolled in the other direction where the phone and clock were. As I picked up the receiver, I was surprised to note I had slept until nine thirty. Doing my best to clear my throat in a prone position, I answered.

"Ms. Billingsley, this is Detective Barbagalatto. You need to come in to the station."

"Sure. No problem. Were you able to reach Inspector Harrison?"

"I left him a voice mail."

"So, after you talk to him, we could..."

"You need to get in here as soon as you can, Ms. Billingsley."

Don't you want to review the fraud file for the existing case first?"

"Case number?" Barbagalatto asked.

Good grief, these guys are bureaucrats. How am I supposed to remember the damned number? "I've got it at my office, and I'll call and give it to you as soon as I get in."

"I'll get it from you when I see you here at ten thirty."

"Fine." I would have a lot of rehabilitation to do in under an hour if that was going to happen.

"Taraval Station at 3205 Taraval, across from the Korean grocery." Barbagalatto hung up.

Replacing the receiver, I sat up on the edge of the bed. I was now awake enough to remember that I didn't have to go *in* to the office. My only remaining office was downstairs off the garage. Shrugging to shake out the stiffness, I rechecked the clock. Next to it in a silver frame was a picture of Joyce. I had dreamed of her last night, as I had done periodically for two decades and would do so more frequently for a while, because murder had reentered my life.

My eyes roamed from Joyce's firm jaw to those fabulous cheekbones. I reminded myself I would have to control my negative feelings about law enforcement today. Here was a category of authority figures which had failed me big time. Inspector Harrison had not triggered my kneejerk resentment, but, then, Barbagalatto didn't have those caramel eyes.

Joyce and I roomed together at Northwestern University and shared living quarters after we graduated, as I began my career in the drug industry and started night school to earn my MBA. Upon completion of my degree, a headhunter found me a plum position at one of the first companies to form in a new industry emerging in San Francisco, biotechnology. I left Chicago and Joyce, not knowing I would never see her again.

A week into my new job, I got the call. An intruder seeking money for drugs had murdered Joyce in our apartment. The Chicago police screwed up the interrogation, broke the chain of evidence, and the killer was freed. Joyce's distraught parents cremated her remains and refused to hold a memorial service. Joyce's mother was soon in a mental institution. I lost touch with her father, but I was sure that by now he had drunk himself to death.

Murder is a big rock dropped in a small pond; the mass disappears, but the circles of water spread out inexorably, disturbing everything before them. I broke contact with the eyes in the photograph and looked out my window to get a solid grip on the present.

My bedroom makes up for many of San Francisco's shortcomings. It is at the pinnacle of the house, an enclosed widow's walk with dust ruffles. When we bought our home, I had the small dormer windows replaced with a large casement. From the vantage point of my bed, I can see the bay, the entire peninsula, and the Pacific Ocean. This lofty aspect gives the viewer a sense of power and control. I took a deep breath. From a control point of view, today would be all downhill from here.

Twenty minutes later, I stood over the coffeepot in the kitchen wearing another suit, a skirted one this time. My blouse only had one button in danger of unraveling.

I'm brown-eyed, auburn-haired, five-seven, and no bombshell, but I have good legs, respectable cleavage, and use my engaging wit to make up for the curves I lack. I looked presentable.

"Earrings would do a lot for that outfit," Janie Belle offered.

"You're right. Don't have time, though. Gotta run." I grabbed a can of Slim-Fast from the fridge and headed for the garage.

As I rounded the corner, I spied Skootch sitting next to the door into the garage, tail wagging. He was giving me a chance to make it up to him.

"No, Skootch. Not now. Maybe we can go for a ride after work today. Be a good boy."

Skootch's brow knitted. He was standing now, and the pace of his tail slowed like a wound down pendulum clock. He moved aside grudgingly as I opened the door and squeezed past.

Barbagalatto operated out of the Sunset Precinct, headquartered in a cigar box of a building. After asking me for a case number and telling me I was expected, a thin young woman escorted me into his glass-walled office. He stood to welcome me and motioned toward a scoop-backed chair opposite his combination desk/table island. A wall module neatly populated with family snaps and citations framed him from behind.

Despite the pads of legal paper aligned on the desk, Barbagalatto extracted from his back pocket the small notebook he used at Fort Funston before sitting. He flipped the pages until a clean one appeared and started asking questions.

"Did Chen have any friends at your company?"

"No, he never formed any relationships with other employees. He had plenty of friends outside the office. He was always getting calls on the office line and his cell phone. In fact, I was planning to speak to him about the time he spent on personal business. It affected his productivity, and I was going to warn him that his performance review would not be pleasant if he didn't shape up."

"Any visitors?"

"I saw one or two of his friends when they came to the office, but their visits were brief and I was not introduced."

"Do you know their names?"

"No."

"Could you describe them?"

I thought this question over. "No, not really. They all wear the same clothes. It's almost a uniform, both men and women. Chunky black shoes. Black clothing. Small tinted glasses. Black leather coats. Nothing to distinguish them, make them individuals."

Barbagalatto changed the subject. "How angry were you when you discovered Chen had been stealing?"

"Pretty mad. Our cash was dwindling fast, and he helped us along the path toward insolvency just when we were facing some nasty business challenges. He was a real heel."

"It must be tough to start your own company and have some creep get in the way of your success. You must take it personally when you're a founder." Barbagalatto's transparent pursuit of my motivation as a suspect irked me. How could they think I would kill anyone? And in such a brutal manner.

"Building a new company is very personal." I controlled an impulse to be snide. "It's your dream coming true, and sometimes your worst nightmare, but it's always your own creation, warts and all."

He nodded, encouraging me to go on.

"It also involves bunker mentality. We're the good guys, and the folks out there are the bad guys. You should hear what we called the venture capitalist who wouldn't give us funding or the British company that negotiated for months and in the end wouldn't partner with us. I fantasize about meeting the VC in a dark alley, but it's just that—a fantasy."

The detective paused before asking his next question, never taking his eyes off me. "Did you kill Chen?"

"No sir. I did not. I hated him. Detested what he did and wished him ill. Now that he's dead, I feel no pity. But I couldn't, didn't kill him."

Barbagalatto waited.

"If you find my Web developer dead, come looking for me. He pushed my buttons so many times I nearly went nuclear. I wanted to strangle him with his own code."

Barbagalatto didn't laugh. I should have known better. This was no time for cracking jokes. This stranger was forming detached opinions about my closest colleagues and me. I had caused him to lose a little respect for me and perhaps to move me up a line or two on his list of suspects.

"Where were you the night before last, after, say, nine o'clock?"

"I was at home with my mother watching television and drinking scotch." Realizing I had an ironclad alibi, I sat up straighter in my chair. Silly I had not thought about this aspect of a police investigation. They'd have to look elsewhere for Roger's killer.

"How old is your mother?"

"She's eighty. Why'd you ask?"

"Just wondered if she had all her mental faculties."

My explosion of boisterous laughter ricocheted down the hall. The thin woman appeared in the doorway to see if anything was wrong.

Taking my outburst as proof of Janie Belle's competence, Barbagalatto waved the girl away and returned to his questioning. "What about the other founders?"

"Dakota, ah, David Comisky and Sally Harford were the other founders. Neither of them is capable of this. Dakota is a gentle man, quiet and kind. Sally heads our marketing effort and has the forcefulness of people in the advertising field. She talks a good game. In fact, she said she would castrate Roger if she ever saw him again, but you mustn't take that seriously."

"How about your other employees? Chen cross any of them? Borrow money perhaps?"

"No, he didn't mix with the staff. He was out the door and gone to the clubs at the end of the day. He didn't buy into the start-up culture. He talked big, but when others stayed late to meet a deadline, Chen was long gone. He told everyone he did a lot of work at home, but the results didn't reflect that. He was behind on several projects."

I began to wonder why I hadn't pulled the plug on Roger sooner. He was a lousy employee. I was remiss in my management responsibilities to let him get away with so much. Distracted by other crises, I had allowed a bad egg the time and opportunity to become putrid.

"I don't think he interacted with many of them and only in the most superficial way in line with his accounting and payroll responsibilities. We had to inform all of them, of course, about the situation because Roger had access to their bank account numbers in order to arrange direct deposits of their paychecks. I'm sure they hated him for the anxiety he caused, but nothing more than that."

"How many employees in total?"

"Thirty altogether, although six of them were based in Washington, DC. I think you can rule them out. The ones worth interviewing are Alice, because she was the receptionist and saw all the comings and goings, and possibly Serge, our IT person. Serge and Roger worked together on our network security and backup systems."

"Sounds reasonable. I'll need to see them and the other two founders as soon as possible."

Although our company was as dead as Roger was, there was a lot to straighten out. I spent the rest of the day phoning suppliers about rescinding contracts. It was an afternoon of unpleasant interactions and unfulfilling phone tag, and at three-thirty,

I decided to call it quits and keep my promise to Skootch by taking him for a ride.

Janie Belle's car was gone. She was probably at the grocery stocking up on bourbon. She could not abide the scotch I drank. Said it tasted of hair tonic. Old Crow Straight Bourbon Whiskey was another matter. Smooth and velvety, with a hint of sweetness. Like a Kentucky morning.

I breezed into the kitchen to write her a note. A grumpy Skootch looked up from the rug. Since he had not been invited to go grocery shopping, he had been rejected twice today. His mood changed instantly when I picked up his leash.

I couldn't bring myself to go back to Fort Funston the day after finding Roger's body. Instead, I drove north to the Presidio, a huge expanse of land at the tip of the city where the bay enters the ocean. In contrast to San Francisco's hippie heritage and No-Nuke policy, the Presidio boasts a long martial history, from the Spanish era to the Vietnam War. There are parade grounds, cannon, bunkers, pillboxes, imposing gates, a military cemetery, battle monuments, and even a military museum.

One of the special places within the grounds is Fort Point, nestled under the southern moorings of the Golden Gate Bridge. The modest fort stands guard over the entry to the bay almost at water level. The sheer force of water rushing past as the tide changes is awesome, approximating two hundred billion gallons a tide. Surging vessels, rough and glistening cliffs, the soaring bridge, and the water make a remarkable sight. However, it is the water that will bring you back. The rushing water rolls into the shape of muscles, strong muscles that could pull you down. You would slip between them, a minnow in a torrent, and go down, down into the cold.

I went to Fort Point because I needed to see the muscles, to be near strength in order to feel in control again. Not that I aspired to that power. It is because no person can achieve such might and beauty that a visit to the fort is therapeutic for me.

Skootch's perspective was more joyful and interactive. The crisp breeze energized him, and he circled the parking lot picking up speed with each lap, a scruffy cyclone in the making. He checked the status of the tide pools and careened off the hill behind the fort. He greeted new visitors as they arrived, left their cars, and braced in the stiff wind. After he ranged over the entire property, he joined me at the channel side of the building to enjoy the waves and sea smells.

I like to watch the tourists get closer and closer to the edge with their cameras, binoculars, and especially their noisy, undisciplined children. I don't want to see them fall or get entangled in the lines of the anglers who fish from the western edge of the bulkhead. No, I want to see them wet. Really wet. Soaked through. Drenched while standing up.

I wait for the big waves, the ones that roll in infrequently enough to catch the novices by surprise. Two kinds of waves drench the tourists. The totems that climb up the side until they are taller than the bystanders, reaching equilibrium in a magnificent instant when they resemble a hand in a horror flick; but, presto, the illusion disappears as buckets of water come down on the unwary. And the bashers, the waves that hit the breakwater with the force of a freight train and slap the crowd with a mammoth membrane of wetness.

The aftermath of these occurrences is delicious. First, the disbelieving pause. Next, the cries, groans, and wails. Then the exodus to the cars. Squish, squish, squish. Mommy-Mommy-Mommy.

It was too late in the day for anglers or tourists. The sail boarders were leaving, but the gulls were in residence. I walked to the end of the breakwater and leaned on a piling, hands shoved in my coat pockets, shoulders hunched to keep my hair on one side so it wouldn't blow in my eyes.

Skootch rounded the corner with something in his mouth. He circled a few times before bringing the mystery thing to me. I took one hand out of a pocket and reached for the prize. No way. Skootch dodged and returned to his circling, faking me out. I leaned on my piling, feigning disinterest. After a decent interval, Skootch returned, coming a little closer. I waited, easing my hand out of the pocket. He stopped. Cocked his head. He danced and made the happy growl.

I lunged and he took off, returning to the circling maneuver. At the apogee, he stopped, trotted to a large puddle near the breakwater and dropped his prize in the middle. For a minute, I thought he was going to wash the thing in the manner of a raccoon. But he took off and ran along the side of the building.

Guess he wants me to go get it. I pushed off from the piling but halted almost immediately. A mature Western Gull, a real bruiser, floated down next to the mystery thing and gave it a tentative poke. Two more birds followed suit, landing in the puddle and eyeing the prize. The first bird gave it a proprietary nudge. Satisfied, it tore a piece away from the object and gulped.

Horrified, Skootch turned to face the interlopers, growled, and lowered his head.

The action was too near the edge for my liking. Skootch could go over. I started to run.

"Skootch, no!"

As more birds landed and the original discoverer tore another piece from the blob, Skootch went into action. Head lowered, he bore down on the ringleader, fierce as a bull in the corrida. Sliding on the wet surface, I tried to get between him and the gulls. One of the more timid recent arrivals took off, smashing me in the face with a powerful wing. I went down on a knee. The leader bird spread his wings in protest and protection for the soggy thing. Skootch lunged and snapped at a wing. Stampeding birds knocked me flat as I attempted to rise. Skootch was behind the leader now. Unfortunately, a supporter was behind him. The sneak let out a piercing shriek. Skootch jumped in reaction, lost his balance and his hindquarters went down with a splat. This pause in the action allowed me to regain my footing.

"Shoo, shoo," I said. Several of the birds took off, but the bird with Skootch's mystery blob persevered. Mustering his courage, he charged the dog. Two other defenders fell on the soggy mass in his wake.

I shuffled around the feeding frenzy and headed for the combatants, reaching Skootch as the heavy bird went airborne. Rising vertically, like a Harrier jet at a Memorial Day air show, the creature squawked at Skootch. I grabbed the dog's collar as he jumped at the feet above. He was pulling hard and near the edge. As I tugged, his body lifted up and his front paws flailed over the precipice.

I leaned my body away from him and down to put more force behind my intention. That's why I didn't see it. The rapid departure of the gulls would have given me a clue if I had been facing the other way. When the wave fingers rose above the edge and grazed the tips of Skootch's paws, the dog figured the tussle with the avian bandito was over. He stopped pulling against me, which resulted in my third fall for the day, and made a beeline for the remains of his prize. Sitting spread eagle, I looked up in time to see the full majesty of the wave before it collapsed on top of me.

The massive waterfall carried the prize over the side of the breakwater and would have taken Skootch along with it, but the dog had doubled back to assist me. I clutched at his silky, soaked coat to get purchase to stand upright.

Together we made a slow progress to the car. As we rounded the corner of the building, a park ranger greeted us. We made a strange pair: a breed of dog not known for its water retrieving prowess and a wet, disheveled woman in a clinging business suit, carrying one dripping dress shoe and limping on the other.

"I hope you realize that you shouldn't venture close to the edge." The haughty functionary crossed his arms beneath his badge. "We all need to respect nature and be more careful. We might have had to rescue you and your dog."

"Not without a fight," I whispered.

* * *

CHAPTER 3

My cell phone rang while I teetered on a ladder in my garage, putting boxes on a shelf to make a wider passage between the detritus of my former business so I could get to my tool bench. I did not make it down in time, but the caller ID showed the call was from Serge. I punched redial and waited.

"Hey, Serge, how's the new job?" I greeted my former IT manager.

"Well, the pay's good, but this is one dull company. I guess you've got to take some boredom along with the stability of a mature firm. One thing about our outfit; it was never dull!"

"True. I guess you got the call from the police."

"Yeah. Was that weird about Roger or what? What a way to go. I didn't like him, but I wouldn't have wished that on him. I have an appointment to be interviewed tomorrow, and I, uh, sort of wondered if you'd help me with what I should say."

"Serge, just say the truth. Tell them what you know, which, I assume isn't much. After all, Rog didn't hang with us, did he? He was usually out the door, faster than a rabbit with a ticket to a carrot convention. Besides, I can't coach you, you know."

I knew the interview would be painful for Serge. He had difficulty talking to non-geeks.

"No, I didn't want that. I just thought. Well, I actually know some things about Roger outside of work." Serge's voice sounded guilt-edged. "Do I have to mention that, or should I stick to the work environment?"

"You should tell Sergeant Barbagalatto everything, no matter the context, even if it seems insignificant to you. Some tiny piece of information could help the police figure out who killed him."

"OK. It's just that my wife, remember, she's Chinese-American, we sometimes go to the South of Market clubs where the Chinese hang out, the young professional crowd, not the moms and dads on Clement Street. The Extreme Lotus is really trendy. The place is a knockout and people wave a lot of money around. It wouldn't be my choice, but Marta and her friends love to go there. Marta likes to dress up and dance. I guess I like the dancing part, too. Anyway, we saw Roger there a couple times. He couldn't dance worth a damn, which was a shame because his girl was hot and she had some good moves." Serge paused. I sensed he was wondering if this was the kind of conversation you had with an ex-boss.

"Roger and his babe had their own circle. He saw me once and kind of waved, but he didn't come over and introduce his lady or anything. His crowd looked fast. I didn't feel they were people I wanted to meet. I think they were popping pills over at their table. Better stay away from all that.

"At work, the day after I saw him, he asked me not to mention it to you." Serge's voice dropped lower. "I don't know why I agreed. I thought he was afraid you wouldn't like hearing that your accountant was hanging out in a fast, expensive club. Later, after you found him out, I realized that the slick suit he wore and that babe's gold chains were bought with our development money. I was too ashamed to tell you. And maybe, just a little, I thought you'd wonder about me, hanging out in a flashy club on my salary."

"Serge, I know you. The Internet café is more your action! Don't feel bad about not telling me. How were you supposed to know what his game was?" An image of Serge clutching his ubiquitous laptop while trying to gyrate on a crowded dance floor came to mind. An involuntary smile tilted my head back, and I bumped my skull into the doorjamb.

"I feel lousy, that's all. When I think back on it, Chen was flashing cash like a lot of those guys. It should have dawned on me the only way he could do that was to develop a set of sticky fingers. I shouldn't have been so dense!"

"Forget it. Just go and tell the sergeant what you remember. And let's get together sometime. I don't want to lose touch. Who knows what next year will bring? Maybe I'll find a venture capitalist in my Christmas stocking!"

"Can't do stockings anymore. Wife's turned me into a frigging Buddhist." Serge was Russian American.

I flipped the top back on my cell phone and surveyed the contents of the garage. It would take more venture capitalists than Santa had elves to resurrect this business.

Retrieving another file box from the top of my workbench, I knocked something off. It landed on my instep, and I dropped the box to grab the injured foot. My gas valve wrench was lying on the floor. When the next earthquake comes, San Franciscans are supposed to run out to their gas valves and turn them off with these trusty wrenches. Unfortunately, most residents can't remember where they put their wrenches. My wrench was, of course, still in its original packaging. While other citizens are blown sky high searching for their wrenches, I will be bourn aloft trying to penetrate the stupid shrink-wrap with nail scissors.

As the throbbing in my foot subsided, I heard the doorbell ring. I limped toward the stairs to the foyer.

Janie Belle was shutting the door. "That was the mailman. You sure did get a lot of mail at that company of yours."

She placed the pile on the hall table and began to sort the pieces with her right hand. In her left was a small parcel. I took the box, noting that it had been forwarded from my old business address.

I saw stamps from Thailand and the name of the parcel's intended recipient, Roger Chen. The return address on a colorful sticker introduced The Ancient Turtle Company. I picked up my mail and headed for my office.

I set the stack of envelopes on the desk and lowered myself into my chair. Should I open this? I wondered. Given the origins, it could be illicit drugs. Wouldn't the post office have found real narcotics with sniffer dogs? The package weighed next to nothing. A customs stamp with some illegible pen marks appeared on one side.

"Well, you paid for this; you have every right to open it." I reached for a pair of scissors and used one blade to slice through the tape on the lid. I pulled out a plastic bag and slit that as well. Inside this bag was an envelope containing a smaller plastic bag and a cheaply printed brochure. The contents of the small bag resembled marijuana, but they were the wrong color.

I sighed, placed the herbs on my desk, and perused the brochure. The instructions, written in abominable English, advised the user to ingest the herbs three hours before sex. The leaflet promised miraculous results that would improve with each subsequent administration. The company could supply the customer with bulk shipments of the elixir at attractive prices, or ship him monthly installments to ensure optimum freshness.

I should have figured Roger for a sex fiend, I thought, eyeing the little bag of minced leaves. How could he spend my money on this crap! I started to toss the box into the trashcan but had an idea. I turned to my computer and hit the Internet icon on my desktop.

On my third search engine, I found them. The Ancient Turtle Company. The graphics were poor, but I expected, the clientele did not care how the splash page looked. The company offered an array of herbs, spices, roots, barks, ground bones, minced body parts, and combinations available in powders, creams, concentrates, suspensions, and tonics. Some of the product descriptions contained cursory warnings that the ingredients were banned in certain countries, but it was clear from the slap-dash wording that the owners of this site did not care about endangered species import regulations.

As I surfed around the site, I realized that the technology behind this portal was more sophisticated than the graphics suggested. A state-of-the art database was in evidence. The site contained powerful search tools and a full-featured shopping cart. When I looked at the corporate contact information and the legal disclaimers, things deteriorated again. These sections were skimpy afterthoughts. I saw, however, that while the company's headquarters were in Thailand, it maintained an office in the city of South San Francisco. The site lacked the helpful links to trade associations, health information sources, or patient advocacy organizations generally provided by health-oriented vendors of even the most rudimentary variety.

What a business! I wondered if they got any venture capital. Almost all the venture capitalists were men; they probably did. Men were definitely behind this business, given the prominence of penis-propping products. Oh, well, somebody had to pay for the powerful site structure behind the tacky graphics, murky product photos, and poorly written content.

I scrolled down the home page and found an unattractive blinking counter. The number flashing at me from the register was 19,062. They weren't paying for their site architecture with sales.

The phone rang. The call was quick. No, my company was not interested in lease space with a view of PacBell Park. I clicked back to my homepage and studied my stock portfolio, a pastime that used to be fun. Now, with the crash of the technology sector, it was the financial equivalent of attending a teetotaler's wake.

* * *

CHAPTER 4

I had set aside Friday for reconnecting with old colleagues in the biotechnology industry, a sector that was still afloat but bailing water frantically in a sinking market. I had made two appointments, one with a financier and the other with a hyper-networked public relations maven.

The financier was working from home, a turn-of-the-century mansion on Nob Hill in the shadow of Grace Cathedral. An elderly houseman answered the door and ushered me into a long, dark hall. A pair of ancestor paintings adorned the wall of the broad staircase, set off by the warm glow of foil wallpaper and burnished woodwork.

The old man disappeared to announce me to Rupert Fong Lee, a respected venture capitalist whose firm topped the competitive pecking order on Sand Hill Road, the enclave on the Peninsula that was the headquarters of the most prestigious VCs in high tech and biotech. Rupert usually drove down Interstate 280 in his Jaguar to his office there, but today he was working in his home office with the drop-dead view of Golden Gate Bridge.

My gaze fell on a venerable, carved mahogany table, but my contemplation was interrupted by the spectacle of two Asian-American teens bounding down the elegant stairs swinging their backpacks perilously close to the fragile paintings.

The slender, pony-tailed girl reached the final step. "My teacher is really bitchy, giving me a paper to write in place of my exam because we're going to France."

Punching a Palm Pilot, the younger boy took the last three steps in a bound. "I hate Provence. Why do we have to go back? It's so boring! If Dad wants French wine, why can't he order it over the Internet?"

They almost collided with me before realizing a person stood between them and the door.

"Hi, Nola!" The boy grinned. "Dad's on three!"

The girl swirled to show off snappy white shoes with blinking lights. I mugged my approval, and they were out the door with a rush of air and a slam.

A feeling of regret for my childless state filled the void left by the retreating siblings, like the rising damp in an ancient cellar. I fussed with my jacket collar to shake off the emotion.

The old gentleman returned, signaling for me to climb the stairs. He knew from previous experience I preferred the stairs to the discrete elevator in the butler's pantry.

Since the ceilings in Rupert's house were fourteen feet, the two-level climb felt more like three stories. I paused before starting the second flight and looked up to admire the stained-glass skylight. The subject was a reclining female with diaphanous clothing, tendrils of light hair and those plump expanses of rosy skin popular with Western artists of the last century. She offered a seductive occidental contrast to the Asian maidens in the screen next to me on the landing. These ladies were completely covered in silks, feet rendered as two black props, hands tucked in sleeves, faces lowered modestly.

These women would share a dislike of modern female dress, a uniform of black pantsuit, chunky pumps, and matching leather backpack. Wondering what they would say about black nail polish, I arrived on the third floor and turned to go back to the front of the house and Rupert's office.

The room was a complete contrast to the rest of the house, an electronic wonderland accentuated with modern furniture. Rupert was behind his desk, kneeling on an ergonomic chair. The desk itself was a vast plane of thick beveled glass supported by chrome pillars.

Rupert stared intently at his flat-screen monitor but acknowledged my presence. "Hey, Nola! Glad to have you back. Sorry your dot-com didn't make it, but we missed you while you were off doing your Web thing."

"The next time I get some crazy idea about starting a company, have me committed, OK!" I settled into a leather chair and dropped my bag on the floor.

"Actually, I thought your strategy for Timely Capsule, Inc., had real potential." Reflections danced off the designer glasses perched atop Rupert's head. His delicate hands moved over the keyboard with the abandon of a virtuoso. "Your basic subscriber news bulletin had value, and the customized products providing information specific to a company's field of development were a real management timesaver, especially when it came to the regulatory stuff. The corporate profiling work you performed for your high-end customers was spectacular. It's a wonder you didn't have every hedge fund in the sector lined up at your door."

"Gee, Rupert, you actually read my business plan. I'm flattered."

He finally peered over the screen at me. "Nola, I'm sorry we couldn't provide financing, but we had cut and run from the Web sector by the time you came around."

"I know. Business is business, right?"

"Yeap, and timing is everything. How much did you lose?" Rupert pulled the sleeve of his navy turtleneck down over his Rolex.

"Two years of my life and half a million of my own money. The founders worked for nothing, and our staff got a pittance plus stock options; still, we burned through two million altogether. Of course, the lawyers got a chunk of that."

"Don't they always?" Rupert smirked.

"Enough of this depressing talk. What's happening with bioscience start-up financing? What are the VCs hot under the collar about?"

Rupert chuckled, and his eyes almost disappeared as his cheeks rose and his crow's feet fanned out. "Well, the screening companies finally fell out of favor. In the end, the investment community always comes back to companies developing new drugs to treat nasty diseases. Compared to that, service companies can't maintain the allure."

"So, what has replaced screening technology?"

"It's the story of what's old becoming new again. Monoclonal antibodies are now all the rage. Monoclonals were out of favor for a decade. However, the FDA approves a couple products and all is forgiven. Fortunately, my firm built positions in two of the original humanized antibody companies when their shares were in the toilet. Now our bottom fishing is making heroes of us with our investors."

"I remember Wall Street's first love affair with antibodies. They were going to cure everything from cancer to the common cold. Then the first products entered human testing and problems emerged. Pop went the bubble."

"We, ah, lightened our positions in the companies you're remembering just before they entered testing." Rupert rocked on his haunches.

"They don't call you Light Horse Lee for nothing." I recalled the nickname he'd earned for charging out of risky positions fast as a cavalry officer galloping through a hole in infantry ranks.

"So, listen." I changed the subject. "Got any assignments for me? I need to get back into consulting to bill my brains out and get some positive cash flow."

"You bet!" Rupert pulled a pad over and jotted a few lines. He ripped the page off and pushed it across the glass.

"Both these companies need your help as of yesterday! I think you'll like the first CEO. He's personable and understands what he needs to accomplish. The other guy is brilliant, but a mad scientist all the way. The needs of lowly investors are lost on him. I want you to make him see he must relate to these people or he's not going to raise enough capital to develop his technology."

Rupert described the technical premises of the two companies, the milestones each needed to achieve, and the financing strategies each was pursuing.

"Nola, it is great to have you back. You're the best fixer in the industry. When a company's business plan, positioning, communications strategy or execution is off the mark, you are the one to straighten the mess out."

"Well, thank you. I try to be a good translator of science and business concepts."

"Translator, my ass. You're a genius with words and perceptions. Many of our science geeks find communications outside the lab painful, but you're at home in both worlds."

"I guess I have dual citizenship. I'm a geek and a scribe. I appreciate these leads, Rupert, and I'll do my best with your companies." I leaned over the desk to grasp Rupert's hand in both my own. He was a great colleague and friend.

Bouncing down the stairs, I met Rupert's daughter coming back up. She waved a CD jewel case at me as she pushed open her bedroom door. I marveled at how much Brenda resembled the rest of the Lee family. Rupert and his wife had had difficulties having children. They decided to forego the fertility clinics in favor of adoption.

The Lees had contacted one of the their relatives still living in China. As it happened, a distant cousin was committing the sin of too many babies, a real problem in the Chinese Republic, because couples are restricted to a single child. The first child born to this couple was female, and the husband was determined to have a son. The inquiry from the American relatives came at the right time. The girl child was spirited out of China through Southeast Asia, Lee money greasing palms along the way. The parents told the Chinese authorities the girl had died. When the second child, a boy, was born, everyone was happy.

While this chain of events would send a Stateside feminist into ideological orbit, the Lees saw no contradiction in solving the childbearing conundrums of their global clan. A year later Lola Lee became pregnant and their natural child, Bobbie, took his place beside sister-cousin, Brenda.

My biological clock was still ticking, but I wondered about my fertility. If I was going to find Mr. Right and start a family, I needed to pick up the pace.

My public relations contact worked on Spear Street. Her office on the seventh floor faced The Embarcadero, affording a postcard view of the Bay Bridge and Alcatraz.

I let go of the pole and jumped off the cable car before it stopped at the bottom of California Street. Only sissies and tourists waited for the conductor to say OK. Dodging a line of cars, I headed for Market Street, catching the green light as I reached the intersection.

An administrative assistant wearing a skirt that must require surgical removal when she changed clothing ushered me into Georgina Fildes' office. A Brit who came to the States for a degree in biochemistry from Berkeley, Georgina married a nice Jewish boy from Manhattan. Together they discovered Birkenstocks and cerebral sex in a flea-bitten cottage on the flats northwest of the Cal campus. Their marriage did not survive his first postdoctoral year.

Georgina, a statuesque brunette, didn't even break stride. In months, she had clinched an account executive's job with the largest public relations agency in San Francisco, trading a hovel in the flats for a flat in chic Pacific Heights. A New York firm acquired her agency, and her new bosses liked Georgina's looks, savvy, and knowledge of bioscience. Soon she was running their entire West Coast technology practice.

Georgina's new digs were courtesy of a ruthless headhunter we both knew. Steve had lured her to a well-funded new firm specializing in investor relations. A partner, Georgina directed the growth strategy of the business. She was in her element and, at thirty, making her mark.

Just as I had done, Georgina earned her stripes and was a card-carrying member of the biotech clan, a close-knit community of entrepreneurial scientists who formed and built the gene-splicing companies, and the financiers, lawyers, accounts, clinical testing experts, and communicators who helped keep the industry moving at a breakneck pace of innovation. It was a world of uncompromising, driven professionals who measured success by Nobel Prizes, issued patents, medical breakthroughs, and billion-dollar valuations. Within this rarified society, members espoused the values and goals of the group to save lives and improve the quality of life of millions by inventing and applying elegant science and using capitalism to deliver it.

"Hurrah, the fixer is back!" Georgina flew into the room. "You have been missed! We have tons of clients in need of help."

She sank into her executive desk chair and spun to face her computer. I waited as she scanned the stock prices of her clients. She punched buttons on her phone, sending incoming calls directly to voice mail, nestled back in her chair, and looked at me expectantly.

"Thank you for fitting me in," I said humbly. "Your assistant said you were overbooked. I wanted to touch base, let you know I'm available, and get your perspective on what's happening."

Georgina leaned forward and put her elbows on the gleaming surface of her immaculate desk. "I'm going to put the word out that you're back in the game, and you'll be flooded with inquiries. Biotech has held well through the dot-com fallout, but the market is sagging and the companies that need to raise capital are scared. Many of the biotech VC firms had lots of money in Internet companies, and they are in big trouble. Rumor has it that Klamath and Parsons is going under. Can you believe it? Such a venerable firm."

Georgina sighed, pushed back from the table, and crossed her elegant legs. "There is no venture money to speak of, and the market for initial public offerings is a distant memory. There's a real premium on good communications with existing investors."

Georgina tilted her chair back. "I'm touring four clients through New York as we speak, and three of them need your assistance on delivering their story more effectively. I'm going to e-mail their CEOs and insist they call you. One bloke in particular is in hot water with his largest investors. He's an awesome scientist, but he babbles about the latest brainstorm had over breakfast and investors think it's a real program. When they inquire about the project later, he's off on another tangent. Someone needs to ride herd on him and make sure he speaks publicly only about product candidates the research and development team has actually advanced into testing."

I rolled my eyes. "I know the problem! One of these days they'll find the entrepreneurial gene, and when they do, they'll discover it's sitting right next to the run-at-the-mouth gene."

"Seriously." Georgina composed herself. "Why didn't you get your degree in biochemistry? I mean, your current career works out fabulously for me, but I have often wondered why you're not leading the charge to clone the next great thing instead of writing about it."

"I did do well according to my professors. They had visions of me doing my doctorate and pursuing an academic career, but there's a difference between being good at something and being truly creative at it. I knew I wasn't Nobel material. And I loved to write. My friends said that if the chemistry final had been an essay, I'd have been a shoe-in for Phi Beta Kappa."

"That's why you transferred to journalism?"

"Yeah, that and some personal stuff. A man I was sweet on died in Viet Nam. His loss was a wakeup call to me that you need to live your life according to your own rules, not somebody else's. "

"And the MBA?"

"Just another set of tools for my tool box. Now I write not only about science but science-based companies."

Georgina's assistant darkened the doorway as best she could with her pencil figure and pointed to her watch. Georgina's posture returned to its usual erect, elegant position. She stood, pulling her suit jacket down with a snap. I rose as well, and we met and shook hands at the end of her long desk.

As we exited her office, she shook a manicured finger at me. "Be ready for all those phone calls."

I waved as she accelerated down the hall, her assistant mincing in her wake. With friends like Georgina and Rupert, my consulting calendar would be full in no time.

The rhythm of my days would be different. I would miss heading my own team, but I would not miss the obstacles and the crises associated with employees and assets. Now, I would advise, but the implementation would be someone else's headache.

Confident I had planted enough seeds to sprout into some gigs, I felt I had earned a drink. I started toward Market Street, heading for the lovely little bar at Campton Place Hotel, but my feet slowed as I remembered Serge's remarks about the club where he'd seen Roger. Bob Harrison's voice overlaid the scene I conjured of Roger dancing with the Internet whore. Harrison had called them lifestyle criminals. People who lived to pursue a certain hip existence, to be a Big Man or Woman in a world evoked in trendy magazines and dark movie theaters. People who plugged themselves into this scene just as addicts plunged a syringe in their veins.

I needed to see this for myself. I was not far from the South of Market district. Stepping to the edge of the sidewalk so that people would not have to careen around me, I flipped open my cell phone and dialed Dakota.

Dakota was still looking for professional work and in the meantime had a job at a Starbucks on Portrero Hill, not far from the fixer he shared with his partner. While it hurt me that a talented designer should have to brew lattes, I was amused at my colleague's choice of interim employment. Dakota never drank coffee, only Mountain Dew. I offered to treat for dinner at The Girder, a restaurant nestled amid the clubs but catering to an older clientele. We agreed to meet in the bar at six. Then I called Janie Belle to say I would not be home for dinner.

"You're goin' to a club," she said. "Is it a date?"

I squeezed my eyes together, rubbing the bridge of my nose as I explained to her that my date was Dakota. Maybe I should ask Rupert to arrange an adoption for me. An instant granddaughter might take Janie Belle's mind off my marital status.

Dakota and I walked the four blocks from The Girder to Extreme Lotus as penance for four courses of California cuisine. South of Market, or SoMa, does not look interesting in the day and doesn't improve much at night. The sidewalks are uneven, and people take a laissez-faire attitude about parking.

We took our time because we were still early, although the neighborhood activity had picked up. Cars cruised by, the thumping of their radio basses rising and falling as they passed. A server sprinted from the bus stop pinning on a nametag as he approached an alley entrance to one of the clubs, and a muscle-burdened bouncer preened in the doorway of the Latin dance club across the street.

Dakota and I reached the block where Extreme Lotus was located. In pauses between traffic, I heard the music emanating from the club. Rap or hip-hop? My grasp of music after Elton John was tenuous. My companion was a Madonna fan.

The bouncer at the club started to say something, but I gave him a motherly look and shoved two twenties in his palm. Dakota and I passed by quickly before he could change his mind. If it had been the weekend, we would have been turned away for terminal dullness.

The interior of the club was Jackie Chan on steroids. The decorator had done everything he could to enlarge the myth of the Macho Ninja. High on pedestals, agile men dressed in black struck exaggerated martial poses. Huge black-and-white enlargements of martial arts experts doing impossible leaps and flips adorned the walls. Nubile females scurried through the growing crowd with drink trays. Their attire also was black—what little there was.

No wonder young men loved this place. Their egos were safe here. I tried to flag down a server but realized after three tries that Dakota would have to do the ordering. A woman with an empty tray zeroed in on him. His discomfort bloomed as she moved with obvious intention into his personal space. He gave her an order, but pretending she could not hear, the server leaned almost to his chest to get him to repeat himself. Dakota looked miserable, and I regretted dragging him into my scheme.

We strolled around the edge of the filling dance floor. The music mixed anger, ugly language, and sex–things that should not go together. As I watched the gyrating crowd, my ears throbbed and my forehead began to get a tight feeling, a prelude to headache. Why had I come? If these were Roger's musical and sexual predilections, so what? I had discovered nothing that achieved closure for me. I pulled Dakota away from the dance floor's edge and shouted in his ear, "Do you have any aspirin?"

He extracted a small tin from his pocket, pinched it, and poured two generic aspirins in my palm. I pointed toward the restroom sign and left him leaning against the wall. The hallway leading to the restrooms was devoid of lighting, but it did have the advantage of a reduced sound level. I reached my hand up to feel along the wall and was surprised to find a surface textured with pictures.

Snapshots of various shapes, sizes, and film types layered the wall. Newer additions obscured those placed earlier. I was surprised at this smarmy practice in a sophisticated, image-conscious establishment. Yet, when you got right down to it, these were images, pictures taken of people in their party duds, arms draped around their equally done-up dates.

I continued my progress toward the ladies' room. A woman brushed roughly past me to get to the same destination, shoving me forward toward the picture wall. My forehead almost touched, and in that moment, I saw Roger. Posed with one hand in his slacks pocket and the other arm wrapped around a petite Asian beauty in an expensive cocktail dress, he smiled at me from the wall. For a second, I was surprised that his date's face was not that of the Internet whore. This girl had a lovely face, although her smug expression took something away from her looks. Examining the pictures in the immediate vicinity of the first photo, I found three more with Roger in them. Another with Roger and this woman. A photo of these two with another couple. And finally, a photo of Roger, his date, and two other men.

I entered the ladies' room, used one of the stalls, and took my time washing my hands. After drying them, I removed a small nail file from my purse and returned to the passageway. When I had the hall to myself, I loosened the photos and placed them in my purse. Older snaps were underneath the pictures of Roger, and the wall looked untouched to the casual observer. I returned to the main room and collected Dakota, who was more than ready to leave.

He walked me to my car, and I opened the door to trigger the cabin light. "Look at what I found. Our trip to Extreme Lotus was not in vain."

Dakota eyed the snaps. "I think you've developed a morbid fixation with Roger."

"These pictures are evidence." I figured the best defense was a good offense. I'll take them to Barbagalatto, the detective managing the murder case. They might lead him to some of Roger's associates." Dakota had to admit this was a prudent thing to do.

After reaching home, I poked my head into my office before going to bed. The red light blinked rhythmically on the phone. Apparently, Rupert and Georgina have been true to their word.

I tiptoed into my bedroom aerie. The moonshine from the casement windows highlighted a black-and-white rump. A head swiveled around at the other end, and two eyes fixed on me.

"Urmph." The owner of the rump turned his face away. I was in deep, deep trouble with a certain pointer dog.

* * *

CHAPTER 5

"Nolaaaaaaaaaaaa." Janie Belle chimed from the bottom of the stairs. Gad, what an awful sound. I flung my feet over the side of the bed while remaining in the prone position. I resembled a model in a cheap mattress commercial.

After a shower, I downed two extra-strength aspirin and looked in the mirror. Man, we must have looked out of place last night; my face had more wrinkles than the grooves on an LP, but only people with wrinkles knew what an LP was. Figuring I would spend the day returning calls, I slipped into some jeans, a turtleneck, and my battered cross trainers.

I had six phone messages. One was from Georgina telling me I would be getting two calls, one from a current client and one from a client of her previous firm. Executives from these companies had left messages. Both companies Rupert mentioned also had called. Finally, there was a call from Barbagalatto.

Remembering my plan to turn the photos in my purse over to the detective, I decided to copy them first. Placing each image on the copier in turn, I duplicated the pictures and shoved the pages in my desk drawer.

Activating the answering system, I listened to the messages, but before returning the calls, I checked out the companies on the Internet. California Antibodies, Inc., was Rupert's hot monoclonal antibody company. CAI had advanced three products into human clinical testing, and the company would file one product with the FDA shortly. Wall Street liked this outfit, and the stock charts and analyst recommendations reflected this positive view.

Rupert's other company was OncoCon Biosciences, Inc., a company developing drugs to treat cancer. This company's technological claim to fame was an ability to identify and exploit novel differentiating targets for major cancers, including breast, ovarian, and prostate. Their discoveries received significant play at the big oncology meetings. The science was first rate. Of course, once you have a good target, you still have to develop a drug that works on that target. The financial analysts covering OncoCon were unanimous in their concern that management did not have the skills or experience to take a drug through the development, testing, and regulatory phases required before marketing a pharmaceutical. This company was the one run by the brilliant scientist who had trouble talking with investors.

Working with the CEO of CAI would be gilding the lily, but I could add real value at OncoCon if I taught this guy the proper way to communicate with external audiences. I called and made appointments with the executives, and phoned Rupert to thank him for the leads.

The first of Georgina's companies, Precision Probes, Inc., was a superbly managed operation focused on the DNA probe diagnostic business. This company had a solid business plan and delivered on milestones. Their problem was that they couldn't get any respect on Wall Street because they weren't a drug company. I called Precision and reached the chief financial officer, who agreed to set up a meeting the following week.

I had trouble finding the information I needed from the last company's Web site. Screen Leaf Biosciences, Inc. was based in South San Francisco. According to the company's cryptic site, Screen Leaf had an extensive library of rare botanical compounds compiled from Asian and Pan-Pacific sources. The company's mission was to provide access to this library to pharmaceutical companies with important targets. If the client company found a compound of interest, Screen Leaf would license it to them and provide the purified compound for research and development. The company was not public yet, and no information about founders or venture investors appeared in the content. This was not unusual, as many private companies were secretive, enjoying a few years of peace before exposing themselves to the unrelenting scrutiny of the public market.

I did find it odd that no "contact us" mechanism was offered on the site. No information on the current management. No e-mail addresses for senior managers or for a designated communications person. I called the phone number and was troubled that no directory was available to guide me to an appropriate manager, just a general mailbox. I left a message explaining my purpose and providing my office and cellular numbers.

Then I rang Georgina's office.

"Hey, Nola! I'm stuffing my briefcase for an investor road show in Chicago. You are going to love Precision's management team; they're a great group to work with. We need to bump their communications efforts up a notch. The content is there, but it needs more polish and pizzazz."

"And Screen Leaf?"

"That one is a company I know nothing about. I gave your name to a former colleague at Brown & Epstein. That client is a recent acquisition for them, and my friend, Lynda, is already frustrated. Don't know what the problems are specifically, it wouldn't be ethical for her to fill me in, but it sounded as if they needed a lot of work. It will be a good billing opportunity for you. And I'm still going to have that other CEO call you when he returns from the New York road show. Listen, must fly. I'm keen to reach Chicago and get my hands on some deep-dish pizza. Cheers!"

I made one more phone call before leaving my office, arranging to meet Sally Harford, the other founder of the e-business, for an after-work drink at a watering hole on Battery Street. Sally now worked for a marketing research firm in an old section of the city noted for antique stores, the original assaying office from Gold Rush days, the corporate headquarters of Levi's, and mercurial restaurants.

In an effort to make it up to Skootch, I put him in the car for the run over to Barbagalatto's office. I selected the station wagon to accommodate the pooch, who propelled himself into the backseat quicker than a fastball hitting a major league catcher's mitt. As I coasted down the hill to Ocean Avenue, I called Barbagalatto's office on my cell phone, reached his voice mail, and explained about the photographs.

Compared to most parts of San Francisco, parking in the Outer Sunset and Richmond districts is actually achievable. I pulled into a parallel space across the street from the police station without having to back in. I jaywalked across Taraval, skipping over the trolley tracks and slipping between two parked cruisers to the sidewalk. At that moment, Barbagalatto and another man exited the station. The other man was Bob Harrison.

Acknowledging my presence, the two men stopped. Barbagalatto spoke first. "We decided to get together and compare notes on Chen. You have to follow through on all the loose ends, or something could be overlooked. Let's see those pictures."

I fished in my bag and handed him the pictures. Harrison, who was much taller than Barbagalatto, looked over his shoulder at the images.

"Yup, well, our boy looks a lot better here than in the morgue photos," Barbagalatto said. "What club did you say these were from?"

I repeated for his and Harrison's benefit the circumstances under which I had acquired the snapshots.

"I didn't figure you for the glittering nightlife of SoMa." Harrison smirked.

I started to defend my presence at Extreme Lotus when Barbagalatto interrupted. "Hey, I gotta be downtown in thirty minutes. Listen, Bob, I really appreciate you coming out and filling me in on the fraud cases. I'll take it from here, and Ms. Billingsley, thanks for the pictures, but I hope you're not getting it into your head to start investigating on your own. Citizens need to leave these things to the professionals." With that, he turned on his heel and rounded the corner on Thirty-second Avenue to reach the police parking compound.

Harrison and I looked at each other. "How about a sandwich?" he said.

"Works for me."

Although ample parking existed at Taraval, as San Franciscans, we were always strategizing about the next parking challenge. It was a cool day, Skootch was asleep on the backseat, and the windows were down an inch for circulation. We agreed to go together in his car and come back for mine after lunch.

"Wow, this is one sweet car!" Harrison handed me into a restored '57 Chevy. As I waited for him to walk around the vehicle, I ran an appreciative finger along the edge of the massive steering wheel and experienced a flashback to my early dating life, imagining Janice's "Piece of My Heart" on the radio.

Harrison eased into the driver's seat. "I really like the better leg room in the older cars. Picked this up in an impound auction. Guy who owned it got busted for entrepreneurial pharmaceutical sales to minors over on Mission."

Harrison headed west to the ocean. Expecting a fast-food chain, I was surprised when he headed north and U-turned into a parking space at the Cliff House. It was a magnificent day, and despite the usual crush of tourists, our wait was only ten minutes. The host seated us at a deuce at the window overlooking Seal Rock. We laughed when we ordered the same thing, a Dungeness crab sandwich and iced tea.

While we waited for our food, I updated him on the closing of the Internet business and my return to consulting.

"I'm glad to hear you're moving on," he commiserated. "You can't dwell on the e-commerce collapse. Many people crashed and burned when that sector blew up. Fortunately, we live in an area with other industries. Say what you will about tourism. It's low tech, but it employs armies of people. And biotech is great."

"Yeah, it's the feeder system for the pharmaceutical industry. We all want to stay healthy, and the older we get the more help we need."

"You know anybody working on a sinus cure? Ever since I moved here, I've been stuffed up."

"Can't help with that yet. Most biotechnology companies are working on diseases that kill or severely debilitate the victims. You don't look particularly debilitated to me."

Indeed, he looked anything but. Broad shoulders, flat stomach, just enough muscle, and the right amount of chest hair peeking out from the vee of his open-necked shirt. He had a reasonable tan for a desk jockey. It was the perfect shade to accent those caramel brown eyes.

"I guess you realize that with Roger's death, the cases against him will be wrapped up and closed."

"You don't mean to tell me that the district attorney was actually going to proceed? Our district attorney, the one who adores publicity but not at the risk of actually doing any work or, gasp, possibly losing a case?"

Harrison smirked and pushed back from the table, arching a hip to extract his wallet. "Pity we're not in the business of prosecuting dead people. A stiff couldn't put up much of a defense or counter the DA's dazzling close."

Now that our professional relationship was over with the untimely passing of the perp, Harrison let his guard down. "You never really had a chance because yours was a crime against property." He layered bills on top of the check. "Now, if Rog had knifed you on his way out the door, you'd have the DA's attention. And if you had been pregnant, you'd have zoomed right to the top of his list."

I scooped french fries from my plate into a paper napkin, and we headed for the door. Harrison drove me back to Taraval, depositing me next to the station wagon. I glanced into the backseat as I slid behind the wheel. Skootch was in his inverted position. Back legs splayed, front legs bent at the wrist, ears resting on the seat, tongue lolling. I set the fries silently on the passenger seat, but I was powerless over their aroma. As I snapped my seatbelt in place, the thrashing in the back intensified. Before I could put the car in reverse, a silky head shot between the seats, and black lips fixed on the edge of the napkin. A determined jerk emptied the fries onto the seat. By the time I had guided the car into the traffic lane, the fries and the seat were vacuumed. I peaked in the rearview mirror and saw a smiling doggy.

"Urp," said Skootch.

"Don't mention it, big guy." I backed the wagon and changed gears.

A visit to my office revealed a blinking light on the phone. I pushed the play button.

"This is Casper Wong, CEO of Screen Leaf Biosciences. I want to talk about your services. Please call me back on my cell." He left the number. I called as instructed and reached the voice mail of his cellular provider. I left another message.

I thought I had better change before going downtown to meet Sally. In my bedroom, I pulled a taupe pantsuit from a cleaner's bag and found a white silk shell I figured I could wear one more time.

While I changed, I thought of Harrison and his choice of luncheon locales. The Cliff House was a romantic spot. Could he be interested? Was I interested in him?

The Internet business debacle had taken a lot out of me, including my libido. Running a start-up is not good for your private life, especially your sex life. Long hours, anxiety, and lack of attention to fitness or healthful food is the rule. I had not had a man in my life since the founding of the company. My mother reminded me of this with numbing frequency.

"Well, are you interested in Bob Harrison?" I asked the face in the mirror lipstick poised at the ready. The eyes in the mirror winked yes. My juices were flowing again. I wondered about that partner of his who had died in Baltimore. Was she attractive? Was she young? I penciled in the eyebrows nature had omitted and streaked on blusher. Pulling my hair back in a low ponytail, I fastened it with a tortoiseshell clip.

Somehow, it was four thirty; I picked up the pace. When I returned to my office to collect my bag, the answering light was blinking again. I listened to the message while I examined my manicure for dings. Casper Wong again. He suggested a meeting tomorrow afternoon at three o'clock and asked that I leave him a message, one way or the other, on his cell. I dialed the number and replied in the affirmative. Grabbing my bag and my Saab keys, I headed for the garage.

Sally breezed into the bar in a red two-piece I particularly admired. Always cold, she had a black jacket thrown around her shoulders. She waved at the waitperson as she settled into her seat. "Great to see you. I've looked forward to venting ever since you called. I am sick to death of researching demographics on eighteen-year-olds. Give me an aging baby boomer any day. Boomers buy early and often, and they are brand loyal. These kids don't know a brand from a viral infection. Were they born or hatched? That's what I'd like to know."

The waitperson arrived. He was slightly older than the demographic Sally had been researching. This produced a glower and a barked order, "Martini. Beefeaters. Up. Donate the olive to Greenpeace."

The young man was taken aback, but he recovered and turned to me. "I'm Chad, your server," he beamed at me, scribbling Sally's order on his pad and awaiting mine.

"Dewar's on the rocks with a twist, please."

"In a jiff!" Chad whirled and sashayed toward the bar. He was wearing a chic Cossack blouse with the neck unbuttoned. His earring had a discrete dangle.

I turned to Sally. "Imagine Chad in a tsarist prison."

This produced a guffaw and the first smile of the afternoon. We caught up on our lives. In Sally's case, this was no small feat owing to the exploits of her three dogs and four cats. She named her pets after New York department stores. The cats were Bonwit, Teller, Lord, and Taylor, while the dogs were Bergdorf, Goodman, and Macy.

We were laughing over the escapades of her delinquent collie, Bergdorf, when I glanced up and saw Roger's babe. She was standing in the queue in the entry waiting for a table. A sage silk business suit and a red knit halter-top had replaced the cocktail dress. Two men, one of whom could have been in the photos I purloined from the club, accompanied her. I could not be sure. She was talking with him while arm in arm with the other man. Oh, Roger, how quickly you have been forgotten.

"Don't turn around, but I want you to see somebody." I quickly told Sally the tale of the club visit. I described the girl's outfit, and Sally excused herself to go to the restroom.

Chad cruised by and I signaled for another round. Sally returned quickly because she didn't really have to go. She settled into her seat in front of the empty martini glass.

"Don't panic, I've sent our server for more booze. Do you suppose his earring might be called a hanging Chad?" We were still giggling when the intact Chad served our drinks.

Sally was quick with her assessment of Roger's girl. "She is attractive, I'll give her that. I didn't expect old Rog to have such taste. They were talking about genes when I walked by. Your kind, not my kind." Sally's company was doing research for the Levi's brand. The company's loyal but aging baby boomer customers was spreading around the middle and opting for more forgiving fabrics than denim.

"Really? She must be sharp as well as sexy," I said. Biotech companies boasted doctoral and master's degreed personnel.

The woman and her companions were escorted away by a host in Russian blouse, nose ring, and crimson hair.

Sally had to cut our evening short and return to the office to finish a report for a tight deadline. We agreed to meet at Fort Funston on the weekend to run the dogs. I strolled down to a favorite sushi bar in the shadow of the Transamerica pyramid and had a guilty pleasure of a dinner. Janie Belle and Sally abhorred sushi, and Dakota would not get near seafood in general. I had to indulge my passion for it alone. I wondered if Harrison liked raw fish. After all, he came from the oyster capital of the world.

* * *

CHAPTER 6

I spent the morning surfing the Internet for information on screening technologies in preparation for my afternoon meeting. I took a break at ten thirty and called several biotechnology analysts. My colleagues were generous with their time, but not one of the three I reached had much to tell me about Screen Leaf. Only two recognized the name, and only one placed the company in South San Francisco.

Janie Belle and I enjoyed a lunch of ramen. Skootch thought this was a poor choice because it produced no treats. No bread crusts, no leftover fries, no croutons. To make it up to him, I took him for a short walk around the neighborhood.

My home is one block from the Chinese consul's residence. Skootch liked the residence because of its canine denizens. For reasons that were lost on me since our neighborhood was crime free, sufficiently affluent for neighbors to resist swiping the consular shrubbery or garden figures, and enlightened enough to refrain from expressing our political views in gate graffiti, the Chinese chose to deploy a pair of pit bulls to police the grounds. Odd choice of dog. Chows can be formidable, can't they? Skootch meandered along the length of the wrought iron and masonry wall as the two pit bulls paced him on the other side. He almost never looked in their direction. At the end of the wall, he peed a long and satisfying pee, secure in the knowledge they could not get out to mark over his scent. We turned downhill toward Monterey Boulevard and circled back to Plymouth.

After depositing Skootch in the backyard, I headed upstairs to shower and change for my afternoon meeting. Refreshed and clad in a mid-calf length black sheath, matching jacket and paisley scarf, I passed through the living room on my way out.

Janie Belle paged through the San Francisco Chronicle in search of the bridge column. "That Barbajello fellow is quoted about your employee's case in the front section. He says he has a lead."

I snapped up the section resting on the couch beside her. I flipped to page two and found the headline. Scanning the article, I located the quote she had referenced and was disappointed. Barbagalatto said the police were seeking a young female associate of Chen's who had been seen with him at a local nightclub.

"This is the lead I dug up for him!"

"How nice of you to help the police! How come he didn't mention your name?"

"Now that's publicity I can do without." I dropped the paper and headed for the garage.

Driving south on Highway 101, I admired the windsurfers traversing the cove above Oyster Point. I exited and eased off to the side to consult the map and directions I'd pulled off the Web that morning. South San Francisco, known as the Industrial City, is home to many companies, including the most famous in my industry, Genentech. The successful, well-financed companies were housed in shimmering high rises or commodious single-story light industrial buildings with attractive signage, landscaping, and neatly patterned parking areas. My map took me away from these sections to a strip of Class C commercial space along a neglected side road across an abandoned rail spur. I had difficulty reading the faded and broken numbers on the units.

I passed the number I was looking for and backed up to enter the designated parking area. Turning into a space, I glimpsed the Screen Leaf logo on the door in the recessed entry. I grabbed my bag and portfolio and locked the car.

The reception area was cheerier than the building's exterior. The reception desk obscured all but the crown, part, and barrette of the occupant. I leaned on the top of the counter, and a smiling face greeted me. The diminutive receptionist handed me a check-in clipboard. Signing my name and the time, I told her I was to see Casper Wong. She dialed Wong's office, announced me, invited me to sit and assured me the wait would not be long.

After ten minutes, I began to riffle through the magazines on the coffee table in front of me. After twenty minutes, I began to pace. At twenty-three minutes, I attracted the attention of the receptionist. She dialed Wong's office again and informed me it would be a few minutes more.

I remained at the counter, and her eyes darted to the door to the inner offices and back to me. "I'm sorry for the inconvenience. Our CEO has a lot of meetings and often gets behind by the afternoon."

I returned to my pacing. I do not respect executives who will not control their schedules. Chronic lateness is not a good trait for a corporate leader. It is a character flaw that screams, "Look at me! I am important." These personalities also make poor consulting clients.

I was about to tell Smiley to call and say I had to leave for another appointment when the inner office door burst open pushed by a trash barrel on wheels. Propelling it was a gum-popping, overall-wearing janitor with a broom in his other hand. He used his hip to push the barrel forward and press the door closed. I had to step out of the way of the gliding receptacle as it made good progress on the polished surface of the reception area floor.

The janitor made a few ineffectual sweeps with his long broom. He propped the broom against a fake banana tree in the corner of the sitting area, and reached behind the reception desk for the trashcan. His movements were clumsy and loud. Smiley shrank from that side of the desk. He took the can to the barrel and shook the contents out, leaving the plastic bag liner to do its duty for another day.

A small, corrugated box plopped on top of the mound in the barrel, landing with the label facing me. It was the Ancient Turtle Company label. The same one that graced the box with the strange herbs forwarded to my home. The image of Roger looking up at me from his desk where he had been enjoying the Internet porn came, unwelcome, into my mind.

An unpleasant coincidence? All it meant was that there was at least one male chauvinist in this company who wanted to prop up his performance. Maybe not even that. After all, some elixirs on the Ancient Turtle Web site were intended for other purposes. A better night's sleep. Longevity. Improved memory. Or maybe, Smiley had bought it as a gift for her main squeeze.

A noise caused me to turn around. The janitor was gone and had been replaced by the CEO's assistant. "Ms. Billingsley." She shook my hand. "Mr. Wong will see you now. Please follow me."

I trailed her through the door into a narrow, undistinguished hall. We traveled about half the length of the building and turned left. Going right would have taken us into the labs. White-coated personnel crossed the hall carrying roller bottles, stacks of ninety-six well plates, and other lab ware.

We passed through a nest of cubicles and down another, shorter hall to the executive area. Wong's office door faced a glass-walled meeting room where several people listened as a colleague spoke to a PowerPoint presentation.

Wong turned from contemplating his wall of bio-art. He had a series of expensive framed prints of electron microscope images. In one striking picture, a sinister macrophage cell prepared to ingest an unsuspecting intruder.

"I'm sorry I made you wait," Wong said, gesturing toward a long, low sofa under the macrophage picture. "I had to take a call from Benjamin Gordon, and this was the only time we could connect today."

I crossed the room and took my place on the sofa. I couldn't shake the feeling that the macrophage was preparing to reach for me.

Benjamin Gordon was the head of investment banking at Lerner Brothers and the most famous banker in the biotechnology sector. Wong knew I knew who he was. And I knew he knew I knew. "Not a problem," I lied. "Mr. Gordon would be a good reference for me. He knows my work well. How may I help you, Mr. Wong?"

"As you probably have guessed since I let slip that we are talking to investment bankers, we are contemplating a public offering. We haven't made up our minds. After all, the market is not the best, but we need to move in that direction." Wong sat on the edge of his desk, swinging a Cole Haan loafer in a circle as he talked. "I am proud to say that we have been secretive about our novel technology and library. We have a library that is brimming with compounds that are truly innovative. This asset will drive our valuation in the offering and accelerate our partnering initiatives."

I tried not to roll my eyes. "There are many companies with compound libraries. It's a long way from a library to a drug approval, and today's investor is well aware of the pitfalls along the way."

Wong smiled. "I think we can make our case to the institutional investors. I'm talking to the cream of investment banking houses, and once we've decided on our underwriting team, we'll make it clear we only want to present before the most knowledgeable institutions. They will see the value of this library."

Wong adjusted the cuff of his designer shirt. "I, of course, am planning to do the lion's share of presentations, but we need to retain you to work with our chief financial officer and chief scientific officer, who will do portions of our slide show and answer the occasional question. The CFO, in particular, needs work on speaking skills. He's dry and dull."

"Do you have an existing presentation? I'd prefer to review as many materials as possible about your company. Your Web site wasn't much help."

"Yes, we intended our Web site to be vague to discourage people we don't have time for. I can't be bothered with those reporters from the biotech newsletters. So tedious. I'll have my assistant get you a copy of our confidentiality agreement to sign after which she may give you a packet of materials. She'll set you up with meetings with managers as well."

"Whom do you consider to be your competition from a technical point of view?"

"We don't have any direct competition." Wong eyed his watch. "Our library and our screening approach are different from everything out there. You won't have any problem differentiating us from the pack." He reached in the direction of his phone to call his assistant.

"Before you do that, perhaps I should tell you how I like to work. I have my own contract, and I'd like to go over some of the points with you before we begin working together."

I slipped a draft agreement from my folder and slid it across the table toward him.

He flipped the document around, thumbed to the last page, and scrawled his signature without reading anything. With that, he stood, punched the phone intercom, and summoned the assistant.

"Look, I'm pressed for time. Another banker wants to see me up in the city. Cindy will get you everything you need. I'm pleased you're going to be working with us."

I half stood to clasp his offered hand and almost dropped my papers and pen as he whirled on his heels and breezed out the door. Cindy had to skip to the side to avoid being struck like a bowling pin.

As I exited the building, I questioned whether I wanted to work for Screen Leaf. The arrogance of the chief executive and the man's complete lack of understanding regarding the needs of investors were enough reason to decline this engagement. The slimness of the packet Cindy had given me was another. I would have my work cut out for me.

I reminded myself I didn't have much in the way of income. As I started the engine, I resolved to do more research on my own and meet with the other managers before jumping to conclusions. Many start-ups had crazy founders backed up by sensible people, the folks who turned the flights of fancy dreamed up by the geniuses into real products.

Wheeling out of the parking lot, I came to an abrupt halt. A truck delivering water bottles was blocking the street. I caught a glimpse of the driver guiding his pushcart around the corner of the building across the way. The other end of the street was a dead end. I backed up into the lot and swiveled in my seat to see what was behind me. Fortunately, an alley offered egress from the back of the property. I turned the car into the alley, shifted gears, and proceeded along the back of the building leased by Screen Leaf.

If the front of this structure was depressing, the back was appalling. Piles of debris teetered against the back wall. Grass grew in lush profusion from gapping cracks in the pavement. Pools of brackish, oily water occupied depressions in the roadway. My pace diminished to a jerky crawl.

The facilities housing most biotech companies are spotless. After all, they are baby drug companies. Even new-minted firms that cannot afford any but the cheapest available space keep it orderly and clean. More evidence that Screen Leaf might not make the best client.

The alley wasn't straight. I swung the wheel hard to the right and eased the car around the elbow between the Screen Leaf building and the adjacent structure. The Saab seemed to suck itself in on the right door panel to avoid touching the rundown edifice on the inside of the turn. I straightened the wheel as the car slipped into the shadow cast by the taller structure. This leg of the alley was narrower than the first. I was encouraged by the light denoting the street ahead and breathed a sigh of relief as we exited the alley, but cut it short as I realized the two vehicles parked on either side of my escape route were too close together to allow me to pass.

I backed up into the alley to afford pedestrians room to get by my hood, and then climbed out of the car. I took note of the car makes and surveyed the block. The entrance to the building across the street must be around that corner, I reasoned. The buildings in the Screen Leaf block faced the other way. That left the tall building. I studied the front of the dilapidated structure for signs of life. A door relieved the monotony of the facade, but there were no windows. No business sign adorned the door, but a 696 was stenciled in sloppy fashion over the entryway. I was intrigued that this company did not choose to display its name on the exterior of the building.

I moved down the sidewalk until I was standing in front of the door. As I reached for the handle, a man burst through, almost knocking me flat. I jumped back as he glanced at me and, without changing his pace, crossed the street to a BMW.

No point asking rude guy for help. I turned, grasped the door handle, and pulled, but it had locked after him when it closed. I looked for a buzzer, but none appeared. Well, it was quitting time now; maybe I wouldn't have to wait long. I didn't. The door opened and three workers exited. I noted how well dressed they were. I also noticed that the cars along the street, although not BMWs, were newer and pricier than you would expect given the surroundings.

I grabbed the door before it closed again and entered the lobby. While the reception area was spare, it was a lot newer than the exterior. The owners had gutted and renovated this building but made no investment on the outside. A uniformed guard sat next to an inner door, which required a swipe card for entry. Bored and no doubt near the end of his shift, he slumped on his stool, favoring the hip that did not support his sidearm. Smiling, I approached him and explained my situation. He said that since it was five o'clock, the place would empty soon and my situation would resolve itself when one of the owners of the offending cars removed their vehicle. As if to underscore the veracity of his assertion, the door began to open rhythmically as people left work. Soon the flow resembled salmon swimming upstream. With a grunt, the guard rose from his perch and unlatched the second door so the crowd of workers could exit faster.

I pressed myself against the wall to prevent being swept out on the tide. The doors were held wide now by the constant stream of bodies. I looked over their heads and saw a large open plan work area. The arrangement of cubicles and computer equipment would be familiar to anyone who has ever been in a high-tech company. These employees were computer geeks similar to those employed at Oracle down the road. What they did paid well, hence the nice clothes and cars.

When a break opened in the stampede, I inserted myself into the flow and returned to the sidewalk. Success! Both of the cars were gone. I returned to the Saab, started the engine, and moved into traffic. As I edged up to the intersection, I noted the name of the street I was leaving. It was United Nations Way. Pretentious, for a down-and-out street. The United Nations, of course, was founded in San Francisco. Perhaps this area was being developed when that happened.

As I turned on the larger road, I realized I had seen that street name recently. But where? The name was memorable.

"Alzheimer's!" Janie Belle exclaimed. Because she was eighty, she had her share of senior moments, and she delighted in a younger person's memory lapse. If only for a moment, it leveled the playing field.

I'd told her when I got home about the street name that was nagging at me. I could not for the life of me remember where I had seen it.

"Well, you're not getting any younger. Of course, you've been under a lot of stress lately, but mostly you're not twenty anymore."

"Thanks, I needed that." I rolled my eyes. "I've gone over all my old clients in my mind, my e-commerce connections, and the new referrals from Rupert and Georgina; and that address does not relate to any of them."

"It'll come to ya." She thumbed through the TV listings. "Remember that time before I moved out here when we couldn't think of that actress's name. It went on for weeks and weeks, but finally I called you in the dead of night."

"Yeah, I remember. It was three in the morning, and I was getting my first good night's sleep after a series of miserable deadlines. The phone rang and I thought sure somebody was dead. I picked it up and you said 'Susan Hayward' and hung up. I want to remind you that I never got back to sleep that night. I'm biding my time, and one night when you least expect it, I'm going to sneak into your room and..."

"I am an old woman. You should be more respectful of my advanced years." Janie Belle clicked the channel changer with a superior smirk.

Skootch is an almost perfect canine, but he does have one glaring fault. He passes gas. We keep him away from any dog food with corn in it. We keep trashcans turned backward to prevent him from rifling the contents. We try, or at least, *I* try to keep his treats to a minimum, but nothing works. He can clear a room. What am I saying? He can clear the 49ers' stadium.

We keep air freshener positioned throughout our home. These accommodations allow us to live together in relatively fresh air. Until the night. The Olympic gas passer is my bedmate. There is nothing like being wakened in the middle of the night by a pssssssssssss followed by an unspeakable aroma wafting in close proximity to your face.

I sat bolt upright gasping for air, and fully awake, regretted I had inhaled at all. I struggled with the covers, trying to reach the side of the bed for tissues to hold over my nose and, if our housekeeper had not moved it, a can of lifesaving lily-of-the-valley aerosol.

The commotion woke Skootch, who grunted and rolled to a sitting position. I grasped the tissue, flicked on the light, and propped myself up on the pillows, leaning casually toward the bedside table.

I let my hand drift toward the can and deliverance.

"Grrrrrrrrrrh."

All boy, Skootch, does not approve of floral air fresheners. In fact, he disapproves of aerosol of all kinds. Someday, a clever company will come out with *eau du steak* and, perhaps, Skootch will reconsider his attitude. Until then, he will remain steadfastly anti-spray.

I tried to distract him by plumping my pillows and arranging the blanket. He slid down on his elbows. I patted him on his head with one hand and reached for the aerosol with the other.

"Grrrrrh."

"Skootch, gimme a break."

His tail wagged. Now it had become a game.

Since I had spied the can, I judged its location and turned the light off. Pretending I was going to sleep again, I rolled on my side and reached for it.

"Gruggggggggrrrrrrrr."

"Damn you, you overbearing, overeating dirigible. I'm going to get you a cork."

Unconcerned, Skootch rolled on his back and sighed.

I sighed, too, wide-awake now. The casement was ajar, and I smelled the night jasmine from my neighbor's backyard, a welcome scent given Skootch's indiscretion. Relaxing into the pillows, I closed my eyes, imagining I also smelled the aroma of peanut sauce from the Thai restaurant down the hill.

"Thai!" I sat up. "That's it!" The address was from the Web site of the Ancient Turtle Company. Their headquarters were in Thailand, but they had a local office in South San Francisco. Now, I remembered that address had been United Nations Way.

Tomorrow, I would go on the Internet and check the street number. I considered sneaking down to Janie Belle's room and intoning, "Thai," like a Buddhist gong until she woke up.

Pssssssssssssssssss.

"Geez Louise, Skootch!" I leaped out of bed, snatched the can, and laid down a floral fog to make the San Francisco Botanical Society proud.

* * *

CHAPTER 7

"Youhooooooooo!" I stood in the kitchen which was empty except for a bolt of sunlight illuminating the dust mites that hovered over Janie Belle's hooked rug in front of the sink.

"I'm in the dining room," a muffled voice replied.

I poked my head around the corner and spied two derrieres, one tailless and one with its tail contentedly waving. The owners of the derrieres were genuflecting in the china cabinet.

"You looking for something?"

"I cannot find my deviled egg plate!"

Skootch swung his head around. The sparkle in his eyes meant he had understood the word *egg*. His head returned to the search position.

Janie Belle pushed him out of the way as she crawled from the left to the right side of the cabinet. Her head and torso rose and descended, an elevator cab, as she perused the shelves.

"I must have it for the church bridge luncheon."

"Well, your odds are good, because you have one and you gave me one as a gift when I moved to California."

"Every Southern gal has to have her own deviled egg plate. You never know when you might have to prepare deviled eggs." The resonance in Janie Belle's voice was enhanced by the bounce from the cabinet interior.

"Right, deviled eggs fit right in with sourdough bread, goat cheese, organic greens, Northwest salmon, and chardonnay. I'll leave you to it. I'll be in my office."

I plopped down in my office chair, grabbed the mouse, and doubled-clicked on the Internet icon. I relocated the Ancient Turtle Company's Web site and found the address. Sure enough, the address was 696 United Nations—the building with the no-name entrance and the security guard.

I sat back and rocked the chair in reflection. Of course, this would explain why I'd seen an Ancient Turtle box in the trash at Screen Leaf. Probably, an employee from Screen Leaf had met an employee from Ancient Turtle while out back smoking or jogging around the block during the lunch hour. Their conversation turned to their work, one thing led to another, and the Ancient Turtle employee offered to liberate some herbal elixir for the Screen Leaf worker to try.

But the building I had visited looked nothing like an herbal company; it resembled a computer company: rows of workstations, several mainframe towers beyond a glass partition, data storage media. Nothing biological. No evidence of a shipping operation. I tried to recall a loading dock.

I sat forward and browsed through the product section of the Ancient Turtle site. I selected an anti-wrinkle cream containing an exotic leaf extract and placed it in the shopping cart. Worthless, no doubt, but cheaper than the stuff I buy at Macy's. I filled in the address information and hit the continue button. When asked for my credit card information, I hesitated but entered the number and expiration date and clicked the submit button. A shipping page with choices regarding delivery methods appeared. It was clear from the methods offered and the handling of the tax calculation that the package would not be coming from South San Francisco. How could they make any money? The shipping charge was sixty percent of the cost of the product, and I would have to wait four to six weeks for my face cream to arrive. How many herb-worshiping nutcases could there be? This made no sense. Why wouldn't they have distribution together with their computer operation? And why a slick technical operation for such a business?

The ring of the phone jarred me from my reverie. I pressed the receiver to my ear. "Hello?"

"Ms. Billingsley, I'm glad I caught you! I'm Leonard Price, CEO of California Antibodies. Rupert Lee spoke to me about you and I hope we can get together. Rupert believes you will be a great asset to our efforts."

"I hope he hasn't oversold my capabilities. Do you have any time this afternoon?"

"Yes, but remember, we're located in Emeryville, so you need to allow yourself time to get over the bridge."

"No problem, how about three?"

"Perfect! We're just off Fifty-third Street on Ostrach Avenue. See you then."

I spent the rest of my morning reviewing the information I had gathered about CAI. The company's patent position was solid, and their clinical team and scientific advisors were first rate. I made some notes for questions I would ask Price when I met him.

Before lunch, a messenger arrived with a manila envelope from Screen Leaf. Cindy had managed to find me a few more documents to review, and she had included a schedule for the following Monday detailing appointments with the CFO and the senior marketing executive.

Well, I reflected, these people want to get moving.

I dropped the materials in my office and headed for the kitchen. The deviled egg plate had been found and filled. It sat on the kitchen table swathed in plastic wrap for the trip to the church hall.

I fixed tuna sandwiches and poured the liquid from the tuna can over Skootch's food. The kibbles were history before Janie Belle and I even settled at the table.

"I'm headed to the East Bay and will be coming back across the bridge during the rush hour, so start drinking without me," I informed my mother. "And try not to beat the church ladies too severely at bridge. After all, these events are for fellowship, right?"

"Anything worth doing is worth doing well."

"You ladies don't play for money, do you?"

"Mind your own business!" Janie Belle avoided eye contact by sweeping crumbs from around her doily.

I left the table and proceeded to my bathroom to brush my teeth and run a comb through my hair. When I stood back to look at myself, I noticed a grease stain from the mayonnaise in the sandwich poised on my bosom. I turned to the closet to find another blouse, but nothing seemed right, so I abandoned the closet in favor of the scarf drawer and selected a silk square. Rolling the scarf, I knotted it in the middle and fastened the ends behind my neck. The knot settled into the vee of my jacket, covering the offending spot.

As I skipped down the stairs, a commotion exploded in the kitchen, and a flying pooch shot past me up the stairs.

I grasped the doorframe and leaned around the corner to assess the situation in the kitchen. Janie Belle stood, red-faced, pointing at the egg plate. The plastic wrap was lifted to a tent position and six of the twelve halves had been excised.

"Seems Skootch has perfected a new version of the Lunge." I bit my upper lip to keep from laughing, but my eyes gave me away.

"That dog of yours is not long for this world." The cardsharp shook her head in disgust.

The Bay Bridge is two bridges, the Yin and Yang of the East Bay. The traffic decks are stacked so that your trip toward the east passes through a polluted, dingy chute fashioned from the upper and lower decks.

On the Oakland side of the bridge, the deck descends and cars alight on land, so many ugly ducklings. I proceeded from the bridge into the Bermuda Triangle of highway interchanges, the confluence of San Francisco, Oakland, Napa Valley, Sacramento, and San Jose traffic peppered with Berkeley peaceniks driving beaters liberated from the capitalistic notion of liability insurance.

I swung left with the traffic headed for Berkeley and Emeryville. In the early eighties, Emeryville was a neglected sliver of landfill forming a no man's municipality between troubled Oakland and nuclear-free Berserkley. Artists, junk dealers, and biotechnology companies flocked to Emeryville for its creativity-boosting views and cheap rental space. In those days, one condominium complex huddled on the shore as if it were debris from a shipwreck, and a forlorn Holiday Inn beckoned travelers to stop before they reached the bridge to Baghdad-by-the-Bay.

Today, Emeryville has arrived. Important companies project their logos from gleaming spires. Alice Waters-esque eateries compete with San Francisco restaurants for nods from leading food critics. Condominiums and car dealerships promise a chic, environmentally sensitive lifestyle.

I gazed at the blue, yellow, and white behemoth, Ikea, as I waited for traffic to accelerate out of the northward turn. When the next quake comes and liquefies these flats, the Viking flagship will come loose from her moorings and sail back to Scandinavia using those trendy inflatable armchairs as flotation.

Exiting at Powell Street, I eased into the left turn lane at Fifty-third and headed north to Ostrach Street, where I made a right and pulled into the parking lot at California Antibodies, Inc. No filthy alleys here. The building and grounds of CAI were crisply maintained.

I announced myself to the receptionist and received a visitor badge, filled out in advance. By the time I had added my name to the sign-in sheet, an assistant stood at my elbow waiting to escort me to the office of the chief executive.

Leaving the lobby, we entered a light-blessed colony of cubicles. Employees occupied every cube, and the place hummed with the low buzz of productivity. I felt myself hoping that I would be successful in landing an assignment.

We took the stairs to the next level and traversed a wide hall separating laboratories. People consulted in the corridor, and traffic between the labs was brisk. We paused in front of one door as a technician edged a steel cart with a new piece of equipment through the doorway. It was a sequencer. Beyond the door, a smiling scientist rubbed her hands in anticipation.

What a contrast to Screen Leaf. This bustle and bonhomie was nowhere in evidence at the other company.

Leonard Price, MD, PhD, and CEO of CAI, greeted me at his office door, his gray eyes and silver-flecked blond hair set off by a cheerful checked shirt. He wore cords and suede shoes. His beard was neatly cropped, and his handshake was firm and exuberant.

Price ushered me to a table and upholstered chairs arranged to face a white board. A laptop tethered to a projector was at his elbow. A bulging folder of materials waited in front of my seat.

"Why don't I give you an overview of the company with the PowerPoint presentation we developed for the partnering conference last week?"

"Sure. Perfect." As he talked, I noted how involved in his work this man was. His enthusiasm was contagious, but his humility won you over.

"I am very fortunate to have Hal De Marco and Philip Barnes on my scientific advisory board," Price said. "We have gotten so many good suggestions from them both. Our products would not be as advanced in the clinic without their guidance.

"I'm proud of our discovery research team and also the efforts of our product development group," Price said summing up the technical part of his presentation. "Of course, I have to pay homage to Hugo Deutsch, our crusty old board member, a retired executive from Mertz Pharma, for some of this progress. His sharp critiques of our original clinical testing plan caused us to redirect the project team and save our product candidate."

Here was a man who listened to others, respected contrary ideas, and weighed input objectively. No wonder the company was doing well.

Infected by Price's enthusiasm, I asked a stream of questions. Soon, I was finishing his sentences and jumping ahead with the next logical thought. Thrilled that I was attuned to his technical strategy, Price began to talk about some of the new stuff they had begun to develop.

After ten minutes, Price reached the end of the talk. "What do you think? Of the technology, not the presentation. I know you'll have a lot of suggestions about how to make that better."

"I think your approach is sound, but I think you need to work on your positioning. You should be more differentiated from

Xereba and OmniMabs who are chasing the same problem, but in a much more traditional and, I believe, risky way."

Price was intrigued by this observation, and we explored my ideas for another hour before agreeing to meet the following Monday after I had read their operating plan.

As I left the building, I smiled at the number of cars in the parking lot. It was after six, and most CAI employees were still at the bench. The leadership and culture here were the stuff of success.

I rounded the turn from Fifty-third to Powell and came to an abrupt halt. The CAI employees were still at work, but everyone else in the East Bay was headed for the bridge. I punched the radio button, flipped my visor down, and adjusted the seat lever. It was going to be a long drive home.

* * *

CHAPTER

8

When I got home, the message light was flashing again. I pushed the button and hefted the stack of CAI materials onto my desk. After the announcement that I had a message received at five thirty, the machine entered play mode. For the first few seconds there was no sound, and I assumed that the call was a wrong number, but then the caller cleared his throat and began to speak.

"Nola, this is Bob Harrison. I need to talk to you about something. It, ah, doesn't have to do with the case. I enjoyed our lunch." He left me his home and cell numbers.

I jotted down the two numbers and tapped the pad with the ballpoint, recalling our Cliff House experience. I hit the replay button. Harrison sounded unsure of himself, and I blushed in the semi-dark of my office. It was a sensation I hadn't experienced for a while. I turned around self-consciously to see if anyone was watching.

Silly, I scolded myself, and, gaining resolve, grabbed the phone receiver and punched in the numbers for Harrison's home phone. When the first ring sounded, my determination evaporated, and I moistened my lips while the ringing progressed, beginning to hope I'd get his answering machine.

"Harrison." He was in.

"Hi, it's me. Nola." I conjured up his caramel eyes and wondered what he was wearing.

"Oh, thanks for calling back. What I wanted to ask. Well, I hope you don't take this wrong. Ah, since we don't have a professional relationship anymore, I figured I might. Ask. I've got to go to a banquet, and I wondered if you'd go with me. Be my, ah, date. I should tell you it's kinda fancy. Willy, that's Mayor Brown, is speaking at a Fairmont shindig this Saturday. Our department got a bunch of tickets. My boss got two, but he and his wife can't go now. He's concerned because we were expected to put butts in seats. Don't have much use for the pols, but this event is supposed to have a nice band, and that restaurateur guy Jeremiah Tower did the menu."

I tried to help him out without sounding too eager. "Sounds like fun. What's the attire?"

"Black tie optional. I was just going to wear a dark suit. After all, if any demonstrators show up, I could have to help out the security detail."

"I'd love to go. What time?"

"Well, that depends. I should pick you up, but I've got a meeting that starts at four thirty run by the longest-winded guy in the department. The event starts at seven. This will go smoother if you meet me there, and then I'll drive you home after."

"Sure, that'll be fine. Shall I meet you near the bar at, say seven fifteen?"

"Great! We'll make fun of the pols and go somewhere after for a nightcap."

Well, I thought as I placed the receiver back in the cradle, this is not exactly a perfect reintroduction to the world of dating, going to hear a political speech by Willy Brown, but it is, nonetheless, a beginning. This was a safe date for Harrison because the semiofficial venue obviated the need to be clear about his level of commitment.

Ohmagod! What will I wear? I catapulted myself from the desk chair heading for my bedroom closet. Of course, that meant I had to pass Janie Belle. Should I tell her, or could I leave it for another day?

"You have a date!" she exclaimed upon hearing the news every mother wants to hear.

"It's a quasi-professional thing, not to be taken seriously. As a date, I mean."

"Who are his people? Is he from here?"

"I don't know. He moved here from Baltimore."

"Thank Gawd, a Southern city!" Janie Belle clasped her hands with a smack. "I can hardly wait to meet him!"

Spare me, Lord. Any chance in the world I had for a juicy romance could be snuffed out the moment the guy found out I lived with my mother. Maybe this business of meeting your date on neutral territory was a good deal. What if she decided to wait up for me? Maybe I should ask him to drop me at the corner. What excuse could I use? The house being fumigated? A broken sewer main?

I retreated to my bedroom to avoid further discussion and to peruse my closet for the right outfit. I pushed things along the pole, took a few dresses out, and held them closer to the light for a more thorough appraisal, smoothing wrinkles, brushing naps this way and that, and reaching the inevitable conclusion I had nothing to wear.

Checking my watch, I decided that it wasn't too late to call Sally. She liked to watch Letterman, so there was no risk I would get her out of bed.

"You have a date!" she squealed. This was getting to sound like a broken record.

"Yeah, listen, I've got to do some focused shopping, because there's nothing in my closet that's going to work."

"I'm your woman!" Sally said, and we agreed to meet in the rotunda of Neiman Marcus at four Friday afternoon.

I spent Friday morning playing phone tag with executives at Rupert's and Georgina's other biotech companies to line up meetings for the following week. I also read more analyst reports, bringing myself up to speed on what had been happening while I crashed and burned my dot-com. As Rupert had intimated, Wall Street's love affair with screening technology was over. Screen Leaf's CEO would get that smug smile knocked off his face when the investment bankers started to talk turkey about taking his company public.

I decided to take the trolley into town to avoid driving in the Friday rush hour. At three fifteen, I hopped a bus that dropped me at the Forest Hill station. I took the elevators down to the platform and caught an inbound car containing a mix of students from San Francisco State, financial district evening shift personnel, and older women coming home from domestic jobs.

The intersection of Powell and Market was its usual manic self as I fought my way uphill to Union Square through an undulating crowd of tourists, panhandlers, street musicians, hawkers, and fur protesters.

On Geary, the dress and demeanor of the crowd improved. At Stockton, I stepped around a man buying a bouquet at the flower stand and crossed to Neiman's when the light changed. I spotted Sally checking out the jewelry counters in the rotunda.

I had no luck at Neiman's or Macy's, and we decided to skip Saks because Sally had seen an ad for a sale at Nordstrom's. Somehow, crossing Market Street changed my karma, and I found four dresses in my size worth trying on. I settled on a black sheath with a skirt cut on the bias. The material of the bodice was shot through with gold metallic thread. I had antique gold evening sandals and a beaded bag that would work well with this dress. My chosen frock was not one of the sale items, though. Bummer. Sally hit pay dirt, however, locating a two-piece red silk that was fifty percent off.

We celebrated in the bar at Grand Café in the Hotel Monaco.

"So tell me about your date! You've had a really, really long dry spell." Sally removed the olive from her martini.

"Thanks for reminding me, pal. He's at least six five, brown hair, nice brown eyes. He works in the fraud unit of SFPD, and he had charge of the Chen case before Roger was offed."

"No shit! He's a cop! He'll have handcuffs!"

"Shut up. And don't get too excited about this. Chances are it'll be over before it starts. You know my track record."

"Do I ever. Here's to the Typhoid Mary of Romance." Sally held her half-empty glass aloft.

I grabbed my Dewar's, clinked glasses, and drank deeply. Typhoid Mary, indeed. I was the three-strikes-you're-out queen of couple-dom. Jeff, the first guy I ever dated when I was sixteen, entered the priesthood right out of high school. Talk about putting a crimp in my emerging sexuality. The second guy, my hometown honey while I was away at Northwestern, was the son of close family friends. A gung ho Marine lieutenant and helicopter pilot, John never came home from Viet Nam. I was a while recovering from that. Then there was my engagement to Doug, the Yale-Stanford man, the handsome BMW-driving corporate doctor. Only one problem; he was an alcoholic. I broke that one off before Doug managed to kill himself or go celibate on me.

"Maybe you're a late bloomer," Sally suggested.

"Maybe I should get this guy to sign a release form."

"No, let this experiment run. You mustn't mess with the data. And, speaking of running, gotta go." Sally drained her glass and reached for her purse to settle the bill.

She took a cab back to claim her car from a garage on Battery. I fortified myself with sushi from a cellar restaurant on Geary before heading for the trolley.

Saturday morning I managed to persuade my stylist on West Portal to fit me in so she could return my roots to the same warm auburn color as the rest of my hair. I dashed from there down a few blocks to the Vietnamese-owned nail salon for a sea spa pedicure and manicure. Fresh out of cash from tipping, I dashed back up the street to the ATM and indulged in a frozen yogurt in order to break a twenty. I needed ones for the bus that evening.

I had pushed my Fort Funston dog-walking rendezvous with Sally to the afternoon. By the time I rushed home and collected Skootch, I was a few minutes late. This was fortunate because it took Sally several minutes to decamp from the car, leash three dogs, and untangle the leads. Skootch was much more accommodating than her three, leaping from the car and almost leashing himself by inserting his head in the proffered loop of choke collar. He greeted Bergdorf, the most obstreperous of Sally's brood, with obvious delight and allowed the collie to sniff his privates as he gazed into the wind, tongue lolling.

Off we headed, wordlessly skirting the area where Roger died. It was a glorious afternoon, and San Francisco's canines were out. Shepherds and Great Danes, Weimaraners and dachshunds, labs of every color, English setter puppies, a brace of Irish wolfhounds, a harlequin mastiff, cockers and Chihuahuas—a canine congress on the golden dunes above the Pacific.

"So, this cop, is divorced, widowed, a serial killer? All of the above?" Sally walked at a pronounced angle to offset the force exerted by her canine troika.

"I'm not approaching it as a date. It's a political event. Official."

"Sure, that's why we power-shopped."

"Look, if I work myself into this thing slowly, I'm less likely to screw it up."

"Ah, self-sabotage, the last refuge of those who are afraid to commit." Sally nearly tripped over Bergdorf who had stopped to sniff a rock.

"I'm not afraid, I'm ..."

"Typhoid Mary. Yeah, yeah. Ever ask yourself how Mary got typhoid in the first place?"

I busied myself with Skootch's collar. "I don't know for sure, but I think Bob is single."

Sally turned as Bergdorf coiled his leash around her legs. "Wow, a new model right out of the dealer's showroom!"

We reached a bench, and I sat next to a portly woman with a neck as thick as her Saint Bernard's. Sally made yet another attempt to untangle the trilogy of leashes. Skootch sat with his back to the road watching Sally's charges with a contented expression.

Over the crest of the hill behind Skootch, a bobbing head appeared. Soon it became apparent that the head was bobbing because it belonged to a man on horseback. The rider gained the flat ground and turned to direct the line of riders following him. There must have been twenty riders. The lead and trailing rider and one other horsewoman looked experienced, but the rest, with their poor seats and inappropriate clothing, must have been vacationers. Once the lead rider had them all in sight, he turned forward and guided his horse off the sand onto the macadam that led in our direction. The clop of the hooves on the harder surface got Skootch's attention.

Usually, we visited Fort Funston early or late in the day, never around this hour. In consequence, we missed the trail-riding expeditions offered by several stables situated at the edge of the public lands. The result was that Skootch had never met a horse. Sally was a dressage competitor; her dogs were frequent visitors to the Marin County stables where she boarded her Arabian, Bloomin' Dale. Her dogs glanced at the oncoming entourage with studied ennui.

Skootch was transfixed, frozen in place, a speckled statue. As more and more horses reached the macadam, the din of hooves became a cacophony. Other dog owners took command of their pooches, leading them away from the larger animals. Skootch's hackles quivered and his body gathered. His head moved, angling higher and higher as the first rider approached, towering over him.

The horse-man-thing spoke to Skootch. The horrific specter could talk! And it was talking to him. That was the last straw. Skootch spun 180 degrees and headed due south for the string of scruffy pines on the horizon. The leash ripped from my hand whipping my arm back and cracking my knuckles on the bench. The grip skidded on the pavement in the dog's wake as he made for the trees. He accelerated in the turn, and once straightened out, his ample leg muscles did what they were made to do. The guffawing of the horse people drifted in the air; Skootch's dust cloud was the only reply. Legs pumping, tail ruddering, and ears pulsing on either side of his head, my dog grew smaller and smaller in the distance.

"Skooooooootch!" I wondered if he would stop before he got to Palo Alto. I rubbed my knuckles and looked at my hand. The skin was shredded and reddening, one of the manicured nails chipped.

Sally, her dogs, and I returned to the parking lot and waited. She was a true blue friend. We'd met a year after I moved to San Francisco, at the stables she still frequented. After Joyce's death, I took up a succession of risky sports, starting with skydiving, then mountain climbing, followed by competitive jumping. That was when I met Sally. She beat the jodhpurs off me and somehow this ignited a lasting friendship. As we grew older, she switched to dressage, and I refocused my risk-taking on intellectual pursuits, finally starting my own company. Solving cerebral puzzles was absorbing, but I missed the high I got from the physical tests.

After forty-five minutes, Sally split with apologies, because she had committed to meeting another friend for a movie. I consulted my watch. I had two hours before catching the bus downtown for my big date. I leaned against my car and over the next hour watched the lot empty out.

The light was getting tricky. I thought I saw a pinprick in the distance heading this way. I began to wonder how late I could be before Bob Harrison concluded I was a flighty broad or a self-centered woman who didn't respect him enough to be punctual.

The speck on the horizon began to take shape. It moved forward tentatively, hovered in place, moved forward again, neck craning. It took thirty minutes for the now leash-free Skootch to traverse the dunes and the desolate parking area.

"No more horsies, Skootch! All gone. Skootch, come!"

Skootch came to the car, dejected. He had been scared before, and now he was embarrassed and ashamed. He crawled into the backseat of the car and lay head down between paws, defeated by his confrontation with the equine aliens.

I shut the car door and turned right into one of the hated park rangers as she put the finishing touches on my citation.

"I gotta cite you, lady, for allowing your dog to run free in defiance of the leash law." The ranger whistled around the pen cap she was holding in her teeth. "Now, I'll need his license number and your information."

"OK, OK. I'll get the tag number, you copy my info from my license." I shoved the document into her hands.

I leaned in the back of the car and yanked Skootch's collar over his head. Returning to her side, I held the tag so that the ranger could read it.

"Now, here's your license and here's your citation. You know, there's a real nice off-leash fenced area in Golden Gate Park."

"I know." I ripped my copy out of her hands. "Lovely spot. Downwind of the buffalo corral."

Despite this run-in with the law, I ignored the speed limit on the trip back to the house. My time for dressing was down to fifteen minutes, and I needed every one of those minutes to rehabilitate my fractured nail and wind-savaged hair. Racing up the stairs, unbuttoning as I went, I yelled for Janie Belle to give Skootch a big consolation dinner.

After a short but reviving shower, I pulled on panty hose, bra, and new dress, rummaged for the star earrings, and dragged a brush through my damp, unruly hair. After donning my makeup, I dabbed nail polish reasonably close to the salon color on the ragged chip. Blowing on the nail, I slipped my gold shoes on and made for the stairs.

"How do I look?" I stopped in the kitchen to transfer money, keys, lipstick, compact, comb, and tissue into my evening purse.

"Not bad for a person who was in blue jeans fifteen minutes ago," Janie Belle had her arm around Skootch who leaned into her for comfort.

Faint praise, I thought. "Now, I'll probably be late, so *don't* wait up. I'm perfectly safe; I'm with a bunch of policemen."

Janie Belle did not respond. I headed the front door. Pleeeeease, God, make her really sleepy tonight!

I hoped I would catch a break on train and bus connections. As I crossed the street, I spotted a cab heading toward me, an uncommon sight in our part of the city. I waved and it slowed to a stop. Now I could make up lost time and improve on my makeup. Sliding into the backseat, I caught the hem of my new dress on the cracked upholstery of the decrepit vehicle and pulled a thread. Thanks to the bias cut material, the telltale line ran up to my butt.

"Whir you lika going?" demanded the turbaned head from the front seat over sonic boom decibels of sitar music.

The driver let me off in front of Grace Cathedral when we reached Nob Hill because we could not get near the Fairmont for the limos. I walked the intervening block, teetering along on the dressy but impractical sandals, dodging between shiny black cars to reach the canopied side entrance of the hotel. There was no getting near the main entrance, clogged with people, cars, taxis, and parking attendants. I rushed through the lobby and down the corridor to the ballroom. The crush of people was overwhelming.

Vaguely, I recalled a news broadcast about Hillary Clinton coming to town for a Democratic fundraiser. This had to be it. My shoulders slumped in my little black dress. The San Francisco branch of the Democratic Party was an acquired taste. As I rounded the corner into the elegant foyer of the ballroom, I wondered what Harrison's politics were. Funny, I thought, what's important at different stages of a relationship. Right now, as long as he was not an outright Weatherman, or a member of the Green party, I could deal with it.

Then I saw him. He was standing between the bar and a clutch of volunteers bent over nametags at the corner of the reception table. He towered over the people in his immediate vicinity, and it was, therefore, easier for me to spot him than him, me. The first time you see a guy you're attracted to decked out in a good suit is always a special moment. His chiseled jaw was set off by the stark white of the dress shirt, and the cut of the suit coupled with his erect posture and the hand stashed casually in his pants pocket telegraphed m-a-l-e clear across the room. I was glad I was too far for the pheromones to reach me.

I threaded my way across the crowded intervening space and touched his arm. He grinned at me and, putting his hand at the small of my back, guided me to a clear space near a pillar.

"You look nice. I apologize for not picking you up. I'll have to make it up to you. What can I get you from the bar?" He leaned over me to have a fighting chance of hearing my response. I drank in his aftershave and concluded it was the best drink I'd have all night.

"Dewar's. Rocks. Or any scotch they're serving." He handed me the program before leaving to retrieve our drinks. As he had mentioned, Mayor Brown was speaking. In fact, he was introducing Senator Clinton. Senator Diane Feinstein was on the program as was Governor Gray Davis, a fabled fundraiser for the party. The program also contained pages and pages of ads representing individuals and organizational well-wishers who had donated money to make the event the obvious success it was. In the center of the booklet was a spread listing the people who had sponsored tables.

Harrison returned and handed me my drink. His hand returned to my waist as we made our way through the double doors and into the ballroom with the surging crowd.

"Are we sitting at a sponsored table?" I was careful not to spill my scotch as I was shoved and jostled despite his protection.

"Naw, there are a few tables on the fringes for the worker bees."

When we reached our table, we were able to claim two of the four seats from which you could see something other than the back of a pillar.

One thing nice about a political dinner is that everyone talks nonstop. They talk through the speakers, the applause, the Pledge of Allegiance, and the benediction. Harrison and I spent the time with our heads close together getting better acquainted.

Before the senator's keynote, we took a stroll together. Harrison told me how he scanned a crowd and what to look for. The tutorial made me take more notice of my surroundings, and I began to observe the table groups with interest and a newfound objectivity.

I noticed several well-located tables of middle-aged Asian men. These groupings were conspicuous because of the almost identical dark suits and the absence of women. The tables circling them were heterogeneous, the ladies' dresses lending color and sparkle.

I asked Harrison about the all-male tables.

"Yeah, I've noticed that at other events. Those tables are sponsored by some of the oldest Chinese business families in San Francisco who have been supporting political events in this city for a long time. The older Chinese men don't bring their wives to these fundraisers. This is all business for them. They fill up their tables with clients or suppliers. Now, the young Asian-American entrepreneurs bring their wives and girlfriends. Look over there to the left. See the good-looking kid with the girl in the pink dress? He's a software mogul. But not these older guys. They attend these affairs like monks."

Harrison leaned closer as he talked. "Look at the middle table. Do you see the bald man talking to the waiter? That's William Chen; he's your Roger's grandfather."

"What?" I blurted, stopping in my tracks. A man passing by leaned away, cringing at my loud voice.

"Didn't you know? Your boy, Rog, hailed from quite a prominent family. Don't know why he was stealing from you since his granddaddy owns just about every dry cleaning establishment north of Daly City and west of Vacaville. Look in the program for Smiling Panda Corporation. Surely you know the logo."

Indeed I did. A pile of clothing waited in my closet for the trip to the Smiling Panda in my neighborhood.

We sat through the rest of the program, including the band, although every fourth number was "Happy Days Are Here Again," and waited a decent interval after the crowd headed for the exits before we left. I was surprised when Harrison escorted me in the opposite direction from the exiting attendees through a swinging door into the kitchen of the Fairmont. We picked our way through the legions of employees struggling to bring order to the stacks of used pans, dishes, utensils, and serving trays. Something crashed to the floor in the background, and a raised voice was drowned out by hissing steam. We exited onto a loading dock and down some side stairs—and there it was, the '57 Chevy.

"Hey, this is better than handicapped parking," I laughed.

"Yeah, I thought I'd park with the rest of the working stiffs." He helped me into my side, circled the car, and slid into the driver's seat.

"Damn," he said and got out again. He slipped off his jacket, folded it, and tossed it on the backseat. He struggled out of something and slid back behind the wheel.

"Hold this for a sec." He handed me a pistol in a shoulder holster. I stared at it in my lap, surprised that he was wearing the gun. I had not noticed it before. Once he was buckled in, he took the holster back, shoved it under his seat, and put the car in reverse.

"I thought you weren't working tonight."

"I wasn't, but I came here directly from the office."

"Oh, right. That's a relief. I thought maybe you always packed a piece on a date."

"Ha! With you liberated women, it might be a sound practice."

"I have my own revolver, but I'm not licensed to carry." Target shooting was another thing I'd taken up after Joyce's murder, and I was good at it.

"How about a nightcap?" He glanced at me as he swung the car onto the street and let it coast down the hill toward the financial district.

"Sure, why not."

"We'll go where it's a lot less stuffy than the Fairmont and that crowd."

"Yes, let's!" I rolled down the window to enjoy the night breeze.

We quickly found ourselves on the Embarcadero. We pulled to a stop in front of an unpretentious, clapboard, tin-roofed structure nestled between two of the long piers jutting into the bay. Once a hangout for longshoremen, the bar and burger joint, Scully's Revenge, had kept its soul and its no-nonsense way with food while all around it went nouvelle cuisine.

Harrison got us a couple of beers, and we headed out to claim a table at water's edge. We could see the bumper of the Chevy around the corner of the diminutive shack.

"The banquet was interesting, but I like this place better," I said.

"Yes, it's a big favorite of mine. Have you had their mushroom burger?"

"No."

"You are missing something fine, my girl."

"What did you think of the speeches?"

"Predictable. You?"

"Same. Was this, ah, your political party?"

"I grew up Democratic, but I'm an Independent now."

"I grew up Republican, but I consider myself a member of the Ideas and Leadership party."

"Ha, sounds like we've met in the middle."

"Sounds that way. You ever considered the priesthood?"

"What?"

"Nothing. Stop hogging those peanuts and pass them over here."

We had another slow, intimate drink before we left. The night was chilly, but I didn't care. When we walked out, Harrison put his arm around me. It was warm and strong, and I regretted for a moment that the car was so close.

We drove over Twin Peaks, but Harrison did not stop at the overlook, known as a spot for making out. I was glad. We were too old to do that on a first date. It would have been trite, and I would have felt silly. When we got to my house, he got out and opened the door for me. We walked up the porch steps to my front door.

I fumbled in the little beaded purse for my keys. When I located and pulled them out, I looked up right into his eyes. He smiled and kissed me.

I kissed him back. A sheet of fog eased down off the roof to blanket us, making the porch light left on by Janie Belle go all fuzzy and soft, giving Harrison an indistinct silhouette like those cameo close-ups they use on the soaps. I didn't know where he left off and I or my emotions began.

"I want to get together next weekend. How's it by you?"

"Just fine," said I.

I entered the house as quietly as I could and eased the door closed. I listened for the sound of the Chevy engine intensify and fade away before turning off the porch light. I removed my shoes, returned the keys to the evening bag to prevent jingling, and headed up the stairs.

As I passed Janie Belle's room, a voice intoned from the darkness, "I like tall men."

Damn. She was watching.

* * *

CHAPTER 9

Our paper carrier missed the porch, and the edge of the Sunday paper was just visible in a bed of nasturtiums, which grow like kudzu. By the time I retrieved the paper, my slippers were soaked and soiled by the black earth of our garden, and the hem of my robe was heavy with damp. I trudged back into the house, reducing the kid's Christmas check with every sodden step.

Coverage of Roger's murder was buried on page ten. There was nothing new to relate. The reporter did note that the coroner had approved the release of the body, presumably both parts of it. He described the deceased's family as a prominent San Francisco merchant clan. Must be right out of journalism school. I'm glad he did not label them a dynasty.

His family would not be commemorating Roger's passing with a stately cortège winding through Chinatown, a band playing and a convertible supporting a huge, flattering picture of the deceased edged in fresh flowers. Then I realized there was a chance that Roger's family knew nothing of his antics. The circumstances of his death were very suggestive, but nothing had been proven, no connections made to drug dealers, gangs, or crime lords. I wondered if the police had questioned the family regarding my charges against Roger.

You could call Harrison, my mind whispered. No, you don't want to look like you're calling on a pretext the day after your date. It's Sunday, you ninny. The man deserves a day of rest. I had been dying to ask him if he had any inside information on the case last night, but I didn't want to cast a pall on our first evening out. Now I'd just have to wait.

"More coffee?" Janie Belle extended the urn. I accepted another cup and halfheartedly thumbed the pages of newsprint.

Janie Belle made a study of the grocery inserts, scissors poised. Occasionally, there was a triumphant "ha," and her blades descended on the prized coupon.

The house phone interrupted us.

I shuffled over to the offending device on my still soggy slippers, anticipating a telemarketer. "Hello?"

"How are your sea legs?"

My adrenalin went into overdrive. I edged the receiver away from my mouth so that Harrison wouldn't hear the accelerated breaths.

"Why do you wanna know?"

"Because I was going to invite you to go sailing, and I don't want you to throw up on my friend's boat." His teasing voice sent tingles up my spine.

"Oh" was all I could muster.

"This guy I know is out of town, and he encouraged me to use it. Only hard asset he had left after the divorce. I think he's paranoid that if someone doesn't check on it now and then, the ex will somehow spirit it away, too."

"That sounds great!"

"OK, so here's the thing. I don't want you to think I'm making a habit of not picking you up, but from the tide perspective we should cast off at eleven or so, and I need to go get us some provisions for lunch."

"So I should meet you where?"

"Meet me in the parking lot at Fort Mason at ten thirty and we'll walk to the berth. You can help me schlep the food and beverage."

"Deal. Bye." I was already focused on the attire issue and halfway up the stairs when I finished the sentence informing Janie Belle I had my second date in as many days. A bubbly but indecipherable response lilted up after me.

Once again, I stood in my closet, a supplicant praying for the Macy's fairy to wave her wand and materialize one of those crisp spring catalog offerings of navy and white nautical perfection. I found a pair of chinos, a white T, and a reasonably unwrinkled blue, green, and tan plaid shirt to wear over it. Blue sneakers completed the ensemble. I slipped off my good watch and replaced it with a Timex sports number.

After showering, I rummaged through my underwear drawer trying to find something that looked less utilitarian than my usual garb. I contemplated a pair of skimpy red bikinis given to me by a cheeky employee as a holiday party gag gift. I looked at myself in the mirror over the frilly waistband. What do you think you're doing, you oldster! He's just palling around with you because he's lonely like almost everybody else on the planet. Don't read anything into this. He needs somebody to untie the lines, that's all. I flung the red lingerie back in the drawer and grabbed a relatively new pair of Jockey hipsters.

After a fast trip through the Presidio to Lombard, I reached Fort Mason. I pulled in next to the Chevy, displacing the athletic fellow in the Oriole's baseball cap, T-shirt, and cutoffs who had been standing in the parking space. Harrison held the space for me; my neck and cheeks started to warm.

As I locked my car, he opened his trunk and extracted grocery bags emblazoned with the logo of a trendy food and wine shop on Chestnut. He grasped them in the male way, crushing their upper edges together in his fist, not supporting them underneath.

Harrison playfully shoved one of the bags in my chest, and I embraced it dutifully. He slammed the trunk with his free hand and motioned me toward the sidewalk. We walked briskly toward the marina.

The fog had burned away from the Marina District, and the bay was peppered with an armada of sailing craft. Kites soared and dipped above Marina Green, echoing the movements of the gulls swooping over the tourists who threw breadcrumbs in direct defiance of the signs.

Juggling his bag, Harrison unlocked the gate at the head of the pier and held it open for me. I stepped through and aside to let him resume the lead. We reached the slip, and I was surprised to see that our nautical destination was not a sailboat but a formidable cabin cruiser. Sensing my thoughts, Harrison said, "Jim is a little bit of an anomaly here. He's from Southern California."

"Oh, to a San Franciscan that can explain just about any kind of bizarre behavior, but there are plenty of sail fanatics in the Southland."

"Yes, but before moving to Southern California to please his now ex-wife, Jim was a Chesapeake Bay guy. He grew up fishing for perch, rock, and blues. Out here, he likes to go after the bigger Pacific game. He used to take this baby down to Baja with his bond trading cronies. Check out the stern."

I stepped back and leaned to take in the boat's name. "Ah. Apologies to Desi Arnez." Our ride was Baja Loo.

Harrison left me in the galley to deal with the food. He had purchased some good stuff. Pate, sushi, intriguing wrap sandwiches, and several nice bottles of chardonnay. There also were some very caloric looking tartlets.

"Are we eating aboard?" I yelled.

"Up to you," came the disembodied reply. "We could go to Angel Island and have our picnic there."

"That sounds excellent!"

"Hey, matey, I need you up here to cast off."

"Aye, aye, sir. I'm coming."

We ate on the grass rather than using a picnic table. Sated and sleepy from the wine, we stretched out on an old blanket Harrison found stowed beneath one of the berths in the second cabin. He lay on his back with his hands cradling his head. I stretched on my stomach close enough for intimate conversation, but not so close as to appear clingy.

"Why did you choose San Francisco after Baltimore?" I was careful not to say anything about the murdered partner.

"They had an opening in a fraud unit. I had been working homicide in Charm City, and after what happened, I didn't want to do that again, at least not right away. Since I hadn't done fraud before and was changing jurisdictions, I settled for a lower grade. I needed a change of assignment and venue, and this fit the bill."

Harrison rolled on his side and leaned his chin on his palm. "I've learned quite a bit out here, and I don't regret my decision, but I've started looking around for something a little more senior now. I've had a grade increase since I've been here, but room at the top is limited. My political leanings won't do much for me in this neck of the woods either. That begins to matter at my level and up, and I just can't be as P.C. as you need to be in this burg."

He paused and rolled on his stomach. This new position allowed him to look directly at me. "I've applied for something in the FBI. Some interesting opportunities have opened up since nine-eleven. One of the reasons I chose fraud is the intellectual appeal. Not always, but sometimes you're up against some pretty awesome minds; and you really have to stretch, to use everything you've got, to bring these guys to justice. The technology angle is getting very prominent now, and that really turns me on. I don't know whether I told you, but my undergraduate degree is in engineering."

"No kidding. Somehow, I should have known you were a geek! You said undergraduate. Do you have more than one degree?

"Yeah. Law. University of Maryland."

"Go figure."

"When I was a senior at Hopkins, I thought I wanted to be a patent lawyer, but in law school, I hung with a bunch of guys who were gung ho for criminal law. By the time we graduated, I was sucked in. I also think my macho genes kicked in, and I balked at a desk job in the bowels of the Patent Office. The rest is history."

Although I was more than a little interested in the life story of my lanky, engaging companion, I decided it would be prudent not to appear too captivated. I changed the subject.

"So, when you were investigating the Chen case, did you talk to his family?"

"Yes, but only as a byproduct of trying to reach him about coming in for an interview. I did do research on the family and know a lot about them. It was easy because they're important people. The grandfather I pointed out to you at the banquet is a very successful self-made man. His company, Smiling Panda Corporation, started out in the dry cleaning business, but now it's a holding company with interests in an array of commercial sectors and substantial real estate holdings in California, Oregon, and Washington State.

"He had four children, and all of them made good. His second son, Roger's uncle, Randolph, is board certified in ophthalmology and, in addition to practicing, owns a chain of optometry boutiques throughout the Western United States. Roger's aunt, Esther, is first violin at the San Francisco Symphony. Emily, the youngest girl, married a fellow student at Berkeley who is now head of the urology department at Stanford Medical School. Emily herself is very active in supporting the horticultural work at the conservatory in Golden Gate Park. But the shining star of the family was Roger's father, Jefferson Chen, the number-one son."

"Really, I thought Roger was sort of average," I said.

"Jeff was brilliant. He graduated first in his class at UCLA. He met and married the beautiful daughter of a powerful Los Angeles family. The Shens made their fortune in shipping. People say they just about own the ports of San Pedro and Long Beach if you're measuring by percent of cargo moved. Jeff Chen and his bride settled in San Diego, and he was conducting research at Scripps Institute when the accident happened."

"I don't think I'm going to like what's coming next."

"No, tragedy like this is never pleasant. It might explain why Roger was a mess. Although I understand both the Chens and the Shens did everything in their power to give the boy a normal upbringing. He was an infant when he lost his parents, too young to remember them. His uncle Randolph raised Roger along with his own two children. Evidently, this was preferable to growing up in the home of his grandparents. The older couple probably believed they could not surmount the age gap as well as the uncle and his spouse, who also could offer cousins as surrogate siblings. All of this was easy to find out. The area Chinese community is deeply networked; the Chens are very prominent and the tragic story of Jeff and his wife so well known that anyone from Chinatown can relate the details."

"So, what happened to them?" I asked.

"They were coming down Route 5 from L.A. back to San Diego after a medical conference where Jeff had presented a paper. A gasoline truck driver lost control of his vehicle. His rig went off the highway and swept the Chen's car along with it. They never had a chance. Probably didn't even see the thing coming at them from the side. The way people talk about him, Dr. Chen would have won a Nobel Prize by now. What a waste."

We lapsed into silence, contemplating the fickleness and fragility of life.

Finally, I turned and sat up. It had become chilly. It was approaching four o'clock; the sun had moved behind the Marin headland, and we found ourselves sitting in the shade. I put my arms around myself and shivered from the cold and from the sad story of fate met on the freeway. Harrison sat up as well and pulled the blanket with him. He wrapped it around me and hugged me within it. I leaned into him. The chill was gone, replaced by the electricity of human contact and a special warmth growing in me for this big, complex man with the caramel eyes.

I leaned far enough back to rub my cheek against his. His five o'clock shadow was well on its way, and the bristles of his beard felt achingly male and solid. He turned his head and planted a slow kiss on my cheek. His breath warmed my face, and the sensation of heat ignited other parts of my anatomy. I sighed and turned my head some more. The next kiss was reciprocated.

Our cruise back to the Marina District was a titillating tutorial. We rounded Angel Island and headed for the Golden Gate. Harrison placed me at the controls for the run under the bridge and around the mooring back to our berth. I think he wanted me incapacitated in front of him with the responsibility of the helm so that he could put his hands on my shoulders, my waist, my neck, and finally my breasts while he lectured me on the proper way to skipper a cruiser. Oh, Captain, my Captain!

* * *

CHAPTER 10

Monday dawned, or at least we in the Sunset district infer it dawned, because the fog prevented us from seeing it for ourselves. I dreaded breakfast because Janie Belle would press for details of my date. I lay in bed going over said details in my mind. I started to get the warm feeling again. It started in my cheeks, widened to the corners of my mouth, and then accelerated down the length of my spine to the groin area. It was time to get up and put an end to these sensations since they could not be satisfied today.

An array of sacramental linen greeted me as I entered the kitchen. "You'll have to eat somewhere else." Janie Belle wielded a steam iron. "I need the table space for all this linen."

"Not a problem," I responded. "I'll get out of your hair."

Thanking God Almighty for the church's altar guild schedule which spared me a grilling worthy of the Inquisition, I collected coffee and a breakfast bar and escaped to my office.

There was a message from Georgina's third client, the one just back from making the rounds of investment houses in New

York. Tim Rilke, the CEO of Peninsula Gene Therapy, had a nice telephone voice.

I called his office and made a late afternoon appointment. The rest of the morning, I worked on strategies for CAI and for Screen Leaf. I had an early afternoon appointment at Screen Leaf to meet the CFO and the vice president of Marketing and Commercial Development.

I presented myself to the Screen Leaf receptionist a few minutes before my appointment time. After phoning the CFO's office, she informed me that there would a short wait. This management team took its lead from the CEO, who had kept me waiting before. I asked if I could use the ladies' room, hoping to freshen my makeup. I had just returned to the waiting area when an administrative assistant arrived to escort me.

Ushered into a conference room, I placed my battered briefcase next to my chair and extracted the Screen Leaf file and a couple of business cards. Fifteen minutes later, the CFO breezed in, followed by the assistant with bottles of chilled water.

Hank Ho, dressed in black from head to foot, sported a Rolex that looked real. Hard to tell these days with all the knock offs around. Real or bogus, he would be wise to hide it when the company started making the rounds for its IPO presentations. Investors are always looking for signals that management is spending money on inappropriate accoutrements.

"I'm sorry our VP Marketing can't join us," Hank said. "He's been called away, but when we're finished here, my assistant will arrange a follow-up meeting. She keeps his calendar, too."

"I'm sure it couldn't be avoided," I lied.

The two of us spent an hour going over the company's five-year plan with particular emphasis on the next eighteen months. We talked about investment banking firms, discussing which firms worked well together and what firms I thought would make the best leads for the Screen Leaf transaction. I discussed my concerns about positioning the company in the crowded screening field and Wall Street's disdain for botanical libraries.

At the conclusion of our session, Hank handed me back to the assistant. I consulted my schedule and we booked a Wednesday meeting.

As I settled behind the wheel, I could not shake the notion that I knew Hank Ho from somewhere. Nothing in his history, which he had briefly shared, suggested we had crossed paths. Maybe, this was going to be another one of those connections that comes to you in a flash in the night.

Back on 101, I headed south and exited toward Foster City. I pulled into Peninsula Gene Therapy's manicured parking area and selected one of the spaces designated especially for visitors.

I was escorted into the office of Tim Rilke, the CEO.

"Hello, Nola, I'm the business guy here because I couldn't make it at the bench." Rilke grinned as he pumped my hand. His introduction of himself as a failed scientist was for the benefit of the researchers in the room, who chuckled warmly at their leader's self-deprecating opener. In contrast to Casper Wong at Screen Leaf, Rilke had assembled his senior management for me. I met all of the managers who reported directly to Rilke in one efficient session. This impressive group worked as a team. Egos were in evidence, but they never got in the way of the facts or the objectives of the business.

Rilke explained, "We're having a particularly hellish month because we're relocating our administrative offices and certain research functions to Mission Bay, that new research park next to the San Francisco campus of the University of California. We're filling the space vacated at this location with our growing clinical operations."

"I'm going to absolutely hate my commute from Half Moon Bay," said Karin Mullins. "Think of the time wasted going back and forth that I could be spending in the lab."

Karin was a stellar researcher credited with several of the innovative breakthroughs that were the foundation of PGT's valuation. She was respected and admired throughout the biotechnology community, and she was the target of every recruiter in biopharmaceuticals. Karin's hair, an Irish Afro, bloomed around her head like a tawny halo. Her lawn green eyes were magnified by enormous glasses that she whipped off frequently to jab in the air in support of an impassioned point. A whirling dervish in white lab coat, she was in perpetual motion, even when sitting down.

"You can take the train," Rilke said. "Think of how caught up on your reading you'll become. The rest of us won't have to negotiate that tower of papers in your office."

"It's not a tower; it's more of an obelisk." Karin shoved her specs into the lush red hair.

"OK, OK. Let's not waste Nola's time. What other questions do we need to answer for you? Have we covered everything you need to get started?" Rilke looked at me.

"You've all done a great job. I just have a couple points I need to clarify about the gene therapy applications in the vaccine field, and we're done for now."

Karen jumped in. "Our lead vaccine programs are focused on cancer and can be grouped into two areas: vaccines that cut off the blood supply to certain cells and essentially strangle cancer, and immune system boosters or adjuvants that spur the body to reject cancer cells as if they were foreign invaders. We've been able to make these advances because we've come to view cancer as a genetic disease."

Karin walked me through her latest contributions, which included an extremely robust vector designed to cradle a broad array of genetic material, including DNA, RNA, and proteins, and was easy to replicate.

"As you know, we and our competitors use viruses stripped of their pathogenic capabilities as delivery devices for desirable genetic material. We wanted to select a virus as a vector that was very benign, but the benign viruses are not able to get inside many cells because the cell's surface proteins recognize their outer coats. So, we substituted a coat from another virus that can pretty much get into any cell type.

"We also expanded the payload capabilities of the benign virus. They were minimal to begin with. The original virus could transport about as much material as a little red wagon; what we wanted for our cancer and infectious disease applications were vectors with the cargo hold of a semi. So we borrowed the genetic capacity of a third virus and engineered it into our benign red wagon." Karin waved her glasses in emphasis.

"Wow, that's elegant!"

"Thanks, so now what we've got on a cellular level is a Trojan horse manufactured on the Toyota assembly line. We can deliver whatever we want and however much we want to any cell we want!"

We wrapped up the session, and Rilke and Karin walked out with me. Guessing Karin's age at about thirty-five, I mentioned a few restaurants and stores in the thirty-something demographic to help her warm to the San Francisco move.

"Oh, I'm such a drudge. I almost never do anything but work for this slave driver." She pointed to Rilke, who aped surprise. "I like music, especially Irish music, but I never get out to hear it. I've got a lot on CD, though. I listen to it when I'm trying to solve research problems."

Rilke said his good-byes, and Karin and I lingered on the edge of the lobby as I told her about River Shannon, a Geary Boulevard establishment noted for its live Gaelic music.

We parted by agreeing to go one night after the corporate move was complete and she had put her new lab space in order.

By the time I left PGT, commuter traffic was in evidence. I decided to cut over to Highway 280 and drive home that way. I hit the southwestern corner of San Francisco ahead of many commuters, but not ahead of the fog.

After returning the Saab to the garage, I stopped in my office and emptied my files onto my desk. Janie Belle had placed my mail next to my keyboard. I plucked an envelope off the top but had difficulty reading the sender's name. Noticing how smudged my glasses were, I pulled open the top drawer to my desk where I kept my lens cleaner. I pushed contents around feeling for the small bottle. Figuring my task would be easier if I lifted out the stack of papers in my way, I removed the pile to the desktop.

On top of the stack were the copies of the club photos. There in one of the scans was Hank Ho, the CFO of Screen Leaf, complete with Rolex. So that's where I knew him from—Roger's little group of club goers—the hip, black-clad high flyers. Well, well. Small world.

***

CHAPTER 11

Wednesday got off to a good start with a dog walk on Baker Beach followed by a late breakfast with Sally at Mel's Diner on Geary. We parked our cars next to each other so that Skootch and her dogs could almost touch noses. Sally is a food reactionary. She believes the devil or the Communist Party invented nouvelle cuisine. Her food pyramid consists of five categories: meat, potatoes, snacks, dessert, and alcohol. Mel's is a fifties diner style restaurant with counter space, chrome, and red Coca-Cola signs. The menu runs to burgers, fries, shakes, and sundaes. They do have a breakfast menu, and from that, I ordered egg substitute, turkey bacon, and whole-wheat toast with fruit substituted for the hash browns. Since this was a late breakfast, Sally opted for a double bacon cheeseburger, chili fries, and a chocolate shake.

When the waitperson arrived with our orders, I eyed Sally's, marveling at how she managed to stay thin while eating like a wrestler. She scrutinized the fruit next to my eggs as if the melon balls were harbingers of a plot to take over Mel's by the Vegan Alliance.

"Listen, I need a favor." I peppered my fake eggs. "I need some fast research done on the anti-gene therapy activists. I want to know if one of my new clients is involved in anything that is likely to draw their attention."

"No problem, I've got time right now. I'm done with the jeans project and waiting for more product specs before I start on a major nutraceuticals assignment." Sally got her hands around her mammoth burger. "This client of yours is conducting their gene business by the book, right? No Dr. Jekyll types who might get ahead of themselves?"

I shook my head. Sally was convinced that somewhere among all the brilliant scientists in my industry, there was at least one evil genius ready to play God. "Sorry, I'm working for normal folks who are not planning to clone a human being or release some genetically-engineered vinca vine into the environment."

She wiped a smear of catsup from her chin. "Too many Nobel prizes. People start to believe their own bull pucky."

"There might be an inflated ego or two." I speared the last piece of melon on my plate. Sometimes, those egos had reason to be frustrated with the lack of science literacy among politicians and journalists.

I returned to the car after breakfast only to be met by an accusing look from Skootch. "Where?" he telegraphed with raised eyebrows. I reached in one pocket and extracted the whole-wheat toast, buttered for his benefit. As I headed west on Geary, I reflected that I had managed to avoid the date interrogation from Janie Belle for three mornings in a row. The Altar Guild had saved me the first time, her dermatology appointment the second, and my breakfast with Sally was my life preserver on this the third morning. By the time I returned home to change, my mother would have left to play bridge. If I stretched this out long enough, she might not grill me at all. Right. And the sun will rise in the west.

Back in the Screen Leaf reception area where I once again was told there would be a short wait, I extracted my own copy of *Biotech News Dispatch* from my briefcase. I was determined to put my time to good use. I finished the lead article and most of the breaking news by the time the assistant materialized.

Theo Tan, the very young head of Screen Leaf's marketing and commercial development effort, was not dressed completely in black. His turtleneck was funereal purple, and he wore an earring. I also thought I caught the hint of a wrist tattoo as he adjusted his jacket before sitting. I was relieved to note that he was not one of the other men pictured in the rogue's gallery from Roger's club. Yet he seemed familiar. A wave of guilt hit me as I realized that people who are racially different are harder to distinguish. Maybe I just couldn't differentiate among thirty-somethings, but the green eyes of Karin Mullins flashed at me in reproach. Despite her age, I would always be able to pick her out of a lineup.

I was not impressed with Mr. Tan. His grasp of our industry, and the strategic imperatives facing his company as it neared the day when it would go public, were superficial if not naïve. I fished for details of his prior experience. I learned that after earning his MBA, he had interned at a pharmaceutical company in Taiwan. After that, he had worked briefly for a Santa Clara technology company. Theo had no background that qualified him to serve in the post he held. He must be a relative of one of the founders; otherwise how could he have been placed in this position? I reviewed much of my discussion with his colleague, Hank Ho, and arranged with Theo and his assistant to return the following day to begin reworking the company's investor presentation. I asked if there was a cubical with a computer I could use and I was assigned a work area near the executive offices.

Theo ducked into his office to pick up a small overnighter and walked out with me. "I'm headed to San Jose airport for a flight down to Ontario."

"Well you've got decent flying weather," I said. We walked together to the parking lot. Coming toward us on the sidewalk from the direction of The Ancient Turtle Company was a young woman pulling a roller bag.

"Hey, Margaret," Theo greeted the girl, placing his hand on her waist as she turned and gazed at me. "Nola, this is Margaret Lu. Margaret, this is Nola Billingsley, a consultant working with our CEO." Margaret nodded as her friend's arm and her own luggage prevented her from shaking hands.

"Margaret works at a company around the corner from us," Theo added.

"Nice to meet you." I stood face-to-face with Roger's ex-girlfriend and what appeared to be her new amore, if Theo's hand in the small of her back was any indication.

"I'm giving Margaret a lift to the airport."

"Well, best of luck traveling to your destinations," I said, easing into the Saab. I waved as I pulled out of the parallel space. Then an idea struck me. I pressed my foot on the brake and rolled down the window. Hoping to sound nonchalant, I asked the girl, "Is your company named, ah, something to do with turtles, oh, it won't come to me."

"Yeah," she said over her shoulder. "Totally retro and stupid. Ancient Turtle Company. Like something out of a kung fu movie. Salary's good, though."

So there it was. Elixirs, computer geeks, databases, and dating. This Bay Area operation was responsible for the powerful backbone of the Ancient Turtle Web site. Access to talented Silicon Valley programmers and the latest in technology would be easy albeit costly in this location.

Gosh, she doesn't waste any time. Ms. Lu's former squeeze wasn't even in the ground yet, and she was off for a long weekend tryst with her new love interest. I almost felt sorry for Roger.

Wednesday evening my luck ran out. Janie Belle was lying in wait for me in the garage on the pretext of depositing newspapers in the recycle bin.

"When will you be bringing your young man to dinner?" she asked as an opener.

I hadn't even been allowed to get out of the Saab. I futzed with my briefcase to buy time. "I don't think we're that far along yet, Mother."

"Nonsense! It is never too soon to cook for a man."

"That's a very nice suggestion, but you have to remember that this started out as a professional relationship, and you have to feel your way along more slowly, ah, to…"

"You are not gettin' any younger," she said. A little tap of her foot and a hand perched on either hip implied I'd better pick up the pace, as time was marching on.

I marched to the kitchen and the Dewar's bottle. I was pouring my second by the time she caught up with me.

My first day of real consulting at Screen Leaf began inauspiciously. I was ushered to my borrowed cubicle by Cindy, the executive assistant, who was kind enough to show me the ladies' room, the coffee area, and the supply room. She also helped me boot the computer and oriented me to the company's network as well as the phone system before returning to her desk. She left me with an employee directory, some general company memos, and a short list of officer and director numbers.

I created a folder for myself on the desktop and opened the shared files to make copies of previous slide presentations and available artwork into my file. Over the next two hours, I reviewed these materials and made good progress outlining the new presentation. Feeling I deserved a break, I headed for the coffee area remembering to collect some change from my purse for the candy machine.

After bringing my coffee and Snickers Marathon bar back to my cubicle, I took the time to readjust my chair before beginning to work again. It had been a little tall for my frame, and my back bothered me because I had been dangling my feet. I also wondered if there was a wrist pad handy to place before the keyboard. I opened the nearest drawer to check. There was nothing in the first drawer but pencils, notepads, and a grimy mouse pad. I moved on to drawer number two. Success! A weather-beaten wrist cushion coiled awkwardly in the drawer amid more detritus from the former occupant of the cubicle, including a box of business cards. I selected a card and glanced at the name as I extracted the wrist pad and dragged it into position in front of the keyboard.

I froze. The name on the card was Roger Chen. He had worked here. According to the embossed card, he was the former senior accounting manager. I closed the drawer but opened it again to extract two more of the cards, dropping them together with the one I already had into my briefcase. Harrison and Barbagalatto presumably knew Roger's employment history, but just in case, I would bring them tangible proof of Roger's career move into biotech. Had Roger stolen from Screen Leaf, too? Was he fired for behavior similar to what had caused me to can him? Or had he still been working here when he was murdered?

Cindy startled me when she peeked over the cubicle wall. "Do you have everything you need? Sylvia and I are going out to grab some lunch, and I didn't want to leave before checking on you to make sure."

"I'm fine. I'm making great progress. Thanks for your help." I beamed up at her in an effort to cover my discomposure. She gave a little wave and vanished from view.

I exhaled a long breath to steady my nerves while I considered what to do next. I decided to peruse the public files on the company's network to learn more about the duties of Screen Leaf's senior accounting manager. I found his e-mail address in the distributions list of many employee memos. I even found a memo posted from Roger himself reminding employees to turn in their expense reports. The prize find was a copy of an employee newsletter with a picture of Roger in a group of employees at a beer bash. I hit the print button, then gasped when I realized I had no idea where the printer station was. I stood up and moved to the hall, listening with all my powers of concentration. Luckily, the printer was within earshot, and the telltale whir of a laser printer warming up drew me to the next aisle and a cubicle devoted to two printers and a fax machine. I snatched up the outdated newsletter and returned to my space. Emboldened by my discovery of the printer location, I reopened and printed the memo Roger had issued. As I returned to the machine cubicle, I almost decked Casper Wong, who was not supposed to be in the office, according to Cindy.

"Hey, Nola, good to see you! Is my staff getting you everything you need?" He reached for papers on the printer I was using.

"Yes. Yes, they are. Couldn't be more helpful. I've been loaned a cube right over there." I pointed, hoping to take his eyes off the printer. He would find it suspicious that I was printing copies of old internal memos that had absolutely nothing to do with Screen Leaf's investor presentation. Memos from a dead employee. Memos from an employee who might be dead because of something he knew about Screen Leaf's business.

Wong only glanced away for a second. He returned to the papers coming out of the printer. "Did you print something to this machine?" he asked never looking up from the pile of copies."

"Well, I, ah, printed something, but I'm not sure which printer will print it or where it is in the queue."

"Hmmmm. Well this appears to be my stuff, so I guess I printed ahead of you. My assistant would be doing this, but I can't seem to find her."

"Oh, Cindy's at lunch. Left about fifteen minutes ago with somebody named Sylvia."

"Just great. They'll take a long one since I wasn't supposed to be back today." He turned and walked out of the cube headed for his office. "Bye. Let me know when you're ready to go over the draft presentation."

"Sure thing." I turned to the printer willing it to whir again.

There was a pause, and then the machine went into action, spewing my pages out into my waiting hands. Thank God, these weren't stuck to the back of his document.

I returned to my cube and collapsed in my chair. I was happy that the screen saver had appeared on my screen, hiding the open memo I had thoughtlessly left visible when I exited the cubicle. I closed the file and stuffed the memos into my briefcase.

Was Roger's death connected to Screen Leaf? That was both possible and creepy. Somehow, I believed Roger had not stolen from these people. These men were like him. Living the high life, being cool, hip, or whatever they called it now. He would emulate Casper Wong and Hank Ho. He would bond with them. Maybe that elixir box I saw in the trash the first day had been Roger's. He kept ordering the stuff after he started working here.

Did he know the Ancient Turtle Company was next door before he met Margaret? Or had he met Margaret because of his interest in Ancient Turtle's products? Had Theo met Margaret when she was dating Rog? Presumably. Theo hadn't wasted any time to make his move after Roger's demise. And Margaret had not been in mourning long.

These folks sure had their own set of rules. And those rules could not be called morals—not in a million years. But there were lots of amoral people in the world who managed not to get themselves killed. What had Roger done to lose his head? Was Screen Leaf doing something illegal? What could be nefarious about a bunch of science geeks laboriously screening compounds for signs of biological activity? The executives seemed slick and shifty, though. Had Roger found out something they had done that was unlawful? Had fast-living Rog seen a way to make some easy money? Was he capable of blackmail? Or were the execs just spooked that their new employee knew too much? But kill him?

It might have been his connection with Margaret. Ancient Turtle was a suspicious enterprise if I'd ever seen one. Perhaps he had learned something about that business he was not supposed to know. Had Margaret engaged in pillow talk?

Obviously, I was not going to be able to concentrate on my project anymore today, so I packed up and headed for the exit.

As I revved the Saab's engine, I knew I had to return to Extreme Lotus. I hungered to understand these young people better. With their nightclub values, fast cars, and penchant for recreational pharmaceuticals, these ebony-clad professionals practiced behaviors that held the key to Roger's death. If I could understand what made them tick, perhaps I could figure out what had happened to my former employee.

While I guided the car up the Monterey Boulevard exit ramp, I extracted my cell phone from my bag. Remembering that I didn't have Harrison on speed dial, I pulled off on a side street so that I could find his card. Putting a man on speed dial too early in a relationship is a sure jinx.

"Harrison," I said when he answered in one ring, "you'll never guess what I found out. Roger worked at Screen Leaf, a biotech company I'm doing some consulting for."

"Huh. Small world. I think I knew he was at a lab company. Ran his employment history as a part of the credit checking."

"Well, weren't you going to tell me? I'm in biotech, ya know,"

"Well, I didn't think it was that small a field that every gene splicer would know every other gene splicer. Besides, we don't talk about our investigations with the subjects."

"Subjects! I'm a subject, now?"

"You were a subject. Now you're a, well you're more of an ex-subject, friend, cute kind of person."

"And you're treading on thin ice."

Silence ensued. The traffic noise on busy Monterey rose and fell with my breathing.

"Your nickel," he reminded me.

"Humph. With my calling plan it's probably more like my three dollars." I considered my next words. "Listen, I want to go back to that club where I found the pictures of Roger and his friends."

"Why? You've got to stay out of this thing, Nola. I know you are all excited you found out where Roger was working, but this is police business. We all get the itch, but you won't get to the answer, because you don't have the tools, the authority, or the skills."

"I know biotech."

"Sure. You are a professional in your field. This isn't about biotech, it's about homicide. Have respect for other professionals. Barbagalatto is on this case, and believe me, he will not appreciate the interference of amateurs."

I agreed with his premise but bristled at the term. I decided to move to even less stable ground, our relationship. "I'm asking you out. I hope you are a modern type of man who will accept this as a new page in our friendship. I'm asking you to go nightclubbing with me and some friends."

"Really." After a pause Harrison continued. "I suppose I'm flattered. I'm being asked out by an attractive woman to serve as a decoy so that she can discover more info about a stiff."

OK. That ploy hadn't worked. "Listen, that didn't come out the way I wanted it to, but the point is I'm going to go to Extreme Lotus with or without you. I would like you to come. I really would. But I'm going. OK?"

"OK."

"OK, you're coming? Or OK, I'm going?"

"OK, I'm coming. Are you going to pick me up?"

"Why? You never pick me up."

"That was really below the belt." He was laughing.

Happy to hear the deep-throated chuckle and remembering how the broad chest from which it emanated felt to the touch, I decided to tease him more. "Well, since I did the asking, why don't you do the driving?"

"Then how is it your date instead of my date?"

"Because I'm going to do the buying."

"Sounds good. We public servants need all the help we can get. I will pick you up for your date at ten. Don't forget your wallet just because you have to carry one of those girlie purses. And, Nola, let's be serious about the Roger thing. Lay off the sleuthing."

"I will. I will." I squirmed in the driver's seat. "I just want to get my hands around these trendy thirty-somethings. You were the one who focused me on the lifestyle thing. Now that I'm back in consulting, I'm surrounded by these kids. I just want to know what makes them tick."

"Riiiiiight," he said, and the line clicked.

I punched the phone savagely to bring up my address book. My ex-IT manager, Serge, was surprised to learn that his stodgy former boss was going to Extreme Lotus.

"Sure, Nola, we'd love to meet you there. My wife and I planned to go out and this just settles which club."

"Great, Serge. Let's say you'll meet me and my, ah, date at the club around eleven."

"You with a date? Whoa. I mean, sure thing." Serge disconnected before he could embarrass himself further.

Relieved that I had been able to supply the friends I had referenced in my invitation to Harrison, I returned the cell phone to my bag.

I swung the Saab in a U-turn and executed a right on Monterey. Only eight stoplights between me and the Macy's at Stonestown Mall. Shoes, I needed shoes. And a purse. I really wished he hadn't made that wisecrack about the girlie bag.

Harrison was a man of his word, ringing the doorbell at ten on the dot. Yelling over my shoulder to Janie Belle not to wait up, I just about flattened him on the front steps in my haste to get out of the house. Fortunately, it takes people in their eighties a little longer to get out of chairs, so I aced her with room to spare.

"You look nice," he said as he handed me into the Chevy. I had chosen a simple black dress to blend in with the younger crowd, but I had added an art deco set of black jade earrings, a necklace edged in yellow gold, and a burnt orange pashmina. My girlie bag was a leather clutch edged in alligator. The strategic choice was the footwear. At the Macy's sale, I had snapped up patent leather bitch shoes: three inches of spike and angel-hair-pasta ties with a toe opening to show off my hastily lacquered toenails. I would be holding on to Harrison for dear life all night. Lucky him. Lucky me.

It was the shoes and the way my hips were swaying because of them that got us past the bouncer; either that or the fact that Harrison looked every inch a cop. Once inside the door, I surveyed the place to locate Serge before plunging into the crush of people. I couldn't make him out and decided he must not be here yet.

We moved into the dancing couples in an attempt to reach the other side of the room. The going was slow. I was jostled on my spikes but didn't fear falling; with the crush of bodies, there was nowhere to go. With a shrug of resignation and a grin, my date turned, put his arm around me, and began to dance. I shifted the girlie bag to my left hand and smiled up at him. He leaned his lips to my forehead and pressed a kiss there. The DJ changed selections, and we danced contentedly toward the far side of the club.

"Nola! Nola, over here!" Serge yelled above the pulsing music. He looked even more surprised than he had sounded on the phone. He probably had a hard time recognizing me in this getup. I'm not sure Serge had ever seen me out of slacks. I know he had never seen me with a man. We edged in his direction, and when we reached the border of the dance floor, we were forcibly ejected from the throbbing multitude, like illegal immigrants with forged papers in a Tijuana queue.

"Serge, this is Bob Harrison. Bob, this is Serge and Marta Washington. Serge headed IT at my dot-com." The men shook hands while I embraced Marta. After I hugged Serge, the two men went off in search of libations. Marta and I chatted about Serge's new job and caught up on several other employees of my failed company. Marta looked fabulous in a black satin pantsuit. She was a size two, so she could get away with the bulk and the shine of the material. She slipped the jacket off as we talked, unveiling a minuscule dusky pink halter and periodically revealing a patch of skin above the low-cut pants. Great costume for dancing, I thought, admiring the athletic firmness of her midriff and wondering, as I pictured my waist in a halter-top, if they priced liposuction by the inch or the pound.

The men returned, and we cruised the outskirts of the dance floor for a table. We settled for huddling around a pedestal table that supported our drinks and handbags.

Harrison enjoyed my friends, and the evening passed quickly. Since our first dance was a pleasant experience, we tried again. Serge and Marta met other friends but returned loyally to our table, probably convinced that given our advanced years, we wouldn't last long without their aid and support.

Marta and I eventually made a trip to the ladies' room, and when we returned, I saw a trio of familiar faces standing behind Harrison as he talked with Serge: Hank Ho and Theo Tan of Screen Leaf and, leaning on Theo as she adjusted the heel of her pump, Roger's ex, Margaret Lu.

I didn't have much choice but to greet my new clients as I returned to our table since they were elbow-to-elbow with my date. "Hi, Hank!" I smiled at Screen Leaf's CFO and turned Harrison around to make introductions. That accomplished, I asked, "Theo, was your trip cut short?"

Hank shot Theo a glance as he answered, "Oh, no, I only went for one night. I shuttle back and forth to Southern California all the time. Ontario or, more frequently, San Diego. Lots of prospective biotech clients in San Diego."

"And you, Margaret?" I beamed brazenly. Where Margaret had been going was, of course, none of my business.

Margaret looked confused, and then, remembering, appeared put out to be asked such a question. "I, too, had business," she said, regaining her composure and a distasteful smugness along with it. "We have a broad array of business interests in

Los Angeles. Our CEO sends me down regularly. We should open an office there."

Since she had opened the door to conversing about her company, I edged closer to her and picked up the lead she had given me. Hank, Theo, Harrison, and Serge settled into a superficial conversation. Marta, looking lost, eased away into another group of acquaintances near the bar.

"Your company seems to have a nice operation here," I said. "I presume that you handle all your Internet business in Northern California in preference to Thailand?"

"Yes," she said, alert to my knowledge of the other corporate location. "We find it easier to access technical, marketing, and customer service talent here."

"But it makes more sense to process and stockpile the inventories of botanicals overseas."

"Why, yes, that's about the size of it. Many of the sources for these preparations are in Southeast Asia and India, although we obtain ingredients worldwide from Africa, South America, Afghanistan, Pakistan, and so on."

"Very interesting business. It seems the entire field of nutraceuticals is burgeoning. I have some experience in the area." This was a lie, but I figured Sally, the research maven, would help me become an overnight expert if I needed to bone up. "Do you need any consulting help in communications?"

"That's not my area. I'm afraid I don't know. My boss, the CEO, manages external communications very closely."

"Could you give me an introduction? I'm looking to expand my client base, and I think I could be an asset to your company with my network of industry and regulatory contacts." I figured nothing ventured, nothing gained. Although I have been in business all my life, I am not by nature a pushy person and have always shied away from frontal attacks on clients or prospective clients. I cringe when others use such tactics on me, but I wanted to get inside Ancient Turtle, and chutzpah just might get me there.

Margaret was no shrinking violet, but this assertive approach rendered her speechless. While she floundered, I put forward a suggestion. "Why don't we exchange cards? I'll call you tomorrow, and you can make a phone introduction with your boss or his executive assistant."

"OK," she agreed, relieved to have this conversation at an end.

Of course, neither of us had a card because we were carrying girlie bags. Margaret borrowed a card from Theo, and I begged one from Serge. I avoided borrowing one from Harrison because I didn't want Margaret to know I was dating a cop. We borrowed pens to scrawl numbers on the backs of the borrowed cards.

"What's your boss's name?" I yelled as we waved our good-byes to the trio when they departed for another club.

"Brutus Fang," she said and showed me hers.

In the end, that chauvinist, Harrison, refused to let me pay for drinks. Perhaps he didn't want Serge to see him in the role of a kept man. It was an uncharacteristically clear night when we pulled up in front of the Plymouth Avenue house at two in the morning. This was way past Janie Belle's bedtime, and even if she was coming back from one of those frequent trips to the bathroom, which are her lot as an older person, the porch light was too dim to let her see I was getting a long and very physical good-night kiss in the car.

In the morning, I leaned over the edge of the bed and surveyed the trajectory of clothing that began with the bitch shoes at the door and ended with the panties on the rug next to the bed.

I rolled over and lifted the covers. I was naked. Hmmmmm, you certainly were in a devil-may-care mood last night. I recalled the kiss. Well, that could explain a lot.

Skootch appeared in the doorway and nudged the bitch shoes with his muzzle. Skootch is not a destroyer of shoes, but then I wasn't sure he would recognize the stringy things as footwear, so I bolted from bed and snatched them up before he could make a decision. I continued collecting items from the floor, clutching them to my bare bosom. Straightening up with my hoard, I realized the pashmina was nowhere in sight. The shawl was in the Chevy. Oh, well, another reason to see him. I pranced happily to the shower.

Janie Belle stormed into my office like a tornado into a small Midwestern town. "What time did you get in last night? I mean, I know when you got in because I was awake, but I can't really read those little fuzzy numbers on the clock without my glasses."

"I got in at two or something," I said, hunkering over the computer keys, intently studying the screen as if something important was there instead of my calendar.

"I like his car."

"I thought you said you couldn't see."

"Clocks. I can't see clocks." Her body language inferred that all else was as clear as day to her. "I like a man who drives a big car. It says something about his character. I think we should have him over."

"What's with the *we*? I hardly know the man, and all of a sudden you're building social engagements around him! Slow down. OK?"

Janie Belle's face took on a stony, brooding look, like a visage from Mount Rushmore, but with good jewelry. "I'm off to the church to give the silver a touchup."

"Amen." I turned back to the computer. The door creaked shut behind me, and I sighed in relief—but, alas, prematurely. A short creak announced the partial reopening of the door. My silent prayer that it was Skootch went unanswered.

"For a person who hardy knows a man at all, you sure are a slow good-night kisser."

As the door creaked closed a final time, the screen saver took control of my monitor. Little fishes puttered lazily from side to side. I projected myself into the scene, imagining I was a swimmer out of my depth, going down for the third time.

My meeting with CAI's Leonard Price and his team was lively and productive. Two hours went by in a flash followed by a one-on-one session in the lab of a scientist who would be presenting an important paper at an upcoming medical meeting. Price and his colleagues thought a press release was in order, but it would be a challenge to make sense of this particular discovery in a few paragraphs.

When I returned to Price's office, he invited me for coffee at Peet's, the Berkeley-born alternative to Starbucks. We drove our own cars to the Emeryville Market, and I selected a table while he got our orders. Price returned with lattes, sandwiches, and cookies; and we exchanged industry and university gossip while we ate.

We both had been undergraduates at Northwestern University, and we swapped stories of braving the stiff winds off Lake Michigan on our way to class. I smiled as Price mentioned doing lab work in a building not erected until after I graduated. I was older than my client, but that wasn't a factoid he needed to hear about his new consultant.

Finishing the last bite of a sinfully good oatmeal cookie, I turned the conversation to the press release. "Does CAI have any art that might be distributed with the announcement to help render the science more understandable to the public?"

"We are forever having needs along those lines, so I authorized the hiring of a graphic design person; but it will take a while to get somebody on board and bring them up to speed on our technologies."

"I have a great recommendation." I was thinking of Dakota. "With your permission, I'll have him call your human resources department." I filled Price in on Dakota's capabilities and experience.

Price and I parted in the parking lot, and I aimed the Saab toward Powell Street and the Bay Bridge onramp. My pleasant morning was made even better by the prospect of landing Dakota a job. I reached for my cell phone but remembered that reception on the bridge was lousy. By the time I was off the bridge and able to use the phone, I would be minutes from his place on Portrero Hill. I could bop over there and surprise him with the news. San Franciscans who live in the fog belt always relish a visit to Portrero Hill, with its sunny microclimate and funky shops. I also had a favor to ask of my former employee.

I eased the nose of the Saab into Dakota's driveway and set the parking brake. Dakota's place was a hill dwelling, which explained why the garage's door was below street level, reached by a driveway canted at a forty-five degree angle. If my brakes failed, my Saab would punch out the garage door and propel Dakota's car out the back of his basement onto the roof of the house below. I turned my wheels hard and rested the car's tire against the curb as an extra precaution.

Dakota answered the bell, peering under the edge of the window shade on his Victorian front door.

"What brings you to this side of town?" he said, waving me in as he stood out of the way. The interior was freezing, just as he preferred it. Born in a blizzard, he liked things glacial.

"You mean, what brings me into the light from the dark side?" I teased, shading my eyes with my hand like a vampire caught out beyond the rising of the sun. Dakota and his partner had removed the entire back wall of the Victorian teardown, mortgaging themselves to the hilt, and replaced it with floor-to-ceiling glass. The resulting view of the downtown was worthy of its own postcard. The original workingman's Vic was a shotgun row house, and the effect of the renovation was that of looking through the end of a sea captain's spyglass.

Dakota grabbed bottled water for me and a Mountain Dew for himself as we passed through the kitchen on our way to the patio. He also nabbed his sunglasses from the counter and donned them as he held the door for me and his two beagles, Meriwether and Sacagawea. The reason his parents had been in Dakota when he arrived on the scene was that his father was a cartographer, documenting the Lewis and Clark expedition. This explained the dog's names. Nothing could explain why despite a father in the mapping business, Dakota had absolutely no sense of direction.

We settled into chairs facing the cityscape, the dogs disappeared under the deck, and I filled Dakota in on CAI. He was genuinely interested and promised to call for an interview first thing in the morning.

"And now that I have brought you a fantastic job opportunity, I have a favor to ask in return." I replaced the cap on my empty water bottle.

"Anything! Just ask away."

"I want you to take a ride down to Colma with me."

"Colma? I mean I'll take a ride with you anywhere, and that's hardly a favor, but your destination is a little strange. There's nothing in Colma but graveyards."

"Precisely." I rose from my chair. "Let's go."

Every San Franciscan knows there are no graveyards in the city itself. Of course, there are the military graves at the Presidio, and there may be a niche or two left in the Columbarium, but the fact is that in tiny San Francisco, land is too valuable for graves. As the city grew, its former citizens lying in repose were unearthed and carted south to make room for progress. Now, for modern San Franciscans, there is that last ride down the peninsula to the charming and remarkably quiet city of Colma in San Mateo County. Jokes abound about Colma's population, always quoted as two statistics—aboveground and below. The subterranean citizens far outnumber the living. The city is home to an array of cemeteries representing every religious and ethnic persuasion, perpetuating our city's diversity into the hereafter.

I knew from the newspaper that Roger's funeral was today because Janie Belle had called it to my attention. Along with many octogenarians, she makes a habit of scanning the obituaries. My mother had observed that the notice was extremely brief for so prominent a family. Indeed. Last rites for a black sheep. A problem child who had managed to get himself killed in a very unsavory manner. Hard to hold your head up and carry on with such disgraceful things happening in your own family.

"This is not a good idea," Dakota murmured from the passenger seat as I accelerated down Highway 101.

"Probably not, but I just have to do this. I guess it's closure for me. And I'm sorry, but I needed somebody to come along. We won't intrude, we'll just drive by."

"Great. A drive-by viewing." Dakota sank even lower in the seat.

It took some time to get my bearings. San Francisco is so dense with structures, cars, and people; it can be a little disorienting to arrive in a locale so wide open and unobstructed. We stopped at a florist's to ask directions to the cemetery we sought. Once near our destination, our Western eyes took in the colorful gravesites and exotic inscriptions of the Chinese cemetery. I slowed the car, and we passed the entrance in a sedate fashion. Fortunately, there was only one burial taking place, so we assumed we had found Roger at the end, or the beginning, depending on your theology, of his last journey.

The ceremony was over, and the party headed down the hill toward the entrance. There were about fifty people making their way along the narrow path from the burial site. I spied a parking place on the other side of the road.

My U-turn across the double yellow line gave Dakota yet another reason to cringe and slump down in his seat. At least my chosen vantage point would position him on the side away from the exiting crowd and prevent him from dying of embarrassment at the funeral of his former coworker.

"Well, Roger didn't rate a funeral procession through Chinatown, but there are quite a few people here. They all look older to me, so they are probably family members or people showing respect to the Chens. I don't see any of the club crowd, do you?"

"No, not their scene."

"Look, there. See the older man just turning on to the main path. That's Roger's grandfather, William Chen. He's a very prominent business man."

"You can tell. Look how people treat him."

Dakota was right. The mourners parted to make way for him. He walked with great dignity, acknowledging the condolences with solemn grace. A taller man at his elbow also responded to the crowd. As they neared the procession of waiting limousines, the tall man nodded to a black-suited functionary standing near the gates, holding an ornate box. Red envelopes from the box were distributed to each of the mourners.

"What's that, I wonder?"

"I think it may be money," Dakota said. "The money is given by the family to all the mourners, and they are supposed to spend it. This helps the deceased have a good transition through the afterlife and rebirth."

"Given the many, many sins he committed while alive, Roger can use all the help he can get."

Out of the sea of strangers bobbed a familiar face. Rupert Fong Lee, my venture capitalist friend, received his red packet formally with both hands. He bowed slightly to William Chen and to the taller man, uttering what must have been words of condolence. Rupert's presence underscored the prominence of the Chen family and the close ties of all the significant families in the Bay Area. It was strange to see Rupert in so formal and somber a setting. He was so modern, so involved in high technology; he seemed out of place, but only to me. Here, he had stepped back into a world where he was as comfortable as he was confident in my sphere when talking to entrepreneurs or bankers.

In silence we watched the family disperse into the line of somber sleek vehicles and the other mourners pick their way along the ribbon of parked cars. I lost sight of Rupert in the crowd, not that it mattered. I did not want to be seen by him here. What would I say to him? "Hi, I'm your friendly occidental funeral crasher?"

I reflected on the differences in beliefs and practices surrounding death. Heaven. Valhalla. Irish wakes. Reincarnation. "Gad!" I swiveled in Dakota's direction. "Roger isn't coming back, is he?"

Dakota nearly jumped out of his skin. A man crossing the street toward a green sedan parked in front of my Saab looked through the windshield. Dakota's face turned beet red. "Can we go now?" he whispered, staring at the ignition keys, willing them to engage the engine.

"We're outta here, pal!" I twisted the keys and turned the steering wheel so that I wouldn't have to look at green sedan man.

We didn't really relax until we were back on Highway 101. Finally, Dakota sat up in his seat like a normal passenger, and the tension in the car dissipated. I punched the radio button on.

"Seriously." I tried to lighten the mood. "What do you think Roger would come back as, if he did come back?"

"Well, I don't think it would be human, what with his poor performance the last time around."

"How about something reptilian?"

"Good guess. He liked black and leather. Sunglasses. Yeah, that could work."

"Or how about a beetle? A nice black beetle. Shiny, sleek, disgusting."

"OK, but I don't think he's supposed to come back as something he likes. It's supposed to be more like penance. You know, he has to work out what he did in life. Learn something."

"Jeeeez! How could I have missed the whole point of this exercise, Comisky? He has to come back as a female. A female who gets screwed. A lot!"

At that moment, Elton John's "The Bitch Is Back" blared from the Saab's speakers.

We burst into hysterical laughter. I could barely see to make the turn onto Dakota's street. My back tire rode up on the curb, and the resulting thump set us off again. Dakota pulled himself out of the car and stood, holding his side and gasping for air. "Well, it's been real, I guess. I can't wait to see what your next excursion is like."

We parted after I extracted a promise from him to call after he reached a human resources professional at CAI.

I parked the car in the garage, dumped my briefcase in my office, and danced up the stairs in a cheery frame of mind considering where I had just been.

Entering the kitchen, I opened a cabinet, grabbing a glass to make myself a celebratory scotch when I heard voices. Janie Belle was in the living room with someone. I replaced the glass, since it would be rude to have a libation if others were not drinking. Besides, once I had come home to find the Jehovah's Witnesses ensconced in the parlor chatting away about the loaves and the fishes. They would take a dim view of drinking.

Conjuring up a welcoming smile and smoothing the front of my slacks, I entered the living room. There, sitting serenely on the Chippendale couch was my worst nightmare. Not Roger Chen come back from the dead. It was Bob Harrison sitting next to Janie Belle Billingsley.

"You left your scarf in my car, so I brought it back. This nice lady was kind enough to invite me in for a Coke." Completely out of proportion for the antique couch, Harrison had managed to drape himself sideways so he could rest his arms on the curved back and still hold sufficient hip on the seat to keep from sliding to the floor. One big leg was crossed over the other, the raised foot keeping time to some lively inner tune.

Pert Janie Belle, always more exuberant in the presence of males, said, "Robert is going to assist me with a terrible problem. I am so pleased, because I just didn't know where to turn."

"He's helping you with what?" I shrank inwardly from the implied obligation if Robert aided Janie Belle. Where would it end? Janie Belle would use this as an excuse to entertain him, pumping him for information about his past and his people. She would probe until she discovered some distant Harrison relation to whom we, the Billingsleys, were connected. Then she would chortle that he was family and privately conclude that he was suitable for me to marry.

"You mother got a summons to appear in court."

I stared at him. My brain would not wrap itself around the concept of Janie Belle in court.

"She got a parking ticket," he said to dumb it down.

"Oh."

Janie Belle explained. "I parked behind the church, because the people at the AA meeting had taken up all the spaces in front where I usually park. How was I to know they were planning to sweep the streets? I was in there all morning doing God's work, and I came out and I had a ticket on my windshield. How dare they? Giving tickets outside a church. Stands to reason that shouldn't be allowed."

"Separation of church and state, Mother. They don't care that you were polishing God's silver. The streets belong to Caesar, and you're going to have to render to him, er, the City of San Francisco, whatever the amount is on your citation."

"Am not! Your boyfriend is going to fix it for me!"

My face felt hot. I kept my eyes on her, but in my peripheral vision, I could detect that the dancing foot was bobbing faster. My imagination needed no help whatsoever picturing the grin on the big mug below the caramel eyes.

"Mother, Bob does not fix tickets!"

"Sure I do." Our eyes made contact. "I'll be more than happy to take care of this. It's no trouble. No trouble at all."

Janie Belle beamed at him, reminding me of the floodlight on a redneck's truck when it hits a deer in hunting season.

This was more than a nightmare. This was a cataclysm. I excused myself to go to the powder room. I needed a john and aspirin.

I took my time composing myself in the bathroom. On the one hand, I did not want to leave them alone together too long. On the other hand, I needed a moment to myself to plot strategy. After all, how much worse could it get downstairs?

I applied eyebrow pencil and eyeliner, blotted my skin with pressed powder, and finished up with a subtle shade of coral lipstick. I reached for the cologne spray but thought better of it. Too obvious that I was fixing myself up for him. Smoothing my hair, I exited the bathroom and traipsed down the stairs.

When I returned to the living room, the Harrison fan club had gained another adherent. Skootch sat in front of Bob, smiling his best doggy smile, tongue hanging at a rakish angle. No wonder. I spotted the peanuts in the heirloom dish on the coffee table. Harrison's Coke had been replaced with a beer, and Janie Belle punctuated the air with her bourbon glass as she spoke.

"We'd love to come! What a wonderful idea!"

Sweat gushed through the pressed powder on my forehead like a freight train on a downhill grade. I had been wrong. Leaving them unattended had led to something worse.

"Robert has invited us to be his guests at a Johns Hopkins affair. They are going to have a crab feast! Isn't that marvelous! I just love crab!"

Janie Belle had pumped him for details such as where he had attended school. He'd probably felt obligated to ask us to some alumni event. How many more embarrassments would I be forced to endure?

"Mother, are you sure we're free? You're pretty booked up with church events, and I have client obligations."

"No, no. This is next Saturday, during the day. You don't have client things on Saturday! Robert and I already have agreed on the time and every little thing! It will be such fun!"

"It's going to be real Maryland crab flown out special," Harrison added encouragingly.

Skootch looked from human to human at the mention of another food group.

I was trapped. My new relationship was to be destroyed by a bunch of crustaceans with frequent flyer miles. It is hard enough for a woman to maintain mystique when she is wearing a bib and picking crab shell out of her molars, but to sit helplessly while her date is treated to stories of her ungainly teen years, is beyond enduring. For once, I would not be sabotaging a relationship. My mother was going to do it for me.

* * *

CHAPTER 12

After completing some real work for Georgina's diagnostics client, Precision Probes, and e-mailing it for their initial review, I put the finishing touches on a PowerPoint presentation designed to introduce me and my capabilities in the biotechnology and finance worlds to the management of Ancient Turtle. I copied the file onto a CD. Slipping the disk and some extra business cards into my briefcase, I headed for the Saab.

True to my threat at the club, I called Margaret for an introduction to her management team. Her lack of enthusiasm for talking to me dripped from the phone like pus from a festering wound. She transferred me to Mr. Fang's assistant. Because the phone hand-off happened quickly, I assumed Margaret had not taken the time to warn the assistant off me. I represented myself to her as Margaret's bosom buddy and acted as if the requested meeting with Mr. Fang was a forgone conclusion. My scheme worked, and she fitted me into an hour timeslot on Friday morning.

I parked the Saab on the side of the Ancient Turtle building that was as far away from Screen Leaf as I could get. I owed them a draft presentation, and they were not going to get it today. Client guilt is a major source of nail biting, overeating, binge drinking, and an array of unproductive avoidance behaviors in consulting. I grimaced, sending them a telepathic promise to finish their project on Sunday, threw my shoulders back, and marched toward the Ancient Turtle entrance.

I was ushered from the lobby by the assistant I had spoken with to arrange the appointment. She guided me up a flight of stairs and deposited me in a conference room opposite Brutus Fang's office. Although the room overlooked the sea of computer-filled cubicles below, the shades were drawn. A laptop was open on the conference table, its electrical cord jutting from a recessed console in the center of the custom table. The room was equipped with a state-of-the-art teleconferencing system as well as the more mundane projection equipment I would be using today. The assistant took my disk and launched my presentation, focused the title slide, and instructed me in the use of the remote. Satisfied I could operate the equipment, she exited.

Moments later, a trio of young managers entered with the assistant in their wake, this time carrying a tray with a bevy of water bottles and a dish of mints. I shook hands with and received cards from each of the men. We stood awkwardly waiting for Fang. Margaret was not a part of this group, but she had said she was not involved in communications. I tried to get a handle on the responsibilities of the three managers from their cards but had trouble reading the typeface from the table surface while I was still standing. I was too embarrassed to pick them up in front of these youngsters and hold them where my forty-something eyes could function. Fang's arrival ended the painful interlude.

I did the handshake thing with Fang. He was distant and preoccupied to the point of rudeness, but then I had almost forced myself on these people, so who was I to be critical. He sat at the end of the table nearest the door, poised for a fast exit. The triad of managers gathered around him, leaving me alone at the opposite end. Fang and his associates did not avail themselves of notepads or PDAs.

"Well, I guess I'll dive right in." This remark was met with a wall of silence. I began my introduction to corporate communications and investor relations in the bioscience field. There is nothing deadlier than standing up in front of a group of people who have no interest in you or your product. The minutes seem like eons. Somehow, I made it to the last five slides of the presentation. These slides contained a list of my current and former clients followed by a list of my venture capital and banking contacts. Fang had been in the process of looking at his watch for the millionth time, but his arm settled back on the table as he eyed the screen intently. He shot a commanding glance at his nearest subordinate, who whipped out a PDA as if he had been zapped with an electrical current. My client list was tapped in with digital efficiency.

After my concluding remarks, Fang rose, thanked me for coming, and was out the door before I could traverse the length of the table to shake his hand. The PDA-user took a step forward to prevent me from following his boss. He also thanked me and forced himself to provide me with a little eye contact, his first during the entire presentation. I suggested I would develop a proposal for them and deliver it the following week. He nodded and began to backpedal to the door through which the other two managers were already exiting.

I let out an audible sigh of relief. What a painful experience! You idiot, you wanted to come back, so here you are and what have you accomplished? Zilch, that's what. I returned to the laptop and extracted my disk. I was collecting my things when the assistant appeared. She escorted me down the stairs to the lobby and nodded good-bye as the door closed on me. I was standing in an empty lobby facing the guard who looked up from the paper he was reading. I smiled at him, the first friendly face I had seen, and started to turn toward the street exit. On impulse, I stopped.

"Gee," I said to the guard, "I have a long drive and I really should have asked to visit the ladies' room before I left. Could you let me back in so I can use the lavatory?"

The guard rose, shoved the newspaper under his arm, and punched a code into the keypad. He held the door for me as I entered and gestured to the left, directing me to the restrooms.

Smiling at him for his kindness, I proceeded down the hall and entered the appropriate facility. Selecting a stall far from the door, I entered, locked the door, pulled my slacks down, and sat. What could I have been thinking? I had no follow-through. No plan. What was I looking for exactly? The guard would become suspicious if I didn't return, so I didn't have time to do much. That is, if I could come up with anything to do.

I inhaled and exhaled deeply. I discovered I really had to go. The tinkle of normalcy reduced my sense of panic. I finished my business and moved to the sink area. Washing my hands with great deliberation, I tried to sort out what I wanted to know about Ancient Turtle.

First, you don't believe they are legit. Because you are in the bioscience industry, you are inherently suspicious of herbal companies. Second, you think the disparity of their clunky product communication juxtaposed to their powerful computer technology is weird. Finally, you think their business operations are structured oddly, with the front office in Thailand and the back office here in one of the most expensive operating geographies on earth.

And then there is Roger's death. So what you want to know is what business they're really in. I rummaged in my purse and extracted a lipstick. That pretty much sums it up. You would like to find evidence of a business activity, legitimate or otherwise, that supports the facts.

With that objective, I left the restroom and headed back in the direction I had come. I had to press myself against the wall as a muscular young man pushed a flatbed stacked with cartons past me. As I waited for him to pass, I gazed in the direction of the lobby door. At that moment, Brutus Fang, his assistant following in his wake laden with laptop and shoulder bag and barely able to keep up, breezed through the exit. Well, at least I wouldn't have to worry about running into her.

I turned and followed the cart. We traveled the length of the main floor, and as the stock boy pushed the dolly into the storage area, I busied myself by collecting supplies from some shelving near the entry. I placed my briefcase on the floor and shoved it behind a waste can. Moments later the young man exited, pushing the empty dolly ahead of him. Before the door could click shut, I inserted my foot. Carrying my little selection of folders and envelopes with me for cover, I entered the warehouse. With the unwieldy dolly to push, the clerk never turned around.

As the door closed, I surveyed the largely empty space. This was a warehouse without a purpose. Next to me were the boxes deposited by the clerk. On one side were rows of shelving. On the other side were pallets with unopened cartons. I moved to the first pallet and took note of the shippers. Computer monitors. The next pallet contained desktop CPUs. I moved to another row of pallets. And then another. No Ancient Turtle products. Nothing shipped from Thailand. A quick survey of the shelving contents produced similar results. Cables, surge protectors, memory cards. Everything here was related to a computer systems operation, not a botanicals distributor. I could not find any promotional literature either. No marketing materials. No product inserts or packaging.

My sleuthing consumed ten minutes, but it was a long time for a woman to be powdering her nose. I opened the warehouse door a slit and pushed it wider after seeing that the coast was clear. I deposited the envelopes I had been carrying, retrieved my briefcase, and moved briskly down the hall to the entrance. Unsatisfied with the results of my detective work, I had decided on one more escapade.

Summoning up a winning smile, I pushed open the door and as the guard looked up shoved my briefcase into his unwilling arms.

"Hold this for me will you? I've got to run upstairs for a moment and retrieve my disk from the conference room computer. Silly to have forgotten it, but I have to give another talk this afternoon." By the time I had gotten this out, the door clicked shut again.

Hoping that the briefcase would serve as a sort of hostage for the guard, alleviating the need for him to pursue me, I dashed up the steps and down the upper hallway toward the conference room. I slowed before the meeting room door and veered off to the right. Fang and his assistant were gone, and the door to Fang's office was open. I don't know if I would have had the courage to enter if I'd had to actually open the door. I walked in and shut it behind me.

I exhaled slowly. My heart pounded from the run up the stairs and the thrill of my little deception with the guard. I could feel the blood pulse at my temples just as it did before I left the plane back in my skydiving days.

Like the man, Fang's office was cold. The walls were gray, and the furniture was black leather or smoked Lucite. An abstract canvas in hues of charcoal and mauve represented the one artistic contribution to the room. There was nothing personal on the desk, merely a large and complicated conference phone. The only things that brought color into the room were magazines, so the neatly stacked piles on the edge of the desk drew my eye. Here was the first evidence of a world of interest to Ancient Turtle other than the sphere of cyberspace.

Arrayed before me was every bioscience and bio-business publication of any significance. Every newsletter. Every journal. Even the ruinously expensive market reports that could set you back thousands of dollars. This was the collection of a serious and well-funded follower of the biotechnology industry. I reviewed the titles a second time. There were no publications for nutritional supplements or any of the nonprescription products that were Ancient Turtle's stock-in-trade. These subscriptions were for drug development and genetic technology companies focused on serious medicine. This was the industry my clients called home. That explained Fang's interest in my client list.

A murmur of voices outside the office reminded me I was in a place I was not supposed to be. I eased the door open and scanned the hall in both directions. The talkers had moved away from the executive area. I stepped out of Fang's office and leaned over the assistant's desk as if to write a note. Her desk was littered with stock analyst reports, all written by people I knew. Marilyn Wynn, the Medford & Putnam biotechnology analyst. Dexter Hume, the Bank of Boston analyst.

I straightened up and headed for the stairs. Bursting through the lobby door, I retrieved my briefcase from beside the speechless guard's podium with a masterful dive, and waved thanks to him as I breezed out to the street. I felt a rush as I stepped off the curb and sidled between the parked cars. It was a feeling I never got writing a business plan.

Saturday morning dawned all blue and sunny. I squinted at the sparkling windows. Couldn't it rain so they'd have to cancel the damned crab feast?. The tick-tick of claws on the stair risers announced the impending arrival of Skootch. If I didn't get up, I'd get the shorthaired pointer "rise and shine" treatment, which consists of sitting on the victim and licking her until she heaves you off and races to the strange little room with the big white doggy bowl full of water. Not in the mood for the treatment, I rose and pushed myself to my feet.

Skootch followed me into my closet but grew impatient and left, because I continued to stare at the rack like a zombie. What did I have that was appropriate for a crab feast in Golden Gate Park? Nothing, that's what.

In keeping with the recurring theme in our relationship, Harrison and I had agreed we would meet at the park. The idea of Harrison and Janie Belle in the same car going and coming from the event was more than I could contemplate. I wandered downstairs to see what Janie Belle was up to. She was already dressed for the affair. Today, she was wearing a yachting outfit over a wool turtleneck and après ski boots topped off with a straw sun hat the size of the gunboat Merrimac.

"Are you sure you're going to be warm enough in that?"

"I could take my fur coat."

"No, you can't. We've been over and over this. You can't wear fur in San Francisco. Some dick head will spray-paint you."

"Language! Language! All right, I will just have to take a cloth coat like Pat Nixon. I would love to wear something red. You know, that is the Hopkins color, but as a redhead I can't bring myself to do it. Why don't you wear red?"

"It's a thought." I sipped my coffee. "That way when I slit my throat no one will notice."

"What?"

"Nothing. Nothing. We need to be in the car by eleven forty-five. OK?"

"No problem. I'm the one who is already dressed."

Parking in Golden Gate Park is impossible. It becomes more impossible when events are scheduled. After circling several times near the section reserved by the Hopkins alumni, I dropped Janie Belle at the curb of a sidewalk featuring a park bench without a homeless person on it. I instructed her to sit and wait for me, to hold her purse firmly, and to avoid conversations with strangely dressed persons. As I pulled away, I realized she was a strangely dressed person.

I parked seven blocks uphill. When we were ready to leave, I would have to retrieve the car and pick her up. Perhaps Harrison had parked closer and could drop us at our car. Of course, this would mean risking Janie Belle and Harrison in a vehicle together, but it was only for a few blocks.

I had managed to locate an Oxford shirt at the back of my closet that boasted a predominance of red stripes. I coupled this with a pair of Chinos, some Saucony running shoes that were pleasantly broken in, and a red crewneck sweater thrown over my shoulders. I spent a significant amount of time with my makeup and repainted my nails a dark red. The red deepened the intensity of my dark hair and eyes. Old Caramel-Orbs should be impressed.

I collected Janie Belle and headed for the green where I saw younger alumni of Johns Hopkins University engaged in a lacrosse match. On the periphery of the playing area, a large knot of people in a disproportionate amount of blue clothing congregated.

"Mother, are you sure about the red thing?" I asked as we continued over the grass. "I'm thinking their color might be blue."

"Well, red is for one of those Maryland schools. Oh, I know! It's the University of Maryland. The Terps!" Janie spotted Harrison and waved at him.

Of course, Janie Belle, being a redhead, was not dressed in crimson. Her cruise clothes were etched in politically correct blue. Even her cloth coat was navy.

As we drew closer to the crowd, I could make out Blue Jays on several sweatshirts and caps. Blue it was. I would be the only person wearing the colors of the rival Terrapins. I looked down at my shirtfront trying to detect any blue. A thin line of navy edged the vast expanse of red stripe on my left breast.

Harrison approached in khaki shorts and a Blue Jay t-shirt. This was the second time I had gotten a look at his legs. Muscular and tan with the right amount of hair.

"You playin'?" he nodded at the lacrosse game.

"Me watchin'. You drinkin'?"

"Yeap. How's about you, Janie Belle?"

Janie Belle was already halfway to the refreshment tent. She would order a 7 Up! I had filled her silver flask with Old Crow Bourbon and placed it in her pocketbook. Janie Belle cannot abide beer. Neither can the officials who manage Golden Gate Park. Events scheduled at the park are booked as alcohol-free affairs, but as every sane person knows, you cannot eat crab without beer.

After settling Janie Belle in a folding chair he had brought, Harrison and I sauntered off toward a nondescript van in a nearby parking space. The driver had arrived early to get close in, a good thing, because this was the beer mobile. As we neared the vehicle, the side door slid back, and we scored two cold ones in opaque blue plastic glasses. Sipping contentedly, we strolled back to the crowd.

You can take Johns Hopkins graduates out of Maryland and away from the Chesapeake Bay, but you cannot get the tidewater out of their veins. Graduates are physicians, physicists, engineers, musicians, and public health professionals; and when you put them together, they might not have much in common.

Except for one thing. Blue crab. San Francisco Bay area residents dine on Dungeness, and Alaskan king crab also is abundant in local restaurants, but to a Marylander, there is only one true crab, only one true blue religion.

A row of portable picnic tables had been set up, and several organizers were busy taping layers of newspaper to the tables. Stacks of heavy-duty napkins were placed at each table and anchored with condiment bottles. Each table also was supplied with a bucket for shells.

As I downed the remainder of my illicit beer, someone on the Lacrosse field yelled, "Heads up!"

At first, I thought something was happening with the game, but all action had stopped on the field and the players were loping in our direction. Their eyes and the eyes of everyone in our party fastened on a white SUV that was pulling into the park from Lincoln Avenue. I glanced at the tables and realized that they were filling up rapidly. Grasping Janie Belle by the elbow, I raised her from her seat and force-marched her as fast as her octogenarian legs would carry her toward a partially filled table. We made it just in time to lay claim to three seats. Harrison returned with two more brewskies.

An organizer rushed to curbside and removed two orange cones reserving a parking space. Other organizers gathered near the space as the Explorer pulled in. The driver and a passenger erupted from the vehicle, moved to its rear, opened the hatch, and began passing boxes to the waiting crew. Each box was delivered to a table, slit open, and upended on the newspapers. The people fell on the steamed crabs like vultures.

Silence ruled the once ebullient throng. Crab picking being the serious business it is, the graduates focused on the succulent task. Some attendees had brought their own personal crab tools, the oval wooden handles worn from years, perhaps generations, of use. Thwack, thwack, crack. Suck, thwack, suck.

Satiated, having picked and consumed the meat of four crustaceans, I cracked a final claw and surveyed the crowd. I wondered if the doctors or at least surgeons were better pickers. To my surprise, my survey turned up a familiar face. Three tables down, Leonard Price picked away none too expertly next to a woman who could have commanded top dollar from any seafood-packing corporation on the Chesapeake Bay. I would have to speak to him, but not until after the feast concluded. There was no way I could roust Harrison and Janie Belle from their seats while another carton of crabs was headed our way.

"Aren't y'all glad I remembered to bring our own knives?" Janie Belle did not take her eyes off the large glob of fat she was teasing away from the carcass she held.

"I'm sure glad you did!" Harrison smiled at her. "It gives us an edge. We'll be a dozen crabs ahead thanks to your foresight."

"I hate to interrupt this mutual admiration society, but does anybody want another beer?" I asked.

"Shhhhhhhhhhhhhh!" Harrison scolded. "That's ice tea, and the answer is yes."

"That reminds me." Janie Belle extracted her flask from her purse and dumped another jigger of bourbon into her Seven Up.

As the shells and soiled newspapers were gathered and placed in large trash bags, I introduced Harrison to Leonard Price and was introduced to Mrs. Price, the former Peggy Bailey of Annapolis.

"I grew up on the North Side of Chicago and attended Northwestern, but I did my postdoc at Hopkins, and I met this blond OB/GYN intern who consented to be my wife," Price said. They appeared to be a very happy couple, despite the disparity in their crab handling skills.

While Harrison and Price chatted about Hopkins's lacrosse prowess, Peggy filled me in on her work. She was associated with a group of fertility researchers and served on the faculty of the University of California, San Francisco. The campus of UCSF loomed over us on the hill above the park.

"You can see the windows of my lab from here, three stories from ground level." Peggy pointed at the sleek high-rise. As we strolled on the green, we talked about advances in the field of gene therapy, the study of important proteins, and their likely impact on the medicine she practiced. Intent on this interesting conversation, I failed to notice how chilly it had become until Harrison tapped me on the shoulder and gestured toward the bench where we had left Janie Belle. Chatting to a mother-to-be sitting next to her, she huddled with her arms wrapped around her torso.

As we sauntered her way, I glanced over my shoulder toward the West. Yeah, here came the fog, the proverbial wet blanket. The crowd thinned rapidly now, the picnic accoutrements long packed away. Even the lacrosse fanatics had stowed their gear. Harrison pulled me close as we walked, rubbing my arm in a warmth-producing gesture. I matched my stride to his. He leaned closer and planted a kiss on my head. I wondered if my hair smelled of crab. I turned my head slightly to get a whiff of the sweatshirt he had pulled on as the afternoon grew cold. Ummmm, hint of seafood over essence of testosterone. Suddenly, Harrison's brow wrinkled and his pace quickened.

I looked in the direction of his stern gaze, gasped and broke into a trot. Evidently, the cold had driven Janie Belle to resort to her flask. A member of the park patrol held the ornery octogenarian by the elbow as he tried to confiscate her booze.

"That is a family heirloom!" She struggled to hold it away.

"Lady, you're not to consume alcohol in the park. You're going to have to surrender that and come with me," said the authoritative brown shirt.

"Let me handle this," Harrison whispered. Janie Belle kicked the constable in the leg. Fortunately, she couldn't do much damage with her après ski boots. That would be a good point to make in court to counter the assault charge.

Harrison extracted his credentials from his pocket and shared them with the officer. The two law enforcement professionals discussed Janie Belle's infractions without consulting the perpetrator or me, and reached a compromise. Janie Belle would leave the park forthwith, surrendering the offending flask to the ranger. However, the valued keepsake could be retrieved at the park patrol office on Monday. There would be no citations for drunk and disorderly or for assault with a furry weapon.

Harrison drove us to my car, and I chauffeured Janie Belle home in sullen silence. My indebtedness to Harrison was becoming a problem. It would ruin this fragile, new relationship. Stupid things like this always did. They destroyed the delicate balance. We would be strangers by next week.

As she got out of the Saab in the garage, Janie Belle said, "I have decided to pray for him."

"Harrison?"

"No, Robert Harrison has already been added to my prayer list. I meant that misguided young person who thought I was homeless."

"He didn't think you were homeless, he thought you were drunk."

Janie Belle drew herself up to her full height and turned an imperious glare on me, quite effective in the yachting uniform. "I have never been drunk. I have been tipsy, of course, but never drunk. Robert knows that, if you don't. He said it all had been an unfortunate misunderstanding."

So, it was Robert now, was it. Janie Belle turned on her heels as best she could in her fur boots and sailed majestically up the stairs. She was going to be very disappointed when this relationship ended. I hoped I had enough Dewar's left in the kitchen to get a damned sight more lubricated than tipsy tonight.

The whisky did not have the hoped-for effect. The reason was Harrison. I tossed and turned for two hours. At one thirty, I got out of bed and slipped on a pair of jeans, sweatshirt, and my Sauconys. I signaled Skootch to follow me. We crept down the stairs past Janie Belle's room. Feeling along the sill for Skootch's leash, I grasped the handle and scooped up keys and a battered windbreaker. I let myself out the kitchen door and then the garden gate before fastening the leash to the dog's worn, red collar.

The neighborhood snoozed and the streets glistened with damp. We walked down the middle of Plymouth since there were no cars about. We reached Monterey and strolled toward the St. Francis Wood neighborhood. I usually didn't walk Skootch along Monterey because of the traffic. Since he didn't pass this way often, Skootch peed frequently to mark the territory. We stopped at tree trunks, retainer walls, low shrubs, high curbs, and traffic signs.

Progress was slow, but I appreciated being left to my thoughts. Did I want Robert Harrison? If not, why not? If yes, what next? Somehow, moving relationships to the next level was not my forte. What did he think of me, a forty-something woman living with her mother?

Skootch took the lead down a side street that would take us to the center of St. Francis Wood. The dog snuffled a large pile of leaves and sneezed heartily. He trotted ahead and thrust his upper body through a high hedge. A cat shot from the hedge, traversed the street, and mounted a lattice fence. Skootch did not attempt to pursue the creature, satisfied that he had given it a good scare. The pointer moved on, and we reached the neighborhood fountain. I sat on one of the benches and, deciding to take a chance, let Skootch off his leash. Panting appreciatively, he headed for the expansive green sward between the traffic lanes. After some random sniffing, he trotted another ten yards down the lawn and began to circle. In Pavlovian fashion,

I reached into my jeans for a plastic bag. Oops, no bag. Skootch was to be permitted an illegal poop. I rose as the dog finished, anxious to leave the area in case another insomniac spotted our indiscretion.

The walk home wound uphill. This did not bother Skootch, now back on his leash, but I had to put my back into it. When the going got tough, I let him pull me up. We were on the street of the Chinese consulate, just ahead shimmering in the lamp lit fog.

Skootch also realized where we were and made for the consular enclave. He wants to go annoy their guard dogs, I thought, and tried to pull him the other way. If he got to the fence, the guard dogs would bark, and it was too late to cause such a disturbance. I tugged and tugged, but Skootch was determined.

"Damn it, Skootch, cut it out!" He stopped long enough for me to come abreast and grab his collar. I lifted the collar to bring his head up and began to turn him with my body. The sound of a door opening drew my eyes to the consular entrance. Somebody was leaving the building. A man in a business suit strode out, followed to the gates by a uniformed employee fumbling with keys. I let go of Skootch and allowed him to walk in the direction of the high gates, pulling the collar of my windbreaker up around my face.

The sleepy employee dropped the key ring, and the impatient businessman stamped his feet in frustration as we closed the distance to the compound. The ring retrieved, the underling bent over the lock, found the keyhole, and turned the tumblers. The brusque guest brushed past, almost knocking him down. Bowing in apology, the man closed the door and reengaged the lock. Not knowing whether to wait or retreat, the poor fellow backed slowly down the walkway, and disgraced himself again by tripping over a crack. By this time, the impatient visitor reached his car and, pressing the remote in his hand, disarmed its security system. The car's lights came on and I recognized the late-night caller. Brutus Fang, the chief executive of Ancient Turtle.

The car pulled out from the curb and purred past me. Although I did not think he would recognize me in jeans and running shoes in the middle of the night, I pulled my collar tighter around my face.

* * *

CHAPTER 13

I woke exhausted. The nocturnal exercise had been followed by a mental exercise trying to figure out the real business of Ancient Turtle. My eyes closed as the sun rose, and I slept until nine. A shower helped, but it was going to be a dull day.

Janie Belle had left for church when I entered the kitchen in search of coffee. As I sipped my steaming salvation, I concluded that I needed to return to Ancient Turtle. My mental marathon had not resulted in any deductions other than the obvious one. I needed to know more. I spent the rest of the morning concocting a consulting proposal for Ancient Turtle, my passport to reentry.

I had little to go on because the company had not provided me with any materials. Since the Ancient Turtle Web site also lacked the requisite corporate background, my proposal was a colossal invention, but then, it wasn't intended as a bona fide solicitation of business.

In the middle of concocting this fiction, I got into the spirit of prevarication. I grew bolder with my assumptions and recommendations; my prose left precedent and practicality behind.

Hours later, as I put the finishing touches on the bogus brief, I marveled at my deceitful creativity.

Before knocking off for the day, I left a message for Rupert Fong Lee. I wanted an introduction to the elder Chens. I needed to know what they knew about Roger's last employment and his relationship with Margaret Lu.

I did one more thing. I e-mailed Harrison my thanks for the crab feast and for handling the situation between Janie Belle and the long arm of the law.

A relentless drizzle made Monday morning errands difficult and delayed my getting back on task. My office was clammy because I had left a window ajar. The phone rang.

"Nola!" Harrison greeted me. "Got your e-mail."

"And I got the flask back. Thanks again for your help."

"How about dinner tomorrow night? There's a new restaurant in my neighborhood we should try. I hear it specializes in comfort food."

"Sounds like our kinda place!" I hoped this date would erase the awkward end to the Hopkins outing and put Harrison and me back on the right track to romance.

"I'll pick you up."

"Nawh, I'll meet you. You're already downtown, and I have meetings in the financial district tomorrow. You can drive me home after."

"OK, meet me in the bar at the Huntington Hotel and we'll walk to the restaurant from there."

I phoned Rupert Fong Lee and reached him in two rings. I asked to meet him the following day, and he agreed to sandwich me in at five. In terms of timing this would work nicely for my date, but I'd have to go to Rupert's dressed to the nines.

I fixed myself a light lunch of celery sticks, peanut butter, and Diet Coke and fed Skootch a treat of leftover pasta from a Styrofoam container I found in the refrigerator. Having come of age during the Depression, Janie Belle does not like to waste food and asks for a doggy bag in every restaurant, no matter how elegant. She informs each waiter that we really do have a doggy. The doggy bags migrate to the back of the refrigerator where they grow organisms of potential interest to my clients. Skootch appreciates these intriguing packages, especially when they contain meat. This time he had to make do with fettuccine Alfredo.

After sending four copies of my Ancient Turtle proposal to the printer, I ascended to my bedroom to change into a black suit. I retrieved the copies, placed them in individual folders, and copied the proposal file to a CD. The proposals and disk were placed in my briefcase, and from the case I extracted a diminutive SanDisk USB memory device, tiny storage media for transporting large files in a unit smaller than a Bic lighter. I placed the petite device in my jacket pocket.

When I arrived at Ancient Turtle, the same security guard who had assisted me with my bogus bathroom foray was on duty. I greeted him with my biggest smile and explained that I wished to drop off proposals with Mr. Fang's assistant. When he offered to take them, I explained that I needed to talk to the assistant in person to explain who was to receive copies, and the easiest thing was for me to dash upstairs and instruct her myself. He reached for the intercom to call her, but I reasoned that she would prove to be as much of an obstructionist as he was, so I suggested that if she were not there I would need to write her a note anyway, so he should just buzz me in. By this time, two delivery messengers formed a line behind me with parcels to be logged. The guard looked past me at the impatient delivery personnel and caved in. After grabbing a visitor's badge for me, he escorted me to the door and buzzed me through.

Now what? I had no plan. I took my time climbing the stairs, trying to come up with a way to gain access to the Ancient Turtle computer system. The assistant, intent on a pile of reports stacked as high as her pert little breasts, started when I spoke to her. She did not hide her annoyance as she listened to my request. I pulled the reports from my briefcase I had placed on her desk. The case nudged the stack of reports precariously close to the edge, heightening her consternation.

I asked for some paper to write out instructions for the distribution of the report. She complied and offered me a seat at an empty work area adjacent to her space. Retrieving my briefcase, I carried everything to the unoccupied desk and took a long time to write out my instructions. The woman, who appeared to be readying herself to leave, straightened the pile of reports, gathered her purse, and tapped her foot in frustration. Another young woman approached also carrying a purse. A plan coalesced as the tapping foot picked up speed.

"Am I keeping you from something?"

"Well, no, I was just going on break with my friend. We can make it to the Starbucks and back if we really move it."

"Listen, I've got an idea. I can just e-mail my explanation of the plan to the four recipients, and then all you have to do is distribute the actual proposal. Can I use your computer? Just show me the intranet and you can go." I was already moving toward her desk.

Relieved and without the least hesitation, the assistant vacated her chair and clicked around her screen to show me where everything was that I would need to e-mail the executives. She waved good-bye and she and her colleague made a beeline for the stairs. As their heads bobbed out of sight, I turned toward the screen.

In her hurry to leave, the assistant had abandoned her computer before logging out of sensitive files. Not only was I on

Ancient Turtle's intranet, but because I was sitting at the desk of the chief executive's assistant, I had access to Mr. Fang's e-mail and correspondence files.

I pulled the SanDisk from my pocket and plugged it into a UBS port on the assistant's computer. I would copy as much as I could to this disk and take the materials home. The women had probably exited from the front of the building, and that security guard might realize that the person I was visiting had just left the premises. Why was I taking a chance like this? Had the Chinese government become the ultimate authority figure for me?

While I downloaded Fang's correspondence, I searched the intranet for any connection with Beijing. Perhaps they had a contract with the Chinese for the processing and supply of some herb important to Chinese medicine, so different from the Western variety. But why not handle that connection from their location in Thailand? Why meet in the San Francisco consulate? Perhaps the source of the substance was American. The Chinese went in for some exotic ingredients. Something derived from the liver of the American bison? Try as I might, I could not find any files about supplements, suspect or otherwise, on Ancient Turtle's system. Frustrated that I knew so little about computer architecture, I abandoned my search and checked to make sure the download of the purloined files was complete. Pocketing the storage device, I dashed off the e-mail for the proposal recipients and pressed send.

When I burst through the lobby door and powered across the expanse to the street exit, the frowning guard was assisting a maintenance employee as he changed a bulb in an overhead fixture. I would not be able to cajole him a third time into letting me enter the secured area without an escort.

After dinner, I settled into my office chair with a piping hot cup of tea. Janie Belle would not miss me because TNT was running a Matlock marathon, and she loved that wily Southern lawyer almost as much as bourbon and seven.

I plugged in the SanDisk and opened it on my desktop. Any compunction about the theft of the files dissolved with the memories of Fang's sinister face as he left the Chinese consulate—and the headless corpse of Roger sitting on the bench in the fog.

After the first two hours of reading memos and letters, I stood to stretch. If these people were crooked, they also were careful; I might not be able to find anything to link them to unlawful activity. Even if they were conducting an illegal operation, and Roger found out about it or was involved, their decision to end his life would not be documented in an e-mail.

By midnight, I was stiff as a pretzel and frustrated as a teenage boy in a home economics class. Fang's files were fallow. I cracked my knuckles and rolled my head in circles to relieve the crick in my neck.

For a change of pace, I opened the folder where I had stored the assistant's e-mail files. I was subjected to the effusive ennui of youthful women who work in offices. She gossiped with female coworkers about the young male executives. The young executives e-mailed her, asking her out. She accepted or rejected their offers and telegraphed giggly critiques about the outings to her gal associates. I quickly grew bored with this diversion.

I opened another e-mail entitled Appointment Confirmation. I sat up straight in my chair and stared at the meeting participants. Fang was scheduled to meet Casper Wong, the CEO of Screen Leaf, the company on his block and my client list. So, there was a relationship between these two companies other than simple geography, and it started at the top. Had my client been screening compounds for Ancient Turtle? This seemed unlikely since Ancient Turtle was a peddler of elixirs and potions and, therefore, not interested in serious scientific data. Such companies were interested in promotion, not proof. Perhaps Screen Leaf had initiated the contact, offering to provide information supporting the efficacy of an Ancient Turtle product in return for research fees. I scanned for other e-mails involving appointment bookings and found one involving Fang with both Wong and his marketing honcho, Theo Tan, but nothing else.

Since my clandestine day had produced one tiny thread of useful information, a link between Ancient Turtle and Screen Leaf, I declared victory and took my aching back to bed. As I teetered up the stairs, I resolved to search the Screen Leaf computers for links to Ancient Turtle the next time I was at work in my visitor's cubicle.

Rupert eyed my getup as we shook hands in his office. I seated myself primly on the edge of the chair in front of his massive desk. I was wearing a short skirt. The blouse to the chocolate cocktail suit had a deep V, and I reminded myself not to slump for fear my bra would show.

"You look great. Have you lost weight?"

"A little. How are things in the VC business?" We chatted about CAI. I told him about meeting Leonard Price at the Hopkins event, and my introduction to his wife.

Rupert grinned at this. "I'm in talks with her colleagues about a possible start-up in the fertility field."

It seemed everybody in the Bay Area was an entrepreneur.

"Listen, Rupert. I have a favor to ask, and it doesn't have to do with our industry. In fact, it will seem a little unusual to you. I noticed that you were at the Chen family funeral the other day."

"Were you there?" Rupert asked with interest. "I didn't see you, but there was a pretty good crowd."

"I was across the street." An awkward silence followed this remark. "I mean, I came, but when I got there, I couldn't bring myself to get out of the car and join the mourners." This was not entirely true, but it sounded marginally better than saying I was spying on a grieving family.

"I think I'd better start at the beginning. Roger worked for my Internet enterprise." After hesitating for a moment, hoping I could get away without telling Rupert that Roger had embezzled, I came completely clean about the theft from my company's accounts and the string of purchases supporting Roger's club-crawling lifestyle. I also divulged that I had been the person to find Roger's body.

As I concluded my story, Rupert shook his head. "This is all most unfortunate. I never met the boy, but what a terrible end, no matter what he did. I am sorry for your trouble and very sorry for the Chens. They are a fine old family, and they have done a great deal for the Chinese community here in San Francisco. The boy's death has brought them much pain, but I had no idea Roger had so dishonored them with his behavior."

Rupert clenched his hands. "This humiliation added to the murder itself is a heavy burden indeed, particularly for persons of such advanced years. William and Rose suffered the untimely loss of Roger's father and their daughter-in-law. One would have hoped for a more peaceful old age for two such fine people. But what has all this got to do with you?"

"I would like you to introduce me to the Chens."

"But, why?" Rupert was not able to fathom what earthly good such a meeting could produce.

"I need closure." I had not prepared myself well for this moment. I had not thought through what I would say to Rupert, and now I scrambled for a logical explanation for my need to meet with one of the most prominent Chinese families in California. How unseemly and nonsensical my request must sound to

Rupert. "I, uh, my last meeting with Roger was rushed and uncomfortable. We parted on difficult terms."

"And you are concerned about his unsettled spirit?"

Rupert was more traditional than I had thought. Here was the big venture capitalist talking about the spirit world. "It would make me feel better to express my condolences to the family. I don't know how it would make Roger feel."

Rupert stared at me for an uncomfortable period. "Why don't you send a nice note?"

"I need to do this in person." Another pause ensued, in which I became conscious that my ankles, crossed primly to keep my knees together under the short skirt, were perspiring. Realizing that my current tack was not going to get me to my desired harbor, I tried another.

"Look, I hope this doesn't sound too selfish, but I've discovered that after leaving me, Roger went to work for a company with whom I am now consulting. It's rather awkward, but I don't know what Roger said about his employment with me to this new company. I also don't know if Roger stole from them as he did from my start-up. He may have been fired from this company, or still working for them at the time he died. I don't want them to think we failed to inform them they were hiring a bad apple. I'd like to know where I stand with them. I'm uncomfortable not knowing."

"And you think the family can help you?"

"I think the family can help me with his general employment history and that they have the same desire to be discrete about this as I do."

At the mention of discretion, Rupert sat back in his chair and ran his fingers absently along the beveled edge of the expensive desk. Assessing the body language of my old friend, I knew I had won. He would contact the Chens for me, but this would cost him face. I would be in Rupert's debt.

As he escorted me to the head of the stairs in his massive hilltop mansion, Rupert said he would call when he had arranged a meeting. We shook hands, and I descended the treads with a heavy heart. I had fibbed to a very loyal and supportive friend. I resolved to take on his most difficult companies with the most bullheaded founders and perform wondrous feats of strategic communications on their behalves. The robed figures in the ancestor paintings glared down on me as I traversed the hall, seeming to say that this would not be enough. Not nearly enough.

I strolled the short distance from Rupert's home to the Huntington and slipped into the powder room to freshen my makeup. I pressed the compact puff to my forehead to capture the moisture that had collected there during my touchy conversation with Rupert. A quick check of my watch suggested that Harrison should be in the bar and I could make my entrance.

Harrison sprawled on a banquette at a table for four, filling up both seats on his side. When I reached for a chair opposite him, he sat up straight and motioned for me to join him on the banquette. "You know we law enforcement types always sit where we can watch the door. That way we can see the wise guy and blow a hole in him before he has a chance to do it to us!"

"What a lovely thought!" I punched him in the arm. "So, tell me about this fantastic restaurant. I skipped lunch just to prepare myself."

"Oh, in that case, bartender, get the lady a double! That way I won't have to waste any of my stash of confiscated date rape drugs on you."

"Oh, great, an unromantic cheapskate. I sure do know how to pick 'em."

"You didn't pick me, I picked you."

"You did?" I said, before I could stop myself. He blushed, or at least I think he did, under the beard that had formed during his long day at work. Who picked whom was a conversation for married couples reminiscing for the benefit of their kids, so we both retreated from this topic as rapidly as it had come up. I changed the subject, asking about the restaurant again.

"It's called Off the Shoulder, and it's down the alley next to Shirley's Sushi." Alley streets sprouted like tentacles off Geary, bewildering tourists and theatergoing suburbanites.

After finishing our drinks, we walked down Mason toward Geary and the restaurant. Strolling along Mason is not an easy task, as it is pitched at a forty-five degree angle. However, this provides an excellent excuse to hold your date close so she doesn't fall off her pumps and roll all the way to Market Street.

The competition among San Francisco restaurants is so fierce it makes a battle among Serengeti lions look like the qualifying rounds at the Powder Puff Derby. The intensity of the rivalry causes restaurateurs to go to astonishing lengths to achieve a winning combination of food, ambiance, and buzz. Off the Shoulder was marketed as a nouvelle comfort food establishment a la Bradley Ogden. In Bay Area foodie parlance, this meant the chef would begin with a simple concept like meatloaf, infuse it with mint leaves, pine nuts, quail eggs, and salsa, slice it in rhomboid shapes, and present it on a fan of candied chard and parsnips with a dollop of boysenberry coulisse.

Over the Shoulder's specialties were shoulders and other joints of meat, a lure for big men like Harrison and unrepentant distaff eaters like Sally. However, any resemblance to a traditional mixed grill was obliterated in an effort to achieve the quintessence of trendiness.

I ordered beef ribs, but no bones were in evidence. The meat had been surgically stripped from the ribs and rolled like sushi around a corn and okra hash presented over a puree of beets and garnished with wisps of scallion protruding from a medium Portobello mushroom cap.

My disbelieving eyes found Harrison, who was frozen in his own tableau, knife and fork at the ready. He appeared uncertain as to how to attack his New York strip, which the waiter assured us was recumbent under the dome of soy and buckwheat flour pastry that had been browned to perfection, after a basting with a cognac and apricot glaze, and festooned with little ricotta flowers bearing red caviar centers. His order came with a side of steamed fennel and mine with sieved black beans seated in a caramelized Vidalia onion garnished with the zest of a jalapeño.

When Harrison took a tentative jab at the brown derby hiding his meat with a motion you might use to poke a dead snake, I emitted a shrill giggle. The fashionably attired couple at the nearest table paused over their bread puddings, served in oversized burgundy glasses, iced with crème fraiche, and sprouting spun sugar pine trees, and frowned in my direction. I smashed my napkin against my mouth in an effort to stifle another outburst, dabbing tears with the edge of the linen.

We ate our food. It was delicious. The staff was attentive. The lighting perfect. The table flowers exquisite. The décor lush and the furniture sensuously comfortable. I gave it six months.

We committed the ultimate faux pas, asking for the bones that were attached to our entrees at some point in the preparation process to take home to Skootch ala Janie Belle. With an attitude of resigned distain, the server brought us a parcel of pristine white butcher paper tied with a raffia bow. Skootch would be amused.

Hand in hand, we walked up the alley made narrower by illegally parked cars. "Well, I feel they engaged in truth in advertising," I said. "Everything was off the shoulder or any other bony part."

"I think I'll stick to Izzy's." Harrison referred to a venerable steakhouse in the Cow Hollow district that had outlasted thousands of culinary upstarts. "Listen, I was thinking we'd go to my place for a nightcap."

"Sure." I remembered him saying the restaurant was near his apartment. The dense center of the city seemed an odd place for this big man. I pictured him in Tiburon or Alameda, near the water, with an expansive deck occupied by the extra large Weber. But men often do not choose wisely when it comes to accommodations. It is almost as if the place where they will lay their head is an afterthought. Are they so confident they'll land an obliging girlfriend, they assume they'll be sleeping at her place all the time? Do they rent hovels so we women will take pity on them?

We approached a venerable brick edifice with a stained marble entrance and stepped around the homeless person encamped on the sidewalk who was using the first of the steps as a bumper for his grocery cart. We entered the dingy lobby and waited for the elevator. When it came, I marveled at its diminutive interior. I would not have wanted to be in such a small space with a stranger. We exited on the fourth floor and turned right toward the rear of the building. Reaching the last door before the stairwell, Harrison twisted a key in an ornery lock, pushed a paint-deprived door open, and stood aside for me to enter.

Don't get me wrong, I was flattered and, well, excited to be invited into Harrison's inner sanctum albeit ever so humble, but it was a cramped place for such a big guy. I surveyed the dingy living area that included a Pullman kitchen and a coat closet. We were already in the living space because there was no foyer to speak of, just an Edwardian alcove with an ancient speaking device superseded by a cheap plastic intercom mounted askew next to the light switch. The graceful details of the alcove carving could barely be distinguished through the bubbling layers of economy paint.

Harrison said, "I leased this on my way back to Baltimore when I took this job. I'd heard about the prices here, but still, I was shocked. I didn't want to spend a lot on an apartment, but this was available on a short lease, so I took it. Not much, huh?"

"Furnished?" I prayed Harrison had not chosen the hideous sofa.

"Yeah. That was the other attraction. I stored my stuff back East. I've got some nice furniture. Belonged to my parents."

As he moved to the kitchen to get our drinks, a tiny closet of a room he completely filled, I settled tentatively on the couch. I wondered what the impermanence of his life here boded for our relationship. He certainly was not making any commitments to San Francisco. Well, he had bought the '57 Chevy. That was something.

Harrison brought our drinks, handed me mine, and set his on the stained coffee table. He turned to a brick-and-board bookshelf housing a Costco sound system, slipped in a CD, and punched the power button. The soothing sounds of Michael McDonald filled the room as Harrison returned to the sofa. Easing down next to me, he slid his arm around behind me on the back of the couch. Our eyes locked. He relieved me of my drink and placed it on the coffee table. Freed of its burden, his hand traveled to the side of my face and pulled it toward waiting lips. We enjoyed a long, relaxed kiss.

"You don't waste much time."

"Unuh." He cradled my head with the hand behind me. The next kiss was firmer and more insistent. My fingers journeyed to the back of his neck. My thumb rested on his throat, feeling a strong pulse and the delicious sensation of beard bristle. I stayed close after this kiss so I could feel his chest rise and fall.

"How about moving to the next room?" He phrased it as a question, but it came out more like a command. I must have nodded or something, because we headed in that direction, my hand in Harrison's.

His bedroom was even smaller and darker than his living room. The bed took up most of the space. It was shoved against the wall to make room for a desk holding a laptop, task light, and phone. The bedside table had been expropriated for use as a printer stand. A digital clock was propped on a stack of phone books next to the bed.

We began to engage in the clothing removal ritual preliminary to a first sexual encounter among consenting adults. I undid his things and he undid mine. My chocolate cocktail jacket slid unheeded off the desk chair where he tossed it. When he pitched my bra, it went directly to the pile on the floor. I stripped him of his shirt and tossed the garment at his head. Already erect, his member got in the way when I removed his briefs. Well, how could it not, being so large?

There was no graceful way to get on Harrison's bed given its position in the corner. I did the backward crab walk, and he used his knees. His weight felt reassuring and energizing. I placed my hands on his chest and spread my fingers through the hair, catching some in my ring.

"Ouch!" He settled between my legs. "So you want to play rough."

"No," I moved my hands to his waist. "I want to play fair. Tit for tat."

"Well, the tits are mine, and you'll have to locate the tat on your own." He lowered his lips to my left breast.

I found the tat and guided it home.

As I lay in the dark listing to Harrison's breathing, it occurred to me that the Michael McDonald disk had replayed itself about eight times. I loved Michael, but it was probably time to make another selection.

"Time!" I sat upright, clutching the sheet to my chest. "I've got to go home. What time is it?"

I threw myself over Harrison's body to get a gander at the clock on the phone books. It was 1:55. What would Janie Belle be thinking? Doing the reverse crab walk to the edge of the bed and cursing, I scanned the floor in the dim light wondering where my panties had gone.

"I'll drive you." Harrison groaned as he rolled slowly into a vertical posture.

"Nonsense, I'll get a cab."

"Nope." He stood and shuffled in the direction of his closet.

I couldn't find my panties, gave up in haste, and donned the rest of my outfit. My shoes were in the living room.

We were in the elevator in no time descending to street level. I used the smoky, gilt-flecked mirrors in the tiny cab to rub the migrating mascara from under my eyes. Harrison guided me out of his building, and we jaywalked across the empty street to a garage where he kept the Chevy.

"Was that an earthquake plaque on your building?"

"Yeah, it's an un-reinforced masonry structure. Guess that's why it was so cheap."

I turned and looked at the brick face of the apartment building. After the Loma Prieta quake, San Francisco leaders passed an ordinance requiring property owners to post notices informing prospective tenants and visitors that the property they were entering was unsafe in an earthquake and that they were proceeding at their own risk.

"I take it you are copasetic with this hazardous living situation?"

Harrison shrugged as he helped me into the passenger seat. "I made for damned sure this garage was structurally sound. This car is a collector's dream."

Just like a man, I thought as we coasted down to Market Street.

After he eased the Chevy to a stop in front of my home, his good night kiss was more proprietary. As I walked up the front porch steps feeling for my house keys, I realized our relationship had reached a new level. Was it a step toward a deep and lasting commitment or a plateau surrounded by a steep precipice?

I eased the front door shut as quietly as I could and tiptoed toward the stairs. As I rested my foot on the first step, I remembered I was about to sneak past my mother's bedroom sans underwear. I froze. Suddenly, I needed to pee like Niagara Falls. I dashed to the powder room on the main level of the house and just made it.

While perched on the toilet in the still dark bathroom, contemplating my plight as a loose woman, I noticed a shape in the doorway. Skootch entered the bathroom. Half in, he lifted his nose and sniffed. Once. Twice. I realized he could smell the sex on me. Despite the dark, I imagined I could see the hurt in his eyes. After all, I was his girl first.

I rose from the toilet and reached to pull up my pants, but I didn't have any. "Why are men so possessive?" I hissed at the dog. Skootch left. Now, who was in the doghouse!

* * *

CHAPTER 14

After a breakfast of oatmeal and innuendo with Janie Belle, I took a cup of coffee to my office to work on projects for CAI, PGT, and Screen Leaf. First, I checked my messages. True to his word, Rupert had arranged a meeting for me with Randolph Chen, Roger's uncle, at his offices on Van Ness Avenue. William, the senior Chen, managed operations from the center of Chinatown, but Randolph, who oversaw a thriving optometry empire, had a more modern venue. I marveled at the dispatch with which Rupert set up the meeting. I began to see how the Lees had so efficiently spirited daughter Brenda out of China.

I also had a call from Sally, who had finished researching the animal rights issues. Since I would be on Van Ness for an afternoon meeting, I invited her for lunch to review her findings in person.

I knocked off work at eleven thirty and changed out of my jeans into a black shift and matching jacket accessorized with silver jewelry, and a woven scarf in muted tones of pewter and purple, appropriate garb for a call on the bereaved.

Sally was already at the Italian eatery in Opera Plaza. The waiter finished pouring a generous dish of olive oil as I settled into my seat. I tried to move the heavy chair closer to the table and bumped the leg, spilling oil on the crisp paper protecting the table linen. Sally, used to my gaffs, offered to hold the utensils, saltcellar, and pepper shaker while the exasperated waitperson substituted a new piece. I did my part by balancing the oversized menus between knees and chin while I held the bud vase and what was left of the olive oil.

I ordered a salad with prawns and artichokes. Sally had chicken parmesan with a side of fettuccine Alfredo. She also demolished the breadbasket while I subsisted on a slender breadstick.

"Your client doesn't have a particularly attractive profile for the activist. The bullyboys of the movement will go after more enticing game in the pharmaceutical and cosmetics industries."

"My biotech start-up isn't as juicy a target as a multinational behemoth with a posh corporate headquarters?" I asked in a mock hurt tone.

"Right, the trashing of which makes a great visual on the six o'clock news." Sally handed me a file of articles to look over. "How's your cop?"

"He's good." I remembered the warmth of Harrison's bed and triggered a wave of heat that started in my groin and rolled to my toes. I crossed my ankles.

"No sabotage yet?"

"Nope." I thumbed through the file.

"This could be a record in the making."

"Don't call Guinness just yet."

I waved good-bye to Sally as the elevator door closed on her for her ride down to her car. I decided to walk the two blocks from the restaurant to Randolph Chen's office building and leave my car where it was. Those annoying "first hour" charges could mount up if you moved your vehicle too often.

I strolled up Van Ness trying to compose my thoughts. What exactly was I going to say to Roger's uncle? "Hi, your nephew took me to the cleaners?" Rupert was right; this was a bad idea. I entered the lobby of the mid-rise building and consulted the directory for Chen's suite number. He was on the tenth floor. The elevator arrived, I boarded in a glum mood, and the cab rose swiftly to ten. It was a short walk down the hall to the headquarters of the Smiling Panda Optometry Services. I entered the immaculate waiting area and admired the gleaming cases of fashionable frames. I announced myself and turned to find a seat, but a secretary came for me immediately. In moments, I was ushered into the presence of Randolph Chen.

As I shook hands with him, I recognized the taller man who had assisted the elder Chen at the Colma funeral.

"I am very sorry for your loss, Dr. Chen."

"Your condolences are appreciated by both myself and my family. Please be seated." Chen indicated a leather chair in front of his desk.

He waited for me to sit before following suit, and clasped his fingers together on the leather-bound blotter before him. He wore a beautifully wrought gold ring, its glow set off by the rich blue background of his Hong Kong tailored suit.

"I don't know whether you are aware of this, but Roger worked for me briefly in an Internet venture I founded. He handled our accounting and payroll."

"Yes, I understand." Randolph extracted a check ledger and pen from the drawer beneath the desk. He opened the checkbook, twisted the pen to expose the writing tip, and looked up expectantly.

My mouth was open, but nothing came out. This man expected me to ask him for money. I was astounded and embarrassed.

Chen decided that he would have to worm a figure out of me. "I understand that he embezzled a significant sum from your firm. I am prepared to make restitution of the money my nephew stole from you. Please tell me how much." There was a hesitation before the word *stole* and a blink at the end of the speech. Otherwise, the man was so composed you would never have known we were talking about an unsavory subject.

"No, ah, please put that away. It is not why I've come." I regained my voice, although it was a voice that didn't sound much like mine.

"My family believes in paying its debts. Kindly tell me how much you want." Chen's pen poised over the blank check.

"Mr. Chen, I am very sorry about this misunderstanding. I came to express my condolences and to ask you for some information, nothing more."

Chen did not look convinced. The hand with the pen descended to rest on the desk, but the checkbook remained open.

"I need to know, well, I would very much like to know if Roger was still working at a biotech company called Screen Leaf at the time of his death. You see, after my Internet venture failed, I returned to consulting in the bioscience field. Screen Leaf is a new client. I don't know whether Roger listed my firm as a former employer, but if he did I'd like to know. It would be useful to learn how he positioned his previous employment with me to his new bosses. You may not be able to help me." My voice trailed off as I realized this must sound very improbable to Chen.

In the silence that followed, I felt awkward after my lame and lengthy discourse. "Perhaps I should go."

"Ms. Billingsley, Roger was not a keeper of meticulous records. However, there were some career-related files among his papers when we cleaned out his apartment after the police removed the crime scene tape. I have kept what there was, and I will consult these papers for you. I will contact you if I find anything that bears on your request."

Chen rose. "I do not believe the police took anything along these lines, so I think I have possession of all that there is. I will attend to this in the next day or two."

I stood and reached across the desk to shake his hand. "This is most kind of you, Mr. Chen, and I am sorry to have to ask in the first place. It's just that I don't wish any awkwardness to arise with my new client. Once again, please extend my sympathies to your family for their untimely loss."

"I understand your concern for any false impression Roger may have left with your client. Such matters left uncorrected can have unfortunate consequences. Business is very dependent on relationships built on trust." Chen escorted me to his door.

My last view of Randolph Chen was of a proud man, standing erect in the doorway to his office, framed by pictures of his family on the wall behind.

I left the building with a sense of guilt mixed with relief. Feeling sullied by my mission, I decided to eradicate my remorse with a bracing dose of wasabi-laden sushi. There was a sushi emporium in Opera Plaza where I'd left my car. The only customer at the counter, I got the undivided attention of the sushi chef. I consumed thirty-five dollars worth of sushi before I felt completely cleansed. The large Kirin beer played a key role in my atonement ritual.

* * *

CHAPTER
15

I spent the next two days working on projects for California Antibodies and Peninsula Gene Therapy. On the second day, messenger services interrupted this flurry of activity. The first messenger bore a response from Ancient Turtle regarding my proposal. One of Brutus Fang's minions from the painful presentation meeting wrote to thank me for my efforts but explained that the company would not require my services. I rolled my eyes at this rebuff and tossed the letter in the trashcan. What would I have done if he had responded in the affirmative? I shivered at the notion.

I was settling comfortably back into the consulting game. While I missed the excitement and fulfillment of my dot-com days, working with CEOs like Tim Rilke and Leonard Price was rewarding, and I was making real contributions. To fake a consult for Ancient Turtle would have required Academy Award caliber acting; I never could have pulled it off.

Gazing down at the Ancient Turtle letterhead lying in the trash, I recalled the logotype as it appeared the first time I saw it on the shipping carton containing Roger's elixir. Where was that box? I should have turned the shipment over to Barbagalatto. Well, better late than never.

After ten minutes of rooting around in drawers and boxes and shifting materials on book and cabinet shelves, I located the package behind a stack of *Science* journals. As I turned the box over triumphantly in my hands, the intercom crackled.

"Package!" Janie Belle's voice erupted from the wall console. I had been too intent searching to hear the doorbell. I set the box of elixir on my desk and trudged up the steps to the front hall.

Tearing open the envelope she presented me, I dislodged a business card from a paperclip attached to the folder inside. True to his word, Randolph Chen had reviewed Roger's papers. A note attached to some photocopies informed me that Randolph had found final check stubs from Screen Leaf confirming that Roger was working for the company at the time of his death. The photocopies enclosed were of Roger's resume and a pitch letter he had used to tout his capabilities to Screen Leaf. To say that Roger had puffed up his qualifications would be an understatement. You would have thought that Roger founded my company and not me.

I returned to my office with the folder and Randolph Chen's business card. There, sprawled on the floor was Skootch. Between his front legs were the remains of the box that had held the elixir. The empty plastic bag misshapen and punctured lay next to a speckled paw. A dusting of crushed leaves, not unlike Oregano, trailed from the bag to a spot immediately under the dog's jowls. Skootch's tail wagged lazily causing his torso to sway.

"Skootch, you bad, bad dog." I scooped up the debris, wondering if I could salvage the remainder of the elixir. I grabbed the small brush I used to keep my keyboard dust-free and scraped what I could onto a piece of paper. Managing to save a small amount of the substance, I deposited it in a Number 10 envelope. What, if any, biotechnology program could this stuff be linked to?

Skootch sat up next to my knee, looking for forgiveness. As I stroked his silky head and contemplated planting a kiss on it to show I would not hold a grudge, his nostril began to work. His nose journeyed from my lap to the edge of my desk where the small brush I used to sweep up the elixir rested. Skootch snatched the brush and galloped from my office.

"Damn you," I yelled. That pricy little computer brush was history.

Luck was on my side, and I pulled into one of the best parking spaces at Fort Funston. I slipped plastic bags in my jeans pocket and collected Skootch's leash. It was a cold afternoon, and I expected that the park rangers were nestled close to the heater in the ranger station, but it would be wise to err on the side of caution and bring the leash anyway.

After his performance, Skootch didn't deserve an outing, but I needed some fresh air after two days of projects. I stretched to ease the stiffness in my neck and back muscles from hunkering over computer keys. We walked away from the parking lot and over a slight rise to remove ourselves from observation from the ranger station. In the windswept open area that ringed the tree-lined bunker fortifications where I'd found Roger's body, we joined a clandestine collection of canine owners who shared my strategy for hiding from the rangers. I slung the leash over my shoulder so that I could button the front of my jacket against the sea breeze.

Already in a squat, Skootch was busy depositing a robust pile of poop in the low grass. I pulled a bag from my pocket and walked in his direction. He zoomed off after other dog acquaintances as I collected his prodigious and steaming production in the bag.

"Hey, lady, call off your dog, will ya," piped a guy behind me. Turning on my heel, I was shocked to see Skootch mounted on the back of a winsome Golden Retriever. I was surprised at my dog's behavior because Skootch was neutered long ago. Normally, he was not interested in the ladies beyond scaring up a partner to join him in a run.

"Skootch, stop that," I called as Skootch pumped away with determination. I reached the two dogs and pulled the Lothario off the bitch. I apologized to the owner and herded Skootch to a different section of the field.

After we were far enough away, I released him, figuring he would forget the gal and return to bird chasing. He made a beeline for a becoming boxer. This female was a little less interested in his attentions. She nipped at him and moved away, but Skootch was not to be dismissed easily. He mounted her again, wrapping his paws around her hips to prevent her escape. She couldn't bite him in this wrestler hold, so she moaned in acquiescence, her ample boxer cheeks vibrating with every thrust.

Her reed-thin Pacific Heights owner came to the rescue but stopped short as she contemplated the possible ruination of her full set manicure. I was the one to separate the dogs, and Skootch did not go willingly. When he wants to dig his paws in, he can be a force to be reckoned with. He is as solid as a sack of cement and stubborn as a mule. Once her bitch was free, the owner with the perfect nails shepherded the boxer toward the parking area, looking back occasionally to assure herself Skootch was not barreling down on them.

"What's the matter with you?" I studied the panting pointer. Suddenly I realized, It must be the elixir causing this eruption of libido. I grabbed Skootch's snout and turned his eyes up to me so that he could see my disgust. Just when I thought I had his attention, his sex-crazed pupils snapped to the left, he jerked his head from my hands, and took off.

Recovering my balance, I spied the biggest dog I had ever seen coming toward us out of the mist. While she was very graceful for her size, the English Mastiff conjured up the Sherlock Holmes best seller. Had the Hound of the Baskervilles been a bitch? It was crystal clear from Skootch's behavior that this horsy apparition was all female.

I had to stop him; he'd injure himself trying to mount this Mount St. Helens of a dog. I stumbled in their direction over the tussocks and the rocks, but as Skootch approached her business end, he veered off to the left. Tripping over a loose stone, I went down on my knees and scraped my hands on a nest of pebbles in an effort to keep from hitting the ground with my chin.

Dusting off my jeans after I managed to right myself, I scanned the field for Skootch and his next victim. My dog was making for two men, one of whom was incongruously dressed in a business suit. The more casually dressed man was in the act of handing the sartorial standout an folder. The recipient could not see the pointer as the dog advanced on him. The colleague who was facing in our direction reacted, but not fast enough to warn his associate. Skootch barreled into the unsuspecting man, wrapping his legs around the man's thigh and humping that appendage in frenzied delight.

The man reeled, windmilling his arms in the air and turned in my direction. I recognized Brutus Fang of Ancient Turtle as he managed to reestablish his balance and tried to kick my dog with his free leg. He lost his grip on the folder, and the contents were scattered by the salty, moist wind. The pages blew toward me just as the scent of the elixir on Brutus's clothing must have blown toward Skootch's ultra-sensitive nostrils. Interested in ingesting more elixir, Skootch had honed in on Fang like a junkie on a Mission Street drug dealer.

I limped after the now-soggy papers. My leg hurt from my fall, so I was not a very effective retriever, and I was hampered by the urge to laugh at the fate of the imperious Fang. The other man was scurrying after the papers as well and appeared very anxious about the pages. By now I had recognized Theo Tan of Screen Leaf. I greeted him as he approached and handed him the one sheet I had managed to salvage. His face showed a mixture of embarrassment and relief at possession of the errant pages.

We turned to Fang in time to see him lose the battle for balance and go down on his back. The fall had the effect of freeing him from the pumping pointer, who released the man in order to find a better position for consummating coitus. Fang kicked viciously at the dog. Skootch paused, perplexed that someone who smelled so good could be so mean. This gave Theo and me time to separate the unlikely lovers.

Theo helped Brutus to his feet and tried to brush the dried grass and dirt from the man's suit. He also shoved the wilted papers into Fang's hands. Fang folded and slipped them into the inner pocket of the suit before smoothing and re-buttoning his jacket.

Twisting the dog's collar to hold him in place against my body, I made apologies to Fang. The angry man turned on his heels in the middle of my offer to pay for dry cleaning and set off toward the parking lot. Theo stayed a few moments longer and then, too flustered to think of anything more to say, departed in the opposite direction. I was intrigued that he took the meandering path he did, but remembered that a branch of it came out at a small parking pad near the Coast Highway access road.

Why would these men rendezvous at Fort Funston when their offices were less than a block apart? Here was more proof that the companies were connected, and whatever that association was, it was not above board. Why else meet in this clandestine fashion on a chilly bluff? They had even taken the precaution of parking in separate locations.

These people were being very careful about passing information, and the information Theo had come here to give to Brutus Fang chilled me far more than the wind blowing up my sleeves. When I'd picked up the paper blowing across the field, I could not help glancing at it. I did not read it, but how could I not notice a logo at the head of the page that was quite familiar to me because I saw it almost daily. The logo belonged to my client, Peninsula Gene Therapy. Theo Tan had information about PGT that was of interest to Fang the erstwhile Internet entrepreneur. I shuddered as I realized my fantasies about Fang being involved in cloak-and-dagger doings because he was a dead-of-night visitor to the Chinese consulate were only slightly off base. These people were not involved in government or military espionage; they were trading in industrial secrets.

As I dragged Skootch past several female dogs on our way back to the car, I wondered what this new insight meant for Roger's murder. Screen Leaf and Ancient Turtle executives knew and used Fort Funston, so their choice of this location to murder Roger and dispose of his body was explained. But I still was not sure why Roger had been killed. Did he find out about the industrial spying and threaten to inform the authorities? Naw. Roger was not a nice guy. He would focus on what was in this for him. Maybe he'd tried to blackmail these people. That made sense. These creeps were far too clever and evil for the likes of Roger. He had gotten in over his head. And lost it.

Safely back in the car, I slumped against the driver's seat, exhausted by the events in the field. The car listed slightly as Skootch moved to the side window to get a better look at a frisky English setter crossing the lot to our left. I speculated on the duration of the therapeutic effect of the elixir. I could not take many more of Skootch's amorous overtures.

Realizing that my cell phone was off, I pulled it from my pocket and punched the power button. There were three messages from Harrison. Sex could be energizing even without the benefit of drugs. Yet, if there were enough leaves of the damned stuff left in that envelope at home, I could give Harrison a night he would never forget.

* * *

CHAPTER
16

The morning fog burned off early, suggesting this would be a pretty day. My evening message to Harrison was a simple "I'm returning your call" missive. Disappointed he hadn't called back, I chided myself for feeling ignored. The man had a job and a life. I decided to call him back and left a lengthier message to the effect that I looked forward to seeing him again, and that I needed to speak to him briefly about the Chen investigation. Anticipating that he would suggest I follow protocol and contact Barbagalatto, I said I needed his advice about a ticklish matter.

Next, I contacted Tim Rilke's office and booked a late afternoon appointment. I was presenting him with a communications plan and first drafts of the related materials, but my real priority was to divulge the logo incident at Fort Funston. PGT needed to know that someone might be stealing proprietary secrets. This was a difficult situation for me. After all, Screen Leaf was my client. However, what I had seen was suspicious, and the party at risk was PGT. PGT had completed their move to the Mission Bay complex, so I decided to take MUNI. As an afterthought, I e-mailed Karin Mullins, their brilliant scientist, and asked her if she was free for Irish music at River Shannon that evening.

I spent the rest of the morning working on projects. At twelve thirty I felt hungry, set my files aside, and headed for the kitchen to lunch with Janie Belle. There was no room for lunch, however, because she had stacks of envelopes, flyers, and labels spread across the kitchen table and counters.

"I'm stuffing mailers for the church," said Janie Belle with a self-important air. "We're starting our stewardship campaign early this year."

I grabbed an energy bar and Skootch's leash and headed for the garage. I yelled for the dog to come as I passed the family room. I was in the car with the engine running and had time to check and delete all my phone messages before the sleek head appeared at the open passenger door. The dog dragged himself into the passenger seat. As I reached past him to pull the door closed, he groaned in misery.

"Hung over?" I asked as I backed from the garage. Not expecting an answer, I returned to my driving. Since it was such a sunny day, I decided to visit Fort Point. In any case, I did not feel like returning to Fort Funston just yet. I wanted to be sure the effects of the elixir had plenty of time to wear off before I ventured back to the scene of Skootch's misdemeanors, but the dog sitting next to me didn't seem capable of a good bark much less an attempted rape.

We pulled into the Fort Point parking area and I set the Saab's brake. I had to pull Skootch from the car and coax him along as I walked to the channel side of the main building. The soaring drama that was the Golden Gate Bridge sparkled above us etched by the early afternoon sun. The narrow channel was alive with container ships. Their massive cargoes dwarfed all the other craft and filled the bay with a rainbow of colored boxes and corporate names from half a world away. A full cargo ship riding low in the water passed between the closest bridge pylon and our position by the fort. The ship was so near it bathed us in shadow until it passed our vantage point. On the powder blue stripe adorning the stern, I noted the legend, Shen Import Export, Inc., Long Beach, CA.

My cell phone rang and I opened it, asking the caller to hold until I could run into the lea of the building. Safe in the courtyard of the old fort, I could hear Leonard Price clearly. "Hey, Leonard!"

"Hey, yourself! Nola, I'm planning a birthday party for my wife. Peggy is having an 'O' year, so I'm doing something special with a bay dinner cruise. I'm inviting you and your significant other."

I presumed he was thinking of Harrison, but Price was too PC to suggest what date I should bring to a social event. "I'd be delighted to come, and I'll check with my 'other' and confirm his availability."

"I interviewed your friend Comisky yesterday. He's perfect for us. I've instructed human resources to extend him an offer. For all I know they've probably reached him by now."

"That's fantastic. You won't be disappointed; he's a fabulous designer and an outstanding human being." I concluded the call and pranced in the direction of the car in an ebullient mood. Opening the door to the Saab, I realized I had forgotten something. Skootch was nowhere in sight. I retraced my steps through the fort and out to the edge of the channel. I walked along the edge of the seawall calling the dog's name. Panic set in as I threaded in and out of the parked cars calling and calling. Finally, I walked the perimeter of the parking lot studying the underbrush behind the fort. In a grassy area sheltered by scruffy pines lay Skootch. His snoring had attracted a gaggle of sea gulls, who studied him from the safety of a high wooden fence. The waves crashed on the bulwark in rough rhythm with the somnolent dog.

I was escorted into Tim Rilke's freshly painted office at Peninsula's new Mission Bay digs. He had a view of the ballpark, and I gathered that he must have chosen this particularly because his desk sported two signed baseballs encased in Lucite amid the Lucite cubes connoting banking transactions that are the equivalent of campaign stripes for successful executives in the biotechnology industry. Rilke still had a few cartons to unpack pushed against one wall, but these business and personal treasures were already unwrapped and in place.

We moved to his conference table, and I handed him copies of the plan and materials. I also provided an outline for our discussion. As we took our seats, I weighed whether I should tell Rilke about the Screen Leaf problem first or wait until I finished presenting my work. I decided I should get the touchy matter off my chest.

"Tim, do you have any sort of contractual relationship with a company called Screen Leaf Biosciences?" I put aside my planned agenda.

"Why, yes." Rilke appeared surprised I had asked such a question. "We have them doing some screening for us related to our vector development program. We are always looking for ways to improve the way in which we deliver genetic material to cells. I must say, though, they have not accomplished much; but to be fair, it's a tough area. Why do you ask?"

"I took them on as a client. It was one of those friend-of-a-friend referrals, and I've been working with them for a few weeks. But it's not about my work for them that makes me bring this up. I saw something that perhaps I shouldn't have, but since I did, I can't keep it under my hat."

"I'm all ears."

"I saw one of their employees—a managerial level employee—hand a document about your company to an executive of a foreign-based Internet company." I described the incident at Fort Funston, the papers blowing across the field, and how I'd noticed Peninsula's logo. I told what I knew of Ancient Turtle's business but left out the part about my clandestine visits to their South San Francisco offices. I included the fact that Ancient Turtle and Screen Leaf were located on the same block, so Rilke would see how incongruous the Fort Funston rendezvous was. By the time I finished, Rilke was sitting on the edge of his chair, his arms rigid and hands pressed tensely into his knees.

"This is disturbing. I can't think of any reason for Screen Leaf to be talking with another company about our work together. Our field is competitive enough without contractors sharing our hard won progress with other firms."

Rilke stood up and returned to his desk. Placing his system on speaker, he reached his head of vector research. "Jack, we may have a problem. I believe that one of our contractors is sharing information about your project with others. When was the last time the scientists from Screen Leaf were over here?"

I fidgeted while Rilke and Jack assessed their exposure to the Screen Leaf operatives. Rilke's mood did not lighten when he hung up the phone.

"As you've heard, I've called a meeting in an hour to review this situation with the vector team, R & D management, and our senior IT person. I hope you can stay."

Rilke and I made short work of my materials. It was clear that his heart was not in reviewing my work. After the editing session, I packed up my stuff, and we walked together to the conference room Rilke had chosen for the hasty meeting. We detoured into the break area to collect Cokes and munchies.

I chose a Coke with caffeine and a Snickers Marathon energy bar because I figured this was going to be a long, painful session.

As people gathered, I called Harrison. Earlier I had left him a message about the invitation to Price's party and my plan to take Karin to the River Shannon later that evening. I suggested he meet us there for dinner but now amended my invitation, recommending he call me before going there as we might be delayed at PGT for a while.

I did not have to call Karin because her position at PGT meant she would be present at the meeting. Sure enough, she entered the room as I put the phone back in my pocket.

"My office and lab are a complete disaster. Moving is such a bitch, I can't stand disorder." Karin took her seat. "I mean I know other people think I'm a complete office slob, but I have my own rules of organization, and when they're not in place I'm a basket case."

"OK," Rilke said. "Let's get settled. We have a serious breach of security. It involves our vendor, Screen Leaf. We need to figure out what they know and when they knew it. This includes information we intended to give them because they needed it to complete their part of the project, and information they may have gotten their hands on inadvertently or actively. Jack, let's start with you."

Jack outlined the scope of his department's project with the suspect firm. He described the orientation to PGT's science conducted for the benefit of Screen Leaf personnel who would be managing or working on the project. Finally, he detailed a list of all the documents and materials that had been given to the Screen Leaf team or to which they had been allowed computer access through the medium of shared files and passwords. At the conclusion of his presentation, Jack encouraged his direct reports to add their comments, expanding on his overview as it related to each of their areas of responsibility.

When Jack's people were through, Rilke regained control of the meeting. "Your comments about passwords and file access are a good segue to Larry's area. Larry, why don't you pick up where Jack left off?"

Throughout the meeting, Larry Banks, the IT boss, had been listening with one ear and tapping away on his laptop, a device he was never without, to the occasional annoyance of people sitting on either side of him. His taps became more pugilistic and his frown deeper as the meeting had progressed.

"We, ah, we seem to have more than a problem with passwords." Larry never lifted his eyes from the screen. He lapsed into silence as something particularly ominous appeared on the laptop.

"Larry?"

"Oh, ah. Sorry. It's just that I haven't completely figured out what they've done or—what worries me more—how they've done it. People, we've been hacked. We've been hacked by real experts."

Larry turned his screen so others and particularly Rilke could see the scrolling code on his laptop, not that many of us could decipher it. "See this right here? This is how they bypassed our firewall and got into our culture collection data." He tapped a few keys, and the code flipped to a different but equally dense page. "And here—I'm actually on Rilke's desktop computer now—here they are in his confidential program files. We've been screwed. They know every damned thing we know.

"Well, I guess we can stop worrying about what files were provided to them for the friggin' project," Karin said. "They just went into our network and took whatever they damn well wanted!"

Larry pushed back from his laptop and sighed in frustration. "We've got that consulting firm on retainer, and they've got a big security maven who used to work at the Pentagon, but geez, we're closing the barn door after the horse has gone."

"I've got a different idea." All eyes turned to me. I was an outsider and neither a computer whiz nor a gene therapy expert, so the team was surprised. "I have a contact in local law enforcement. Why don't we call him for some general advice about how to proceed while we're in this meeting?"

"Go for it," Rilke said, and heads nodded in agreement.

Now I was on the spot, not sure whether I could contact Harrison or what his response would be. I used my cell to reach him, asking the scientist sitting next to the conference phone to jot down the call-in number so I could get Harrison to call back on the speakerphone. Dialing Harrison's office number, I hoped I could come up with him and that he would not think my call out of line.

I waited which the departmental assistant who answered his main line found him and brought him to the phone. I quickly covered the basics of our dilemma, and Bob agreed to call back on the speaker.

After the electronic introductions, I retold the story of the Fort Funston handoff. Harrison, Rilke, and Larry did most of the questioning. During the recounting of my encounter with Fang and Tan, Harrison interjected a compliment for my "nice sleuthing" that suggested the next time we got together I was in for a lecture on playing amateur detective again, but otherwise my part of the conference call was over quickly.

Harrison had an impressive knowledge of computer systems, code intricacies, firewalls, and the crafty ways of hackers. Bob and Larry went back and forth finishing each other's sentences as Larry described what he was reading in the code. They soon left Rilke behind, and he joined the rest of us on the cyber-sidelines. They mapped the trail of the interlopers as they'd penetrated PGT's most confidential files. Despite the seriousness of this development and its implications for Peninsula's business, after forty minutes of this, people in the room began to squirm and fidget. Rilke suggested a break, but Harrison had other ideas.

"I'll meet you and Larry tomorrow at your offices; we'll finish the assessment of the damage and devise a strategy for dealing with this. In the meantime, don't do anything that would alert them that you're on to them."

"Of course not." Larry was almost insulted that he had been given such an instruction.

As the group broke up, I said good-bye to Rilke and joined Karin for the stroll back to her lab. She made room for me in her office so that I could work while she finished an experiment she had been running on a gene defect common in patients with aggressive ovarian cancer. Having isolated the defect in mice, she was attempting to replace it with the normal sequence and deliver the revised DNA to a mouse with the defect. I loved this science and the strategies it suggested for solving human health problems, but the actual work to achieve these breakthroughs was exacting and tedious.

After another hour of making note revisions and leaving phone messages for clients, I poked my head around the corner. "Are we coming in the home stretch?"

Karin looked up through her protective goggles with an absent gaze. Her eyes snapped into focus. "Oh! I'm sorry. I forgot you were here!"

She gathered a stack of 96-well plates from the laminar flow hood, spun on her stool, and crab-walked across the aisle to a temperature-controlled cabinet. After storing her work, she removed her goggles and gloves, kicked the stool under the lab bench, and returned to her office.

Karin slipped out of her lab coat, I collected my things, and we headed for the parking lot. The tires on Karin's Toyota were so bald her car could have won an Olympic bobsled competition.

I tried to remember paying my life insurance premium as I settled into the passenger seat. The space for my feet was littered with CD jewel cases, Burger King beverage cups, and junk mail. I tried not to rest my feet on any of the CDs, but it was a challenge. As we skated out of the lot into the traffic lane, Karin launched into a diatribe about scientific ethics.

"I'm sensitive to the commercial implications of what the hackers were planning, but what pushes me over the edge is the temerity of the interlopers with regard to my work. Bastards." As she warmed to her subject, Karin bashed her palm on the edge of the steering wheel. She was a veritable dervish as she danced around her chosen theme, citing examples of scientific thievery and conniving. I clutched the edges of the bucket seat and stiffened in preparation for a crash.

Somehow, we made it to the block of Geary Boulevard that contained the River Shannon. Karin punched the car into a parking space, like a drop into one of her 96-well plates.

We settled for the last unoccupied table. Live music was to begin within the hour. Harrison had not arrived, so we ordered beers and studied the laminated menus. The room was dingy, the chairs uncomfortable, and the table unbalanced, but the Guinness was cold and tangy.

The band was setting up by the time Harrison entered. He still wore his suit, but he had removed the jacket, so he didn't look completely out of place. He scanned the dim room looking for me or for errant members of the IRA. When you are dating a guy in law enforcement, you have to accept that you won't always have his undivided attention. Dating. That still sounded strange to me. We had survived our first roll in the hay and were still speaking.

I introduced Karin to Harrison, even though they had already met in a way on the speakerphone. Over our initial beers, I had filled Karin in on my relationship with Bob and was careful to tell her that this was early days. Karin shook his hand and beamed at him, and when he squeezed past her to take his seat by me, she shot me a conspiratorial wink.

While we awaited our food, we chatted about bioscience in general and its contribution to forensics in particular. We could not talk about the Screen Leaf situation in such a public venue. Karin briefed Harrison on some recent advances in PCR technology, the definitive science behind DNA fingerprinting now universally applied in court cases, and he listened with an intensity to match her own.

All changed with the arrival of the lead band members. Karin might as well have been a snake and the Celtic musicians a trio of turbaned charmers. She brought the same passion and force to Irish music she did to her science. It occurred to me that this was the first time I had seen her still. The hand had stopped slicing the air, and her foot no longer performed a rat-tat-tat on the floor under our table. The only things moving were the wild, scarlet curls that danced in the aura of the spotlight.

Not the aficionado Karin was, Harrison leaned back against the wall, rested his arms on the chair seat, and smiled warmly at me. That was all the invitation I needed. I scooted my chair closer to his.

"You look tired," he said.

"You too. We're working too hard."

"Yeah, I know. Pretty interesting situation your clients are in."

"No kidding." I leaned closer, whispering about my suspicions of a nefarious linkage between Screen Leaf and Ancient Turtle. I filled him in on the rows of computer workstations and the warehouse areas filled exclusively with computers, monitors, and accessories.

His brow wrinkled when I mentioned the warehouse, and I hurried on to my research on their Internet site, the package that had come addressed to Roger, and Skootch's amorous behavior after ingesting the elixir.

Harrison forgot about the warehouse and laughed aloud, earning the attention of Karin, the musicians, and the people at the next table.

Looking apologetically at Karin, he moved closer and whispered, "Got any of that stuff left?"

"You don't need that stuff, fella."

Bob grinned and squeezed my waist under the table. His hand lingered there for the rest of the set.

We sat through a second set before calling it a night. All of us had to work the next day. I accepted a ride home from Harrison, which was a smart choice. I would get some action, and I would not have to risk my life riding with Karin.

Karin thanked me profusely for introducing her to River Shannon, her first official outing in the big city since PGT's move. "If I can listen to live music like this every week, my commute'll be more than worth it."

Harrison and I strolled around the block to the '57 Chevy, parked in an unattended lot behind the Geary storefronts. He dropped my briefcase in the trunk and opened the passenger door for me.

We got underway, heading west on Geary. "Feel like a little necking?"

"Why not?" I tried to sound nonchalant. I was excited because I was aroused and pleased at the prospect of making out at some location other than my house under the watchful eye of Janie Belle.

In minutes, we were pulling into the long access road leading to the Palace of the Legion of Honor, a museum nestled in a park adjacent to a public golf course. Harrison passed the circle in front of the monumental museum. The thick ground fog caused the heavy building to float, a natural trompe l'oeil.

We turned right into the larger of the parking areas. This lot listed down toward a thick coppice of trees enveloped in fog. The Chevy sank into the vapor like a rowboat with a punctured keel. We rolled to a stop when we heard our front wheels kiss the verge marking the end of the macadam. Our view consisted of three dark tree trunks and a mass of black vegetation. When Harrison shut off the engine, all was silence except for our breathing. A more secluded place could not be found in San Francisco. I sighed and looked at the hulky Harrison silhouette.

The silhouette said, "Let's get in the back seat."

Two doors opened, causing twin fog swirls as we got out of the car to get into the back. My God, I haven't done this in more than a quarter century, I thought as I pushed myself back on the ample seat. Even with the guy's arms around me, we had quite a bit of room. The Chevy's bench seat was almost as big as the bed in Bob's dinky apartment.

This was heaven, I concluded, as I came up for air after our second long kiss. The fog rolled against the car windows over Harrison's shoulder, jealous and trying to get in. I lifted my leg over the seat back in response to my partner's urgent maneuvers, and tugged at his slacks to help him in the confined space. He bumped his head on the ceiling, and we collapsed in laughter.

Reconsidering the logistics, Harrison pulled me onto his lap and I began a slow grind. The aromas of man in his prime and venerable vehicle were deeply satisfying. It was definitely OK to be forty-something. How else could you appreciate the effect of maturation on man and machine? As I looked into his eyes and rested my weight on his chest, I realized that backseat sex is wasted on the young. It is a sport at which the experienced can excel, the experienced and those who have acquired the wisdom to laugh at themselves.

I managed a dismount that was, if not graceful, at least not lethal to my still exposed companion. I remained, a little awkwardly, on my knees as he buttoned up. Thus positioned, I faced the rear window of the Chevy and caught a dim flash in my right peripheral vision. Figuring the fog was playing its usual tricks, I reversed position, opened the door, and stepped out.

"Ouch!" I'd lost both shoes during the calisthenics in the Chevy. An obliging arm extended from the car with a pair of pumps. I set them on the ground, leaned on the car door, and dusted the pebbles from the bottom of my foot before slipping it into a shoe.

As I retrieved the second shoe and straightened up, the fog parted to reveal two swaggering punks dressed in baggy pants hanging so low on their hipless forms that they must have kept them up with Crazy Glue. Their T-shirts and jackets were black, as were their high-topped athletic shoes. Their choice of head-to-foot black attire and the loose fit of their clothes almost made them one with the fog, were it not for the gold chains, the metallic clasps on their back-to-front baseball caps, and the soft sheen of the knife blade dangling from the hand of the lead punk.

"S'up, bitch?" the first one said, corralling me in the vee between the open door and the car. Rising panic gripped my throat. I managed a nonchalant shrug and looked the boy in the eye, which was slightly above mine. He could have been as much as four inches taller but favored the slouching, bobbing strut of the street gangsta.

"Ya havin' a nice friendly fuck out here'n the woods?" he said. "Seems like there oughta be a fee foh dat."

The other boy circled the car to Bob's side as the first thug warmed to his theme. "Hey, tell Hump Daddy back there we getting a fee for his fornicatin'. Ha! Yeah, tell him we prefer cash, but we just do her instead, seein' she's all warmed up and everything."

This produced a laugh from the second punk, who had opened the door on Bob's side. He grinned at us over the top of the car, almost resting his soul patch on the roof. He did not see the foot coming, which smashed into his chest and sent him reeling backward until he disappeared in the monster hedge. The rest of Bob followed the foot out of the Chevy.

As my lover stood to his full height, I heard an intake of air from the boy on my side of the car which almost drowned out the thrashing in the hedge. Baggy pants guy stood his ground as Bob circled the front of the car. The boy tossed his knife back and forth from hand to hand. Bob knocked him clear of his weapon with a punch to the jaw. The knife clattered to the pavement, and I retrieved it as Bob advanced on the staggering boy. Another punch put the kid down for the near future.

My date reached the edge of the parking lot as the second boy emerged from the brambles brushing leaves from his jacket. Bob got a fistful of the kid's coat and drove a knee into his gut. When he doubled over in pain, he got an uppercut for his troubles. This took him to his knees. When Bob released his jacket, the punk fell face first the rest of the distance to the ground.

Bob returned to my side of the car and rummaged in the glove compartment. Finding a set of handcuffs, he returned to the first boy and cuffed a wrist. He dragged the kid to the car and cuffed him to the door handle.

"Don't you want to call this in or something?" I helped Bob drag the second boy to the side of the car where the first kid lay.

"Are you nuts? What exactly do you want to tell them we were doing out here?"

Under other circumstances, I would have been thrilled Harrison let me drive his car. Even the most sexually enlightened of men will revert to a card-carrying chauvinist when you ask to borrow his car keys. This was not a true test of Harrison's tolerance, however, because this was an emergency of sorts.

He herded the two handcuffed punks up the parking lot toward the front of the museum. I followed in the car. I had been told not to take the car out of first gear. I crept along behind the car's owner and his charges. It was slow going because the punks lacked enthusiasm. Harrison occasionally prodded the nearest laggard with his fist. Since I had rolled the window down to hear any commands Harrison might issue, the car was as cold and damp as the great outdoors.

After an eternity, we reached the museum entrance. I parked at the curb and waited for Harrison to finish with his prisoners. Harrison made short work of them and joined me at the car. He opened the driver's side door and gestured for me to slide over. My brief role as a getaway driver was at an end.

Since the car windows were down, we could hear the boys as we drove away.

"Hey, man, you can't leave us like dis! We wasn't gonna do nothin' to you. Attsa fack. Come on."

"Jamal. I'm fuckin' cold."

"Shut up. Jackass. Lady! Lady! You tell the man dis ain't right."

Their voices faded as we drove away from the palace along the deserted road that traversed the fairways. Harrison had handcuffed the punks with their arms around the museum's information kiosk to be found in the morning with their noses pressed on the colorful cabaret scenes of the posters heralding the Toulouse Le Trec exhibit. As an added punishment, Harrison had yanked on their pants and the baggy garments, requiring little encouragement given their precarious perch on bony hips, fell down around the boys' ankles.

I was silent for the trip home to my neighborhood. When we pulled up outside my house, Harrison broached the subject of the Prices' party. We agreed on the logistics and after a perfunctory kiss said our goodnights.

As I trudged up the steps to the porch, I concluded Harrison and I had to find a decent place to have sex. Despite the romp in the backseat of the Chevy, we were not kids. We needed a real bed of sufficient size with real sheets in a room bigger than a matchbox. That bed and that room were here in my own house.

As I passed Janie Belle's door, I heard soft snoring. Thank God, she was not waiting up spying this time! Maybe this would be a good time for her to visit her sister back east. Maybe Harrison and I could have sex while she was at church.

A head with obsidian eyes emerged from a black lump on the landing outside my bedroom. Geez, here was another customer who wasn't going to like it if Bob slept over. Skootch was, and had been for eons, the only male occupant of my bed. He might adore Bob in the living room, but the pointer would not take kindly to being replaced as a bed partner. Life was complicated. Sex was complicated. And I was too tired to solve anything tonight.

* * *

CHAPTER 17

I got a very late start. When I shuffled into the kitchen, I found a note from Janie Belle about a bake sale at the church. A sink full of baking tins and batter-covered bowls provided evidence that the note was on the level. Wishing she had left a few samples, I settled instead for cereal.

After breakfast, I treated myself to a visit to Nordstrom's to search for the perfect ensemble for the Price party. By the time I had selected an outfit and shoes, earrings, and necklace to go with it, it was almost lunchtime. With parcels under both arms, I stopped in my office to play any messages that might be waiting. Georgina had called with a reminder about the upcoming biotech conference at the convention center. She had arranged a pass for me available at the check-in desk. Bob had left two messages. The first said last night had been fun and that we should do it again sometime as soon as he saw his chiropractor. The second, left in the late morning, was the result of his visit to PGT to work with Price and Rilke on the hacker problem.

"Hey, babe, you were right. I brought the computer fraud expert from my office, and he and Larry trailed the hackers from here to Screen Leaf. But here's the interesting part: we also tracked back to computers at that other company, Ancient Turtle. We were careful, and I don't think they'll catch on to us over the little snooping we did, but I've called my FBI contacts about this. Bet Peninsula isn't the only company they've penetrated. See you soon. Oh, and I haven't forgotten your little warehouse excursion. It's time to stop amateur sleuthing. Hear me on this, Nola." Click.

I cringed like an overweight teen caught with her hand in the cookie jar.

In the afternoon, I was due at Screen Leaf. I planned to finish their presentation and present it to Casper Wong. I called Wong's assistant and learned that he would be at headquarters in the afternoon, so I booked a presentation time of four o'clock. Although Harrison had warned me, I was not ready to forego my detective work cold turkey. I detoured into downtown Daly City on my way south in order to stop at a renowned Ma and Pa Italian bakery to purchase pastries, including irresistible biscotti almost the size of bananas. I would use these delicacies to get tight with the assistant.

While I knew Roger was still working at Screen Leaf at the time of his death thanks to Roger's uncle, I hungered for more information. What had Roger done to earn himself a one-way trip to Battery Betty? Had he been playing in the big leagues, a willing soldier in this cadre of industrial criminals with a specific role that he somehow screwed up? This scenario had the ring of truth to me. Roger had the ego to aspire to the status of a player, but was little more than a playboy. When the going got tough, Roger would not have what it took. A spineless dandy, he would blink, fold, or puke.

Cindy met me in the lobby and brightened when I showed her what I had brought. Once back in the executive area, she signaled a couple of her cronies, and we convened in an unoccupied cubicle to enjoy our repast. Two other girls joined us, pulling extra chairs into the cube. We ate with our knees almost touching, giggling and licking icing from our fingers.

"Did you know Roger Chen very well?" I asked Cindy, who was sucking on one of the banana-sized biscotti. "He used to work for me. He did accounting for an Internet start-up I headed."

"Sure, he had the cube you're using. Whatta creep. He was a nasty piece of work. Hit on me every chance he got."

In accord with Cindy's assessment, the other girls jumped in.

"It was nice for us when he started hanging out with a girl from another company. Took the pressure off."

"Not! He couldn't keep it in his pants. Tongue hanging down to his knees all the time."

This image sent them into fits of laughter. A nerdy guy poked his head over the cube wall and asked us to keep it down. This precipitated more laughter, and one of the girls developed hiccups. She and her friend left for water.

I focused on Cindy. "So, what happened when he died? Did any of you guys go to the funeral?"

"I was just so wierded out. I mean, he was found without a head, you know. That's sooooo sick. We took up a collection for flowers. We all sorta felt we should do something. He was a creep and all, but he was dead. It was a pain to the max, though. The collection came to about enough to cover the tax on the flowers, so Casper made up the difference."

I kept nodding in commiseration. "Did you have to clean out his desk or anything?"

"No way. Somebody in human resources did that. Can't you just picture it? Handling a dead guy's stuff. Ooooo!" She shivered as she stood up, which helped shake the biscotti crumbs off her diminutive skirt. "Gotta go. Thanks for the treats. That was nice."

Not having learned very much other than the fact Roger's personality had not improved after he left my employ, I returned to my cube with the remains of the baked goods. After loading the disk with my presentation, I checked over my work to make sure it was complete and refreshed my memory of the talk in preparation for my four o'clock session. Once I was sure I was ready, I removed the disk and studied Roger's former computer screen. I opened the file of registered users on the computer. There was an icon for Roger.

I was very thankful the human resources operative had not removed Roger's personal profile. Perhaps they had not gotten around to deleting his files either. Of course, no other person aside from Screen Leaf's IT professional could get to Roger's files without his password, so it was safe to leave this task until later. They were not expecting amateur detectives roaming their premises under the guise of biotech consulting, were they? Well, here I was, but I would need the password if I want to get anywhere.

Whipping out my cell phone, I dialed Serge, my former IT guy. I got his voice mail and left him a request to tell me Roger's password if he remembered it. People were such creatures of habit. I expected that Rog would use the same password or something close to it. If only I could get hold of Serge.

Rocking the desk chair in frustration, I stared at the little phone screen willing Serge to contact me. It was three thirty. I didn't have much time before the meeting with Wong. Drumming my nails on the desktop, I thought of Dakota. Toward the end of my dot-com's life, Dakota had done almost as much system administration on our computer network as Serge. As our economics went into the toilet, people had to wear multiple hats, and Dakota had taken over much of the day-to-day file sharing and employee access issues. Grabbing the phone, I punched in his number.

"Hey, you!" he answered. "I guess you got my message about accepting the offer from CAI. Do I owe you! Guess I'll forgive you for the funeral drive-by."

"Congratulations. Listen, I don't have much time, but I need you to try to remember something. What was Roger's password for his desktop profile?

Silence.

"Are you thinking?" I asked, afraid I had broken the connection.

"Yeah. But, Nola, are you still chasing this Roger thing? I mean, shouldn't you maybe let this go?"

"Dakota, I hear you. I know. I just need to check this one thing, OK? Then I'll leave it to the pros. After this. I promise."

More silence.

"Can't remember?"

"I remember. I just have trouble saying the word aloud. To you. Over the phone."

I was mystified at his response. "You'll only have to say it once."

"It's cunt."

"What!"

"You said I'd only have to say it once."

"Yeah. Yeah. I know I heard you. Sorry. I should have known it would be something disgusting."

"Where are you?" Dakota asked, relieved enough to refocus on what I was doing.

"Not to worry. Can't talk now, but I will call, and we'll get together to celebrate your new position. Thanks for the help!" I disconnected.

Unwisely I had left the profiles on the desktop, I double-clicked on Roger's, and a password screen appeared. Hesitating only for a moment over the keyboard, I typed c-u-n-t. Roger's file folders opened before me. I headed for his e-mails and started reading through what was in the file in reverse chronological order. The process was both tedious and revolting. From a corporate point of view, Roger was a sexual harassment lawsuit waiting to happen. He propositioned his female colleagues with nauseating language and lewd suggestions. In contrast, his work product was mundane and predictable. Here were memos about tax filing schedules, revised expense forms, bank reconciliations, and ledger entries. He was probably stealing from this company, and I'd find evidence of that in his e-mails, not that I cared.

Checking my watch, I saw I had ten minutes left. I scrolled along the document list. Here was an e-mail to Margaret! He said he had something pretty for her. Here we go, I thought. This was probably an expensive item, jewelry or lingerie purchased with company funds. I scrolled down and found another missive to Margaret about a trip to Vegas. Ca-ching, ca-ching—there went company cash for plane tickets and hotels.

Below this e-mail was one directed to Casper Wong. This was the first e-mail of Roger's I had found addressed to Screen Leaf's CEO. To see if this was true, I scrolled up and down the file again. Yes, this was the first. There were several to the CFO, Hank Ho, but in Roger's line of work there would be correspondence over accounting matters with the CFO.

Just as I opened the document, Cindy poked her head around the corner. I jumped, startled at her sudden appearance.

She smiled, touching my arm. We were friends now after the biscotti.

"Mr. Wong is going to be late. I hope this isn't an inconvenience. Do you have a later meeting?"

I smiled intently at her, willing her to keep her eyes away from the computer screen. "No, no problem. I'll just keep working here."

"Sure thing," she said and was gone, but not before helping herself to the pastries sitting next to my briefcase.

Friggin' biscotti were becoming a liability. She could have buzzed me instead of terrifying me nearly out of my skin, but, no, she had to come down here for more sugar.

I turned to the e-mail. Here was a Roger I hadn't seen before. Well, perhaps I'd seen a little of this Roger in his job interview. Roger was selling hard, trying to ingratiate himself with Wong through a scheme that would help Wong's business. But this proposal did not sound like it related to Screen Leaf's client business as I understood it. Roger was setting up a face-to-face meeting with Wong to present him with a program for international shipping.

This was puzzling. Screen Leaf was not Toyota, Sony, or Toshiba. The company had no goods to ship. Its business was screening minute quantities of biological material primarily for US-based bioscience companies. Even if Screen Leaf managed to land a European or Japanese client, the amount of material that would ever be shipped would fit in a Federal Express envelope. Wong must have thought Roger a dunderhead to put forward such a proposal.

I scrolled on. My searching was rewarded with two more e-mails to Wong, both with copies to Hank Ho. In one, Roger talked about the problems with shipping materials via air courier, focusing on the documentation required. The examples he cited centered on importing into China and Thailand. Although there was no mention of Ancient Turtle, the elixir company had operations in Thailand, and I had seen its CEO coming out of the Chinese consulate. In the final e-mail, which would have been the first to be sent in the series since I was working backward,

Roger boasted of extensive and powerful connections in international shipping. Well, Roger, I smiled, you were more of a salesman than I gave you credit for.

I closed the e-mail folder and checked other folders for anything about shipping or anything that related to China, Thailand, or Ancient Turtle. There did not seem to be anything else in Roger's files related to his proposal. I reached for my briefcase to see if I had another empty disk to use for downloading Roger's files so that I could check more carefully later. My hand closed on a new CD, but Cindy appeared to announce that Wong was in his office and would see me now.

I asked for time to collect my belongings and said I would follow shortly. Throwing my stuff in my briefcase and pitching the biscotti bag in the trash, I returned to the computer, logged out of Roger's profile, and turned off the CPU.

Casper Wong was standing when I entered his office. As I greeted him, he offered me the briefest of eye contact. Impatience dripped from the man like perspiration from a spent athlete.

"Where shall we set up my presentation?" I scanned the room for a projector.

"Ah, that won't be necessary, Ms. Billingsley. We've decided that we no longer require your services. I've asked my assistant to prepare a termination letter per your contract. You'll be able to take it with you when you leave. My suggestion for the presentation is to leave me a disk copy or e-mail it to me when you return to your office."

"May I know the reason for this decision?" I was suspended awkwardly between his desk and his conference area. "I don't think you've had a chance to see what I can do for your company."

"Yes, yes. I realize that. We know you're very good, and we appreciate your taking us on. We've just decided to go in another direction. We've postponed our plans for a public offering."

By the time he had finished this explanation, he had rounded his desk and grasped me by the elbow.

"Now, be sure to send us your final bill and we'll handle it promptly. You can direct it to my office, and my assistant will take care of it as soon as it comes in." At this, he all but shoved me out of his office and closed the door. Encumbered as I was with my briefcase, purse, and disk, I couldn't exactly shake his hand in parting.

I stood alone and speechless in front of the Cindy's desk. Puzzled herself, she looked sympathetic as she typed the termination letter.

"This will only take a second more," she said. "Can I get you anything? Maybe some Arrowhead, or I think there are a few Dasani left.

"No, don't worry about it. And don't rush. You can fax me that letter when you're done with it," I said, dismissive of the legal formalities that would sever my business relationship with this undesirable client. As an afterthought, I decided I would part from this young woman in a positive way, preserving our biscotti bond in the event I needed to learn more about Roger's sojourn at Screen Leaf. "I'll miss seeing you, Cindy, since I won't be doing any more work here. I hope we see each other around."

The young woman beamed at this, and after a glance in the direction of the closed door, she said conspiratorially, "He's no prize in the boss department. I'm looking for something better."

"You go, girl!" I smiled and pocketed one of her cards from the Lucite holder on her desk. "I'll let you know if I hear of anything."

My new conquest jumped at the chance to walk me back to the lobby, gushing forth her hopes and aspirations for a higher salary and a post in the financial district.

Back at my car, I flung my case and purse across on the passenger seat. What a weird experience. The guy had fired me before he'd even seen my work. That had to be a first. I reasoned that Screen Leaf's marketing manager had told Wong of our encounter at Fort Funston, and what I had witnessed. I was too much of a liability to have around given what these companies were up to. Unfortunately, I still didn't know exactly what that was, and I was not going to get any more opportunities to learn about their plans by snooping around their offices or using their computers. Of course, there was a growing list of people who would be thrilled that my sleuthing activities had been nipped in the bud. Dakota. Harrison. Barbagalatto.

I headed up 101 back to the city smug in the knowledge that despite their wishes I had cultivated a contact at Screen Leaf who might prove useful in resurrecting my detective career if I chose to do so.

For Peggy's party, Leonard Price had hired a yacht from one of the dinner cruise fleets. When we arrived at the dock, I regretted my shoe choice. The spaces between the boards on the main dock were bad enough, but the floating dock the crew used to transfer guests from the central pier to the waiting yacht was almost unnavigable in high heels. I staggered to our destination with Harrison holding on to my waist from behind. An attendant met me at the gangway, and I threw myself into the fellow's arms as I was pitched forward by the last swell to hit the damp and rolling ramp.

Harrison shook his head as he relieved me of my new turquoise Chinese jacket and handed it to another attendant. "You look so cute; I'd hate to lose you overboard. Do you have any flat shoes to wear with these getups? With you in pants I can't admire your legs anyway; why not be safe and leave the stilts at home?"

"Does this conclude your lecture on haute couture?" I relieved a strolling waiter of a champagne flute, rather than wait for Harrison to serve me. Sometimes you have to put men in their place.

"For now," he said as he ran his hand along the bottom of my hips feeling for the absent panty line.

Seeing Price and his wife on the far side of the main salon, I grabbed Harrison's roaming hand and led him across to greet our host and guest of honor. Peggy's blond hair, swept up on top of her head, was held in place with exquisite combs of silver and turquoise. Southwestern jewelry adorned her slender neck and wrists. Her dress was a simple sheath of terracotta silk. A loose, woven shawl of the same shade graced her shoulders. Elegant boots made of butter-soft leather completed her outfit. Harrison poked me in the ribs and whispered in my ear, "Look. Flats."

Price asked Harrison if he would like to see the bridge as the captain was about to cast off. Abandoning Peggy and me, the men disappeared up a small gangway. Spying my shoes, Peggy took pity on me and settled into a banquette along the starboard side of the large cabin.

"How's the fertility biz treating you?"

"Can't complain. My research is going well. Oh, and my grant was re-approved, so I'm really celebrating two things: my birthday and another three years of funding."

"That's great! What's the focus of this project?"

"We're trying to improve on current techniques of embryo fertilization and implantation so that the number of cases of multiple viable embryos can be reduced. You know, where the parents have to allow the doctor to kill off some to permit others to develop normally to full term. Those decisions are very difficult for parents and tough on medical staff, too."

"I understand. Couples seeking infertility solutions have already been dragged through the emotional wringer."

"Yes, and then they are finally successful. Too successful."

Peggy waved at an approaching guest. She took his hand and pulled him down on the banquette with us.

"Nola, this is Tony Kwan. He works with me at UCSF."

"Peggy's my boss, actually." Tony grinned at his superior. "I'm privileged to work in her lab."

"We haven't seen each other for ten days, because I sent Tony to the International Fertility Institute's congress in Tokyo. We scraped together enough cash from our measly budget to keep him from having to sleep in the subway. Of course, Tony's was the real coup. He got his paper accepted. Pretty good for a postdoc!" Peggy teased.

"How did the presentation go?" I asked with real interest.

"OK, I guess. It is funny though. In this country, everybody in our field is focused on helping infertile couples conceive. Yet, in most countries, the priority is curbing the birth rate. It was a real revelation for me. I've attended more than my share of scientific meetings, but this was the first congress for me with an even split of scientific and sociopolitical presentations. Listening to presenters from India, China, and Africa was a whole different ball game."

"In addition to being a brilliant young scientist," Peggy interjected, "Tony is seriously multilingual. Tell Nola about your personal interactions at the meeting. The e-mails you sent me were very interesting."

Tony blushed at Peggy's compliment. "It wasn't so much my interactions with them during the poster sessions and dinners. It was overhearing them talk to each other in the general sessions or the bars. I didn't mean to eavesdrop, but I'm fluent in three Chinese dialects and Korean plus some Japanese and Thai. The candid remarks kind of spooked me. I've never lived outside this country. I guess I've been taking all our freedoms for granted. Of course, we're very beholden to the federal government for research money, but we do have choices, and we get to propose the ideas for the research. The Chinese scientists in particular have to work on what their government wants them to do. They have to be very, very senior before they can even suggest an independent approach. God, I would hate that. I'm so used to saying what's on my mind and pursuing my own ideas."

"As long as you're also pursuing some of mine in your spare time," Peggy said, laughing. "After all, I'm the one with the funding!"

We all laughed at that. After assuring Peggy that her project was his Job One, Tony returned to his observations at the congress. "I had one direct conversation with three guys from Beijing University who came by my poster. They seemed genuinely mystified at the amount of time, effort, and money we put into solving infertility problems for individuals. Even though I switched into their language to help them understand what I was doing with my research, they had trouble following. Not the science so much as the basic concept. My paper involved research on twenty women between the ages of forty and forty-five who were attempting to conceive, an increasingly prevalent problem in our culture. I finally realized that my listeners couldn't get beyond the idea that we would place such emphasis on helping to fulfill the desires of middle-aged women. I never thought of myself as a women's lib advocate, but I guess I am."

"That would be a good thing for you to be in my wife's lab." Leonard Price rejoined the group along with Harrison.

Their return reminded me to look outside. The captain had cast off and eased out of the slip where the yacht was berthed. He had progressed into the channel, giving us an unimpeded view of the Bay Bridge as its necklace of lights began to glisten in the dusky sky.

Harrison reached my side holding twin flutes of champagne, and I rose to accept a glass. It was time to let other guests sit next to the birthday girl. We strolled across the cabin, and I introduced my escort to several of CAI's management team. I was pleased to see how quickly Bob grasped the science that was the inevitable subject of every discussion in this crowd of researchers. Although his scientific training had more to do with circuits than clones, he was at home with my brand of geeks. I grew a little warm as I realized just how much I had come to like and respect this man.

As the yacht rounded Alcatraz, we were invited below to the dining deck where the buffet awaited. I knew that a line would form immediately made up of the younger managers and research scientists. "Let's go out on deck."

"Good. We'll catch the last of the sunset." Harrison escorted me aft to an exit.

We huddled together at the rail enjoying the brisk air and the brooding hills of the prison island as we drifted past. The body of the island swiftly erased the city lights to the south.

I rested my head against Bob's chest, inhaled and caught a whiff of his aftershave. I wondered if he liked kids, then blushed, realizing I was getting way ahead of myself. Still, at my age, Peggy might prove to be a very useful contact.

We enjoyed the warm glow of the yacht's interior, the laughing crowd silent to us beyond the glass. Surrounded by the chilly breeze and the arms of my lover, the promise of warmth and food was enough for me. Unlike the inmates of Alcatraz, I was a willing captive of the velvet night and the insistent rhythm of the bay.

My companion broke the spell by jingling something in my ear. Cold metal touched my check. "Guess what I've got."

"Handcuffs?"

"You wish! Guess again."

"Hmmmm. Safe deposit key. You've stashed millions in jewels in an obscure Daly City bank, and you're going to drape me in diamonds and rubies before ravishing me within an inch of my life."

"Sounds painful, and you need to take a closer look at my paycheck. No, what I have here are the keys to the dock entry and yacht of my divorced friend. You will recall the craft because we borrowed it previously. You also will recall that it came supplied with sleeping accommodations."

"You sly devil! How thoughtful! How considerate! How practical! I intend to make you very, very happy that you are such a good planner. When do we return to dry land?"

"Your friend Price is a damned good planner in his own right. The yacht will return to the dock at nine thirty to drop off old fuddy-duddies and return to sea with the young folk for more dancing, drinking, and a cruise out under the Golden Gate."

I nodded in appreciation at Price's wisdom and drank in the aroma of aftershave that came to me on the night air. Turning in Harrison's arms, I pressed my breasts into his chest and ran my nose along his bristly chin. "I presume you are counting us among the old fuddy-duddies?"

"Damned straight!" Harrison fished below my waistband and tugged on my thong.

After a fabulous dinner and an even more spectacular dessert of birthday cake, a chocolate caramel confection with a sinful buttercream frosting that should have been declared illegal by the artery police, I wondered how I was going to negotiate the floating dock. Price got raves from the crowd for having Peggy's cake shaped like conjoined male and female symbols. Peggy had chosen to carve the first slices from the male member. Scientific humor can be literal. My crowd likes to leave the subtleties to the English majors.

The yacht company had five of its fleet chartered for the night, and we pulled into a slip reserved for a sister ship. The dock at this mooring was a more substantial affair, and I had no trouble alighting from the gangplank.

Harrison and I made fast work of the distance from the Embarcadero to the side street where he'd parked the Chevy. We turned on Bay Street and made our way to the Marina District and the dock where his friend's cabin cruiser was moored. As Harrison fumbled with the key in the dock gate, I jettisoned my high heels in order to make headway on the wharf without mishap. In minutes, we were in the main cabin of the cruiser, pulling shades down and ripping each other's clothing off.

"Would you like some wine first?" Harrison breathed between kisses.

"Later." I tugged at his belt. We stumbled down through the galley toward the forward berth. Harrison hit his temple on the open door of the adjacent head, and I rammed my hip on the ice chest as I passed through the galley. He entered the diminutive cabin first, and then backed out to let me pass so I could lie down first. He hit his head again when he stood up after removing his shorts. I used my elbows to shove myself back on the cushions like a turtle trying to right itself. Although we were both aroused, we had the presence of mind to open the hatch for some fresh air. Only a sex maniac would not have noticed how close it was in the confined space.

The cabin cruiser was only a slight improvement over the backseat of the Chevy. If anything, the yacht had more protrusions and sharp angles to bang with body parts. Exhausted from the claustrophobic coupling, we lay beside each other. I listened to Bob's breathing mix with the soft lapping of the water as it slapped the hull. I felt for his hand and caressed his knuckles and then his palm. Perhaps his friend would trade up to a larger yacht soon. Wondering how difficult it was going to be to locate my tiny thong in the trail of clothing from taffrail to galley, I sat up and bashed my forehead on the ceiling.

"You OK?" the big, naked guy asked.

"I guess." I rubbed my head as I sank back beside him.

Harrison rolled carefully on his side and leaned his head on his palm. "You know, we've got to find a better place to have sex. I have some printouts from the Internet. I thought we might go away for a weekend. To a hotel. You know. With king-sized beds and those big bathtubs."

"Sweetheart, you are talkin' my language. My behind can't take too much more of this."

"I like your behind."

"And I yours."

"What would you say to Carmel or Monterrey?"

"I say book it, Danno!"

The vision of a king-sized bed with the crisp sheets and the mound of plump pillows had a positive effect on my partner. We both looked down his torso and then back at each other. Without taken my eyes off his face, which had acquired a salacious smirk, I reached for his member.

I did not achieve my objective. The little cruiser lurched against the dock. I rolled on top of Harrison, and then he rolled on top of me as the boat listed sharply in the other direction.

The cruiser groaned and strained against the lines securing it to the pier. It did not right itself but remained at an awkward angle. The prow, which contained our sleeping chamber bobbed oddly, tugging at the bowline.

"What the hell!" Harrison tried to lift himself off me.

"We've been hit!" I gasped now that his weight was off my chest and I could breathe.

Harrison scrambled to the galley and his pants. I crawled on all fours for my blouse and slacks, all thoughts of searching for the thong abandoned.

Harrison gained the main deck by walking more on the handrails than the steps leading up from the galley. As I hung for dear life onto the galley table, I saw him freeze after yanking open the blinds on the stern-facing windows.

"What is it?"

"It's a damned sea lion. A damned sea lion has its fat ass on the swim platform.

San Francisco harbor had increasing problems with these hefty sea creatures. To control the situation, harbor officials dedicated several large floats to the exclusive use of the beasts. The creatures congregated on these platforms in large numbers and provided a novel tourist attraction.

Unfortunately, there are renegades in any community, and occasionally one of these troublemakers would leave the platform and drape himself over one of the docks or the yachts in the nearby marina. Our night visitor was one of these.

Harrison exited to the cockpit area above the swim platform and the corpulent creature. "Get the fuck off my boat, you tub of lard!"

"Ah-ah-ah-ahhhhhhhhhhhhhhh," the blob bleated.

Dressed, I gained Harrison's side as he searched the cockpit for a weapon.

"Gonna damage the boat." He grasped the end of a pole lashed to the side of the deck.

"Wait a minute. Let's think about this." I studied the mass dragging the stern under the waterline.

"Nothing to think about; it's him or us."

"But what if he doesn't like being poked?"

Harrison gave me a look that suggested I was an alien from another solar system. "I'm kinda hoping he doesn't like it. In fact, I'm counting on it!"

With that, my sidekick stabbed the animal in the side with the pole.

Except for a slight ripple of the flesh similar to the movement of a horse's hide when a fly lights on it, nothing happened.

Harrison jabbed harder.

"Ahhhhhhhhhhhhhhhhhhhhh," uttered the creature.

Encouraged, Harrison gave it all he was worth. The pole snapped with a crisp crack, and the wielder almost followed the severed end overboard.

"Now what?" I asked as he righted himself.

Harrison stormed below and could be heard crashing around in the well-stocked galley.

I studied our uninvited guest. Perhaps he was a jilted lover. Or a widower. Or perhaps he was a she. I had no idea how you sexed a sea lion. Or perhaps he was the advance man for a legion of sea lions who would join him shortly. This frightening thought brought me to my feet. I turned to go below and ran into Harrison staggering up through the hatch with an armload of canned goods.

He brushed past me and deposited his ammo on the deck. Taking aim with a can of tomato sauce, he smacked the lodger in the kisser.

"AAAAAAAAAHHHHHHHHHHHHHHHH!"

"Take that, you damned fat ass!"

Lights came on in yachts up and down our wharf and the next.

The next missile missed. The beast bobbed his head, and the can sailed into the water. The next can missed as well.

"Aim at his midsection!" a silhouette two yachts over advised.

Taking the cue, Harrison connected with a can of corn.

The beast was bobbing nonstop now, and the motion sent the little cruiser swaying back and forth in the water. I grabbed at a rail, and Harrison steadied himself again the captain's chair for better aim.

"Hey, mister, hold on, I'm coming?" A uniformed guard headed toward us along the wharf.

Our friendly silhouette yelled to him, "Got fish?"

"You bet! Keep a supply at the guardhouse for emergencies!"

The guard reached a position on the dock opposite our swim platform and the offending interloper. He set the pail he had been toting on the dock and extracted the first fish. With expert skill, he lofted the fish within inches of the sea lion's nostrils.

"AaaaHHHHHHHHHHHH."

"Better hold on," said the guard as he hefted the next fish.

The second fish went airborne, and the creature followed the trajectory with his eyes, nose, and then his entire body as he slid effortlessly from the platform.

When the creature surfaced, the guard let fly with another fish. He repeated his actions along the length of the wharf until the creature was back in the main channel. Bob checked the platform for damage.

I returned to the galley to put what was left of the canned goods away and search for my thong.

A solemn and determined pair made the turn onto Sloat Boulevard at two a.m. "When you get to the house, park one street over," I said.

"Why?" Harrison asked without much enthusiasm.

"Because you're coming in with me."

"It's after two."

"I know what the hell time it is, genius! You're not dropping me off; you're coming to bed with me. We're going to sleep together through the night in a full-sized bed. And in the morning, we're going to have sex. We're going to have safe sex. By that, I mean we're going to do the sex act and not be assaulted by criminals, injured by objects in our environment, or attacked by endangered species."

At this ultimatum, Harrison pulled up at a stop sign and stared dumbly at me.

"What about Janie Belle?"

"What about her? It's my house, too. Besides, she goes to church in the morning. We'll get up after that and have coffee. You'll leave before she gets back. She'll never know you were there."

"Sounds like a plan."

"Damn straight, it's a plan. Now, move it or lose it."

The car glided through the intersection, parting the fog like an icebreaker in the North Sea.

Skootch met us at the back door. Harrison whispered to him and scratched behind his ears as I tiptoed to the pantry for dog biscuits. We left him chewing on a substantial bribe and tiptoed up the stairs to my bedroom without incident.

* * *

CHAPTER
18

The distant but distinct sound of the front door closing wakened me. Janie Belle leaving for church. I rolled on my side and admired the profile of my bed partner. Harrison's beard was darker than his hair except for a sprinkling of gray bristles. I ran my finger along his chin line, gently pushing the hairs in the wrong direction. An eyebrow lifted, followed by a deep intake of air.

"If you continue to do that, something may happen to you."

"I'll take my chances."

Light from the casement windows suffused my bedroom. Harrison rolled in my direction, intent on starting his day with a good morning boink. Ever the gracious hostess, I accommodated him.

The sex was unhurried and sweet. Staying in each other's arms, we drifted off to sleep again despite the bright morning light.

I think I was snoring because I snorted when I was jerked into wakefulness by a strident voice only a few feet away. Grabbing the sheet and pulling it above my bosoms, I sat up and stared at Janie Belle, standing in the doorway to my bedroom, one hand on hip and one grasping a man's shoe by the lace, dangling it before her.

"Just what, may I ask, is this doing in the front hall?"

"I believe that's mine." Harrison had come to a sitting position, and held his half of the bed sheet in the same prim position I did.

"Well, I guess that explains it. However, house guests shouldn't leave belongings strewn every which way where little old ladies might fall over them." She started to place the shoe on the bureau but caught herself, and with her eyes fixed firmly on us dropped it on the floor, turned, and descended the stairs.

After a lengthy pause, I exhaled and turned to my companion. "I guess we overslept."

"Ya think? How the hell did my shoe end up on the first floor?"

"Oh, I think I know how it got there." I listened to the soft click of claws on the stair treads. A bobbing black-and-white head appeared in the doorway. The dog paused at the discarded shoe and snuffled the insole. When his head came up, his face wore a sly doggy grin, the tongue lolling rakishly.

"You naughty piece of work." I said. "You traitor, you turned us in! Harrison, in fairness, you are lying in his place, so taking your shoe was no more than you deserved in his way of thinking."

Harrison pushed himself off the edge of the bed and shuffled around to reclaim his shoe. Examining the leather, he smiled in relief that the surface was not marred by chew marks, and reached over to pet the thoughtful canine.

Skootch rolled his brown eyes up at Harrison as if to say, "No sweat, we're even now," and then, panting playfully, skirted the bed and leaped into the place Harrison had vacated, settling down into the warm sheets.

Harrison was unwilling to challenge the dog for a spot on the mattress. "I'm going to take a long shower while you figure out how I'm going to get out of here."

I ventured into the kitchen in my bathrobe to find Janie Belle tending a battalion of sizzling sausages in a cast iron skillet.

"Do you think these will be enough?" she asked without looking up. Next to the stovetop was a bowl of eggs, beaten and awaiting a scramble, and a tray stacked with freshly made cornbread.

"Good God! Who have you invited for breakfast, Lee's Army of Northern Virginia?"

"Don't be silly, we've a man in the house and we're going to feed him. Go fix the coffee. How much longer do you think he's going to be? I don't want to put the eggs on until I am sure he's coming down."

"I'll start the coffee and then go up and see." I realized there was no escape. We were destined to enjoy a long, calorie-and-chatter-filled Sunday morning breakfast with Janie Belle.

"Is that the only robe you've got?" Janie Belle eyed my patched plaid garment that was two sizes too big. She already knew the answer; she was just making the point that I looked about as much like Loretta Young as a lumberjack doing a pole dance.

Not dignifying her underhanded question with a response, I pushed the brew button on the coffee maker and headed for the stairs. As I passed the door to the dining room, I noted that the table was set for three with Janie Belle's wedding china. I trudged up the steps marveling at her ability to put on a complete show at the drop of a, ah, well, in this case, the drop of a shoe.

I met Harrison on the stairs. He cleaned up very well. I think he'd caught a whiff of the sausage cooking and cut his shower short.

"Don't you want to wait for me?" I asked. "It has been suggested that I'm not dressed appropriately for Sunday brunch, so I'm going to slip into some slacks."

"Naw, I'm ready to face the music." He gave me a peck on the nose. When he reached the bottom stair, he smiled up at me, put on his game face, and disappeared into the kitchen. I heard him say, "Morning, what can I do to help?"

"Not a thing," cooed Janie Belle. "You just take this plate of cornbread into the dining room and sit yourself down with the paper."

I was amazed at how easily they had gotten past the embarrassment of the morning and settled into the comfortable relationship of Southern cook/mother and hungry, appreciative male. I, on the other hand, would need time to reclaim my equilibrium and erase the image of Janie Belle and the peripatetic shoe from my gray matter. Harrison and I still needed to find a safe haven in which to be intimate. Even without the competitive canine, this was not the ideal location for our trysts.

Moscone Center attracts an endless succession of conventions, delivering to San Francisco fresh legions of tourists to fill the restaurants, shops, cable cars, and sightseeing buses.

I made my way from the BART station to the entrance of the convention center. The block between the two buildings of the center was cordoned off with yellow-striped concrete barriers and peppered by an army of police and security personnel. In the post 9/11 world, entering any large public building has become an ordeal, and this morning's admission into Moscone was to be made even more difficult because a major animal rights organization had announced a demonstration against the biotechnology industry. My briefcase grew heavy as I took my place in the long, slowly moving line of dark-suited convention-goers.

After entering the lobby, I joined another queue so that my purse and briefcase could be searched. A surly, overweight woman in uniform and glitter-laced mascara directed me to open my briefcase and slid her elongated fingernails in and around my papers. She OK'd the case and aimed a bored glance at the contents of my purse.

I passed into the check-in area and proceeded to the booth where Georgina said my entry pass would be waiting. I received the ubiquitous canvas bag emblazoned with sponsor logo containing my meeting agenda, floor plan of the exhibit space, and collection of advertising inserts.

After consulting the floor diagram, I strolled in the direction of the Screen Leaf booth. I should have headed directly to the exhibit space of my client, Precision Probes, but I couldn't resist checking out the booth reserved for my ex-client. Fortunately, a major publisher held the island booth across from Screen Leaf's setup. This company published two textbooks to which I had contributed chapters and three periodicals containing articles I'd authored, so I had a legitimate reason to call at their booth. My cover established, I returned the map to the tote and began to pay attention to the people I passed in the aisle.

My progress was slow due to the necessity of greeting and chatting with colleagues. The longer you were in the business, the longer it took you to move up the aisle. By the time I reached the publisher's booth, I was very thankful they had a seating area. I sank into a comfortable chair.

The publisher was distributing some popular reprints and conducting a raffle for an expensive set of reference books. The offer of freebees and the chance to win something valuable had drawn a significant crowd. The milling scientists, jostling forward to reach the table to fill out their raffle entries, gave me the perfect cover for observing Screen Leaf's booth.

Theo Tan straightened the literature on the Lucite podium at the booth's center. A pretty girl dressed in a spectacular gray silk suit stood at the edge of the booth's carpeting with a basket from which she extracted leaves and handed them to passersby. By adjusting my glasses, I discerned that the object was not a leaf but a CD sleeve upon which a leaf had been depicted. This made more sense: they were passing out a presentation about their screening services on disk.

As I watched the girl, she handed a CD to a familiar face. Theo Tan seemed to recognize that face, too, and traversed the booth to shake hands with the man to whom it belonged. He pulled my client, Leonard Price, into the Screen Leaf booth.

A chilling thought formed in my head, as I pushed myself up out of the chair. Peninsula Gene Therapy was not the only company Screen Leaf and the conspiratorial Ancient Turtle were hacking. I moved in Price's direction as he exited the Screen Leaf booth and headed away down the exhibit aisle.

"Hey, Leonard, that was some party. When's your birthday? I figure your wife will have to get even with you for that cake."

Price took my arm and guided me out of the densest part of the crowd to the sidelines where we could talk. Leonard began to talk about a company who released major news at the convention, but I interjected my question about Screen Leaf.

"Yes, we have been a client of theirs for, oh, about nine months. They have taken one of our compounds in-house for screening, and their report is due back to us pretty shortly. I'd have to check with the project manager, but now that you bring it up, I'd say they are overdue."

I dragged the surprised CEO into an unoccupied booth space. "Leonard, Screen Leaf is a rotten apple."

I filled him in without going into details proprietary to my other client about the discovered hacking.

Price's expression turned grave as he listened to the tale of corporate thievery. "I'm going to contact my IT manager to evaluate our own network."

"Caution him to exercise care, and contact Harrison's office before doing anything that might alert the hackers." I gave Price Harrison's phone numbers, and we parted after agreeing to meet later in the week.

I decided I would conduct a survey of my current and former clients to determine how many of biotechnology companies had contracts with Screen Leaf. After several failed attempts, I hopped an elevator to the street level of Moscone to improve cell phone reception.

Finding a quiet corner near the coat check concession, I sat on my briefcase and tote bag, leaned against the glass wall separating me from a brilliant San Francisco afternoon, and started dialing. It took the better part of an hour, but I reached all of the dozen companies I had intended to survey. Because I stayed in one place for so long, I attracted the attention of the security patrol. A heavy, pock-faced man clad in the same uniform as the nail queen who'd checked my purse, patrolled past several times trying to get a better look at the tote bag I was using to cushion my ass against the stone flooring.

All of my clients and former clients had some kind of arrangement with Screen Leaf—all of them except Precision Probes. At least, the administrative assistant I had reached at Precision had never heard of them. I was reasonably sure she would know because she would have seen any contract signed by the CEO, but he was here at Moscone. I needed to go back downstairs to find him because I could not raise him on his cell phone.

Fortunately, I remembered the location of the Precision Probe booth. I found it and identified a manager senior enough to give me a definitive answer. They were not a client.

Because my cell phone battery was in its death throes, I made my way through the crowds to a phone bank and dialed Harrison's office. I filled him in on my discovery that all my clients save the diagnostic probe company were clients of Screen Leaf. Having just returned to his office from a meeting, he had missed Price's call and was about to return it when he took mine. We agreed to meet for dinner, and he promised to call Price back immediately to set up a visit to CAI's offices.

I had time to hit Nordstrom's before we were to meet. I promised the Estèe Lauder maven I would buy the large night cream, another ruinous purchase, if she would do my face.

After a stop at the perfume counter for a spritz of my favorite Tuscany cologne, I sailed out the shopping center door a new woman, and hailed a cab to take me to the restaurant.

Harrison had picked a very romantic restaurant for dinner. Julius' Castle hangs off the side of Telegraph Hill affording diners a spectacular view of the bay from an intimate setting, but it was on the other side of the downtown and we were traversing the city at the rush hour. I settled back on the seat. We did reasonably well through the financial district but bogged down in Chinatown. The street lamps began to glow in the dusk.

I rested against the bench seat, enjoying the colors and clamor. Ducks swung in restaurant windows, aged mamas hefted bags of vegetables, and tourists clogged the sidewalk as they perused street displays of souvenirs. Pedestrians dodged between the cars as we waited for our turn to cross Columbus. My eyes strayed to the entrance to one of the city's older Chinese restaurants. Red Dragon itself was on the second floor, but the carved double doors at street level opened onto a jade and black foyer with an elegant staircase rising to the host station on the level above. I had not eaten at Red Dragon for years and resolved to return soon with Harrison. The food was excellent and the atmosphere, timeless.

A restaurant employee was lighting torches flanking the entrance, but he interrupted his task to hold the door for three older men exiting the establishment. I straightened, recognizing William Chen. I did not know the man in the middle, but it appeared he was the proprietor because he remained on the stoop as the other men descended to the pavement.

The third man I recognized easily. He was a famous San Franciscan, or rather infamous. It wasn't that he was in the papers that often, for he took pains to remain in the shadows. The *Chronicle* and the *Examiner* had file photos of him collected over decades, and they dusted off and reprinted these images every time something of a sinister nature happened in Chinatown. Bartholomew Woo, or Shanghai Woo as he was called, usually in a careful whisper, was reputed to be the crime boss, the enforcer, the underworld law in Chinatown.

Modern Chinatown marched to a new drummer; third- and fourth-generation natives ran for political office, held senior positions in the police and fire departments, anchored the evening news, and rose to prominent management positions in banks and investment firms. Despite these signs of progress, it remained that if anything affected the deep underpinnings of this city within a city, Woo pulled the strings.

I was not surprised William Chen knew Woo or would associate with him. I might think of the man as a gangster, a crook, but the world of these old survivors was more complex and intertwined. They had both lived long enough to remember when the white world was closed to them, when they had to get things done within their own community and protect that community from the excesses of the larger world.

As the restaurant proprietor waved and bowed, the other two men strolled up the street ahead of my cab and turned down one of Chinatown's enumerable alleys. My vehicle inched forward, but when we reached the mouth of the alley so that I could view it lengthwise, the two figures had disappeared.

The North Beach traffic was no improvement over that of Chinatown. We escaped up Telegraph Hill, and as we left the flatland behind, the traffic abated. The driver turned on the narrow, divided street that was the only approach to Julius' Castle and accelerated down the brick-paved route at a speed that made me stiffen in discomfort. He skidded to a stop in front of the Castle's unperturbed valet. I settled with the cabby, and the valet took charge of my briefcase as I made a graceful entrance into the snug bar and Harrison's embrace. After a drink in the cozy retreat, we were escorted to the upper floor and our table.

Seated at a deuce nestled against the window, we held hands and enjoyed the night view of the bay ferries as we waited for our wine. Despite the romantic setting, our conversation turned to business, and I listened as Harrison filled me in on the developments at PGT and CAI.

When he was finished, I said, "The only reason Precision Probes has been omitted from the scam is they are a diagnostics company. All of my other clients are developing therapeutic solutions for major diseases."

"That could be it," Harrison said. "But this leaves us with too big a field of interest."

"Right, it doesn't tell us enough, unless these companies are in cahoots with the Chinese government to steal every therapeutic invention they can get their hands on. That seems unrealistic to me."

"Agreed. The bad guys usually have a specific quarry and a reasonable expectation of turning a near-term profit. If we could see them operate from the beginning contact, we could detect the pattern, be we're not there yet."

Our entrees arrived. I was having salmon and Harrison opted for halibut. As the waiter placed my plate, I pictured the fish flying past the whiskers of the sea lion who had adopted our last love nest as his personal diving platform. That pinniped was having something very similar for dinner tonight somewhere out there in the blackness, and he wasn't paying thirty-five dollars for it. Coming to from my reverie, I realized Harrison and the waitperson were staring at me.

"Harold wants to know if everything is to your satisfaction."

"Perfection itself."

Our attendant retreated, and Harrison poured me more wine from the bottle in the ice bucket at his elbow. I slipped my right foot out of my shoe and ran my toes up the side of his leg. He hit the side of the ice bucket with the bottom of the bottle, drawing the attention of the server who was passing on his return to the kitchen.

"Can I bring you another bottle, sir?"

"Not just yet. We're still enjoying this one."

After the waiter was out of earshot, I apologized and shared my vision of the supping sea lion.

"Speaking of the yacht," Harrison said, "I was thinking we might spend a weekend at the Tartan Inn in Carmel. I don't think we can take too many more run-ins with sea lions or your mother, although I'll have to admit that breakfast she fixed was first-rate."

"OK, but did you win the lottery or something? That place is ruinously expensive."

He grinned. "I get government rate. Anyway, although they don't really have an off season, their prices are slightly less than stratospheric right now, so we should go while the going is good."

"I'm game!"

"Good, I'll reserve for next weekend."

Our plates were cleared, the linen was de-crumbed and our coffees, delivered.

I stirred my coffee. "What would you say if we could lure Screen Leaf and their sidekicks into a screening agreement with a company who was prepped by you in advance? You know, a setup."

Harrison raised his eyebrows. "That could work. If my people were in place beforehand, we could get to the bottom of their game and catch them in the act with their fists in the cyber-till."

"We should get Precision Probes, my one client they haven't penetrated, to approach them about a screening project."

"What about the fact that they aren't a therapeutics company?"

"Yeah, I know, but that can be finessed. The CEO can say they have rights to a compound with therapeutic potential and they'd like to develop it sufficiently for out-licensing to the appropriate drug company. I hear you, though; the bait has to be perfect. I'm sure we can work this out with the team at Precision once they're brought into the picture. Should I make the introductions for you tomorrow?"

He leaned forward. "Yeah, and then, even though this idea is really your baby, I need to ask you to step aside and let the pros handle things. Are we agreed on that?" Harrison reclaimed his credit card from the holder and scrawled a tip on the merchant copy.

I dabbed my mouth with the tip of my napkin, carefully folded the linen, and placed it on the table before answering. I wanted to tell him that sometimes the pros screwed up, like the Chicago police had screwed up with Joyce's murderer, but I couldn't find the words.

"If you insist." I pushed back my chair.

"Oh, I do." Bob rose and reached for my arm.

* * *

CHAPTER 19

I faced the next morning refreshed by a good night's sleep and energized by our plan to ensnare Screen Leaf and its accomplices. Harrison had dropped me off after dinner the night before. We agreed to forego sex until the luxurious weekend in Carmel. We wanted to build our anticipation for a seismic orgasmic experience.

I swung my heels over the edge of the bed contemplating what I would take with me to Carmel. I would have to shop again if for nothing else than the little nothing I would wear to bed. The image of a lime green teddy crystallized in my brain. My nipples hardened.

As I promised Harrison, I called the CEO of Precision Probes, Phil Gephardt, and arranged to meet him later in the morning. Smug in the knowledge Harrison couldn't completely cut me out of the scheme-building process since all the companies involved were my clients, I called Rilke's and Price's offices to line up call times with them after lunch. I would brief them on the plan, find out whether they knew Gephardt, and arrange to make introductions if either of them didn't already know him. This I presumed would be OK with Harrison, but I also intended to arrange for myself to be invited to any meetings between PGT or CAI and the investigators. This *would* be breaking faith with my man.

Placing the receiver in the cradle, I tried to summon up some good old-fashioned guilt for stepping on Harrison's turf so soon after giving him the impression I would back off. I could not muster even a milliliter of regret. Those creeps at Screen Leaf were attacking the biotech brotherhood. This was no time to sit back and leave it to the professionals. Every man, woman, and postdoc should rally to the ramparts and protect our industry. I grabbed my purse and briefcase and headed for the Saab.

Gephardt was saddened to hear about the problems at PGT and CAI and instantly offered to help. I set forth our plan, and he agreed to allow his company to be used as bait.

"I've met Price, but I don't know Rilke."

"No problem. I'll handle the introduction. You'll need to decide which of your managers should be included in the operation."

"I've already decided. I'll assemble this group at the end of the day to brief them on the sting."

"Great, I'll be back for the meeting."

Back in the Saab, I headed for the mall. I had just enough time before I had to make my calls to Rilke and Price to do a little teddy shopping.

My conversations with the two CEOs went well. I was impressed that both men offered to cooperate with the other companies. This is a competitive business, and yet they were willing to share information and scientific talent. Despite the value of their top scientists' time, the two young leaders moved past their own needs to confront a communal threat.

Back on Ocean Avenue on my way home, I called Harrison to report in and line him up for the session at Precision.

"Good. I'll see you there," he said. "Once these guys are brought into the picture, we'll have to find a place to get the right people from all three companies together to work out the details. I don't think we want to convene them at any of their own operations or here at headquarters. We need something off the beaten track."

My progress along Ocean was slowed by a trolley. As I listened and drummed my fingers on the steering wheel, my gaze shifted to the bell tower of St. Agnes Episcopal Church, the establishment where Janie Belle spent so much time polishing silver and bilking church ladies out of their bridge money. "Don't worry, I've got just the unlikely place you're looking for."

I closed the cell phone and placed in on the seat next to me. My hand brushed the Victoria's Secret bag. My sortie into the mall had proven successful. Even if Harrison got a little steamed at my meddling, I knew how to divert him.

The briefing at Precision went well, and two days later we convened representatives from the three companies, San Francisco law enforcement, and the FBI in the parish hall at Saint Agnes Church.

"Geez, these deviled eggs are outstanding, I don't think I can recall a meeting where we've been served deviled eggs." Karin Mullins used her laptop to push a Play-Dough bust of Jesus away from her place at the meeting table.

"It was the quid pro quo for getting my mother to book the hall," I explained. "I had to let her cater the event."

"I think you should set her up in business." Karin popped another egg in her mouth.

"Only one entrepreneur per family, thanks." I spied Janie Belle coming from the parish kitchen with Harrison in tow. She had pressed him into service to carry a tray of sandwiches.

"I'll be right back with the cookies. Tell your folks the coffee urn is almost done perking." Janie Belle was in her element dishing out calorie-laden goodies to the multitudes.

The computer guys overcame the lack of sufficient outlets in the church hall by stringing a web of extension cords around the tables. The attendees, who could not function in a meeting without a laptop, swarmed to the power strips and plugged in.

"OK, everybody, listen up," Harrison said. "You all know why we're here. I want to spend the first part of the meeting hearing from our CAI and PGT colleagues on what they've learned about how the bad guys operate. We'll cover how Screen Leaf penetrated the security systems, what they took, and when. Then we'll move on to our sting setup. The Precision Probes team is going to present a scenario for snaring these turds. I want everybody to torture this plan until we get it right."

Fueled by Janie Belle's sandwiches and sweets, the group tore into the data. Everybody had theories and suggestions. Harrison fought to control the flow of ideas.

"OK, let's summarize." He signaled for silence. "Screen Leaf gains its first access by being given their own account on your system to facilitate sharing their screening data on the compounds you've consigned to them from your scientific team. With this Trojan horse inside your operation, they build themselves a bridge for getting back and forth through your firewall. Once they've established their clandestine electronic tunnel, they begin replicating all your data files. Am I right so far?"

The CAI and PGT representatives nodded in agreement. "That must be the point at which Screen Leaf hands over the keys to your cyber assets to Ancient Turtle. Then Turtle operatives suck proprietary data out of your company and into their servers."

Karin piped up. "That's about when they start taking actual compounds, stealing materials that are not subject to the contract between the companies. By then they know where we keep everything from our cell lines to our clinical samples."

"Those assets have to walk out the door," Harrison said.

"Yeah, but they're pretty small, so it's no big deal to slip something in a pocket or briefcase," Karin said.

"Is there a pattern to what they're taking?" I asked. "Do the data and samples suggest what they are working on?"

"I think they're working on methodically acquiring the assets of the entire U.S. biotechnology industry." Leonard Price's voice was solemn. "Let's face it, the Chinese are not known for their respect of intellectual property or rigid regulatory controls. They knock off all kinds of goods from designer shoes to movie DVDs and conduct human testing that would never be permitted in the West."

"That's a tall order. It'll take them years to sift through what they've stolen," I said.

"They're ambitious, ruthless, and they take the long view," said Harrison's FBI liaison. We all turned in his direction, but he offered nothing further to enlighten us.

"You sure it isn't something more specific?" I persisted.

"Oh, I'm sure they have their priorities, but I can't discern what they are from what we know at this stage," Price said. "Why is it important? We've established that they're acting illegally."

"I just thought it would help us design our sting with Precision Probes if we knew what they're most interested in."

"Nola, they seem to jump at any chance to steal experimental results and biological samples. Don't over think this,"

Harrison snapped. My active participation was getting under lover boy's skin. Our deal was that I was to introduce all the players and get lost. I settled into sullen silence.

"Let's move on to Precision and setting the trap for Screen Leaf," Harrison continued, looking over my head toward the far end of the table where the Precision managers waited with their PowerPoint presentation. "Remember, we need to catch these guys after they've stolen samples and before they pass the samples and data to a consular official we can't touch. Preferably, the samples will be for materials not detailed in their screening contract, and the moment of capture will occur when Screen Leaf hands over Precision's proprietary stuff to an Ancient Turtle manager. OK, Precision, let's see the scenario."

Two hours and about six hundred calories later on my part, we nailed down the details of the sting. While people packed up their laptops, I headed for the kitchen in search of Janie Belle. I found her sound asleep over a half-finished hand of solitaire. The army of Tupperware containers used to transport our repast half-circled the cards like a polyethylene Stonehenge.

* * *

CHAPTER
20

We made it through San Jose's Friday afternoon traffic in good time and breezed south on Highway 101 toward Carmel and our weekend at The Tartan Inn. When Harrison collected me and my indiscreetly small piece of luggage, it was the first I had seen him since the parish hall strategy session.

Much had been accomplished. Precision's exec had called Screen Leaf the next morning to discuss a possible contract. A Screen Leaf contingent arrived at Precision the following day, a contract was signed, and Screen Leaf began work on the project at Precision's facilities conveniently ensconced in two spare cubicles mere steps from the company's R & D storage laboratories. An array of electronic monitoring devices were rigged and systems alerts programmed to detect the penetration of Precision's security and document the thefts of data and samples. Now all we had to do was wait for Screen Leaf to act.

Our room at the Tartan Inn overlooked the ocean and boasted a private spa tub with its own picture window, a mountain of plush towels, and enough eucalyptus-scented oil to zonk half the koalas in Australia. We opted for room service and donned our complimentary robes and slippers. Harrison chose the champagne, and I picked a dozen of Puget Sound's very best oysters. We waited impatiently for the food, figuring we didn't have enough time to get anything amorous accomplished before its arrival.

The sunset blushed pink haze like a soothing balm over the surf, and the shore birds settled in for the night. A lone human gathered his jacket collar around his ears and quickened his pace on the wave packed sand. What a peaceful backdrop for a storm of sexual passion, I thought as I rested my head against Harrison's arm. His hand grasped my shoulder and turned my body to face his. A soft rap on the door, heralding our bubbly, interrupted our kiss.

The spa temperature was a perfect hundred two degrees. I dropped my robe, shrugged off my specially purchased teddy, stepped in, and settled seductively into the warm, turbulent water. Since men get naked a lot faster than women, Harrison was already there, watching me. I reached his side, and he stroked my pleasantly full tummy. I stroked his pleasantly full something else.

I wakened to the sound of gulls. My buttocks touched Harrison's, so I didn't need to turn to know he was still in bed. A wiggle of my cheeks elicited a gruff moan from him. Bob rolled over, slung an arm over my body, and felt for a convenient nipple.

At last, we'd had civilized, adult sex straight through from start to finish without any interruptions. I smiled remembering just how satisfying our lovemaking had been. I detached

Harrison's fingers from my nipple so I could roll in his direction. Kissing his Adam's apple, I mumbled, "Breakfast or more sex?"

"Both."

A cell phone rang across the room. On the second ring, we determined that the sound emanated from Harrison's pile of discarded clothes. He kicked the sheets off his legs, hit the floor, and retrieved the phone as it started its fourth ring. I turned away, tuned out his voice, and concentrated on the wave and avian sounds welling up from the shore. I did not want anything to break the magic spell that protected our little trysting heaven. Lulled by the sea sounds, I started to drift off.

"Hey, babe, they took the bait." My companion yanked the covers off me. "Your friends at Precision Probes have reported the theft of samples beyond those offered to Screen Leaf per the contract. Their IT people detected the presence of Ancient Turtle hackers inside their data storage server."

Harrison grabbed his watch from the bedside table and headed for the bathroom. "I'm gonna take a shower. We need to head back. I don't want to miss the closing of this particular trap."

"Me neither!" I sat up and stretched.

Harrison stopped in mid stride. "Remember our deal. You're sticking to the sidelines. Way to the sidelines, right?"

"Ummm," I muffled my reply by bending over to search for my hotel-supplied slippers.

We were out of the hotel and in the car with takeaway coffee and buns in under thirty minutes. I sighed as we drove past the Tartan's entrance and blew a kiss to the façade. My recent bed buddy glanced at me and smirked. "It was a great night, wasn't it."

"Better than great. The sea lions thoughtfully kept to their part of Monterey Bay, and there wasn't a single street thug booked into this establishment. It sure pays to go five stars."

We drove north in an amiable silence shared only by new lovers or old friends.

As we left the built-up area north of Monterey and entered the large agricultural buffer between that coastal enclave and the San Jose metro area, I had a thought. "Could we make a quick stop and get Janie Belle some strawberries and artichokes?"

"Sure, no problem."

I glanced to my right and took in the calm sea glistening in the morning light. The bank separating the shore from the adjacent fields was lower here than at Fort Funston.

"Harrison, why do you suppose Roger's killers dispatched him at Fort Funston? He was killed there, right?" I remembered all the blood on my pants.

"Yeah, they killed him there. The spot has the advantage of isolation at night when the park is closed."

"OK, but why behead the guy? Why not shoot him or strangle him?"

"This has all the earmarks of a professional hit most likely committed by an Asian outfit. Think Ninja sword. San Francisco's Hip Sing Fong gang is second only to New York's in size. Youth gangs also are used for added muscle and mayhem. Perhaps the Wah Ching or United Bamboo. The Chinese sometimes employ Vietnamese gangs in murder for hire exercises."

"Gives me the shivers. An Asian gang, then. And placing him so he could be found easily means they were sending a message, but to whom?"

"Nola, you're going to leave the interpretation of that particular message to Barbagalatto and his team, right?"

"Yeah. Yeah. I know. It's just so puzzling. A Rubik's Cube right in my own backyard."

Ten minutes up the road, Harrison spotted a roadside market. So had about fifty other tourists, and we had to wait for a car full of jostling kids to back out so we could squeeze into a vacant space in the dusty, unlined parking area.

I scored a spectacular flat of berries. The artichokes were picked over, but I managed to unearth two acceptable specimens and settled with the vendor for my finds. A large bag of pistachios under his arm, Harrison methodically picked through a pyramid of corn ears.

"I'd like to go back to the car. Can I have the keys?"

Harrison nodded at his right pocket, and I reached in and retrieved his key ring.

I placed my purchases on the backseat, spreading some newspaper under the berry flat to prevent any juice getting on the upholstery. This accomplished, I settled back in the passenger seat and closed my eyes. I'd almost drifted off when something bumped against the car.

I was staring at the derriere of a very large woman trying to negotiate the space between the Chevy and her own truck with two bags of produce. A person of normal girth could have sidled through, opened the truck door and, after ridding themselves of the vegetables, gotten into the passenger side of the truck; but there was too much flesh on this lady's carcass for that to happen. She tried to turn in my direction and almost impaled herself on a rearview mirror. She had wiped the dust off the length of the truck chassis with her breasts and abdomen, and her ruined blouse now pressed ominously against Bob's window. The Chevy rocked again as if to get away.

I looked down in my lap at Bob's keys and up at the ignition. The only way that poor woman was going to get in her truck was for me to move the Chevy. Harrison let me drive his beloved car at the art museum. I figured he wouldn't mind if I just backed it out and re-parked it. I got out on my side and circled the vehicle to tell the lady I'd make her life easier.

I stepped past her and slid behind the wheel. The Chevy roared to life. I shifted into reverse and eased my foot down on the gas pedal. The big car responded nicely. I glanced over my left shoulder at the corpulent woman who waited behind the truck's lengthy, covered cargo bed, resting a grocery bag on the high bumper. She smiled encouragingly. I twisted in the other direction to assure the way was clear and backed into the makeshift aisle between the ragged rows. I came to a stop mid-aisle and gestured to the woman to get in her truck.

She headed for the door. Pressing one bag on the running board with a dimpled knee, she reached for the handle, opened the cab door, turned back to retrieve the sack, and screamed.

"*Halta, halta!*" She squealed. The kneed bag slipped and split, spilling its contents on the ground.

I felt the impact and heard the sickening discord of metal on metal. I swiveled to my left and stared up the butt of a Cadillac Seville. I could not see the driver because a mosaic of fruit and vegetables took up the entire back window of the Caddy.

The Caddy shuddered from a gearshift change and eased forward to the tune of tinkling headlamp glass and the subtle thud of a chrome wing inset as it fell to the ground from the side of Harrison's Chevy.

A cranium with a vast but sparse comb-over emerged from the driver's seat. When the figure stood, the head just peeked over the car's top. The senior, who wore his pants up to his rib cage, used one age-spotted arm to steady himself on the Seville as he teetered in my direction. Since I couldn't open the damaged driver's side door, I slid across and exited on the passenger side. By the time I managed this maneuver and rounded the back of the car to meet him, he had acquired a Greek chorus of pastel-haired ladies from the Seville's passenger seats, one of whom brandished a lethal looking faux leopard cane. Senior comb-over dropped his wallet while fumbling for his insurance card, which I very much doubted he had the eyesight to read, and I squatted on my haunches to retrieve the dusty license and cards spilled from his billfold.

Something blocked the sun, and I looked up. There towered Harrison, clutching a bag of corn ears, the silks trembling in the breeze. It was the only thing about him that moved.

"My car," he finally managed to say. "My. Car."

"I owned a Chevy Bel Air once," said Leopard Cane brightly.

We reached Morgan Hill, a southern suburb of San Jose, before I could bring myself to say anything. In the backseat, the Chevy's severed chrome appendage rested against the strawberry flat. I apologized and offered to pay for anything the old man's insurance did not cover, but nothing was going to improve Harrison's mood. Our idyllic escape was ruined in a flash with a crash.

I decided to try another subject. "How are you guys going to apprehend the perps now that they've got the physical samples and the data?"

Harrison was silent for a while. I figured he was weighing whether to share any details with me. It wasn't that he didn't trust me with the information; he just didn't trust me to stay out of the way.

"I've promised not to meddle," I assured him. "It's just intellectual curiosity."

"It better be. We figure that Ancient Turtle not only collects but also organizes the data from the subject companies, perhaps even providing interpretation, annotation, and cross reference. They then copied these data to disks. Screen Leaf steals actual samples and delivers them to the gang at Ancient Turtle whose CEO, Fang, has the connection at the consulate. He delivers the disks and the samples to the consular operative, and the stuff goes to China in a diplomatic pouch."

"Why couldn't they just transfer the data electronically?"

"They could, but they would be taking a significant risk. Their transmission needs are significant and ongoing, and Homeland Security, which monitors international Internet traffic, could discover them."

"They snoop into file transfers?"

"You're surprised?"

I was surprised, but I didn't want to let on to Harrison. I was pretty naïve about espionage stuff.

"So their risk aversion actually gives you an opportunity to catch them red-handed."

"Yes, but it's not going to be easy. We figure they don't hand off the stuff near their operations despite how simple it would be. Both companies have a large number of employees who have no idea what the real purpose of their firm is, and our perps would like to keep it that way, so they manage the transfer somewhere else. Unfortunately, we have no idea where that might be. We have round-the-clock tails on the players, and we're using devices on their vehicles, but they could shake us for long enough to pass the samples."

"They'll use Fort Funston again."

"No. You spotted them there. They'll pick another location. San Francisco is a big city. Lot's of places to chose."

"No. It'll be Funston. Fang is too arrogant to be threatened by me. I'm just a useless, annoying woman to him. But that's not the reason they'll pick Fort Funston again."

"OK, I'll bite. Why will it be Fort Funston?" Harrison navigated onto 280 North.

"Simple, it's the only spot in San Francisco you always know you'll find a place to park."

In an awkward role reversal, I held the door for Harrison as he climbed out the passenger side of his damaged car. Once he extricated his lanky frame, he handed me the flat of strawberries and grabbed my luggage and artichoke parcel.

"Gotta use your john," he said as we entered the foyer. Harrison took the stairs two at a time, and I headed for the kitchen with my purchases. Janie Belle had neat stacks of envelopes lined up on the kitchen table, and was applying pressure-sensitive stamps while listening to her favorite Glenn Miller CD.

"Please take that dog for a walk. He's driving me out of my wits!"

I looked for a safe place to deposit the strawberries. Mailing materials covered everything.

"I'll just set these on the washer on my way to the car. Skootch needs a run to burn off his pent up energy is all. Harrison's upstairs using the facilities."

The last remark proved unnecessary as the sound of running could be heard, and a second later, a head poked in the kitchen, followed by a shoulder and a hand gesturing with a cell phone.

"It's going down. See you later." Harrison was in the foyer and out the front door before I could respond.

I shrugged and headed for the laundry room. Skootch was stretched out in the hall near the place where his leash hung. I reached for the leash, and he burst into action, tail wagging, tongue flapping, feet dancing. He raced through the garage and bounced impatiently next to the driver's door.

As I backed the Saab out of the garage, I struggled to see what was behind me because Skootch obstructed my view. I recalled my last unsuccessful backing experience. When the furious knock against the window came, I nearly fainted.

"Open up. My car won't start. Move over." Harrison yanked my door open, and I was barely able to get out of his way as he got behind the wheel. As it was I impaled myself on the gearshift. Rubbing my sore hip, I was slammed against the car seat as Harrison floored the Saab and swerved onto Plymouth Avenue.

"Hey, careful with my gearbox."

"You're telling me to be careful, after wrecking my car?"

"I didn't wreck your damned car; some other jarhead of a male did that. A bullheaded man who thinks he can still drive even though he can no longer see over the dashboard. Typical."

Powering down Sloat Boulevard, Harrison ignored my male bashing. Skootch lost his balance and rolled on his back when Harrison hit the turn south toward Fort Funston.

"So it is going to be Funston; I was right," I said as we ran another light. Skootch righted himself and pointed his head between the front seats like a furry hood ornament.

We pulled abruptly off the road into a service area and parked between two unmarked cars. I recognized Harrison's FBI colleague trotting down the hillside toward us.

Bob was out of the car in a shot, but before slamming the door too decisively, he poked his head back in and leveled a steely glare at me. "Stay in the car, and that goes for your little dog, too, Dorothy. Got it?"

I fumed as the two men trotted back up the hill toward the main plateau in the center of Fort Funston. A whimper of disappointment came from the backseat.

An hour passed. The whimpers had turned into insistent moans. "I know, Skootch. I want out, too." What could be taking so long? I thought about calling Harrison on his cell but realized how stupid that would be. Surely, they had taken the crooks into custody by now. What reason would there be for me to remain here when the action was finished?

I grabbed Skootch's lead and hooked it to his collar. When I opened the door, the dog climbed across my lap in his haste. I was barely on my feet when the first stream of pee sprayed a nearby fencepost. "Sorry, boy. Didn't know you were in such urgent need of relief."

We followed the path of Harrison and the FBI guy up the hill. Skootch zigzagged from tussock to tussock, smelling and marking. When we crested the hill, I saw no evidence of law enforcement personnel or vehicles. It was a nice day, although the fog was starting to come in, and there were more people strolling back toward the parking lot than heading out on the meandering trails. Puzzled, I paused in place and let Skootch rotate around me.

Where could Harrison be? Then I saw them—Margaret and Theo and another of Fang's managers from my ill-fated pitch meeting at Ancient Turtle. No out-of-place business suits this time. The corporate lieutenants were dressed for strolling in the park. I was disappointed Fang wasn't here himself. Margaret had to be present so the new guy could recognize Theo. The body language of the young lovers also provided cover. Holding hands and mooning at each other, they did not look the part for corporate skullduggery.

The trio turned in my direction. Realizing the three should not see me, I turned and headed for the back of Battery Betty. The approach to the bunker from this side was festooned with trees, bushes, and tall brush. I wondered if I could get Skootch to hunker behind a bush and be quiet.

"Pssst. Get the hell up here, Nola." Harrison was using a pile of fallen tree trunks as cover. Joining him, I crouched behind the logs and we placed the dog between us.

"What's taking so long?" I whispered.

Harrison spoke without taking his eyes off the advancing trio. "The third guy was late. The couple has been here for a while. They seem pretty nervous. I hope our cover isn't blown. There are enough people in the park today that they'll probably use the battery to do the handoff. Shush, here they come."

Sure enough, the two men advanced into the tunnel. Shivering in the cool breeze, Margaret remained behind in the open as lookout. Harrison, who had drawn his weapon, signaled FBI guy, who crouched behind a dense bush higher up the hill. He turned to alert someone else we could not see from our vantage point.

The executives passed out of sight into the tunnel where Roger had met his end. In moments, there was a shout, and the two men ran out from the passage, speeding off in different directions. Margaret began to run in yet another direction. Harrison took off after Theo, who had chosen a path near us. Another athletic law enforcement type shot from the tunnel clutching a fat manila envelope, and pounded after the Ancient Turtle manager I didn't know. FBI guy, whose perch was above me, slid past, never stopping his commentary into a headphone mouthpiece, and sprinted after Margaret.

I stood but was pulled off balance by Skootch, who, excited by the chase, yanked the lead from my hands and pranced down the hill tail high. I fell painfully on my knees.

Shaken, I skidded down the remainder of the incline. Safely on the path, I picked up the pace enough to see Margaret apprehended. I also could see several other officers converging on us. Harrison's head and then Theo's bobbed up the path that led down to my Saab and the unmarked cars. Theo's hands were already bound behind him.

I turned to locate Skootch. My dog powered past the officer with the manila envelope and closed on the Ancient Turtle exec. The man had gained the highway that separated Fort Funston from the grounds of the exclusive Olympic Club.

Skootch reached the road just as a large truck crested the rise. The driver braked mightily. I screamed. He swerved. Spooked by the noise of the brakes, Skootch dodged and circled, narrowly avoiding a sedan approaching from the opposite direction. The running man jumped the ditch and disappeared into the woods lining the club's golf course.

"Skootch, come!" I yelled, running. Now on the shoulder of the road, the dog stopped and looked in my direction. He looked back wistfully at the woods where the running man had vanished. He looked back at me.

"Come, boy." Panting, I continued toward him.

The officer with the envelope found his interval between the cars and sprinted across the road. This was too much for Skootch. He accelerated after the running man and was almost hit by a vintage VW microbus sporting a faint haze of psychedelic paint.

As the dog disappeared into the woods, I gained the shoulder. A swarm of cyclists in Lance Armstrong garb, their helmeted heads down, thighs pumping to master the hill, interrupted my progress across the road. Fists clenched in frustration, I heard Harrison call my name in the distance.

At last the cyclists whizzed by, and I sprinted across the road, down the ditch and into the woods. I emerged onto a fairway.

"Hey, get those trespassers out of here," somebody yelled. About a hundred yards ahead, a crowd of people collected at the edge of a green, where a man squatted in contemplation of his lie, his caddie whispering advice. I spotted the winded officer at the edge of the respectful fans because he was still grasping the envelope. I trotted in his direction.

As I neared the throng, a marshal grabbed my arm. "Lady, you don't belong here. I'll escort you to—"

"Sorry." I yanked my arm from his grasp. "I've got to find my dog. You don't want a pointer interrupting your tournament." Before he could answer, I put some distance between us and made a beeline for the officer.

"Did you see where my dog went?" I asked when I reached his side.

"No, I lost your dog and my man in this damn crowd."

Someone in the front said, "Shhhhhhhhhhhhh."

Quietly, we circled the outer edge of the spectators searching for the executive. I pointed to another knot of people just visible about two hundred yards ahead at the next green. I looked over to the tee box pointing down the fairway. We were on seventeen. Going that way would take us in the direction of the eighteenth green, clubhouse, and the exit.

I pointed. "That's the surest way for the fugitive to escape the grounds." We began to trot toward the eighteenth green.

As we neared our objective, we passed the back entrance to the cart return area. A golf cart zoomed along the neat rows of parked carts with two attendants in pursuit. A golf bag broke free from the cart strap and crashed to the pavement, sending one of the attendants sprawling. The other man dodged the clubs, crashed into a parked vehicle, and doubled over. Free of pursuers, the stolen cart climbed a manicured hill.

Tongue pulsing and ears flailing, Skootch broke from behind a high hedge and galloped across a carpet of petunias. He caught up with the cart but fell hard on his first attempt to jump on to the passenger seat. His second try was successful, and a struggle ensued. The cart paused, poised just below the crest of the hill. The chassis rocked. Skootch was on top of the driver. The man alternately beat at the dog's head and tried to push the canine off.

"Hey, you bastard! Hit my dog again and I'll kill you." I hurdled over a clump of lilies like a horseshow contestant in my equestrian days.

The officer had gained his second wind and reached the vehicle well ahead of me but dodged out of the way as it tipped over and slid down the hill on the driver's side.

"Skootch!" The cart canopy faced me, so I could not see my dog. I ran the last few yards and flung my upper body over the edge of the canopy. The man was crumpled on the ruined grass beneath the cart. Skootch's body draped over him, the dog's nose resting in his crotch.

Oh, please God, no. My grip tightened on the canopy. Then Skootch moved and snorted. He shifted his position and rooted in the man's trouser pocket.

"Get'm off me!" The man shoved the dog.

The officer leveled a semiautomatic at him. "You heard the lady; don't hit the dog again."

Skootch teased a plastic bag from the pocket and tore at it with gusto. The oregano-like mulch sifted all over the captive, and Skootch licked up the leaves wherever they landed.

"The guy's a doper, too?" the agent asked.

"Nope, those leaves are some kind of natural Viagra. If Ancient Turtle's management had just tested and gotten FDA approval for the stuff, they'd all be living large in Pacific Heights rather than heading to the penitentiary to punch license plates."

Skootch sighed as the elixir began to take effect. After the disheveled executive was extracted from the cart and taken into custody, the Olympic Club was kind enough to lend me a groundskeeper and utility cart to transport the stoned dog back to the Saab.

* * *

CHAPTER 21

I finished my recommendations for Precision's new investor presentation late Monday night a week after the sting went down. I proofed the file, saved it, and took a final look at my e-mail before turning in. There were no messages from Harrison.

I reflected on the prior week's events. Margaret, Theo, and Fang's other lieutenant were in custody, the two business operations seized. Evidence of theft at more than eighty bioscience companies had been found. Unfortunately, the principals, including Brutus Fang and Casper Wong, had eluded detection. The usual apprehension strategies were implemented: checking all the airports, rental car agencies, credit card usage, cell phone numbers, but no leads had turned up yet. Or Harrison had not chosen to share anything substantive with me.

After the Chevy disaster and my meddling in the case, I needed a personal strategy for putting Harrison's and my relationship back on steady ground. Wondering what deals were available for Las Vegas weekends, I pulled down my favorites menu to select my travel site. There at the top of the list of saved sites was Ancient Turtle. I selected it. Up came the Ancient

Turtle home page. I was surprised that the site was still online. The authorities seized the company, but no one had thought to take the site down. Remembering that Ancient Turtle had overseas locations, I surmised operatives at these distant facilities were keeping the Web presence alive. No, the computer operations of this company were definitely in South San Francisco. The crime tape might be across the door, but the servers were still connected to the Internet.

I rocked in my chair, studying the screen. On the other side of this portal were the answers to all my questions about Roger and the data thieves. I didn't need to meddle with anything, I just needed to look.

But what about Harrison? An image of Sally mouthing the word, sabotage, danced in front of my conscience. Well, I thought, removing my glasses to clean a smudge on the lens, if I don't learn anything, he'll never have to know.

I put the glasses back on and checked the clock on my toolbar. It was a little after ten thirty. I picked up my handset and dialed.

"Talk." A preoccupied Karin answered her lab speakerphone.

"I figured you'd still be at work."

"Because I'm taking a breather from my whirlwind social life?"

"You have a social life?"

"Remind me not to call you when I'm depressed."

"Listen," I cut to the chase, "I need your help and I need it fast." I told her what I had in mind.

Karin bought into my plan and offered her lab as a rendezvous location for our band of proposed coconspirators. Her rapid enlistment and apparent enthusiasm for what was a risky and ethically questionable gambit gave me pause.

"Listen, Karin, I really appreciate your willingness to help, but I need to know you fully understand the problems with what I'm suggesting. I don't know how many laws we'll be breaking, but it has to be a bunch. I'm a bullheaded baby boomer. My idealism and general disrespect for authority would almost get me through this on its own even without the added incentive of nailing corporate bad guys and maybe solving a murder, but this is not your fight."

"Get real," Karin interrupted. "This most assuredly is my fight. We're the biotech brethren. This is our industry. These are our inventions the bastards are screwing with. We're pursuing the greater good here. Some of the science they've snatched is pretty powerful stuff. Such tools in the wrong hands could do a lot of harm."

"You don't think we're being arrogant?"

"So what if we are, if we're right? And you do believe you're right about this, don't you?"

"Yeah. I know it. I know I am."

"Well then, what are we waiting for?"

Karin enlisted Emily Takataru and Fred Kim, the two senior scientists who reported directly to her, to be part of our little scheme. She also called Larry Banks, the IT expert at PGT, and arranged for him to join us at the end of the following workday. I corralled Dakota, Sally, and Serge.

By six o'clock Tuesday evening we were jammed into Karin's already cluttered office next to her new laboratory. While I had briefed Karin on the scope of my plan, I now engaged in full disclosure with the rest of the team. I wanted to be facing them when I explained what I wanted to do. Relying on their friendship, loyalty, and intellectual curiosity, I persuaded them that we needed to find the underlying cause of the industrial thieving conducted by Screen Leaf and Ancient Turtle.

"These companies were involved in systematically stealing America's biotechnical bounty. While this is unscrupulous enough, I believe there are nuances to this conspiracy that are eluding the police, subtleties that biotech specialists can ferret out. By discovering what the creeps are really up to, we can aid the authorities and help our industry protect against similar incursions in the future,"

I studied their sober faces. "The police are happy that they have broken up an industrial espionage ring. They will continue to pursue the leaders who may or may not be hiding in the area. What they won't do is delve any further into the science. What were these people really interested in? It can't be just money. They're already engaged in manufacturing knockoff pharmaceuticals with the same efficiency they apply to handbags and running shoes. My gut tells me there is more to this than the theft of secrets and samples.

"I believe that if we get a look at their data and the way it is stored, we'll discern a pattern and learn what the real goal of this complex subterfuge is. The only evidence I can offer to support my theory is my knowledge of Screen Leaf's client list. Their current clients are not a good fit with their business model. Not even close. They should have pitched Genentech or Amgen, not companies like yours. The same would be true if they were stealing drugs to copy."

Serge shifted his position in the narrow space between Karin's desk and file cabinet. "And we're not exactly going to get an invite from the police to come in and look at the data they've confiscated."

"No, that's for sure." Larry Banks caressed the laptop clutched to his chest. "We'll have to hack our way into their system the same as they did into ours."

"Yeah, and I need to know everybody here is OK with that." I looked from face to face. "You really need to accept what we're about to do and decide if you're comfortable with it. Nobody in this room is going to think any less of you if you walk out right now."

The whir of the refrigerator backed up to the wall of Karin's office dominated the silence like a mechanical mantra. Eye contact in the little room became as scarce as debutants at a hog-calling contest.

"Why don't we set up in the lab." Karin slapped the top of her desk and rose. "There certainly isn't enough room for us to work in here. Emily, you show them where to plug in their laptops, and, Fred, how about calling Antonio's for pizza. Interfering with a police investigation is bound to make me hungry." Karin popped out from behind her chair and plowed through us to the door.

Freed from moral inertia by Karin's action, our gaggle of geeks emerged from the tiny office and spread out along the isles of the lab. I followed in Emily's wake as she indicated usable network connections and shoved lab notebooks aside to make room for computers. Larry settled into a spot, squeezing his laptop between a sequencer and a PCR system. Serge huddled behind him as his fingers flew over the keys. They grunted as things began to happen on Larry's screen and conversed in low tones without looking away from the action.

Karin and Fred, who had quickly placed the pizza order, emerged from a closet at the far end of the room pushing a projector console. They pointed the projector toward the lab's windows. Seeing their purpose, Emily pulled down the opaque window blind which would serve as a makeshift screen.

I asked Sally to do a rundown of Chinese science and foreign policy in the news to see if this suggested anything to the group.

Positioning Dakota on a stool in front of the projector, and using his script-capable laptop for data input, Karin and I began to dictate to him a rough diagram of what we knew about Screen Leaf and the clients it had duped.

"I think we'll call ourselves the RNA Irregulars," Karin said as she studied the makeshift screen. "We're all about translating messages and synthesizing ideas which are what RNA does. Without it a gene's work would never get done."

"Ha, and our industry already comes with its own Dr. Watson." Emily referred to the co-discoverer of the DNA double helix.

"Enough, you guys, let's focus," I said.

By ten o'clock, we had consumed the pizza, salads, and spumoni Fred had ordered and cleaned out the vending machines on two floors of PGT's building. The coffeemaker in Karin's office was on its fourth pot, and the supply of Starbuck's grounds was exhausted. It had not taken Larry and Serge long to find their way inside Screen Leaf's operations and only a little longer to breech the Ancient Turtle security. Larry took quiet satisfaction in following the same cyber path the interlopers had used to get into Peninsula in reverse. The challenge facing us was what to look for, where to look for it, and how to interpret what we found. We assigned Larry to research and development files and Serge to administrative and operational files.

"Dakota, gimme that cord," Larry said twenty minutes later. "I want you guys to see this index I found."

Dakota obliged, and Larry's computer was hooked to the projector. Once the image appeared for everyone to see, he began to scroll down the massive list.

"Hey, stop." Dakota pointed. "Can you click on that link?"

Larry did as asked and the link opened.

"That's frightening." Dakota riveted his eyes on the screen. "You guys are looking at files of a very important CAI project that has not been announced publicly yet. I'm working on illustrations for the scientific paper, but it won't be submitted for another month. That's why I recognized the file name."

"Well, we knew these guys stole from you and from us and from other companies, but look at the scope of this. It's massive." Karin shook her head. "Go up a level, Larry, I want to get a sense of how all this is catalogued."

Another hour melted away as Larry clicked and clicked opening file after file and following link upon link. We stood in a little arc around him staring at the makeshift screen and occasionally asking that a particular folder be opened.

"Gosh, can anybody name a biotech company whose data we haven't seen tonight? My back is killing me." Karin pressed her knuckles into her sides and arched her shoulders. "Let's take a break."

"Sally, anything turn up from your end?" I asked.

"Not really. Trade issues. Human rights issues. Blustering at Taiwan. MacDonald's in Beijing. There's a touching article about some poor woman who had a second child against the State's policy and was penalized severely. Some Panda coverage. The only things really medical are about avian flu and acupuncture."

Karin and I strolled out of the lab and along the corridor to the restroom. "I don't think we're going to find what they're up to in the headlines," Karin said.

I sighed. "I just hoped we'd get a fresh idea somehow. Some of our biotech colleagues are working on flu vaccines. There was a file in there on Enza Biologicals."

"Point taken." Karin pushed her stall door shut.

After everyone reassembled, I asked Larry to go back up to the master index so that we could look at it with fresh eyes.

"OK." I marched to the front of the room and gestured at the screen. "Here we have the files organized by company, here by project, and here by industry category. Over here, they've organized and cross-referenced the same information by disease. Geez, these guys are thorough. This file groups the data by medical specialty. We've been doing the needle-in-the-haystack drill all night. Maybe instead of looking for something, we should look for the absence of something."

"Yes," Karin said, "but if we're going to do that, we'd better not start with the company or project files. They would be too complex. We'd never notice the omissions. Why not start with diseases and disorders? That way everybody can play."

Larry clicked open the specialties file. Silence ensued as our weary group stared at the screen.

"Fred, get the Merck manual," Karin ordered. "At this hour, we're not above using a crutch. Merck'll be our Cliff's Notes."

Fred returned from Karin's office flipping the well-worn pages of the manual. "Infectious disease," he intoned.

"Check," said Karin.

Immunological and allergic disorders."

"Check."

"Cardiovascular disease?"

"Uhhuh."

"Pulmonary Disorders?"

"Check?"

"Liver?"

"Yeap."

"Metabolic?"

"Right."

"Endocrine?"

"Hold it."

As one, we edged toward the screen.

"There's no file for endocrine," Karin said.

"Wait. Let's not get too excited," I cautioned. "Read the rest of the list."

Fred turned back to the Merck index, continuing with hematology and oncology and concluding with venomous bites and stings. We were frozen in our places transfixed by the screen, only now Karin had a grip on my arm that was turning my fingers numb.

"Notice anything else missing?" she hissed.

"Yeah, even a non-scientist would notice this," Sally said. "There's no gynecology and obstetrics."

"Right on!" Karin squealed. "Larry, do a keyword search and see if you can find endocrine stuff stored anywhere else on their server. Check for hormones produced by the endocrine system. Try follicle-stimulating hormone or just FSH or maybe luteinizing hormone. That's LH for short."

"I've got an idea! What time is it?" I flipped the clam on my cell phone.

"Ten minutes to the witching hour," Sally said, "but who's counting?"

I paused for a moment realizing I'd probably be rousting the Prices out of bed. "Oh well, I could lose a client over this." I punched Leonard Price's home number.

Price answered on the third ring, and it was obvious from his slurred speech that I had awakened him from a deep sleep.

"Leonard, I'm really sorry to call so late, but is your wife there?"

"Nola? What the. Yeah, Peggy's right here. Beside me. In bed."

"Pass the phone to her and go back to sleep. You're getting a day's free consulting for the insult."

Sheet ruffles and mumbles were all I could hear. I think Price dropped the receiver. My phone went dead. I stared at the readout and noted that the timer had stopped. Before I could redial, the unit rang. "Hello?"

"Nola, this is Peggy. What's wrong?"

I fumbled through an expurgated explanation of the night's activities, realizing that it all sounded farfetched. "Basically, Peggy, we want your take on how interested the Chinese government might be in learning about the hormones that support fertility."

"They'd be very interested, but for the exact opposite reason I would be. My team at UCSF is trying to help infertile couples become parents. In Western society, the fertility problems we have are associated with couples not being able to get pregnant or women unable to sustain a pregnancy to term. In contrast, the Chinese have an overpopulation problem. They would like to manage fertility down, to reduce the number of births. They've been addressing it at the policy level since the seventies. Yet they still do not have as low a birthrate as Japan or Thailand. Legislating penalties and engendering cultural approbation for having more than one child have only accomplished so much. A particular problem occurs when a couple has a girl child. They want a male no matter what the government says. Since legal and social approaches haven't completely accomplished their goals, the Chinese authorities might be looking for scientific ways to prevent fertility."

"Bingo, FSH worked." Larry alerted Karin behind me.

"Would they be interested in follicle-stimulating hormone?" I asked.

"Sure," Peggy said. "The pituitary gonadotropins, FSH and LH, are governed by gonadotropin-releasing hormone or GnRH, and are responsible for regulating follicular development and ovulation in women. The same hormones play a role in male fertility. If you interfered with the timely secretion of these hormones, you could achieve something like medical castration or, in the case of females, oophorectomy."

"Wow, how would you do that?"

"Oh, it's actually being done," Peggy said. "People are perfecting long-acting inhibitors of the master regulator GnRH. Today, proliferative diseases that are hormone-dependent are treated with such products. Endometriosis, breast cancer, and prostate cancer are examples.

"I suppose you also could focus on an Inhibin strategy," she continued. "That's a peptide secreted by cells in the ovary that prevents the secretion of FSH and thus the maturation of germ cells."

"I think we're on to something here." My mind was racing.

"I have to caution you, though," Peggy said. "The interaction of hormones and steroids in fertility is extremely complex. In addition, the Chinese would be looking for something that could be applied to the mass population so it would have to be easy and very, very cheap. There has been significant progress in developing orally available versions of the new therapies, but how are you going to get people to take a drug that will render them infertile on a mass scale? That would be the fertility equivalent of Jones Town. If people were that docile, wouldn't they dutifully take birth control pills or just follow the rules about having a single child?"

"I don't think they're intended to know they are getting it." I recalled Sally's reference to the non-compliant woman who had the second child in defiance of state edict. "How long-acting are these GnRH agonists? If you could get them in the body, would they prevent fertility over an extended period? Could they be administered using vaccine technology? Are they candidates for use with gene therapy? Or maybe a timed-release implantable technology?"

"Ah, now I see where you're going. Well, the current agents aren't there yet, but a focused development program could probably get them to the point where they could be accommodated within an annual public health vaccination program of some kind. Longer-term gene therapy would be the way to go. Perhaps inducing the body to produce ineffective protein versions of FSH and LH would be the right methodology. The nice thing about this hormone-targeted strategy is that you could apply it to men and women. With these technologies, you could inoculate large numbers of people who think they're being immunized against the annual influenza epidemic when what you're really doing is genetically sterilizing them until they're too old to have kids. This conversation is giving me the creeps."

I apologized again to Peggy for the late-night call. I would have to beg forgiveness from her husband in the morning because I could hear his snores in the background."

I rejoined Karin and Larry, who were delving through the special storage area on the Ancient Turtle server they had unearthed with the keyword search. There it all was. The companies who had made advances in hypothalamic and pituitary hormone research were all grouped in this exclusive file. And there with them were the leadership companies in the vaccine technology and gene therapy fields. Foremost among the latter was Peninsula Gene Therapy and the work of its leading scientist, Karin Mullins.

"Those bastards are planning to use my new vectors for their slimy, underhanded, anti-feminine crap." Karin slammed her fist on the lab bench. "I develop this stuff to save lives, and these scumbags pervert my discoveries! Self-righteous, controlling bastards! I haven't even published these findings yet."

"Calm down, boss," Fred said. "You're gonna pop an artery. Let the cops deal with the creeps. Our work here is done."

"Not quite," came a triumphant voice from behind us.

Larry and Serge divided the work in order to speed the file-searching process. While the sleuthing through the research and development files assigned to Larry had taken center stage all evening, Serge had been equally busy but largely ignored as he perused the electronic business records of the Screen Leaf and Ancient Turtle operations. Now, it was his time to shine.

I studied his find. "Serge, you've discovered a massive inventory buildup of late stage development and manufacturing equipment. This is far beyond anything Screen Leaf could have required to run its operations."

"No kidding. I've been analyzing their invoices and shipping manifests, and I think I know where this inventory is kept."

Now that they had Karin's nifty vector technology, our Chinese friends were ready to scale up their fertility control scheme. I had much to report to Harrison. The warehouse with the inventory of production goods was located in Oakland. In all probability, the missing executives were hiding there among these pharmaceutical production assets.

Despite the urgent need to apprehend Fang and Wong, I decided I would wait until morning to call Harrison. I was so tired, I could no longer string a coherent sentence together, and I had awakened enough people for one night.

We made halfhearted offers to help put Karin's lab back in order, but Fred and Emily shooed us out saying they'd handle it the following day.

* * *

CHAPTER 22

Although I was bone-tired from my long night, I rose at seven. Janie Belle brightly inquired about my whereabouts the prior evening and was miffed when I brushed her off. I had to get to Harrison with my team's explosive news.

I punched four of the numbers to his cell phone before I came to my senses. I was about to tell Harrison some important information that would break open the case, but I would also have to tell him how I obtained this knowledge. He would not be a happy camper. There was no way I could avoid his displeasure, but by composing my thoughts and presenting my case in the best possible light, I could mitigate his anger.

Grabbing a legal pad and pen, I began to make a list of bullet points I could tweak into a logical argument. My computer issued a ping, heralding the arrival of e-mail. It was from Sally. She had been up early doing more research on the Chinese. Her message was packed with data. China's State Family Planning Agency had instituted its one child policy in the late seventies. Over the ensuing decades, they had driven the fertility rate from 2.9 in 1979 to 1.7 several years ago, but the rate drop had stalled. The state planners needed something dramatic if they were to drive the numbers to the next level. Other countries in Asia had been successful at achieving lower numbers: Japan was at 1.38, Singapore was at 1.04 and Hong Kong was at 0.91. That last one must be a thorn in their side. It also was not lost on me that China's political and economic situation was light years from Japan's. That was another reason they would reach out for a technical solution to narrow the gap.

I incorporated Sally's data into a new bullet point on my pad and consumed another fifteen minutes completing my argument. It was quarter after eight, a perfect time to reach Harrison. I called his cell phone and got message mode. I called his office phone and ended up in voice mail. Just in case, I placed a call to his apartment. I didn't leave a message on that phone. There would not be anyone at reception until eight thirty. Now that my remarks were prepared, I was anxious to deliver them. I punched the number for the front desk at his office, and the recorded message answered. My shoulders slumped back against the chair. In my exhausted condition, it was going to be hard to stay pumped. I pressed the redial key. The message played again. My computer's clock said 8:31. Damned city employees. Can't even spell the word punctual. I hit the redial again.

"Hello?" The receptionist spoke through a mouthful of something. Despite my impatience, I politely asked to speak with Harrison. "Oh, he's in his staff meeting" was the muted response followed by a swallow. The next bit was clearer: "They usually run about an hour and a half. Is there a message?"

After ascertaining that the meeting had started at eight, I left Bob a message to call me as soon as he got out. Disappointed and feeling the effects of the previous night, I rocked in my chair and wondered what I could do for nearly an hour to keep myself from dozing off.

I read my e-mails, checked my home page for the day's weather, and scrolled through my stock portfolio. Some of my picks were performing quite well, but in my present mood, this couldn't cheer me. My eyes started to close. I shook myself awake. I would need to do something more active to stay alert.

Clicking to my favorite search engine, I typed in Ancient Turtle and scrolled the links that came up. I clicked on a promising link and found myself on the Web page of a professor of religion at UCLA. In rich, academic prose, the scholar reviewed the myths associated with the turtle reaching back into earliest Chinese history. Representing long life, wisdom, steadfastness, and immutability, the turtle was variously the protector god of the north, the bearer of the universe, and the symbol of winter and water, whose shell was the very vault of heavens. The turtle mated with the snake, the original yin of the creation myth. While the creature's long life could attain for him infinite wisdom and oracle powers, the female's habit of leaving her eggs unattended forever linked the turtle to the concept of bastardies. The beast also was known as the Black Warrior.

I wondered which aspect of this rich anthology had appealed to the founders of the Ancient Turtle Company. Probably the sexual angle. Mating with a snake would appeal to Fang. Brutus's face swam unbidden into view. His body elongated and slithered across the top of his desk. A turtle logo on the front of a company brochure lying on his blotter began to grow. The logo presented the turtle from the bottom and the creature that emerged from the image was on its back. It fought to right itself as it continued to grow. The thing managed to flip over before it got so big it would not fit on the desk.

As it continued to morph, the turtle fixed an eye on me. I could not move my arms or turn my head away. I could not even close my eyes to avoid its reptilian stare. My eyes followed as its head rose. The body stretched, compressed, and reformed in a fluid and unfocused progression.

I tried to breathe, but my chest would not rise. I felt as if I were in a shell, a shrinking, constraining shell. Now fully formed the Black Warrior stood before me. He reached behind Fang's desk and drew out a broad, gleaming sword. His eyes, obsidian, continued to fix on me. I fell from my chair to the floor still unable to breathe. The warrior stepped closer and raised the gleaming sword over his head. I watched helplessly as the blade descended.

The phone ring scared me awake, and I knocked my coffee cup and a large stack of journals from my desk. The falling journals unseated the handset from the cradle, sending the phone spinning to the floor between the desk and my file cabinet. I crawled under the desk to retrieve it and banged my head as I answered. "Hell. Ouch!" was what the greeting sounded like.

"Nola? What are you doing?"

"Harrison. At last. Ah, I just knocked the phone off the desk, that's all. I kind of dozed off and you startled me."

"Sorry. But I'm returning your call. Or calls, I should say."

"Yeah. I really needed to talk to you."

"Well, have at it."

Here goes nothing, I thought. All my energy from before was spent. The dream had left me even more drained. My legal pad with the bullet points was somewhere under the pile of journals. "Ah, my colleagues and I thought you could use some help with the, ah, more scientific dimension of the investigation."

"Really."

"Yeah, we felt there was more to this thing than just industrial secrets."

"Go on."

Given this much of an opening without any negative feedback, I launched into a detailed explanation and justification of our sleuthing. I gathered steam as I went, and by the time I finished off the anti-fertility plot and progressed into the warehouse buildup, I was almost as peppy as I had been when I first called his office.

"So you see, the real purpose of their plot is directed at their own people. This is why they've taken such risks and why you'll be able to capture Fang, Wong, and their associates. They couldn't leave here because they need to arrange the transport of the stuff in the Oakland warehouse. They need to do this secretly not just to avoid apprehension on this end, but so they can keep things under raps on their end too."

I rocked back in my armchair, satisfied. "I think I've covered everything. I'm fagged after our near all-nighter, so maybe you'd like to ask some questions now. That way I can clear up any fuzzy bits."

"Oh, I think it's pretty clear. You and your little band of CSI-wannabes hacked into the servers over at Ancient Turtle that we purposely left up and running to monitor activity from additional bad guys.

"Ah, that explains why the site is still up."

"And then, you muck around in what will be evidence when any of these people are brought to trial, and I might add that much of the intellectual property in those files belongs to other law-abiding companies who may be your competitors and who would be unappreciative of unauthorized persons stomping through their data uninvited."

"We would never divulge any—"

"That's hardly the point is it, Nola?"

"Look, we wanted to help, and thought we had expertise to bring to the table."

"You just don't get it, do you? Miss Fix-it. You're too smart to be this naive. This is blatantly willful on your part."

This was not going well. "I really respect what you do and—"

"You don't respect what I do. I can't believe you just said that. And I see that I can't trust you to stay out of my business."

This was worse than I had imagined. Your lover not trusting you couldn't be good for a relationship. I needed to make amends and pronto. "Harrison, listen, I…"

"No, you listen. I'm getting off the phone now. I'm going to follow up on that Oakland address you gave me. I will be getting back to you later, but listen up and listen good. I want the names of every person who was a party to your little operation. You are to drop whatever you were planning to do next and call each one of them until you reach them in person. Tell them they are not to even think about going back into Screen Leaf or Ancient Turtle. They are to make themselves available for debriefing by my people. I will be collecting their laptops."

"And, now, as for you, Nola," Harrison's voice grew cold and slowed to a scary crawl. He spat my name out like a bad tasting mouthful. "If you do anything, and I mean *anything* more that touches on this investigation, I will arrest you for obstructing justice. You might not respect me, but believe me, you will respect the justice system up close and personal."

The line went dead. I cradled the handset in my lap. The lack of sleep, the disturbing dream, and the thorough dressing down my lover had just given me proved overwhelming. Tears slid down my cheeks, coalesced at my chin, and dove like suicides onto the hard case of the handset below.

I had taken my entrepreneurial spirit into a place it had no business going. Huddled in the cold room, I saw myself as he must see me, a self-important dilettante with no boundaries. Ego trumped judgment and the result was the loss of a very special man. I felt myself shrinking, knowing there was no rabbit hole in which to escape.

Humbly, tail between my legs, I called the members of my sleuthing team to let them know that the police did not appreciate their assistance and ordered them to cease and desist. Dakota, Emily, and Serge were terrified. Larry and Fred were mystified. Sally was insulted. Karin was unrepentant and downright belligerent.

"Where do they get off telling us to butt out?" she boomed into the receiver. "It's my technology that's being subverted. Harrison is turning into a tight-assed martinet. He's got some nerve."

As her decibel level rose, my spirits lifted a little. Why had I shed tears over this guy? I tried to lend him a hand, and he slapped it away. I rose and began to pace as Karin bitched on.

"He can't see the DNA for the amino acids. If he gives us any more grief, we'll get a lawyer and sue his sorry ass."

"Hang on, Karin, all the lawyers you know are patent guys."

"Not so. A fellow who lives downstairs from me is a bona fide ambulance chaser! Not everybody I know is a biotech nerd."

"Listen, girl, I want you to know just how much you've cheered me up. I got you in trouble, and I've definitely ruined a perfectly good sexual relationship, so I was doing the dance of depression. But you've been as good as a life preserver in a sea squall."

"Holy wild-caught halibut, woman, you've got nothing to apologize for. Lift your head up and square those shoulders. Let him stew by himself without any nooky for a while. He'll come crawling back. Bank on it."

I placed the handset back on its cradle. I wasn't ready to picture Harrison crawling, but Karin had lit a tiny candle of hope. Still standing, I surveyed my desk and tried to focus on client work that needed doing. The long night at Karin's lab and the explosive interchange with Harrison had erased all thoughts of business obligations. I struggled to remember what proposals and presentations I owed and to whom. Realizing I needed to FedEx my plan to Precision, I opened the document and directed three copies to my printer. I grabbed a FedEx envelope and mailing label and filled in the required information. Suddenly full of nervous energy, I was anxious to get out of my office and hit the road, but it would take a little longer for the copies to print. I swiveled frenetically in front of my computer, fingers drumming on the wrist rest in front of the keyboard. The printer labored on.

A conviction formed in my mind. Harrison might dismiss my thesis about the Chinese government pursuing a plan to use genetics to sterilize their own citizens, but I knew people who would take it seriously. Very seriously.

I pulled myself closer to the desk, opened a new e-mail message, and began to type. Outlining the conspiracy my colleagues and I unearthed as cogently as I could, I closed with the deduction that the authorities on this side of the Pacific would not pursue this avenue because of the difficulties in proving anything and the diplomatic sensitivities. I typed Rupert Lee's e-mail address in the recipient slot and reread what I had written. I made a few edits and read the paragraphs a final time. Satisfied, I moved the mouse to press the send button.

A little voice whispered that I might want to reconsider sharing this information. Pausing, I remembered Rupert's wonderful daughter, Brenda, bounding down the stairs of the Nob Hill house. How many fantastic girls like Brenda would not be born because an overreaching government had decided to interfere in the most intimate of life's decisions. I clicked the button and the message leaped from my screen like an electronic Paul Revere.

"One if by land," I said.

I collected and stacked the proposal copies, encased them in the folder, and slipped the folder carefully into the shipping envelope whose transparent sleeve already contained the completed label. I stripped off the tab and sealed the package.

Halfway to the door, purse in one hand and envelope in the other, I halted.

"And two if by sea."

Dumping the purse and package at the door, I returned to my desk and rummaged through the top drawer. The card I was searching for had worked its way to the back. Opening the message I had just sent, I copied the contents and pasted it into a new e-mail. I copied the e-mail address on the business card into the send window of the duplicate e-mail, pressed send, and tossed the business card of Randolph Chen, Roger's uncle, back into my desk drawer.

* * *

CHAPTER 23

"I am sooooooooo glad you're coming to church tonight." Janie Belle put the finishing touches on her makeup in the hall mirror. "You haven't been in ages. I am always making excuses for you with the rector."

"I'm sure he's not losing sleep over the condition of my immortal soul." Feeling guilty about neglecting Janie Belle for clients and clandestine crime solving, I had, in a weak moment, agreed to an evening of church followed by dinner out. I followed the octogenarian to the garage.

It took several tries to parallel park in front of the church because the space was just big enough for the Saab. An impatient driver behind us gunned around my hood, causing Janie Belle to emit an unchristian epithet.

We entered the dank and dimly lit nave, settling into an empty pew midway up the center aisle. Janie Belle preceded me in, deposited her handbag, pulled out a kneeler, and began to pray, no doubt asking God to forgive her sinner daughter for a burdensome list of offenses, at the head of which was my stubborn insistence on remaining a spinster. As for the rest of the list, I hoped her knees held out.

The service began. The celebrant was our assistant rector, a newly minted priest. An exuberant fellow, Andrew embraced his new role as certified cleric with gusto. He seemed determined to practice until perfect every sacrament, chant, blessing, and collect in the Anglican armamentarium. Since his ordination, the congregation had been subjected to daily Eucharists. The Altar Guild was, according to Janie Belle, about to mutiny. The fair linen was being worn out before its time.

A zealous parishioner had donated a costly thurible and aspersorium. Andrew, the newbie, was overjoyed. The acolytes were drilled in the swinging of the censor, and there had been two fires so far. Andrew reserved the aspersorium for himself. With my spotty attendance record, this would be my first opportunity to witness his sprinkling skill.

As a rule, Episcopalians aren't sprinkled a lot. We like our clergy to remain up in the chancel. Sure, they can come down from the altar to the center aisle and bring us the Gospel. The Gospel is an old friend, and the chosen passage is printed in the bulletin, so there are no surprises.

I let my mind wander and absently followed Janie Belle's cues as she knelt or stood or sat as required. I wondered what Harrison was doing. Before we left for church, I had received a terse text message from him reporting the seizure of the Oakland warehouse but the failure to apprehend the company executives. No matter, I still advanced his investigation, and someday he'd thank me.

I resolved to tell him about my roommate Joyce Strand's murder and how I had never gotten over the botched handling of her killer's case. Hell, I had never gotten over Joyce's slaying in any way, shape or form. I wasn't trying to be disrespectful of professionals and certainly not of him; violent death just made me a little crazy. Perhaps Bob could connect my feelings of loss and frustration with his own over the death of his partner in Baltimore, conjure up a little sympathy, and maybe some forgiveness.

Janie Belle tugged at my elbow and sidled toward the middle of the pew. Pulled from my reverie, which had segued from a contemplation of Harrison's investigation to total recall of his physique, I glared at her for interrupting. She gestured for me to move with her. I ignored the summons.

"It's your funeral," she hissed.

I glanced up the aisle and saw the procession descending the steps. Andrew was resplendent in the most florid of the church's vestment collection, a number with a gilt cruciform edged in flames made of red and orange beading. When the material shifted with the motions of the wearer, the effect was less like flames than feathers. I wondered if anyone else thought the garment evoked an Incan high priest in exotic bird plumes. The birdman was abreast of me, facing the congregants across the aisle. As I lifted my eyes from the beads to his face, Andrew turned and slung an aspergillum full of water in my face.

I sputtered and almost spat back before I caught myself. He had gotten my glasses and my mascara. A black streak slithered down my cheek, and the rest burned my eye. I reached down and fumbled in my purse for a tissue. One was thrust at me at bosom level. I took it and dabbed my lashes, but not before noticing with my one functioning eye the water stains across the front of my silk blouse.

Janie Belle was at my side. She'd sidled back because Andrew had made the turn and was coming up the side aisle rendering her mid-pew position no longer safe. She pressed against me, almost pushing me out of the row as he passed our pew in his progress toward the front of the church.

"Can't be too careful." She held her open prayer book up for protection. The trajectory of his blessed drops, flung earnestly as he passed, fell short of our location.

I shook hands decorously as we exited the church and resolved to deposit my cleaning bill in the plate next time I came to services.

Getting out of the tight parking space was going to be a challenging. I idled the car discussing restaurants with Janie Belle, hoping that another parishioner would come and remove one of the vehicles that hemmed me in. "What about the Italian place? We haven't been there since it changed hands."

"Isn't that the same banshee who passed us when we parked?" Janie looked beyond me.

I turned but wasn't quick enough to make out the car she referred to. The streetlight ahead was not operating, and during the service the fog had rolled in. "Sorry, I missed it." I turned back to her. "Want to do Chinese?"

We settled on Tsing Tao, a reliable restaurant on Ocean Avenue, and a fellow churchman extracted his venerable Mercedes from the slot in front of us, only dinging us once in the process. We eased out behind him and left-turned our way back to Ocean.

The restaurant's proprietor seated us in a choice window alcove. Cars hissed by on the wet pavement, but traffic was light and the lamps and their reflections softened by the growing fog made a pleasant Impressionist scene. We ordered drinks along with the Imperial appetizer platter and studied the lengthy, well-thumbed pages of the tasseled menus.

"There he goes again!"

"Who?" I looked up from the pork section.

"The driver from in front of the church."

"Now you're imagining things. You've gone too long without bourbon." I shook my head and returned to the menu.

The proprietor took our order personally. If we weren't regulars we'd have been flattered, but we knew the reason was that our server couldn't speak a word of Engresch.

The appetizers were scrumptious, our excellent entrees came up quickly, and we ordered green tea ice cream for dessert. Janie Belle poured us both tea and extracted a packet of artificial sweetener from her purse.

"Mother, you don't put sugar in this kind of tea. Please don't embarrass me again. Can't you just sip the stuff the way the Chinese intended it?"

Ignoring me, Janie Belle signaled the waitress. "Honey, I could use some cream for this." She pointed at the teacup. The girl bowed and smiled the frozen grin of the clueless. She whirled around and minced in the direction of the kitchen.

Moments later, she returned with a fresh pot of piping hot tea. She placed it on the table and reached to remove the cups of tepid brew before us. Having sweetened hers to treacley perfection, Janie Belle swept her cup out of her reach. The girl looked perplexed but recovered and removed my cup and the old pot.

"Miss, miss! You haven't brought the cream."

"Gleam?" said the girl. Janie Belle nodded excitedly. The girl disappeared again.

I chugged my tea as if it were scotch.

The girl returned to our table. "No gleams," she said. "You tekka clabba?"

"Clabber? Why in heaven's name would they be offering clabber to customers?" Janie Belle repeated, mystified. "OK, kid, I guess it'll have to do."

I ignored the cultural abyss yawning before me, retrieved my credit card, and signaled for the check. The owner rose from his station by the cash register, but our waitress intercepted him. She launched into rapid fire Cantonese. Finally, the proprietor got a word in. The server listened and headed for the kitchen.

The man smiled across the restaurant at me and gave me the universal palms up gesture for wait-a-second. Resigned, I sipped more tea.

Shortly, the owner approached our table and deposited our check on a lacquered tray with fortune cookies. The swinging door to the kitchen burst open and our attention was drawn to the two emerging employees. One was our waitress, and the other was the cook.

"I so glad you order this dish," he began as he reached our table. "Only Chinese order this. No Western peoples. You like." The girl placed a large plate of steaming food in front of Janie Belle.

The owner beamed. "When Missus Belle order the crab, chef was really pleased. He fixed it for her Hakka style. Very fancy. Sorry, we're out of clams. I thought it strange you want seafood after ice cream, but my son, he study for business degree at San Francisco State, he say customer is always right."

I glanced at the bill just presented to me. The last item entered before the revised total was crab something. "Well, that explains the clabba mystery," I said, handing the owner my credit card.

"Oh!" said the cook, handing me an envelope, "A man bring you this to back door. Said give to lady in window."

I tore the flap and extracted the single piece of paper contained therein. "We've got to go." I slid out of the booth.

Leaving was not that easy. Janie Belle insisted on taking the crab dish home in a carton. The chef carefully packaged his culinary masterpiece along with an extra helping of rice and more fortune cookies.

"Hey, careful!" Janie Belle cautioned as I all but shoved her into the passenger side of the car. "I don't want to upset my crab whatsa."

"I'm sorry, Mother, but I've got to drop you off and get somewhere fast." I jumped behind the wheel and shoved the gear into reverse. I made a U-turn on Ocean and traversed the slick streets of the residential stretch between the commercial enclave and our home rather faster than I should have. I pulled into the garage, threw my door open, and grabbed the food bag to hasten Janie Belle's exit from the Saab. I unlocked the house door for her and handed her the parcel.

"I'll be back late." I hustled to the car.

"Where are you going at this hour?"

"Presidio." I was almost knocked off my feet by a flash of fur. Skootch gained the driver's and then the passenger seat before I could stop him.

"Shit!" I said getting back into the Saab; I'd just have to take him. Janie Belle was transfixed by the headlights as I backed from the garage.

I peeled out on Plymouth Avenue and careened toward Sloat Boulevard. The piece of paper said the men I sought were in the abandoned enlisted personnel housing on the Baker Beach side of the Presidio base. The shadow car of Janie Belle's imaginings was real. We had been followed. The men hiding out in the crumbling housing on the former Army base could only be Fang and Wong, but I had to be sure. If I gave Harrison another lead in this case, it had better be accurate or I would not succeed in getting my ass out of the sling it was in.

As I straightened the car out of a swerve executed to make the light on Nineteenth, I realized Skootch was whining.

"Sorry, boy." I rolled his window down. We sped north, Skootch's elegant ebony ear snapping in the aggressive night wind.

I gritted my teeth as the car's tires made noise in the gravel of the weedy parking area below the ribbon of base housing.

I coasted the last thirty feet, and the Saab came to rest at the edge of the lot against an overgrown hedge. When the Presidio had been under military control, the grounds were clipped like a recruit's buzz cut. Now that the Park Service was in charge, things looked neglected.

The disposition of the base housing, as with all things in San Francisco, had taken a turn to the controversial. Officer housing was reserved for park employees and what was left was leased to lucky outlanders. The fifties-style enlisted housing was not deemed worth the renovation required to achieve code standards. However, homeless advocates targeted these structures as ideal for the grocery-cart-driving dispossessed. Encouraged by organizers, squatters had taken up residence in several units. The police and park officials left the trespassers alone while negotiations evolved. Human activity randomly dispersed throughout the otherwise abandoned row houses created an ideal environment for criminals on the lam.

"Skootch, you'll have to stay here," I said to the contented dog. Skootch gazed happily into the darkness, hoping for a glimpse of a rabbit or raccoon.

Squinting at the overgrown path that jutted upward from the parking area, I realized how alone I was out here in the dark. There were patrols circling through the Presidio, but this was a sprawling expanse with a multitude of roads and footpaths. What was I thinking coming out here solo?

"Skootch, how is that somebody as smart as I am gets herself into such stupid situations?" Too smart for your own good. Too smart for Harrison. He wants a woman who is more, more what? Compliant. Feminine. Less cerebrum. More pituitary.

The dog panted softly. It was so quiet in the secluded lot, I could hear my own breathing. I pulled open my purse and extracted my cell phone. Someone should know I came here in case something happens. But it wasn't going to be Harrison.

Determined to avoid another volcanic eruption induced by this interloping civilian, I punched Sally's number. No answer. I severed the connection as the answering machine came on, not wanting to leave my whereabouts as a message. Next, I tried Dakota.

"Dakota, its Nola," I said in a rush when he answered. "I'm about to do something naughty, and I need to tell somebody in case things don't go as planned." The suggestion that I had any kind of plan made what I was about to do seem even more ludicrous.

"Hope it involves good sex." I could hear Sacagawea or Meriwether yapping in the background.

"No such luck. I got a tip that the bad guys are holed up in the Presidio in the abandoned housing, but I don't want to hand this information over to Harrison and his buddies unless it's true, so I'm going to, ah, tiptoe around and look in some windows. If I locate Fang or Wong, I'll call it in immediately.

His tone changed to concern. "Nola, you're crazy. What if they see you first? You could get hurt."

"I only need one sighting; then I'll come back to the car and split."

"I'm afraid for you. Those guys know you, Nola. They killed Roger, right?"

"Yeah. It sure looks that way. I'll be super careful."

"Nola, the police warned us to butt out. What part of cease and desist don't you understand?"

"I created a mess, I know, but it's like I put myself in a tunnel and the only way out is forward."

"Can't I talk you out of this? This is a very bad idea."

"No, you can't, but what you can do is hang by your phone for a while. If anything goes wrong, I'm going to hit redial and alert you immediately, and you can call for reinforcements."

A sigh of resignation on the other end of the line. "I'll be right here." Dakota's tone was glum and unconvinced.

"Good, hang in there! I'm going to start with the units that are just above Baker Beach, and my car is parked in the lot that is halfway up the hill." I disconnected before he could try to persuade me to abandon my course of action

"Stay, boy." I opened the car door, shoved my cell phone in one pocket and the car keys in the other, and shut the door as quietly as I could. Looking at my leather shoes, I realized how inappropriately dressed I was for sneaking up on bad guys. Remembering that my gym bag was in the trunk, I weighed exchanging the leather flats for my Sauconys but rejected the idea because of the sound I would make shutting the trunk.

I started up the unlit path. As I felt my way along, my eyes began to adjust, and shapes emerged from the gloom. I could make out a railing, a helpful assist because the path was beginning to climb. A branch brushed my face, depositing chilly dew on my cheek and jaw. I wiped and trudged and wiped again as another branch slapped my forehead. Drops of dew joined the holy water on my ruined blouse.

I was winded when I gained the summit. Leaning against the rail, I listened for human sounds among the murmurs and creaks of the surrounding night. The row of units immediately in front of me appeared completely dark. I edged along the end unit until I gained the rear yards. The backyards of the next line of houses abutted these. Those units also appeared to be deserted.

Perhaps my informant had been wrong. Maybe it had been somebody's idea of a joke, and the funster, snuggly tucked in at home, was even now chuckling at my discomfort. What if it was Harrison, teaching me a lesson for meddling in official business?

Maybe I'd just started with the wrong cluster of houses. I trudged along. This police work was drudgery. They were not kidding about the shoe leather it took to track down miscreants.

Ahead and to the left, another row of housing loomed out of the mist. The butt end of the row was facing me, so I couldn't see any of the windows. I found the beginning of a sidewalk that would take me around to the front of these units. Shivering from the cold in my little suit jacket, I stepped carefully to avoid noise and the possibility of tripping. Rounding a hedge that defined the edge of the nearest yard, I saw a light in one of the windows. The illumination came from the first floor window of the last unit at the far end of the row. I stepped off the sidewalk onto the grass and approached the house.

Perhaps these were some of the homeless folks, I thought, trying not to get my hopes up. There was no car anywhere in sight. How did these people get back and forth when they needed a carton of cigarettes or a six-pack? Maybe there was another parking area on the far side of these units, and I couldn't see it because of the way the land slopped. Maybe, being homeless, they had no cars. Their shopping carts could be around back.

As I neared the lighted unit, I traversed the patchy lawn and placed a steadying hand on the side of the building. Landscape shrubs grew in front of the units but had been planted away from the façades to make painting the siding easy. I was thankful for this because it allowed me to stay very close to the structure as I approached the window. I couldn't tell from the halo of light whether there were curtains or not. The lack of lumens could simply mean that the bulb was of low wattage or that the light source was far from the window.

Moving deliberately, I gained the space behind the bush in front of the end unit. I leaned against the façade, careful to avoid touching the shutter affixed to the exterior of the window frame. Wooden shutters are notorious for coming unhinged. Resting my back against the house, I took comfort that homeless people ware rarely violent. If I peeped in and they saw me, I would be treated in all probability to a deranged diatribe as

I made my retreat in the darkness. And if spotted by Fang or Wong? What then?

A thump from the front room of the occupied unit made me jump. I almost fell into the shrub. Regaining my composure, I realized I could hear faint conversation and that the occupants I wanted to see were immediately behind me, sitting on a couch or chair that had bumped against the wall causing the thump. In order to get a look at them, I needed to be on the other side of the window.

Crouching down, I eased ahead. Actually, I'd have to traverse the window and the entry door. Fortunately, the stoop at the front door was low, and there was another scraggly shrub to give me cover on the other side. Because the picture window was at hip level, I could hunker along under the sill until I reached the entrance.

The low-key conversation continued, and I gained the far side of the window without detection. I felt electric, as if all my nerve endings had floated to the surface of my skin. Now, there was nothing for it but to ease up and take a quick peek. With a steadying hand on the side of the house, I began to rise.

I had been concentrating so hard on my objective, I had tuned out the other sounds around me. There were footfalls approaching on the sidewalk. I crouched down immediately, shaken by this new development. The walker aided his progress with a small flashlight. His pace telegraphed that he knew the path and was anxious to reach his destination.

Trying to make myself invisible, I held my knees and my breath. The walker reached the stoop, shifted a bag onto the hip closest to me, and rapped on the door with the butt of the flashlight. The sounds inside changed, and the door opened, bathing the stoop and lawn in a cone of light. I shrank from it like a vampire. The occupant and the new arrival seemed completely at ease and unconcerned about detection, speaking in normal tones and pawing at the groceries like participants in a Friday night poker game.

I guess it was that sense we all have that someone is watching us or a presence is near that made the man turn toward me; or perhaps I made a noise, I don't know. He turned and swung the small, intense beam of the flashlight in my direction. He was genuinely surprised when it crossed a human face.

Casper Wong stared at me dumbfounded. "You!" was all he managed at first. Then, as I scrambled up from my knees and ricocheted off the sheltering shrub, he launched into rapid-fire Chinese directed at the occupants of the house.

As I struggled around the bush, I realized that Wong was between my escape route and me. Not that I had an escape route, but he was between me and the way back to the car. I would have to run in the other direction, and I had no idea where that would take me. I hoped I could circle back to the path down to the parking area and the Saab. The row of houses the executives had chosen abutted a forested area. As I rounded the end of the building, hoping to reach the backyards and a path back in the direction of the other houses, I heard the backdoor of the end unit open. Someone was going to cut me off from that direction. I had no choice but to enter the woods.

I crashed through dense foliage holding my arms in front of my face. The overgrown hillside was oppressively dark and saturated with moisture. I sank to my ankles in vegetation and started to slide more than run down the incline. I heard commotion behind me suggesting that others had entered the dripping coppice. Repelling off tree trunks to keep from picking up too much momentum, I managed to reach a flat area. I stumbled leftward, heading for the car. Making safer progress on the level ground, I picked up the pace and reached into my pocket for my cell phone. It was time to ask for help. Actually, it was way beyond that. It was time to scream and yell for help.

I flipped the clamshell up and ran my finger over the buttons. Redial was nine. I raised my other arm to fend off a branch that came out of nowhere, and suddenly I was airborne. I fell forward and down, hitting a solid surface full force on my shoulder. On impact, the phone flew from my hand and bounced out of sight. Reeling from the pain in my shoulder, I pushed up off what must have been a service road. That was the good news. I was on a road, not much more than a lane, really, but a road must lead somewhere. The bad news was that I could not see my cell phone. I followed what I thought was the trajectory of the phone toward a thicket of bushes on the opposite side of the road and peered into their depths. Voices approaching from the hillside interrupted my search. I would have to call Dakota after I regained the car and fled immediate danger. Right now, I had to run, I hoped in the direction of the car and Skootch.

I pounded along the service road, keys jingling comfortingly in my pocket. Maybe I should call Skootch's name. The car window was open and his hearing, acute. He could bark me back to my objective. Better not risk it; they'd hear me. My side began to throb. My shoulder ached from the fall. I burst from the side road onto a macadam surface and stopped to gain my bearings. This stretch of road, or what I could see of it in the blackness, was unfamiliar. Woods stretched uninterrupted on either side. I had to make a decision. I started running down the road to the left. My leather soles slid on the wet surface, and I almost lost my balance again. Gasping for air, I ran, one arm pressed to my aching side.

A crash followed by the sound of running feet echoed behind me. I glanced over my shoulder. Two men sprinted after me. Despite the hitch in my side, I accelerated. Over my ragged breathing, I could hear more rustling in the wood to my left. There were at least three of them. More than a match for me.

I don't think the shot was very accurate. The report of the gun scared the hell out of me, though, and I jumped into the ditch on the right and scrambled up the other side into the sheltering trees. I pushed through a brace of saplings and freed myself but with too much force, pitching away from the trees and over an embankment. Crashing into a canopy of branches, I sank into the crotch made by two closely growing eucalyptus. Scratched and shaken, I struggled for footing. My right toe touched ground, and I edged my torso out of the trees and collapsed to the ground.

Breathing in painful jerks, I looked up and immediately knew where I was. The little handmade tombstones jutted from the earth, tilting in crazy directions. Although I couldn't read inscriptions in the dark, I was certain they said Beloved Muffy, Fluffy, or Faithful Duke. I was in the Presidio's pet cemetery, the last resting place of hundreds of companion animals of military dependants. I had ranged far from Skootch and the Saab, but I wasn't that far from the exit gate on the Marina District side of the park. I would make for that exit and flag down the first car I saw. As carefully as I could, I skirted the lovingly crafted little headstones. A road bounded the cemetery to the east, and once I gained it, I could safely run again.

I hefted a leg over a low picket fence and froze. How could they have outdistanced me so easily? Two men loped along the road I was heading for. I remained a statue, praying that my distance from them and my black suit would protect me. They passed my location and continued their trot toward the gate. One cradled a cell phone as he ran. I would have to go the other way. I lifted my leg back over the fence and felt my way to the rear of the graveyard.

Climbing up a partially cleared hill, I reached another road that traversed the park from south to north. It turned west above Fort Point and provided me a direct but lengthy route back to the Saab if I did not come up with a park employee sooner. I brushed myself off and began to jog, trying to remember the location of some of the former officer housing now domiciling park managers and their families. If I could find an occupied house, I could find safety and a phone.

I reached the section of road where it curved west. I could just see the access road to Fort Point roll away over the steep incline that descends to water level, and the gleam of lights coming from a Civil War era residence perched on the rise above me. The glow from the high windows illuminated the porch wrapping the structure and a coach lamp marked the beginning of the walk to the house and my rescue.

"Don't move," a voice barked as a hand closed on my upper arm. I turned to face Brutus Fang holding a semiautomatic. The damp Presidio air weighed on my lungs, and I felt as rooted in place as a granite statue.

Fang shoved me in front of him and began to walk toward the Fort Point access road. He poked me in the back with the muzzle and talked into his earpiece, alerting his comrades to my capture. They could pass the site of the Letterman hospital and the Burger King, traverse the warehouse area, and join up with him on the side road that merged into the lane where we were. Once they reached us, I would be out of options.

Fang sauntered behind me with a smug, chauvinistic gait, the gun carelessly waving in no particular direction. He seemed mighty sure he could control me and not very schooled in the handling of firearms. Maybe it was lucky that Fang and not his goons had apprehended me. I decided it was time to be annoying.

"It appears your little scheme has come to a sorry end," I said, edging back in line with him. "Now you've even lost all that stuff you stashed in your Oakland warehouse."

"Shut up. Stupid woman."

"I know about your real plans, Fang. I know about the anti-fertility strategy."

This got his attention. So much so that he failed to make me get back in front of him. "You know shit," he shot back.

"I know your government intends to use genetic technology to destroy the fertility of its own citizens without their knowledge."

"And how are we to accomplish that?"

"By employing the vector technology perfected by Karin Mullins."

Fang's eyes narrowed as he realized I really did understand his plot. "Stupid fucking woman. You'll be dead soon."

"Like Roger, you murdering thug!"

"Huh?" Fang's pistol listed to the right. His hesitation was the opening I needed. I rammed into him high on the torso. He tried to balance, but his right foot stepped off the road surface and on to the spongy vegetation at the edge of the hill above the pet cemetery. One more shove to his ribcage sent him over.

"Don't disturb the animals." I started to run. I had to get off this road before the other men arrived. I looked longingly up at the residence. If I ran up hill, my progress would be slow and they would see me, but if I headed down the Fort Point access road I'd be out of sight in seconds.

Arms pumping, I picked up speed, but I was so fatigued, I felt like I was moving in slow motion. I crested the entryway to the fort, but not before I saw the men approaching from the east. I prayed they hadn't seen me. My burning legs wobbled on the steep downward incline. I could see the dark fort and the fluorescence of the swelling seawater. I came here so often with Skootch I felt I was greeting an old friend. I'd hide on the westward side of the garrison. They would never look there. Nobody went there but raccoons, skunks, and the occasional pointer dog.

Protected from view by the fort, I leaned my back against the reassuring bricks and focused on slowing and deepening my breathing. Every part of me ached. I could see the undercarriage of the Golden Gate Bridge and hear the distant hum of traffic. Every one of those cars had a passenger with a cell phone; I longed for the smooth feel of mine in my palm and the sound of Dakota's voice. The ambient noise, a complex mix of bridge, channel, and woodland sounds, calmed me. The skydiver highs had carried me. Now exhaustion in the wake of the multiple adrenalin rushes weighed me down. I slid down the bricks and settled into the fecund mulch at the base of the old building.

I tried to clear my head, but my thoughts refused to string together. There was Janie Belle saying Susan Hayward over and over. And Skootch performing the Lunge.

I don't know how much time elapsed, but I was alerted by the subtle, unmistakable snap of a twig. I fought to snatch sharpness out of my groggy stupor and struggled to see into the middle distance. Another sound came from high on my left. I more imagined than saw a figure near the cyclone fencing that prevented trespassers from reaching the footings of the majestic bridge. A dozen feet from me, a rock crashed into a stump. I jumped, and my involuntary movement caught the attention of the figure at the fence. He started to descend, striding down the slope in my direction while the rock thrower edged along the side of the fort.

I made for the channel side, pulling myself onto the apron of cement using a rusty fencing stake. I walked swiftly toward the other end of the building and the adjoining parking lot. Perhaps I could outflank them and get back on the access road, or failing that, I could ease over the ledge of the bulwark and hide myself between the overhang and the rocks. My alternatives were getting bleaker by the minute.

As I passed the massive wooden doors of the fort, now closed and bolted, a figure emerged from the parking area. His coat festooned with leaves, and pants torn at the knee, Fang had a grim sneer and a much more effective grip on his pistol. He motioned for me to move away from the building.

"Get on your knees and place your hands behind your neck, bitch," he said as he reached the center of the seawall. His sharp words disturbed a gull asleep on a piling. The bird eyed him with detachment, spread its wings, and coasted to the surface of the incoming tide.

Out of options, I did as he asked. Harrison had been right. Amateurs should leave policing to the professionals. Fang strolled forward, but not any closer. I had gained some respect from pushing him down the hill, and he wasn't going to take any chances with his first shot. He could come closer after that and finish me if need be.

Harrison. How I longed to look into those warm caramel eyes. Touch that scratchy stubble. I'm sorry, Bob, so sorry.

Fang's colleagues emerged from the wooded side of the fort. He waved them on, and they continued to the parking lot, their part of my termination completed. It did not take three men to finish one meddling female. Fang pulled the slide on the semi-automatic and took very deliberate aim. He was enjoying this. A cold possibility caused my heart to sink. He was angry enough and mean enough to gut shoot me just for spite. I could writhe around a while in agony before he dealt the coup de grace.

"Got any more theories for me now? How about a theory about body decomposition in salt water?" Fang's teeth flashed in the moonlight.

He was so delighted with torturing me that he didn't hear the rushing sound. This one was a tower wave, a horror film hand rising high behind him. I forced my eyes to stay on him and not follow the trajectory of the water, so I would not call his attention to what was building behind him. My peripheral vision would tell me when the wave reached equilibrium.

The descending wall of water hit him like a two-by-four, and then cascaded around him like a shroud. I flung my body away from his gun hand. If the pistol discharged, I couldn't distinguish it from the roar of the water. He landed at the edge of the concrete apron with one shoulder hanging in space. The retreating wash had enough volume and force to pull him over into the roiling muscles of water surging in through the mouth of the bay.

Rising to all fours, I was knocked flat by a pointer dog.

"Skootch, Skootch." I wrapped my arms around the dog's muscular neck, "Am I glad to see you."

"His howling helped us locate your car." Harrison stooped to help me up. His hand supported my cheek and his thumb traced one of my deeper scratches.

"How'd you know to look for me?" I sputtered, recalling the lost cell phone.

"Dakota called. He told me he couldn't wait any longer for your call and he was afraid to call you for fear the ringing would bring attention to you at the wrong moment. It's a good thing you have some sensible friends, or we would have had to fish you out of the channel tomorrow." Harrison tried to look stern, but the corners of his mouth edged up into a grin.

I shivered as I remembered Fang's taunting remark. We rounded the corner of Fort Point in time to see Barbagalatto place his hand on the head of one of Fang's associates and guide him into the back of the police cruiser.

"Dakota tipped you off, and you found Skootch and the Saab?"

"Yeah, and Skootch found you. I opened the car door, and he got away from me. Took off down through the woods. Fortunately, we had enough squad cars in the park that we just radioed them to keep tabs on the pooch. So we listened to the chatter reporting his sightings as he made his way across the park. He doubled back a few times and got a little confused, but for a field dog he turned out to be a pretty good tracker."

Harrison shrugged off his jacket, wrapped it around me, and squeezed. The jacket was warm from his body and smelled of him. When we reached his car, we were far enough from the other detectives for intimacy. Hands on my waist, he turned me to face him and slid his arms around me. "I thought you were a goner. First, I was mad at you, and then terrified, then both. You sure are a troublemaker."

We kissed, and then Bob crushed me to his chest. He rocked me back and forth in rhythm with the waves. I tried to lift my chin so that I could see his face, but my neck hurt something awful, so I mumbled into his shirt, "You know I think I might have learned my lesson this time. You wanna know why?"

"Uh huh."

"It's because police work is harder on your body than Chevy sex."

* * *

CHAPTER 24

Four days later we met for the celebration at Scully's Revenge. The conspirators called it the un-celebration. Sally, Serge, Dakota, Karin, Larry, Fred, Emily, and I gathered around two tables pushed together at waterside, swilled beer, and picked through an expensive mound of Dungeness crabs, except for Dakota who never touches seafood. He huddled over his hamburger plate, protecting it from contamination from encroaching crustaceans.

"Well, the papers were full of the capture but short on the facts about what the corporate culprits were really up to." Karin pointed a crab leg for emphasis. "The way the story in the Oakland paper reads, you'd think they were trafficking in illegal immigrants. So much for accuracy in reporting!"

"Oh, I think they do, they're just being led astray by the authorities," I said. "The feds can't let it be known that a foreign government pilfered the nation's bioscience treasure and then not engage in some sort of diplomatic retribution, and they can't really afford to do that. Besides, the Chinese would deny responsibility for their own operatives. Fang, Wong, and their ilk are expendable."

"Yep." Sally cracked a claw. "Their handlers have already written them off."

"Let's just enjoy our good deed among our own little group!" I raised my glass. "Here's to the RNA Irregulars!"

"OK, who can chug their beer faster than I can say deoxyribonucleic acid?" Karin dared.

"Finished." Sally waved, and the server returned to our table with two more pitchers.

By the time I got home, I was feeling no pain. I probably should not have driven, but the afternoon traffic was sparse and easy to negotiate. I had a date with Harrison in the snug bar at Julius' Castle. This would be our first meeting since he, Skootch, and the rogue wave rescued me from Fang. Bob had called me, and I was hoping this was a rapprochement on his part, his way of forgiving me for meddling in the case. I'd apologized on the phone and promised never to do anything like that again. I was disturbed, however, that there was no invitation to dinner and, more importantly, bed. Perhaps he was traveling later in the evening. He could not be working, or he would not be planning to have a drink. Maybe I was to be punished for my transgressions. Denied sex for a week or two, sort of a probation strategy. From a law enforcement type, this sounded plausible. Now that I had a theory, I felt better.

I tried to take a nap, but my growing excitement for seeing Harrison prevented me from dozing off. Finally, I opted for a long shower to shake off the effects of the beer and the scent of crab.

Selecting a slimming, dark green sheath with a slit that was flattering to my legs, I pulled a multicolored shawl from the closet and slipped into open-toed pumps to show off a hint of red polish. I brushed on rather more blush than normal and rooted in my lipstick drawer to find a dark red stick I'd received as a gift-with-purchase.

I walked into the kitchen and executed a dramatic whirl to elicit Janie Belle's approval. "My, aren't we gussied up! Your scratches are healing nicely."

I looked down at my legs. The taupe hose I'd chosen covered the scabs on my legs, but a survey of my forearms revealed several unsightly gashes. "I'll just make good use of this big shawl. What are you working on? Is that what I think it is?"

"Yes, I am afraid so." Janie Belle fingered the garment spread across the kitchen table next to her open sewing basket. "One of the acolytes set Andrew afire this morning. When he raised his arms and saw his sleeve burning, he ran straight down the center aisle, and two ushers had to tackle and roll him on the ground to put him out. I don't know if I can fix this. What a shame."

There lay the singed remains of the pagan Inca priest vestment, its flaming feathers done to a crisp.

He was waiting for me on the little bridge that connects the valet parking area to the restaurant entrance. The walkway hangs out over the northwestern precipice of Telegraph Hill, shielded from the wind by a panel of Plexiglas. He leaned against the railing with his back to the drop, something that with my touch of vertigo, I wasn't sure I could do. Harrison handed me out of my cab and guided me along to the door and the cozy welcome of the snug bar.

"You look nice." He seated me and took a chair next to mine. He gave our order to the barman and took my hand. We sat in silence for a few moments just looking at each other.

"You do, too," I said, finally.

"I do what?"

"Look nice."

"Oh, thanks. That scratch on your chin. I can't see it at all." He brushed my chin with his fingers. I silently thanked Estèe Lauder for her latest foundation formula.

Our drinks came and we clinked glasses. "To us," I said and sipped.

His eyes blinked and he looked away. I immediately regretted my toast. Remember, idiot, you're on probation. Don't push it.

Harrison looked back at me, leaned forward, and placed his glass on the table. He scooped a few nuts into his hands, turning them between his fingers like Captain Qwig with the ball bearings.

"I've been offered a position by the FBI. I always intended the fraud unit thing to be temporary, although I didn't have a set timeline. I worked closely with a number of the federal people on this case. There are many opportunities at the national level now. Actually, one of the people I knew in Baltimore is in the bureau's L.A. office."

So, this was it. I wasn't on probation; he was moving on and I was getting the brush off. I tried to think of something neutral to say. "The work you will be doing will be much more important and interesting, I would think."

"You could say that. The resources they have are impressive. I like the people, too; they think big picture."

"You mean they're less provincial than the SFPD."

"Aw, the guys here are all right. I'm just ready for something more."

I felt boxed in. I couldn't very well ask if that meant he had gotten over the death of the woman in Baltimore. I could not bring myself to inquire where he would be located, although I had a hunch it wasn't San Francisco.

As if reading my mind, he offered, "I'm not sure where I'll be based. I think it's going to be Los Angeles, but I won't know for sure for several weeks. I, ah, have to leave tonight to go back East for orientation."

"Well," I managed to get out, "I guess congratulations are in order." I lifted my glass, but it was empty. I had drained it during this depressing dialogue. Harrison saw my plight and signaled the bartender for another round. He appeared happy to have something to do for me. It must have been the look on my face.

"I'll call you as soon as I know what's what. I'm sure it will be L.A. That's not far. We'll be able to see each other a lot."

"Of course we will." I tried to sound blasé. I smiled broadly and insincerely at the barman as he delivered our drinks.

It didn't take us long to down the second round. I think we talked about the challenges of finding a good living situation in the City of Angels. I really can't remember. An aching numbness set in.

"What time is your plane?"

Harrison grasped this opportunity as if it were a cue in an off-Broadway play. He looked at his watch and waved to the barman for a check. He extracted his wallet. "Actually, I've got to get going. I'll drop you at your place on my way south."

"No thanks, I'm going to get a cab." I rose and on my way to the powder room requested a taxi from the maitre d'. As I freshened my lipstick, I half wished Harrison would be gone when I returned to the bar. But when I retraced my steps, he was waiting at the door, hands in pockets, impatiently rocking on his heels. Prior to tonight's revelation, I would have found this endearing.

He handed me into my cab and kissed me.

I made a last-ditch attempt at humor. "Do you say break a leg to FBI types? Probably not. I'll just say good luck, then."

"Bye, Nola. See you soon."

I twisted in my seat and waved to him through the back window, a big smile engineered on my mug.

"Yeah, right."

I forced myself to wait until the cab gained the top of the hill and turned down Union Street before I allowed the tears to escape. If there is one hard and fast rule in the over-forty dating game, it is this: never let them see you cry.

The cab driver had no change, so I was forced to over-tip him. He didn't deserve a tip given the way he drove and the state of his shocks. My backside, which still bore a few tender spots from my experience at the Presidio, was jostled and battered all the way home. I trudged up the steps as the driver pulled away, praying that Janie Belle, exhausted from her mending project, was sleeping. I eased the front door shut and removed my heels. My effect on men was, if anything, consistent. At least Harrison was not dead, nor had I driven him to the bottle. That was something. After all, I did sincerely wish him well.

Standing alone in the shadowy stillness, I realized I was wide awake. Awake and depressed. No point going to bed just to lay there and stew. I deposited my shawl and bag and headed for my office.

Not bothering with the room light, I opened my e-mail and studied the list of messages in the dark. Sally had e-mailed a collection of links to E-zines and trade publications that covered the capture story. Next, I opened a message from Rupert Lee.

"Hi, Nola, I've just come up for air from the most intense negotiation of my life. I've been going round and round with this professor and his two postdocs at the University of Chicago who want to start an inflammation biology company. We've been at it for two straight days battling over the details. While all this was going on my laptop died, so I've been incommunicado. We reached agreement this morning, and I caught the first plane out. When I got home, I got your message. Rest assured this information will get into the right hands. I'll want you to take the new company on as a client. Call me ASAP."

So, Rupert had just gotten my e-mail about the Chinese plot. That meant he wasn't responsible for the tip about the base housing. I was sure it had been Rupert with his far-reaching network of contacts who had come up with the location of Fang and Wong.

It must have been Roger's uncle. Randolph Chen had seen to it that I learned the hiding place of the guilty executives. With his ophthalmology business and rigid ethics, he didn't seem the type to dabble in underground information. I pictured him in his neat office, his back ramrod straight, his manner patrician, the family pictures carefully framed.

Of course, another member of the Chen family would not hesitate to reach out to the underworld to obtain information he needed. One person whose perspective was Old World. Whose orientation was ethnic and cultural, not legalistic and moral. The old man had the contacts to find anybody in San Francisco no matter what rock they tried to hide under.

I opened a new message and typed, "Thank you for getting me what I needed to see that justice was done. And please thank your father."

I pressed send.

The weekend promised to be sunny and warm. Perhaps it would help lift the gloom that had settled over me with the departure of Harrison. Other than taking Skootch for a walk at Fort Funston, I had only one commitment, and then the entire weekend was mine. I thought about inviting Janie Belle for lunch in Sausalito or Tiburon. The drive would be pretty, and we could do a little shopping after we ate.

For once, the kitchen was devoid of church materials. Janie Belle sipped coffee, riveted to the television set. "Come look at this, they're filming in our neighborhood!"

Sure enough, there was the front of the Chinese consular residence and the fence that Skootch peed on as he baited the watchdogs. The camera zoomed in on a youthful Chinese American man who thrust forward a placard reading *Genetic Atrocities*. The reporter intoned into his microphone that demonstrations like this were occurring in Los Angeles, Seattle, Chicago, and the nation's capital. A clip of downtown San Francisco now appeared. Police tried to direct traffic along Geary Boulevard around a crowd of demonstrators who spilled off the sidewalk in front of the consular offices. Car horns blared and bullhorns crackled.

I left the kitchen, traversed the hall, and opened our front door. Our street was clogged with parked cars. A news van was parked half on the sidewalk, and a cinematographer struggled with a magazine as he balanced his camera against his thigh. My ears picked up what sounded like chanting from the direction of the consular residence. Rupert had been true to his word. The Chinese would be the target of global condemnation.

I returned to the kitchen and was greeted by talking heads. The network medical reporter was interviewing a molecular biology guru from UCSF; I knew the professor because he served on scientific advisory boards of companies for whom I had consulted. I was acquainted with the reporter, too. He would do an excellent job of explaining to viewers the use of vectors to deliver altered genes encoding proteins central to reproduction.

Janie Belle declined my offer for a drive up the coast. "Father Andrew is back after his sojourn in the emergency room. I want to see him perform the Eucharist with his arm in a sling."

As I merged into the left-turn lane on the Great Highway, the driver of a vintage Ford Futura, who was rubbernecking the wave action on Ocean Beach, almost rear-ended me. I crossed the southbound lanes and drove along the center aisle to the parking area. Skootch switched sides in the backseat so he could face the water and the gulls. I found a parking space and grabbed Skootch's leash.

Skootch and I strolled to the stone stairs and descended to beach level. The going was rough until we reached the packed sand near water's edge. The happy dog stopped to sniff each pile of seaweed. Glancing back, I saw a Lincoln Towncar pull in from the north. The driver stopped opposite the stairs, and a tall man in a Burberry got out of the car. A magnificent Chow followed him. The dog trotted obediently as the man walked down to the beach and established a trajectory that would intersect with mine in thirty yards. Skootch and I continued down the sand inspecting debris as we went.

"Good morning, Ms. Billingsley." Randolph Chen greeted me at the place we had agreed to meet. "This is my daughter's dog. She's away at school, and he doesn't get much exercise."

Skootch trotted forward to greet the newcomer, but a low growl stopped him in his tracks. He diverted to an unsniffed pile of seaweed and began to go over it with great care. I walked over and undid his leash. Freed from the presence of the antisocial Chow, he headed for the water.

"I appreciate your giving me the chance to thank you in person," I said. "I really don't believe the police would have apprehended Fang and Wong if you hadn't acted."

"That is kind of you to say. They would have been caught eventually. I thank you for telling me about their intended crimes against the Chinese people. A most heinous plan. I hope your interference has prevented them from moving forward with it."

"I hope so, too."

We walked along in silence. The gulls circled hopefully as many people came to the beach with bread for the birds.

"I also trust your father is pleased," I said.

"He was pleased to help take such criminals out of circulation."

"Well, yes, but I mean in seeing to it that the people who killed Roger were caught."

Chen frowned and stopped. His Chow and I stopped as well two steps beyond. When I turned back to him, he was studying me.

"Of course, the cops may not be able to prove they did it."

At this, Chen looked out to sea. The death of his nephew was still an open wound. I had been insensitive to mention to it.

I watched him in profile as he inhaled the sea air. His nostrils flared and his chest rose. He held the breath for an unnatural interval, and then exhaled a long, cleansing lungful as if some inner yoga class had come to an end.

Chen turned to me. "Those people didn't kill my nephew."

"They didn't?"

"Roger died because he forgot who he was. He brought shame to his family. What was worse, he had begun to engage in activities that would have brought dishonor and shame to his mother's family."

The Shens, the shipping family, the Southern California dynasty who controlled the fleet of container ships.

"He was going to ingratiate himself to Fang and Wong by offering to use Shen Shipping to get scale-up materials to China." I said it more to myself than to Chen.

"If he had only dishonored our family, we would have found a way to punish him. Perhaps we could have turned his life around. We discovered he used his familial connection to bribe and control some of the Shen's captains and dockside operatives.

He was well on his way to involving his mother's people in this dirty business. That was unforgivable."

I said slowly, "I see. Once they started down the scale-up road, they could no longer slip a sample or a diskette in a diplomatic pouch. They had to find a way to transport equipment, supplies, and intermediate products to China undetected. What better way than inside a container on a Shen ship."

"I'm glad my brother didn't live to see this." Chen kicked at a discarded water bottle. Then, he stiffened, realizing he had said something personal. "I must go. My father is waiting in the car."

"No, he's not." I looked back at the seawall. The elder Chen was at the opening where the stairs began. One hand on the wall, the other on his cane, he stared not at us, but westward. With his back to America, my America, with its new culture, its melting pot, its political correctness. His aged eyes fixed on the horizon, the thin line that contained all of the Orient. His culture, his values, his honor.

"Why did you choose to tell me this?" I asked.

"When you came to see me, I was sure you would ask me for money. Later I realized I had misjudged and insulted you. I hope I have made amends."

Randolph Chen shook my hand and trudged back up the beach to his father and his duty.

The old man studied his son before turning to the Towncar. You tough old patriarch, I thought with dawning realization, you made a call to your cronies in Chinatown and had your grandson executed just as surely as if we were in the Forbidden City. You have nothing to fear from me or the police. Shanghai Woo will see to that. The executioners are as untraceable as the ripples on the receding tide. But you did this in such a way and in such a place that your grandson's body could be buried with the family.

The gleaming car edged out of the lot and accelerated into the traffic lane. The black windows glistened in the sunshine that promised to stay for the whole of the weekend.

I turned back to the westward view. The sky was turquoise and the sea was jade. A Coast Guard cutter headed north to the channel. Another boat top-heavy with tourists cruised toward the Farallon Islands. Two surfers in wetsuits bobbed, waiting for a challenging wave. I recalled the embrace that was my reward after the tower wave swept Wong off the Fort Point landing. Harrison's face came back to me commanding in its masculinity. God, I missed that man.

Well, said a voice in my head, here you are back where you started, struggling uphill through the sand, forty-something, dateless, and living with your mother.

I gained the wall and used it to support myself while I emptied sand from my shoes. As I straightened up, I saw him heading for me. Legs pumping and ears snapping. I grabbed both his jowls and shook his solid head from side to side. The deep brown eyes open to me as always, brimmed with love and trust.

"You're here in the moment, aren't ya, fella. No memories. No regrets." I jingled the car keys in my pocket. Skootch did the dance of joy.

As we pointed the Saab south on the Great Highway, I thought that maybe things weren't so bad. My consulting business was back on track, and I pretty much called my own shots. I was involved in the most exciting industry on the planet. I lived in the most beautiful city in the world—wacky, but beautiful. I had the best short-haired pointer in the universe.

Buoyed by this assessment, I reminded myself Harrison had joined the FBI, not the priesthood.

"Would you like to see L.A., Skootch?"

Now, Skootch is a born and bred San Franciscan, and as such, he has heard some pretty awful things about L.A., but he

Grover, Al Halluin, Mark Hanamoto, Wolf Hanisch, Bob Havranek, George Hersbach, Brian Issell, Ed Kenney, Bez Khosrovi, Joe LaCob, Filippo LaMonica, Frank McCormick, Kary Mullis, Michael Ostrach, Jeff Price, Hollings Renton, Joe Rubinfeld, Jim Rurka, Peter Staple and Tom White, it is important to add, there were a few good men. Thanks, also to staffers Janet Williams and Evelyn Evans for keeping all those slides straight before PowerPoint was invented.

* * *

I could not have written this book without the expert instruction, support and encouragement of the faculty and staff of the UCLA Extension Writer's Program. Not only the novelists, but the short story writers, nonfiction writers and the poets made essential contributions to my process, my project and my sanity. I owe Jerrilyn Farmer a particular debt of gratitude because she suffered through the entire manuscript of *A Pointed Death* at a very early stage in its development. Kudos also go to my fellow students for their helpful critiques and enthusiasm.

Special thanks also go to Ron Ruelle who brought Nola and Skootch to life in cartoon form.

Finally, I want to thank Dale Johnson, Sally Willis Rogers, Doug Given, Devon Giacalone, and Jane Russell, who worked with me in a start-up I founded, and to remember Gigabyte and Wysiwyg Rogers, our spokes-animals. We lived the dream.

* * *

Palm Desert CA
June 2010
http://www.pointermysteries.com

Made in the USA
Charleston, SC
05 January 2011

likes to keep an open mind. L.A. has beaches. L.A. has food. L.A. has freeways for riding in the car car car. What's not to like?

"Urrrrrrrrrffff!" said Skootch.

* * *

ACKNOWLEDGEMENTS

This is a silly, escapist book. I have tried to produce a *good read* for professional women to take along on those long, lonely flights. Although what I wrote is a light, irreverent story, it is set in a very serious industry that has produced enormous value, especially in the healthcare field. *A Pointed Death* is intended as sort of a cockeyed tribute.

I was privileged to work in biotechnology from the early days through a quarter century of amazing discovery and progress. Women were a part of this journey from the beginning, and it was not exactly a smooth road. I channeled these women when I created Nola Billingsley, and that is why she is spunky, witty, clever, persistent and unafraid. I have published *A Pointed Death* under Kath Russell because I am working on more serious literary projects that will be published under my full name, Katharine A. Russell. However, I intend to return to the wacky world of biotech I have created in this first pointer mystery, because I miss the culture, the characters and the impossible situations of startup companies. To the degree my fictional people resonate with readers, it is because they have been faithfully replicated from the real hurly-burly of entrepreneurial bioscience.

I want everyone in bioscience today to remember the pioneering females, not just the scientists, but the managers, bankers, venture capitalists, stock analysts, fund managers, journalists, lawyers, accountants, lobbyists and communicators who helped build a new industry. I know I am going to leave some important early woman out. Too many amyloid plaques are accumulating in my grey matter these days, so I will apologize now and humbly ask that you send me a strongly worded e-mail.

These books are for all who remember the Pier 66 Hotel in Fort Lauderdale with affection, and, looking back, a certain awe: Roxanne Bales, Karen Bernstein, Judy Blakemore, Annette Campbell-White, Nancy Chang, Marilyn Chase, Shirley Clayton, Lisa Conte, Abla Creasey, Ellen Daniell, Wanda DeVlaminck, Devon Giacalone, Denise Gilbert, Kathy Glaub, Sarah Gordon-Wild, Carol Hall, Joan O'C Hamilton, Jennie Hunter, Ruth Kunath, Janice LeCoq, Nola Masterson, Jennie Mather, Linda Miller, Jean Ann Mire, Abbey Meyers, Tina Nova, H. Stewart Parker, Lisa Raines, Cynthia Robbins-Roth, Jackie Siegel, Mary Tanner and Alison Taunton Rigby.

To the next generation of women who made their careers in the bioscience industry, including Angela Bitting, Jana Cuiper, Nicola Fildes, Elizabeth Gard and Sylvia Wheeler, I say this: Your path was made wider and brighter and your success greater and more visible by the great gals above, who are forever the charter members of the Sisterhood of the Traveling Genes.

* * *

I got my start at one of the first two genetic engineering companies, Cetus Corporation, and owe my career to my colleagues there, both female and male. For Brian Atwood, Ed Bradley, Ron Cape, Pete Fernandes, Bob Fildes, Bill Gerber, Michael Goldberg, Jay